MOUSE Trapped

SATAN'S DEVILS #9

MANDA MELLETT

AUTHOR'S NOTE

Mouse Trapped is the ninth in the Satan's Devils MC series, but can be read as a standalone.

If you're new to MC books you may find there are terms that you haven't heard before, so I've included a glossary at the end to help along the way. I hope you get drawn into this mysterious and dark world in the same way I have done—there will be further books in the Satan's Devils series which I hope you'll want to follow.

If you've picked this book up because, like me, you read anything MC, I hope you'll enjoy it for what it is, a fictional insight into the underground culture of alpha men and their bikes.

Road Name	Role/Status	Other Name
Drummer	President	Rick Felis
Wraith	VP	Scott Remington
Heart	Secretary	Dale Norman
Dollar	Treasurer	Todd Bishop
Peg	Sergeant-at-arms	Ronald Rinter
Blade	Enforcer	Jack Sharples
Joker	Road Captain	Josh Wilkinson
Mouse	Computer expert	Tse Williamson
Adam	deceased	
Beef		
Bullet		
Buster	deceased	
Dart	transferred	Colin Lowe
Fergus	Prospect	
Hyde		
Jekyll		
Lady		Scott Flintstone
Marvel		
Matt	Prospect	
Paladin	(was Marsh)	
Roadrunner		
Rock		
Slick		Jeff Andrews
Shooter	(was Spider)	
Tongue	deceased	
Truck	Prospect	
Viper		

Cast List of Characters

Old Lady	Children
Sam	Elijah (Eli)
Sophie	Olivia
Marcia	Amy, Jacob, Isabel
Darcy	Noah
Carmen	
Alex	Tyler
Becca	
Ella	
Sandy	

CONTENTS

Author's Note...
Chapter 1..1
Chapter 2..10
Chapter 3..18
Chapter 4..28
Chapter 5..37
Chapter 6..46
Chapter 7..54
Chapter 8..61
Chapter 9..70
Chapter 10...78
Chapter 11...86
Chapter 12...95
Chapter 13...105
Chapter 14...118
Chapter 15...125
Chapter 16...132
Chapter 17...140
Chapter 18...148
Chapter 19...157
Chapter 20...166
Chapter 21...176
Chapter 22...182
Chapter 23...191
Chapter 24...199
Chapter 25...210
Chapter 26...217
Chapter 27...225

Chapter 28..238
Chapter 29..251
Chapter 30..258
Chapter 31..271
Chapter 32..281
Chapter 33..295
Chapter 34..305
Chapter 35..314
Chapter 36..325
Chapter 37..341
Chapter 38..350
Chapter 39..358
Chapter 40..367
Chapter 41..377
Chapter 42..388
Chapter 43..399
Chapter 44..408
Epilogue...417
Other Works by Manda Mellett...
Glossary..
Acknowledgements..
Stay In Touch..
About the Author..

CHAPTER 1

Mouse

Glancing at the monitor in front of me, I pass a hand over my reddened eyes. Nothing changes or leaps out at me. This code has beaten me for hours. The ashtray is full to overflowing, and my stomach growls reminding me just how long I've been sitting here.

Reluctantly I pull my gaze away from the screen and roll my neck, trying to ease the stiffness, only now hearing the muffled sounds wafting in from the clubroom that's just a few feet away from my office door. Outside will be a collection of my brothers, both those who remain single and the others with old ladies. Though, with Peg recently getting hitched, the former group, of which I'm still a loyal member, seems to be shrinking.

Outside is a world of camaraderie, of support, of love. All I have to do is step out of my door to be part of it.

A part of something. The reason why I joined the Satan's Devils. To have a place where I could feel a sense of belonging. My hands reach back and untie the leather thong keeping the strands together, letting my long dark hair hang free. Running my fingers through it, I tie it back neatly once again. The hair that reminds me of my heritage, a mix of Anglo and Native American blood, a visible sign I'm neither one thing nor the other. The juxtaposition of my two lives sometimes jarring, often causing a bone-deep restlessness inside me.

It's not that I'm bored, never that. How could I be when I have the whole world at my fingertips? Power beneath my hands that I make the choice to use wisely. The dark web, the deep web, those nefarious depths where black and white merge into grey. Where I delight in my solitude, stepping in then back out without leaving a footprint. Where I can escape from the disquiet in my soul. Something's missing, but I can't put a name to what it is. *Purpose?* What I do for the club is invaluable, I know that. Putting aside my usefulness, there remains a hole in my soul, which I don't know how to fill.

What day is it? What's the time?

Another roll of my stomach reminds me it must have been hours since I've eaten. Unwinding my long limbs, I stand and stretch, trying to get the kink out of my shoulders. Even I realise it's unhealthy to keep going on like this, burying myself away, hiding from the camaraderie just outside my office, preferring solitude to socialising with my brothers. *Something has to give.*

Taking a breath, I open the door and step out into another world. It's bright, I blink rapidly. While my office has windows, the blinds are constantly pulled down. The way the light falls suggests it's mid-afternoon, so the sunlight shouldn't surprise me, but it does. *How long have I been in there?*

"Hey, Mouse. Wanna game?" Rock's playing pool by himself, but I'm not feeling companionable.

My gut gives a loud grumble as though trying to answer him. "Nah, Brother. Going to get something to eat."

He waves his hand, and goes back to practising shots again.

Heading in the general direction of the kitchen, I take a second to divert to the bar where a bored Jill is standing, and wave to the sodas. As though I'm putting her to great trouble, she pulls her eyes away from the pool table behind me, and at last takes a bottle from the cooler. A dark stare has her opening it. I'm teetotal by nature. My late teenage years were spent on the Rez of the Navajo Nation where alcohol possession is illegal. Not that there weren't ways to get a hold of it if you wanted to bad enough. There may have been a couple of times that I'd partaken, but for the most part, I learned to go without it, and that's become habit.

Marijuana, now that's my drug of choice. A mellowing sensation, but without the hangover.

Sophie, the VP's old lady, is in the kitchen, plating up something for Olivia, her daughter. "Mouse." She gives a broad smile when she sees me. "If you've come for food, there's not much, I'm afraid. Oh, there's pizza left over from lunch." After her comment, she goes back to her daughter who's starting to fuss.

Ruffling the kid's head as I pass, I go to the fridge, cutting myself a slice of the sad looking said pizza. I lean against the counter and start eating. Consuming leftovers doesn't bother me, on the Rez nothing was wasted. As the food goes into my mouth, I occupy myself by watching the only other people in the room. Ollie's a cute kid, and Sophie makes a great mom. As I eat mechanically I ponder how it doesn't bother me that my brothers are hooking up with old ladies. I don't mind the kids in the clubhouse, even if I can't see any of that in my future. Why bring another person into a world that will surely fuck them up?

I must be frowning, because Sophie's brow knits. "Is that okay for you, Mouse? Want me to rustle you up something else? I don't mind."

The VP's woman wouldn't, she's a good sort like that. "Nah, I'm fine. Just wanted something to take the edge off."

"You going to be around for dinner later? Going to be bloody good. Got one of Ma's recipes to try."

"Nah, I'm going out," I tell her. "I'll make do with whatever's left over."

"Ha! If it's anything like normal, these guys won't leave much. Want me to put something aside for you?"

I give a grateful chin lift as I go out the door. It couldn't hurt. Today I don't feel like sitting around the table, conversing with my brothers.

Apart from Rock, there are only a few others in the clubroom so my progress is unimpeded as I make my way past, only having to slap a few backs in the process, earning reciprocal ones on mine. Then I'm outside, sliding my sunglasses out of my cut as I stride toward my bike.

Matt, the prospect, is on gate duty. He must have heard my engine, as he slides the barrier open in time so I don't even need to slow down. Raising my fingers from the clutch, I send him my thanks as I roll on by.

The wildfire, a couple of months back, ruined the surface of the track that leads to the clubhouse, but Viper and Bullet's crew have laid new asphalt and now it's good and smooth. But I don't pick up speed until I'm out on the highway, then knock up through those gears until I'm in top. My Harley rumbles beneath me, the wind blows through my hair. A sense of freedom all by itself, however, today it's not my steel steed I'm going to enjoy the most. I'm looking forward to a different type of ride.

I don't need to travel far. Soon I'm pulling in to a rough-looking lot, carefully manoeuvring my bike over the worst of the jagged stones, coming to a fairly level area where I kick down the stand, turn off the engine, and step off.

My sunglasses back in my cut, the cut itself safely stored in my saddle bag, I saunter over to the office. The door's ajar, the room's empty. I'm not surprised. Taking a familiar path, I go around the back, walk past a corral, and over to the stables.

"My friend!" Jacob is lifting a bale of hay on his shoulder. It overbalances as he turns to greet me, but my hand's there pushing it back in place. "You here to ride?"

I grin, pulling a loose strand of hay from the bale and slipping it between my teeth. "Well, I'm not here to shoot the shit," I agree, speaking around it.

"Huh." He pretends to be offended. "Not me you come to see. Just that fucking horse."

"And how is my boy, Niyol?" I'd named him the Navajo word for wind when I was helping Jacob break in the young foal. Jacob's blamed me ever since for being the reason he goes like his namesake. Too much for the paying customers who Jacob takes trekking in Sabino Canyon to handle.

"Like always. Causing havoc amongst the mares." But the softening of Jacob's eyes shows me the respect and love he has for the stallion. He tilts his head to one side. "Fucking horse knows you're here, Tse."

Before I was forced to leave Tucson, here's where I first learned to ride. It was one of the few areas where my Navajo mother had gotten her way. My Anglo father wanted me brought up as a strictly white all-American boy, but he gave in on the riding, something for which I've always been grateful, especially when I discovered I had an innate ability, and a deep love for horses.

Like my MC brothers, I love the freedom of my metal steed, but a flesh and blood one? Nothing can top that.

Alongside Jacob, as a fourteen-year-old boy, I had worked with Niyol for a year, breaking him to the saddle. He'd been a wild one then, and though now he must be in his late teens, he hasn't much calmed. Sometimes Jacob rides him, less often he'll let an experienced customer mount the stallion, but mostly Niyol's not worked until I come around. Something I try to do at least once a month.

"You taking him out?"

I nod, my eyebrow raised as I wait for permission.

"Knock yourself out. I'll be taking the *paying customers* the usual route. Got some novices…"

"I'll keep clear." I avoid the reference to the fact money doesn't pass hands when I take his horse for a ride. I've invested enough in these downtrodden stables over the years. Don't need thanks, which he's well aware of. We say what we have to by trading insincere insults.

Slapping the old man on his back, leaving him to prepare for what sounds like a boring trek to see the sunset tonight, I grab a rope halter and go to the furthest corral. There, already stamping his feet with impatience, is the sixteen-hand black stallion I've come to think of as mine.

The whites of his eyes are showing. *Like that, is it?* "Hey, boy." I stand at the fence, just waiting. "Can't come every day, you know. And Jacob doesn't neglect you, so don't give me that look."

Another stamp.

I dig into my pocket and pull something out. "Got a carrot with your name on it."

An impasse. He doesn't move, neither do I, as we play the game we've played ever since I returned to Tucson, some eight years ago. I'm sure he can read my every expression, as I can his. I do nothing as I wait for him to approach me. I don't smile, don't speak, and definitely don't frown. With a shake that starts at his nose and ends at his tail, at last the black stallion moves.

When he's taken the carrot, I climb the railing. Standing alongside, I stroke my hand down his neck. "Up for having some fun?" I croon softly, as I slip his halter on.

With Niyol content to munch on hay, I groom him until he gleams, taking care to stand at his side when I brush his tail out. Usually with me he's calm and patient, but if he's in a mood, he can have the tendency to kick out. I only had to learn that lesson once, a nice horse shoe print bruise on my thigh something to be avoided. When he's ready, I untie the halter and loop it around his neck. He accepts the bit in his mouth without too much head tossing, and calms as I put the saddle on his back and clinch the girth tightly. Then he starts stamping impatiently.

Without delaying, I leap onto his back, taking up the reins quickly. "Whoa, give me a moment, boy." He prances while my feet find the stirrups.

As soon as my heels touch his flanks, he's off. I give him his head, knowing he's as full of pent-up energy as I am. Steering away from the route Jacob will be taking, I head off on a different, less used track.

Niyol's flanks are heaving and covered with a sheen of sweat when I slow his pace, leaning forwards and patting his neck. *Just horse and man enjoying the solitude, the quietness.* Letting my body move as one with his, we plod on, covering ground, heading onwards.

The air feels fresh, the sky above me darkening as the sun starts to drop over the mountains. Old friends, knowing each other well, I'm now walking with a loose rein. Suddenly Niyol rears. I throw myself forward, easily keeping my balance. When his four legs are back on the ground, I look around, wondering what had startled him. What's that? *I thought I heard something.* I did. The finer-tuned ears of the horse had picked it up first, but now I can hear it clearly. The sound's not far away. It's screaming. A woman.

We're off the main tourist drag. There shouldn't be anyone out here. I strain my ears, nope, can't hear anyone else. *Doesn't mean she's alone though.* It's the panic in the next scream that gets me dismounting, looping the reins around the branch of a tree. I'd rather approach quietly and discreetly on foot until I find out what's going on. *Could be screams of delight. A lover's tryst I'll be interrupting.* But that's not what it sounds like. I've experienced enough cries of fear to recognise one when I hear it.

Silently, using tracking skills I learned as a youth, I walk up the path, then push quietly through the undergrowth until I come to another little-used track, then stop. My brain is analysing the situation as fast as any computer I use. A woman standing tall, her backpack held over her head, waving it at something standing in front of her in a clearing…

A *bear*. A *fucking bear*. She looks like she's going to scream again at any moment.

Noiselessly I approach her from behind. One hand going around her mouth, the other holding her still, imprisoned against my body. She struggles, her writhing brings her ass into contact with my cock. Ignoring everything, I bend my head to speak into her ear, "Listen to me. I've got you, okay?" As I talk, I straighten my legs, making myself as tall as I can. Taking the backpack from her I hold it high and still with my free hand. I tower above her smaller frame. She stiffens.

"I'm not going to hurt you." Raising my voice so the bear can hear, I use a tone similar to the one I use on Niyol when he's in a spat. "You just got to be quiet and calm down. Gonna remove my hand now. Don't say a fuckin' word. I'm letting the bear know we're human, and that we're not a threat, but also, too much for him to take on."

The slightest nod of her head. Keeping her flush to my body, I use my now free hand to slide my gun out of its holster. Don't want to shoot a bear, but if she's enraged it, it could either be it or us. And I'd rather it not be me.

"We're going now, Mr Bear," I say calmly. Keeping my voice steady, I instruct her. "Turn to me, sideways, so we can keep an eye on the bear. We'll back away so he knows we're leaving him alone." In the distance I can hear Niyol's feet stamping, the far-off jingling of his bridle. Time seems to stand still, but at least she's obeying me, and slowly we're putting distance between us and the threat.

The bear stares at us, two sets of eyes watch him back as we edge away. "Look at the ground, not at him," I whisper, trusting she's doing as I ask. "That's it. I've got you. Just follow the lead of my body."

She relaxes slightly, I take a step back, then another. Then risk a glimpse up over her shoulder. The bear's on all fours now, no longer standing up. *Could mean we're no longer a threat, could mean he's preparing to charge.*

Another sideways pace to my rear, another glance up. *Leaving your territory, brother. Didn't mean to bother you.*

As if he can sense my thoughts, the bear snorts and turns, then goes back the way he'd presumably come, his black pelt quickly being swallowed up in the twilight.

Still I'm holding her close, breathing in a perfume that makes my nostrils twitch, nothing fancy, just soap, shampoo, and her. *Her fear. I can almost taste it.*

I wait, hearing the sounds of the bear retreating until the rustling fades. My adrenaline now starts to recede, its place being taken by anger. *What the fuck is she doing here? Alone, and in near darkness. Is she crazy?*

CHAPTER 2

Mariana

An angry looking bear is a few yards in front of me, a very masculine body far too close in my personal space at my back. *Extremely close.* I get the sense of a hard cock pressing into my rear. I'm pinned to his chest, a hand with the odour of horse over my face, and I've no idea whether it's the bear or man I'm in danger from most.

Until a voice speaks into my ear, "Face up to bears, but keep calm. Screaming scares them into making an attack."

Jesus. He's right. In my panic my only thought had been to make the bear frightened so he'd go away. But it appears the one most scared had been myself. Mr Bear there, or Mrs, what do I know? Well, he looked completely in control of himself.

The man behind me is saving me. Rescuing me. When he takes his hand away, I've learned my lesson and don't let out another scream. Not one damn peep. Forcing my taut muscles to relax, I move back with him. Distracted, I focus on the bear, then reluctantly lower my eyes when instructed.

Another few steps back, my feet fumbling to stay out of the way of his, and to avoid putting more pressure on his groin. Then I can't resist opening my eyes and peering through my eyelashes. *Thank the Lord. The bear is moving away.*

I'm breathing fast, the blood rushing through my ears is deafening. I'm shaking, the arm holding me relaxes, but now I need the support to keep myself upright. *I'd been terrified.* I'll be the first to admit it.

The arm loosens again, and now I lean forward, placing my hands on my knees and taking long deep breaths. I'm just starting to calm, recognising I'm now out of danger.

"What the fuck are you doing out here? Are you alone? Is someone with you?" I glance up, seeing a face looking around me as if searching for somebody hiding.

"If there was anyone they'd have fucked off," I hiss back. "What kind of friend would they have been to just leave me?" I pull myself upright for the first time, able to properly see the features of the man who's rescued me. *He's gorgeous. Native American by the look of it.* His long black hair reaches down to his waist, tied back with a leather thong. His pupils are so big and dark, there's almost no white in his eyes at all. His tanned looking skin is dark against my more olive shade.

"You haven't answered my question," he demands in clipped tones, anger making his cheeks blaze.

It makes my temper rise too. "What the fuck is it to you?"

He rolls those beautiful eyes. "My business, if I make it. I suspect you wandered off the trail, got lost. Now I've got options. I can leave you here, or take you back to civilisation. There. My offers are on the table. Make your mind up. I haven't got all day." He pauses and looks around. "All night," he corrects.

His words draw my attention to the fact it's getting darker by the second. Where a short time ago twilight lit the area around me, now it's hard to make out anything. The sky above is clear, but there's no moon tonight, and though stars are starting to appear, they give off next to no light.

He tsks a little impatiently. "Well? Have you supplies in that backpack...?"

Interrupting him, I tell him the truth. "You're right. Came out for a hike, ate everything I had around lunchtime. I got a little distracted, got off the path, then couldn't find it again." I'd been lost before the bear, and then my rescuer, found me. Now that the wildlife danger has dissipated, my previous worry about my main predicament returns. *I'm lucky he came along. I could have been walking around in circles all night.*

He lets out a sigh as if this wasn't the way he saw his evening, and says a little grumpily, "Come then. I'll take you back." Immediately he turns, and within seconds has been swallowed up in the darkness. Instead of following what I know is a small, if little-used path, he's gone straight into some bushes.

At my squeak, the bushes part again and he reappears. This time he takes my hand, and I can do nothing more than hold on and follow him. Over in the direction he's leading me, I can hear the sounds of a bridle jangling, a horse snorting, and a hoof hitting the ground as though in impatience. *Is it only him? Or is somebody else there waiting?* While I'm grateful not to be alone any longer, I start feeling nervous about who exactly has rescued me. *What am I getting myself into here?* If that horse I hear is his form of transportation, I'll need to explain I've never been on such a beast in my life. I'm just about to ask him when his arm shoots out again and stops my progress.

He waits. Beneath us, in the quiet, I hear a slithering noise.

"What is it?" I whisper.

"Rattlesnake. Still too hot for them to hunt during the day."

"Are you going to shoot it, or something?" I'd felt the bulge of his holster and gun when he'd been holding me earlier.

He sucks in a breath. "It doing anything to hurt you?"

I shake my head, realise he can't see it, then reply, "I suppose not." Only the fact it's alive and near me. I press closer to his back as though, like he did with the bear, he can protect me.

Instead of continuing to be annoyed, he reaches back his other hand and squeezes my arm. "It's gone now. Hoping to find its dinner for the night, which wouldn't in any case have been you. Doesn't deserve death just for frightening you."

I start to deny I was scared, then snap my mouth shut. He can read me too well. Even in darkness.

Onward progress again. Soon we're on a proper path, then approaching that massive annoyed looking animal. My gasp startles it, the horse jumps back, the reins tautening where its bridle is attached to the tree. *It's going to break. It will stampede. Crush me...*

"Hey, fella. Calm down." Letting go of my hand, he expertly untangles the reins. "Shush, boy. Bitch ain't gonna harm you."

Bitch?

Lithely he puts his foot in the stirrup, does a little jump, then he's miles above me sitting comfortably in the saddle.

"Er, I'll just walk alongside."

"Nah." Kicking his foot out of the stirrup, he indicates it. "Place your foot in there, then jump up behind me."

He's got to be joking. Mount that wild beast? I take a step back, then another.

"For fuck's sake. Okay, follow the path and walk yourself out. You'll come to civilisation, eventually." He gathers the reins again. "If you don't get bit by a snake." He kicks the horse; it starts to move away.

He's leaving me alone? "No!" I cry out, trying to match my pace to that of the horse. The horse which gives a little jump in front of me. I, instead, fall flat on my face, my human eyes not good enough to see the branch blocking the path. The desert sand, at least, is soft to land on. But I swear I felt something run over my hand. "Please, please..."

I don't need to run to catch up. He's already turned back, has stopped and is waiting.

"I'm scared," I admit.

"More of the horse than the desert at night?" I think he's chuckling.

I bristle, then give a nervous look around. A slight breeze is making the leaves rustle, or is it the bear coming back? I shudder. "Both. But the sooner I'm out of here the better." The fastest way is to take the route he's offering.

"For fuck's sake." Now he's dismounted again. He leads the horse over to me. The animal doesn't look impressed. Then he's pointing to the stirrup. "You get up first."

How?

Trying to copy him, raising my leg as high as I can, I place my foot in the leather holder. Before I can do anything else his hands are under my backside, shooting me up and … almost over, but not quite. The horse prances as I land. Terrified I'm going to fall off, I open my mouth to scream when a body lands behind me, pushing me forwards in the saddle. There's barely room for us both. My groin is pushed tight up to the horn, his cock, tight to my ass.

Second time tonight. Is this usually how he gets his rocks off?

The horse starts to move as the stranger's still sorting the reins out in his hands, one going each side of me, a fleeting touch to the side of my breast which I hope is accidental. I squeal at the movement of the horse, or at least, I think that's what makes me cry out. Then I grip his arms.

Putting the reins into one hand, he fixes the other around me. "You're safe. I've got you. Not going to let you fall off."

"But who's got you?"

He chuckles again. "Niyol's got both of us," he reassures me. Then he makes a clicking sound, and the horse quickens his pace. "You'll be back soon. Just relax and enjoy the ride."

But back where? Where is he taking me? I'm riding with a real live Native American in the dead of the night. Do they still capture women and take them back to have their wicked ways with them? Scalp them? Realising I'm letting my imagination run away with me, I try to normalise the situation. "I'm Mariana," I introduce myself.

"Tse."

Even his name sounds foreign. "Tse?" I ask.

"It's Navajo. My mother got her way and named me. I'm half Native American. My father was an Anglo." He offers this by way of conversation. Probably talking to keep me calm.

I don't respond. I never give too much away about myself.

Sensing I'm not going to answer, he goes quiet. The horse, Niyol, plods on into the night, the muffled beat of his hooves almost hypnotic. The sooner we're back out of the canyon, the sooner I can leave this strange enigmatic man, collect my car and get back on with my life. *My car.*

"Er, are we going near the parking lot at the bottom of the canyon?" I ask, realising I've no idea where he's taking me.

"Guessed that's where you'd have parked. Nah, it's well over the other side. I'll drop Niyol off, get him sorted out. Then, don't worry, I'll get you back to your car."

That's something at least. I hope it's not far, my pussy is chafing against the seam of my jeans where it's pressed hard into the leather. The motion of the horse makes it more erotic than uncomfortable. My reaction is *stupid.* Isn't it? *Perhaps not. I've got a handsome man riding behind me, who's also aroused.* I make a concerted attempt to get my head out of the gutter. I was in danger, now I'm safe, my body is overreacting, is all. *But that masculine odour surrounding me.* Is it possible to be attracted to a man you've barely seen? Just because ever since I met him less than half an hour ago, his arms seemed to have been around me, or he's been touching me.

When we're crossing a field, and approaching a lit barn, I'm not sure whether I'm more relieved or disappointed. As the horse picks up his pace sensing home, I settle on the former, wondering whether I'll be able to walk straight once I get down.

The horse needs no instruction to stop in front of a gate. Tse expertly positions him, leans over, and opens it, unbalancing me so I'm again clutching at his arm. His hand brushes my chest once more as he rights me. *Can he feel my nipples are erect?*

An older man's walking out on hearing the footsteps. He glances up, then barks a laugh. "Only you, Tse. Only you could go out and find a girl. In distress, was she?" He holds his hand up over his eyes. "Or a wood nymph? Wouldn't put that past you either."

Suddenly there's no one at my back. He's off, and I'm still up here. "No spirit, a flesh and blood woman who was facin' off a bear."

"The bear won, I take it?"

"Luckily, it was a draw. Darlin'. Swing your leg over to me. That's it. I've got you."

I do what he says, land *again* in his arms as he holds me to steady me.

"You ridden before?" the older man asks.

As I shake my head, I have a fleeting moment of pride, thinking my graceful dismount had impressed him, when he disavows me of that illusion.

"Thought not. Looked like Tse was unloading a sack of potatoes."

Tse starts laughing. At the same time, he puts the reins over the horse's head. The older man undoes the girth and puts it over the saddle. "Leave it, Tse. I've got this. You look after your desert sprite."

Placing my hands on my hips I glare at them both, then realise how much I owe to Tse. "I'm sorry. I spoiled your ride, didn't I?"

The light from the building shines on his face. I was right. He's the most beautiful man I've ever seen. *In other circumstances…*

The light must be lighting my features too, as I catch a flare of interest in his eyes. *Not going there. Can't afford to.* "Thank you for bringing me back. Now, if you could just take me to my car?"

A fleeting pause, then, "Sure, darlin'. Let's get you back." He points with his hand, then when I'm turned in the right direction, puts it to the small of my back. His warmth settles through the thin material of my tee. I walk around the building, then to the small parking lot. It's empty of cars.

"Where's your…?"

"There."

I know it's dark, but a car would have been big enough to see. *Oh no.* My eyes suddenly alight on what I realise will be my mode of transportation. *A motorcycle.* A big metal beast that looks, in its own way, every bit as scary as the horse I'd just gotten down from.

CHAPTER 3

Mouse

It was only when we'd gotten back to the stables, and Jacob had led Niyol away to rub him down and give him a feed—jobs which I should have been doing—that I realised why the old man had volunteered. Having seen little more of her than a view of her back up to now, for the first time I get a look at her face, and realise she's fucking gorgeous.

Long dark hair, similar to mine and also tied back, large brown eyes in an olive-skinned face. *Hispanic.* I don't know why that surprised me, nearly half the population in Tucson has that heritage, but it did. Maybe it's her perfectly spoken English with no trace of an accent. Yeah, Jacob hadn't thought I should let this one get away. That's why he gave me space. *He could well be right.*

My cock's been half hard ever since I first pulled her back against me, painfully so while I'd been pressed up against her in the saddle. I'd taken advantage of feeling the swell of her breasts against my hand, her peaking nipples giving away she's not immune to me.

Now she'll be the one behind me, hanging onto my waist, her tits making contact with my back. I grin as I relish my anticipation, and also at her reaction to my bike. Which is about the same as when she'd first seen the stallion. *Yeah, it's time for another first tonight, Mariana.* Watching her face go through various expressions of horror, I wonder what she'd look like in the throes of passion. And whether there's any chance I might be able to find out. Doesn't hurt to hope.

Approaching the bike, I take my cut out of the saddle bag and slip it on, hearing the audible gasp behind me. Yeah, babe, I'm a real biker. *Will she be intrigued? Scared?* I guess I'll soon find out.

"I'll walk," she offers, decisively.

Looking around incredulously, my head shaking side to side, I exclaim, "You fuckin' what? It's miles if you go by the road. If you try to go cross country, you'll get lost. Or come face to face with snakes and fuck knows what else. Nah, darlin'. Won't take long. Hang onto me and you'll be fine."

"Doesn't the old man have a car? Perhaps he's going into town…?"

"Nah," I interrupt her. "Jacob bunks down here. His eyes are failin', he doesn't drive in the dark." They are. Good enough to handle a car in daylight, but at night he gets an attack of nerves. *Man's getting old.* It's not the first time the thought has struck me. *Maybe I should do more to help out.*

Time to move this along. I swing my leg over the bike, and settle on the seat. Holding out my hand, I instruct, "Come on. Get up behind me. Just hold on tight and we'll be back at your car in no time."

Still she hesitates, then says words that enrage me. "I can't, you're a criminal, you're in a gang."

"What the ever-lovin' fuck?" I dismount again and stalk her, getting up into her face. "I'm a member of a motorcycle club. We're not criminals." Or not the way she's imagining. "I should leave you here, would fuckin' serve you right, if you take one look at my cut and think you know me." My head shakes again. "Should have left you to that fuckin' bear…"

"I don't mean that!" she exclaims. "I've got nothing against you. You're right, I know nothing about your… club. But…" she clamps her mouth shut. For a second I get a glimpse of shuttered eyes before she looks down at her feet.

There's something she isn't telling me. Things which don't add up. But that's what I do. Solve problems. Just haven't got enough data to process yet. *But give me time. I'll learn her secrets.*

Why I should be thinking I want to know what's behind her unusual reactions, her lack of explanations, I'm not quite sure. Maybe it's the thrill of the chase? That she's holding back only makes me want to get to the bottom of what she's hiding. Or it could of course simply be that she's a beautiful woman who's got my cock throbbing. He's a fussy organ. I could have pussy any time I want, but I refrain from using the sweet butts back at the club. Sex isn't something I want handed to me on a plate. The woman herself has to interest me. It's starting to appear that Mariana fits that bill nicely.

She's turned to face the track leading to the road, as though calculating her chances. It's pitch black now, the light from the stables behind only illuminating the first few yards. The way she's biting her lip does nothing to calm my dick.

"Fuck it!" I walk over to her and take her hand. "Minutes, just minutes. Down this track then up the tourist road to Sabino Canyon. Minutes, darlin'. Then you'll be safe at your car and can go on your way."

Another nibble with her teeth, then she tilts her head and grimaces. "You must think I'm very ungrateful."

"I think you've got problems you don't want to share. But the least of those should be worries about ridin' behind me. I've ridden a bike for fuck, I don't know, thirteen, fourteen years? I'm safe, darlin'." Or at least a safe rider.

Suddenly I see her shoulders draw back. I realise it's the first time I've seen her smile when she turns, white teeth gleaming in the darkness. "I'm sorry. Thank you. Let's do this then." She strides to the bike.

I shoot my hand out, touching her arm, and hold her back. "I get on first. Not anything to do with manners, it just better balances the bike." Moving past her, I reseat myself. She takes my offered hand, and awkward with the unfamiliarity of it, situates herself on the pillion. Grasping her fingers, I pull her arms tight around my waist, only just north of that growing appendage I can't seem to bring under control. "Hold me tight."

She grips me loosely, until I raise the stand and the bike moves off. The path is gravelly and rutted, so I have to take it slowly. The way she's grabbing onto me now, you'd think I was going a hundred miles an hour.

I was right. It doesn't take long until we reach where she's parked her car, only a handful of other vehicles remaining in the parking lot. She gets off just as ungracefully as she got on. *She needs more practice.*

Taking her key out of her pocket, she unlocks the door, then turns. "Thank you, Tse. Thank you for all you've done today."

I accept her thanks with a nod. In truth, facing up to a bear and rescuing a maiden in distress has put a spark into my day, as well as a longing in my loins. The latter not being helped as she shows me an outline of a perfect heart shaped ass when she gets into the driver's seat. Then the door shuts, leaving me with the feeling I'm being excluded. *I know nothing about her. Except her first name.* An unexpected sense of loss takes me unawares. *I'm not ready for this strange encounter to end.*

As she fumbles to get her key in the ignition, I eye the car, realising fast what a piece of shit it is. When she starts the engine it neither purrs nor roars, but stutters in a slightly disturbing way, then stops. She starts it again, this time it draws away with a lurch. Wondering how far she's got to go, and whether it will get her all the way, I decide to follow her, just to make sure she gets home safe.

I hold back, intuitively acknowledging that if she's been so reticent about herself today, she'll probably not want a stranger to know where she lives. It's harder to keep back than I would have thought. She's driving so carefully, keeping one or two miles an hour under the speed limit. Slowing down well before lights have a chance to change to red, proceeding so cautiously across junctions. I've seen some careful drivers in my day, but she takes the prize. Uh oh, she's slowing down even more. *Hold back, Mouse. Got too close there.* Well, fuck. She doesn't give a damn about her security, hasn't looked in her mirror once, or perhaps she is just ignoring an anonymous motorcycle head-lamp. I shoot past when she turns into a run-down trailer park. By itself, that's not unusual, many people live in such places around here.

Making a U-turn, I head on back. It doesn't take me long to spot her car. *Hell, this is a shithole.* I've seen trailer parks before, of course I have. But this is one of the very worst. Looks like something I'd more likely see on the Rez.

I draw up as she's entering through a chain-link fence, climbing the two steps which take her into a small trailer. What drives me, I'm not sure, but I want to learn more about her. And, for a start, warn her about her car. Yeah, that gives me a valid excuse to be here.

She's padlocked the fence behind her, but I have that piece of crap picked in seconds. Now I'm knocking on a flimsy wooden door.

There are two concerned voices behind it. A couple of minutes pass. I knock again. The door's opened, and Mariana's standing there. Her face has drained of all colour, her eyes are wide, her nostrils flaring. Her chest rises and falls as she inhales air rapidly into her lungs. *She's fucking terrified. I did that to her.* The crime rates around here must be sky high.

"Hey." I hold up my hands. "Didn't mean to scare you."

Resting her hand on the doorframe as though to hold herself up, she bows her head, looking like she's making an effort to control her breathing. When she at last looks at me, her expression is a combination of scared and angry. "What are you doing here?" she hisses.

"Who is it, Ma?" a male voice asks.

Ma? Is she married? With kids? I start to back away, when I realise the voice had squeaked as though not completely broken. *A teenager?* How fucking old is she?

"No one," she calls back, without taking her eyes off me. "Well, why are you here?"

I wave toward her car. "You've got a brake light out. Noticed it immediately. Thought you'd want to know." She has. Normally I'd just ignore that shit, but it's given me the perfect excuse.

What I didn't expect was her reaction. Her hand covers her mouth and she looks like she's going to be ill. Her words, though, they're what really surprise me. "I can't thank you enough. Oh my God."

"Ma, what is it? Who's there?"

Not a husband, thank fuck. I notice immediately as a head pokes around the door. Features similar to Mariana's. She surely can't be old enough to have a son that age. *A younger brother, perhaps?*

"Who are you?" the kid, taller than Mariana I notice as he comes to stand beside her, demands. "What do you want? We've got no money…"

While I'm admiring the way he's standing up for her, she admonishes him. "Drew. This man helped me today."

"Helped you?" I was right, his voice squeaks on the second word. "Helped you with what?" His dark eyes, so much like hers, view me with suspicion.

Wondering whether she's going to tell him, one side of my mouth turns up. Her lips twitch too. "Drew, this is Tse," she introduces me. "Tse, meet my pest of a brother, Drew. Tse rescued me from a bear."

The kid's eyes go wide in his face. Then he chuckles. "A bear? This I've got to hear."

She looks at me, I look at her. I've delivered my message, there's no reason for me to stay. There's just something that makes me linger.

A pregnant pause, a sigh, then, "Look, you might as well come in. He'll give me no peace until he hears the full story."

A chance to get to know her. I won't turn that down. I step inside the trailer. *Fuck. I didn't realise people outside the Rez lived like this.* It's clean, but the furniture is worn and well used. There's nothing here worth stealing, only an ancient television and I doubt you could give that away. But I swallow my amazement, and take the seat that's offered to me on the only piece of furniture made for that purpose, a two-seater couch. I hadn't realised how small this place was from the outside.

Drew, the Hispanic with the very Anglo name, stands with his arms folded. "So, the bear?" he prompts.

Her mouth quirks. "You know I did what I've wanted to do for ages? I went to the canyon today." As she starts filling him in, she picks up the kettle and waves it toward me. Yeah, I could do with a coffee. I nod. She continues to speak, as she goes to the sink. In only a few short sentences she's brought her brother up to date. He's howling with laughter as she turns on the tap. Nothing comes out. Replacing the kettle on the stove, she leans forward over the counter, sighing.

"No water?" I ask unnecessarily.

"Third time this week." Drew seems totally unfazed. A common occurrence it would seem.

Without looking at me, Mariana speaks. "I've only soft drinks, I'm afraid. No beer."

"I don't drink. A soda would be fine."

Now she turns, with one eyebrow raised, and her face breaks into that beautiful smile again. "Seems I should stop making assumptions about bikers."

I chuckle. Her statement doesn't require a response.

"Noticed the leather," Drew begins, sending a censorious look at his sister.

Mariana looks flustered. "Don't you have homework to do? We'll talk later, Drew."

"I've got plenty of time for that."

"Drew." Mariana's voice deepens.

"Ma," he throws back.

I sit watching how the scene's playing out. *Data.* No parents around—this place is too small to hold more than the two of them. Only one bedroom if I'm not mistaken. He calls her Ma, which could be a shortening of her name, or to reflect she's got the parenting role, or both. *How did that happen?*

Not much money here. She must support the two of them. But how?

Placing her hands on her hips, Mariana swings around. "If you want that scholarship you've got to work for it. Go do your homework now."

"Don't like leaving you with him."

"For goodness sake, Drew. You're only in the bedroom." She stares him down. With a shrug toward her, a warning glance my way, he takes himself off. Bet that kid will be listening to everything she says. My cock's given up for the night. Won't be coming out to play in this cramped place with no privacy.

Mariana gets two sodas out of the fridge and brings them across the few short steps to the couch. From her awkwardness as she views the empty seat beside me, I doubt she often has visitors. Just her and her brother. And now I've entered her domain. Shifting up so I'm pressed against the arm, I give her room.

She sits, but doesn't lean back, making sure no part of her touches me. Propriety. I can respect that. Looking around as though seeing the surroundings through my eyes, she gives a self-deprecating smile. "It's a hellhole, I know. But it's all I can afford."

I suspect, barely that. I raise and lower my shoulders. "Seen worse."

"I doubt that."

"Hey." I half turn so I'm facing her. "Lived on the Rez a few years. Many hogans aren't much better than this. Some worse. Don't need to apologise to me for poverty."

"I work." She sounds indignant.

"Expected that." I point to the closed bedroom door. "You responsible for him? No parents?"

Her voice breaks slightly, "It's just us." Her lips purse. "Now I've got to find some way to get to work in the morning."

"It might have sounded rough, but your car got you home." I'm planning to get Blade to look at her car and sort that dying engine out if it's possible to extend its life.

"The brake light's out."

"Drive it to a shop and get it replaced. Hell, it's only a bulb…"

"I can't drive it anywhere."

She's the most careful, most law-abiding driver I've ever met. "If you're headin' to the nearest shop, cops will probably let you off. 'Specially a pretty thing like you."

Clearly unconvinced, she looks like she's going to cry. "If you hadn't told me, Tse, I wouldn't have known. I'd have driven, been pulled over..."

Data, Mouse, data. Why is she so worried about being stopped? Why does she drive so fucking carefully?

The answer hits me in a flash as my computer like brain joins the dots, ignoring the things that don't fit, sifting through those that do. "You're illegal."

CHAPTER 4

Mariana

"You're illegal."

I knew I shouldn't have let Tse into my home. Knew I should have shut the door in his face. If he hadn't been so kind today, or looked so beautiful, making my lady parts tingle in ways they never had before, I probably wouldn't have let him inside. Now he's guessed my secret. For the life of me, I don't know how he's been clever enough to put it together.

Staring at the opposite wall, I want to know, realising I'd do myself no good to deny it. "What gave it away? How did you glean that from just a broken brake light?"

He grins. I don't know how old he is, but when his face relaxes, it takes years off him. His eyes seem to twinkle. "I've a talent for sorting through facts. No, it was more than your brake light. Little things that might have passed other people by, like your reluctance to say much about yourself." He moves a little closer, and his slim hand with long slender fingers reaches out and touches my chin, a gentle persuasion to get me to look him in the eyes. "Let's get your mind eased on one thing. I'll go get you a new bulb, fix it, then you can stop worryin' about getting to work. But on one condition."

"What's that?" Is he going to ask for something I'm not prepared to give?

After a rapid shake, as though he's guessed what I'm thinking, his head tilts to one side. "I'm curious. I'd like to know how a young woman like you ends up lookin' after her brother. My price? Your story."

If I tell him everything, he could turn me in to the authorities. I bite my lip. I've tried so hard to stay under the radar, been so careful. Done everything by the book. But nowadays, the book seems to have been tossed out of the window, and I'm the only one following it. He could stir up trouble…

"Stop what you're thinkin'." His voice is sharp. "I'm not going to turn you in, even if you're not supposed to be here. I'm in a one-percenter club. We don't agree with citizens' laws."

"But how do I know I can trust you?" I feel my cheeks start to glow. "And why the hell should I say anything just to satisfy your curiosity?" He goes to speak, I shut him down. "It's dark, you haven't seen the graffiti which I'm sure has appeared again today. Everyone hates illegals, they all hate me. Why should you be any different?"

"I'm Navajo," he leans back on the seat, "well, half of me is. Believe me when I say I understand discrimination."

I breathe in. "As a Native American you've got more reason than anybody to want people like me out of your country."

"Doesn't work that way." He's dismissive. Then he points down the trailer. "Drew get much shit at school?"

He doesn't. There's a reason for that. Standing, I go to the fridge, thankful that at least that's working, then bring two more sodas back. I stay on my feet for a moment, undecided, before taking my place beside him again.

I pop the tab on my drink, then just hold it. "I'm from Colombia," I start. "My first memory of my dad was good. It's not clear, but I sense him loving his little girl. That was before he enlisted in the army." I pause, even as young as I had been, I'd noticed the change. "Some of what I think I remember, I was told by Mom. The things he was asked to do. Government-sponsored wiping out of villages. They condoned, *encouraged,* soldiers to rape the women. I suppose it affected him mentally, but you could say he brought his work home. He became violent with my mother."

I pause, risking a look at his face. His mouth is set, and his dark eyes flare.

"Very violent. He'd grab her by the neck and try to strangle her. When he turned on me as well, she knew she had to get away. She knew it was only a matter of time before he went too far. She'd seen it with a friend of hers who'd left it too late. Her friend and her young children died. The cops did nothing. Like my dad, her husband was a member of the army, somehow protected. They were too good at what they did, had been trained extremely well by American forces."

"So she ran. With you and Drew?"

"With me," I confirm. "The last night before we ran, my father had broken my arm, then turned on her. He raped her. She didn't know she was expecting until she got to America."

"Drew was born here?" His face suggests he's quickly sifted through the data again. "So he's an American citizen."

"He is," I say proudly, then the corners of my mouth turn down. "But I'm not."

"Your mom? What happened to her?"

I close my eyes, it's still too raw and painful. Blinking back tears I explain, "She applied for asylum. The case dragged on and on. She'd managed to smuggle out some of her family's jewellery. It was all sold to pay for a lawyer to progress a case that was surely cut and dried. If she went back to Colombia, my dad, who'd apparently risen in rank, would find out about it. He'd kill her for running."

"He know about Drew?"

I shrug. "I don't know. I hope not."

His hand covers mine. "Continue."

"She lost her case." Tears come to my eyes and I brush them away. "Even after ten years when we'd asked nothing from society. Both me and Drew were doing well at school, she was working three jobs to pay for us. They came and took her. Didn't care that she had kids she was leaving behind." Again, my hand wipes over my face, clearing away the tears that have escaped. "They took her while we were at school. Got home, she wasn't here."

A sharp inhale comes from my side. "Surely they came back to check you were okay? She must have told them about you? Did you have relatives? Friends who could help?"

Moving my head side to side, I let him know. "No, no one. No one from the authorities came, they either ignored or forgot about us. We had no close friends or relatives. You see, when you're flying under the radar, you don't know who to trust. I did the only thing I could, I decided to do my best for Drew. I had to keep up school, knew that. But got what cash-in-hand jobs I was able to find. Just about managed to keep our heads above water. You could say I grew up fast."

"How old were you?"

"I was fourteen, Drew coming up on nine."

"Fuck." His eyes, slightly unfocused, look into the distance. "What happened to your mother?"

"She rang," I explain. "We still had a phone then. She was held in a detention centre. I couldn't visit as there was no one to take me. She impressed on me, whatever happened, whoever spoke to me, I was to say nothing. Not tell anyone about Drew. And never to leave the US. Guess she didn't want my father to learn of his existence. Then," again my voice breaks, "I didn't get another phone call. I presumed she was deported without being able to tell me."

"And after that?" His face is set, his aquiline features standing out as his muscles tense. "Did you hear from her again?"

"I had some letters. It hadn't taken long for my father to find her. With no money, she'd had no option but to stay with her mother, her one surviving relative. It took him no time to track her down and force her to go with him. She warned me. Her situation was even worse than she'd expected. He'd found out about Drew—seen the scar from the caesarean operation and forced her to tell him. She warned me to stay hidden. Then the correspondence ceased. After that I heard about her. Not from her." I try to suppress the sob that rises into my throat. When he goes to comfort me, I wave him back. "From her mother. Mom had died. My grandmother didn't give details. I think I know the reason for that."

"Ma, why are you telling him?" Drew's agonised voice is closer than I thought. With my head in my hands I hadn't heard him leave his room. "You've only just met him. You've only got a few years…"

Beside me, Mouse stands up. "A few years for what?"

"Ma," Drew warns.

Ignoring him, I tell Tse. "I'm what's known as a Dreamer. Became one when I was fifteen. Get the paperwork renewed every two years. I should have protection for another year, until it's time to renew again. That's, of course, if I can. Who knows how things are going to change?"

"So you're not technically illegal?"

"I am, but with a certain degree of legitimacy. Unless I do something which puts me on the wrong side of the law."

"When I'm twenty-one, I can sponsor my sister," Drew puts in, almost proudly. "She should be able to get her green card."

I smile at him, but know it's unlikely. Apart from all the other impossible hoops I'd need to jump through, to be a sponsor, he will need to show he earns an income sufficient to support me. We'd need to pay a lawyer to take us through that minefield. It's expensive, and I earn no more than what allows me to keep a roof over our heads, and a growing boy fed. I shoot Tse a look, luckily he interprets it. Drew seems old for his age, but he's still just a boy of fifteen.

Tse sends me a look of understanding. Instead of asking for more details, he suggests, "I'll go out and get that bulb, shall I?" Pausing, he looks around the trailer. "Lock the door after I've gone."

"How did you manage to get through the fence?" Drew asks, his eyes narrowing.

"That reminds me," Tse grins. "I'll buy a new padlock while I'm there. The one you've got is too easy to pick."

When the door closes behind the biker, Drew shoots the dead bolts. It's more for show than anything else. If someone was determined they could easily kick it in. But no one around here owns much, nothing worth stealing. Unless you keep drugs or alcohol in the home, which we don't, there's no point breaking in.

Taking the place Tse's vacated, Drew sits beside me on the couch, and pouts like only a fifteen-year-old can. "Didn't like you talking to him, Ma."

Drew calls me Ma as a joke. A shortening of my name, and a reference to me being his mom since he was nine. I'm so used to it, I don't even notice.

When I don't respond, not sure myself why I'd told Tse all that I had, Drew fills the silence. "You see that leather he was wearing? The Satan's Devils? They're criminals. You can't risk being seen with the likes of them."

He's only echoing my fears of earlier. For some reason, I feel the need to justify myself. "I saw what he is, Drew. He's also a Native American. Neither of those things suggest he'd want to turn us in. If he hadn't followed me home to tell me my light was out, I wouldn't have known, and the police could have stopped me at any time."

"Having a brake light out isn't a felony, Ma."

But in this world we live in now, it could be enough to determine me someone not of good enough character to stay in the US. The only country I've ever really known, too young when I was brought here to remember anywhere else. As Drew busies himself putting his completed homework away, and I wait for Tse to return, I lean back my head. When I'd arrived with Mom, I'd had no idea we'd entered the country illegally. What child of four knows about visas or passports? All I knew is that my mother encouraged me to speak only English from the day I'd arrived. I already knew the basics, she herself was bilingual, and had spoken to me in both languages from the day I was born. Her way of separating us from the other Hispanics. Important not to stand out, but fit in. English is so natural to me now; I've forgotten what Spanish I'd ever known.

Drew never learned to speak anything else.

I think back to the day she was taken. Were it not for the fact I had Drew to look after, I don't know what I would have done. But with him, I couldn't allow myself to descend into despair. Having the responsibility of my brother, I just picked myself up to move forward. I tried to get advice from Mom during those phone calls, but it wasn't enough. Could never have been enough.

I went through her meagre savings quickly. Tried to get a job, running a mile after I was first asked for my paperwork. It was only at that point I realised what being undocumented truly meant. But I managed eventually to get employment, working at well below minimum wage. I washed dishes, washed cars, anything I could do where people appreciated my English and weren't fussed about seeing any documents. When I was fifteen, I applied for the Deferred Action for Childhood Arrivals program, just pleased at the time to have some kind of protection, not worried that it meant I'd entrusted the authorities with my fingerprints and all the personal information I had. At least it meant I was no longer at risk of deportation, of leaving my brother abandoned in this country where he had legal status and I had none. Two siblings, the same blood running through us.

My delight lasted for those first few years. I worked myself to the bone, got my driver's license and bought an old jalopy, the same one that's on its last legs and outside the trailer now. Then the political arena started changing, and I realised my DACA status was no longer the protection it once had been. The policy was set up for people such as myself who, through no fault of their own, were brought to the States illegally as young children. It doesn't mean I've got a route to citizenship, but it does allow me to get a work permit and, up to now, has been renewable every two years. Now that renewal is likely not to be automatic, and the illusion of legality it gives me is no longer a shield against deportation.

As I watch Drew frown, putting his homework away, I just hope I can stay with him long enough for him to become independent, wanting to give him the teenage years I never had. Already he's old for his years. *Heaven help me if I return to Colombia.* I'm under no illusions what my father will do. He's an evil man, capable of murder.

I continue to reminisce. Homework. Yeah, I did that too. As well as the jobs, barely able to fall into bed for more than six hours, and that was if I was lucky. I got my GED, then got into nursing school. Soon I'll be qualified and able to get a proper job. *Unless my quasi-legal status is revoked.*

A rattling of the fence, a knock on the door. Drew puts his fingers to his lips and goes to the window. "It's your friend."

"Let him in."

Tse enters, his tall frame immediately making the trailer feel smaller. He's brushing dirt off his hands. "All done. Give me the keys and I'll check it's working. Drew, want to come help?"

Drew looks at me, I silently nod. Two minutes later both return, Drew's smiling. "All the lights work fine, Ma, and look." He holds out a box. Seems Tse's bought spares for all the bulbs. "We'll check them regularly, okay?"

It was kind, thoughtful. I tell him so. Also appreciating that this time he's come to the trailer park, he's removed his cut. *Doesn't want to draw attention to me.*

Tse's fidgeting, moving from leg to leg as though awkward. Drew's sat down in the place he was sitting, as though making a point there's no room for him here. *There's not. Foolish daydreams to think I could have made a friend. Got to keep existing day to day, keeping everyone at arm's length. Far safer.*

I stand, but I'm not certain what to say. Tse fumbles in his pocket and brings out a card. He hands it to me. *SD Computer Security* it says on it. With a phone number. No address.

He taps it. "Call me. If you need anything. You call me." His intense dark eyes stare into mine. "Call me," he repeats. Only when I give a half-hearted nod does he look toward Drew. "Look after your sister, Drew."

"Sure." My brother waves his hand in agreement without looking at him.

Another glance at me, a rise and dip of his chin. Then he's out of the door, through the fence and out of my life. The roar of his bike fading into the distance has the mark of finality.

CHAPTER 5

Mouse

It wasn't her home circumstances that got to me, the poverty she and her brother endured. I'd spent a few years on the Rez, seen my mom's people eking a living from the earth, some without electricity, living hand to mouth. Nah, I could cope with that. What I hated was the thought even that could be taken away from her. Just one bit of carelessness, needing help from a stranger like she had today. What if she trusted the wrong person who had a vendetta?

To live with the knowledge she could be stripped of the little she had, of her only remaining family. That the government hadn't even cared, they'd taken her one parent away, confirms to me how right I am to live outside society. One thing about the Satan's Devils is that we look after family. Like Heart. When he wasn't in the right mind to care for his daughter, we'd stepped up. Weren't going to let the child suffer for the things her father had done.

Mariana had had no choice in whether she came to the US or not, just dragged along with her mother at an age when she wouldn't have understood anything. Not that she'd have been better off in Colombia, not with a violent rapist for a father. What fucking sorry excuse of a man breaks a four-year-old's arm? If they send her back, it sounds like it would be to a father who most probably had killed her mom.

I'd have liked to look into that for her, investigate further, see if there was any way I could help. But as I ride back to the compound, I realise I don't even know her last name. Would she have even given me her real one? Then I feel like hitting myself in the head. *I know her address and car registration number. Bound to be records.* Yeah, I'm the master at finding out things I shouldn't know.

I'd done more than change her light bulb. I'd topped up her oil and water, and checked the state of her tires. While I'd earlier thought I'd had preferred Blade to have given that heap of a car a once over, now I don't feel I can draw any more attention to her than I already have. That's why I, for the first time I can remember in Satan's Devils territory, took off my cut when I returned to the trailer park. I'd never forgive myself if something happened to her which could have been prevented if I'd left well enough alone.

Yeah, she's pretty. Got backbone. I suspect today's outing was one of the few occasions she's ever done something simply for herself. It's not just my cock that finds her attractive, my brain does too. But it's obvious a relationship wouldn't go anywhere. She's got to keep squeaky clean if that plan with her brother is to come to fruition. Consorting with what the cops see as a criminal gang wouldn't be in her best interest.

By the time I'm close to the compound, I've convinced myself. Despite the interest my cock has in her, I won't try to see her again. I won't interfere. Sure, I know ways of getting her fake papers, but what if I do, and something goes wrong? Nah, she's doing it legal. She's survived this long, hopefully she'll stay out of trouble until Drew's old enough to sponsor her.

I don't like it, strangely feeling I've ridden away from something, someone, who could have enriched my life. I can't see a way around it. The Satan's Devils have a lingering reputation in Tucson, one we can't seem to shake off, the echoes of a drug and gun running past still sticking to us. I'm the last person she should be consorting with.

I've given her my card. If she calls, needs me, I'll do what I can to help. But the ball's in her court now.

I turn up the track leading to home. Matt's still minding the gate, and opens it when he recognises me. *Guess Truck must still be on his shift.* It's a fucking shame we lost Fergus. I spare a quick thought for the promising prospect who had to leave to go help his terminally ill mom. Truck's good, but with all the shifts he has, Matt is left bearing the brunt. The man's only been prospecting a short while, and I wonder if he knew what he was taking on. Instead of ignoring him, I nod my thanks as I ride past.

After backing my bike into its normal space, I walk into the clubhouse. It's late. The men with old ladies have obviously come and gone, the few remaining single men are making good use of the sweet butts. I dodge my way around the tables, returning chin lifts from those not otherwise engaged, and make my way to my office.

Having checked my systems, I reopen the program that was beating me earlier in the day. A good ride on both horse and bike seem to have cleared my head and the erroneous line of code jumps out at me. I change it and sit back with a satisfied smirk on my face. *Got you.* I roll a joint and light it, inhaling deeply. The smoke absorbed by my lungs mellows my mood as I again think back over the evening.

Pulling my tablet toward me, before I consciously know what I'm doing, I'm tapping in the little I know about Mariana. Then I stop myself, reaching over and lighting the joint again instead. I might not like her situation, but there's fuck all I can do about it. What would knowing more about her situation help her or me? I need to stay away from her, put her right out of my mind. Last thing she needs is a man like me getting into her business, and possibly causing her problems. I live in Arizona after all, and it doesn't take much for an illegal to be gleefully taken off the street by the cops and handed over to Immigration and Customs Enforcement, ICE, who can be as cold as their name.

I'm restless. On edge. Off balance. Whether it's just my lingering sensation from earlier today, a horse ride I hadn't been able to lose myself in, or meeting the woman who I'd have loved to see again but my common sense tells me I can't, I'm not sure. Logging out of the programs I don't need running, I stub out the joint, and take myself off to my suite.

All the brothers who live on the compound have their own room and bathroom, together with a balcony from which can be seen the most stunning views, the benefits from the club having bought a burned-out vacation resort and restoring it. Going outside I watch a late summer storm flash lightning over the distant mountains, only returning inside when the first heavy raindrops start to fall. I need space, air. I'm starting to feel suffocated here. *It's time to get away.*

Decision made, the next morning I go to find Prez. He's in his office, his son, Eli, with him. I grin at the sight.

"Starting him early, Prez?" I take the seat he points to.

Putting Eli on the floor to play with some toys, Drummer looks down at his son fondly. "Never too soon to let him know he's a Satan's Devil."

Little prez in the making there, I suspect. If he's anything like his father.

"What can I do for you, Mouse?"

Leaning forward, I put my hands on my knees. "Need to take off, Prez."

His eyes narrow, and his hand rubs at his beard. "Like that, is it?"

I've tried before to explain what I can't put into words. The two sides of me warring constantly, the Anglo and Navajo not coming to terms. The need to find myself, restore balance once again. It's hard to express, and harder still for Drummer to understand. I think, by now, he's given up trying. For an answer, I raise my chin.

"You'll keep in contact?"

As far as I can, yes. "I'll have my laptop with me, and my phone. I'll check in for messages and do whatever you need me to. There's not much I can't do remotely." When I pick up his messages, of course, as where I'm going that can take some planning. But he's giving me time off—oh, I've no doubt he'll agree to it—and I'll do my best to ensure I'm not leaving my brothers in the lurch.

"Stay in touch, Mouse. You'll be missed."

"I'll let you know when I'll be comin' back."

"Appreciate that." He nods, just once.

I stand and take my leave. This time of the morning the clubroom is empty. Returning to my suite I pack what I can into my saddle bags, send a quick message to Jacob explaining I'll be gone for a while and to look after Niyol for me—which he'd do without the reminder -then I'm on my bike and off on my journey.

As I ride north, I let my mind drift back to the first time I went to the Rez. I hadn't wanted to go. Absolutely no fucking doubt about that. But then, in the first fifteen years of my life, I'd never even considered the possibility I'd be changing the streets of Tucson for the area bounded by the four sacred mountains.

I was brought up as an Anglo in Tucson. I went to school, had friends, was a quarterback on the football team. If it wasn't for my mom, or my skin or the features that I'd inherited from her, no one would have known I wasn't totally white. I spoke English, and a smattering of Spanish I'd picked up from the Hispanics in class—mostly swear words. I had my life planned out in front of me, and nothing could happen to make me deviate from that path. I had my eye on a football scholarship, maybe eventually joining one of the big teams.

My father was white with a ruddy complexion. He'd met my mother when she'd been selling some blankets she'd woven by the side of the road when he'd driven through the reservation. It had been, apparently, love at first sight. Though he had no need for more, he'd gone back for blankets time and time again. Until one day she'd agreed to get in the car with him, and leave everything she had ever known behind.

I'd come along pretty quickly, but due to complications with my birth, had been their only child. The mom I'd always known seemed happy, content to keep house, a quiet unassuming woman. It was only later I realised she'd burned her bridges, and how much she must have missed her previous life.

My father had given her one stipulation, that I was to be brought up as a white boy. They might not have been able to change the darker colour of my skin, but I'd never considered myself as anything other than Anglo. As I grew older, I realised English wasn't my mother's first language, and that she looked different from other boys' moms. But with the number of Hispanics in Tucson, she didn't look out of place. I was much older when I first heard the term Navajo, but soon learned not to mention it. Navajo were *Indians* to the kids I did tell, and for a while I was subjected to whoop-whooping noises whenever I passed. A move to middle school, where I put a zip on my mouth, thankfully left that behind me.

My father must have been disappointed, but never said a word as I grew to resemble the heritage on my mother's side. My mentality, though, well that was all white.

I pull up for gas. With my tank topped off I get back on the road, and allow the memories to continue to flood over me. My hand tightening on the throttle as I remember exactly how and when my life changed, which led me ending up at the one place I never expected.

All caused by the truck slamming into my father's SUV, pushing it into a flooded wash in one of the summer monsoons. Injured from the crash, possibly knocked out—we never knew for certain—the car had been swept away and my dad died before he could be rescued.

Mom didn't even try to survive in the Anglo world without him. Even before the funeral she was packing our bags and ending the lease on the house. Fuck, I'd hated her for that. For wiping everything they'd been together out of existence. Now I'm older, I imagine it was the only way she thought she could cope.

It's always hard on a boy to lose his father, especially when they've had a good relationship. I'd felt adrift, lost in wild seas without anything to anchor me. My sixteenth birthday only weeks away, I couldn't get my head around the loss. *My dad's gone. He's never coming back.* I was now the man of the family, but not entitled to be involved in any decision making, it would seem.

"We're what?" My head shakes with incredulity, only a few minutes since I'd come home from school, unable to believe what I was seeing and what she had just told me. "Mom? What's going on?"

"We're moving, Tse."

Looking at the boxes packed and labelled, I can see that. "Yeah, but what did you say? To the reservation?" My head keeps moving side to side as I look around in disbelief. "These are labelled for the thrift shop, Mom." It looks like we'll be taking little more than our clothes with us.

"We're moving in with my parents. Your grandparents. We haven't got room for everything."

A crow's flying alongside me. It stares at me for a moment, a man on his own on his bike on the road, and then it flies off into the desert as if mocking me for being even freer. Yeah, I had to leave everything behind. An Xbox would have been useless on the Rez. Fuck, how upset I'd been. I was going somewhere I'd never dreamed of visiting, let alone living there. Meeting people I've never met, and only occasionally heard of. I didn't know why my father had wanted my Navajo family kept away from me, but that's what he'd done. To a fifteen-year-old boy it was like my mother was transporting me to a different world. A place I couldn't begin to imagine. I hadn't made it easy for her.

"My friends are here. My school…"

"There are schools on the reservation. You'll make new friends."

I know it won't be as simple as that. A new kid on the block, one who can't even speak the language, is likely to be picked on, not welcomed. I pull my shoulders back. "Mom, I'll leave school. Get a job. Support you…"

"Oh, Tse," she sighs. "I can't survive in Tucson. Not without your father by my side. It's time I returned to my family. And past time you learned about your culture."

"It's not mine. It's yours." With that shout as my parting shot, I walk out of the house, go to my friend's home, and spend the evening sharing my woes.

No argument I put forward can persuade her. One morning a man, not looking unlike myself, parks a truck outside our house. Mom opens the door, and is in his arms, making me glare, remembering the recent loss of my father. They speak in rapid fire Navajo, a language I've never heard used in conversation before and one I don't understand a single word of. Voices rising and falling, making it impossible for me to identify syllables. Hearing them brings my fears back in full force.

I don't interrupt, just wait until Mom remembers I'm there. She spins around, a smile on her face for the first time since we lost Dad. "Tse, this is my brother. Your uncle. He's come to take us home."

We are home, I think as I glare. But at least there's an expla-nation for the emotional display.

My uncle steps forward, nodding toward Mom. "Sorry bout Fatter. Muttah reddy ta leave." His heavy accent confirms all my fears. I'm going somewhere I don't even understand what they're saying.

As my eyes go wide, Mom slaps his wrist. "Stop it, Roy, please. Tse's worried enough as it is."

A wink toward me, then her brother holds out his hand. "Pleased to meet you at last, Tse. Ready to get going?" His accent has all but disappeared.

I later learned it was a trick they played on tourists, playing the part as expected. In time, I'd come to find most Navajo spoke English no differently from anyone else I'd ever met, except maybe in their excitement pronouncing th as tt. That morning, I was just relieved that despite my concerns, I was probably going to be able to comprehend everything said around me.

CHAPTER 6

Mouse

Riding automatically, I don't notice the scenery rushing by, still lost in the past and in recollections of the first time I made this journey. A kid who hid his fear beneath a sullen mask. Who could blame that scared child/man?

It was a new chapter in my life. In some ways like being reborn all over again. Taken from the loving home I'd first entered as a baby, uprooted and then set down in a primitive eight-sided hogan made of logs, staying with my grandparents and mother, all sleeping in one room. There was no electricity in our house, we were too far off the grid.

For a boy brought up in Tucson, it was a complete culture shock. No wonder Mom had given away my Xbox.

The move had been as bad as I'd feared. There I was, a stranger, someone not from the Rez despite looking like I belonged there. Most of the kids expected to spend the rest of their lives on the reservation, so they didn't bother to keep up their grades, many dropping out of school early. Me? I saw education as a way I'd be able to escape, and, with no friends and nothing much else to do, something to occupy me. So I threw myself into my studies, quickly finding I had an aptitude for using computers for something other than games.

I wasn't the only outsider, there were a few white kids who attended the school too; children of teachers, nurses, and other Anglos who worked on the reservation. My natural inclination was to gravitate to them, but I wasn't part of their tribe, and any friendship I made would only set me apart from the Navajo. I didn't fit in. Anywhere.

A windblown frown comes to my face as I continue to remember. I'd gotten my ass kicked more times than I care to remember, my food dumped off my lunch tray. My tennis shoes once stolen so I had to walk home barefoot. I was as miserable as anyone could be.

One Saturday morning, I was sitting outside the hogan, just kicking my feet, not knowing what to do with myself. Oh, the boys here played football, just like I had in Tucson, but obviously I hadn't been picked for the team. It seemed no one knew how to treat me, which wasn't surprising, I hadn't gone out of my way to make friends.

Until I got my own head out of my ass.

"Got room there for me?"

I inch over to make room on the log for my grandfather to plant his ass next to mine. He stares into the distance, and for a time doesn't speak. Then he clears his throat. "Your mom ran off with the white man. Didn't settle easy with me. Knew she had a son, hoped she'd bring you to meet us sooner. Didn't happen that way."

It hadn't. Just as well. There'd have been nothing here for me then, as much as there isn't now.

"Not good, a boy growing up not knowing his family or his history."

I shrug. It had suited me just fine. Until Dad died, I'd had all I wanted in Tucson.

He gives me a sideways glance. Unlike my long hair, his was trimmed short. I was surprised to find not many Navajo wore their hair long nowadays, but I'd refused to cut mine just to fit in. Refused to do much to help myself. Just pig headed, another sign I was unwilling to do anything to make my life easier. Kept hoping it was all a bad dream and I was going to wake up and find myself back home. In Tucson, where I belonged.

"You ever hear about your great-grandfather?"

I shrug again. He wouldn't mean the one on my father's side who'd fought in the second world war.

"Heard anything about the Navajo Code Talkers?"

"Some." I vaguely remember something in history, but it wasn't a subject I was interested in.

"Navajo's one of the most difficult languages to learn." My huffed laugh, having already discovered that, rolls past him. "Well, the Navajo had been treated badly by the US Government, but it didn't stop them joining up to fight alongside Anglos in the war. It was something bigger than this country, something that threatened the whole world." His eyes, unfocused, look my way but don't seem to see me. "At that time, the number of non-Navajo people who could speak our language could be counted in tens. And few at that. So, using a code based on Navajo, and using Navajo Marines to translate it, was proposed as a way to organise the troops without the enemy knowing what the American army was doing."

My shoulders rise and fall, my head shakes. Okay, so they sent and translated messages in code. Big deal.

"They played an invaluable part in being able to beat the Japanese in the Pacific Theatre. Before the code was used, the Japs always got wind of what the US were up to, and what they planned to do. Wasn't always easy though. Navajo looked like Japs to some of the US troops. Ended up they needed to be paired with a white man to keep them safe. They didn't sit in an office; they were out on the front line. Saved those Marine asses."

"And my great-grandfather was one?" My interest begins peaking.

"One of the original twenty-nine."

"Cool." For the first time, I realise that part of my history has played an important role in the world. Perhaps the Navajo have more to offer than I thought.

"Was he ever in danger?"

Grandfather grins, looking much like he's caught a fish on the hook. Now he's got me wriggling, he continues, "Sure was." My interest caught, I eagerly listen as he rambles through some old stories, a boy intrigued by tales of war and fighting.

That was my first talk with the old man, but certainly not the last. Through him I started to learn about my Navajo heritage, their beliefs, their understanding of the world and the way it worked. Some things I scoffed at, some things made sense. We spent many a time on that log. Me absorbing an education I wasn't aware I'd been learning. I smile at the memory as I back my hand off the throttle.

I'm here. I stop my bike at the sign denoting the reservation of the Navajo Nation, killing the engine, listening to the peace and quiet, breathing the air that at one time I never thought would make me think of as signalling I've come home. Above, a hawk is flying, dipping down as though to welcome me back. My Navajo blood seems to run freer through my veins. I shake out my hands, stiff from the long ride, then start my engine again. I've still got a way to go until I reach my destination, the reservation covers over twenty-seven thousand square miles of land.

Surprisingly, it was the one thing my mom had encouraged me to learn back in Tucson that started me on the road that would see me being accepted by my contemporaries.

"Hey, Tse. Navajo ride horses. Let's see whether you're a natural."

My eyes sharpen as I look up from my book. Billy and Thom aren't exactly my friends and I don't immediately trust them.

Well, none of the boys here are my friends. But maybe this is where I've got something up my sleeve to surprise them.

I've been here a few months now. Summer's turned into winter the likes of which I've never previously experienced. Down in Tucson the dark months were mild, but here there's snow and ice, and the wood stove is kept burning. Like any human I yearn for company, so gradually I've started trying to fit in. My initial aloofness I realised was a mistake as it had come back to bite me. Knowing now it was going to be an upward struggle to get Navajo boys to become my friends.

I stand, putting down my book. "Yeah, I can ride a horse."

They mockingly laugh. "Sure you can." Billy slaps my back. "Sure you can, White Boy."

Yeah, because my habits were 'white' to them, I've picked up a nickname.

I follow them to Billy's house, and to a corral out back. Then come to an abrupt halt. Hmm. I can ride, but not a fucking unbroken paint horse. But I committed myself when I told them I could. Can't back out now. Not without looking like a pussy. Can't be much worse than breaking Niyol back in Tucson.

As Billy approaches him with a bribe of an apple in his hands, I see the horse accepts the halter at least. But I also note the white in his eyes. My hands clench by my sides. I can do this. In my head, I see myself calming the mustang, bringing him under control, and back to my friends fully broke. One side of my mouth turns up. I got this. I'll be the one to tame him. I'll show them.

Picturing that image in my head, I saunter down to where the horse is now being led toward a gate.

"You sure you want to do this, White Boy?" Thom, at least, has a look of concern on his face. Billy's just grinning widely.

"Said I would, didn't I?" Without hesitation, as though I've been rodeo riding all my life, I take the rope of the halter, then lead the horse the final few steps to the gate. Climbing the rails, I

sit on top, then in one smooth movement, lower myself down gently, and quickly have myself on the back of the horse.

A split second's warning is all I get before the beast takes off, bucking and broncing across the corral. The space isn't large, obviously not big enough for the mustang's liking. Aware of horrified exclamations behind me, before I know it we've jumped the fence and are galloping out over the reservation.

I've no saddle, I'm just using my balance, having nothing to grab but that long mane for support. Tugging on the rope attached to the halter does nothing to slow the speed. There are moments when I can enjoy the rush of air through my hair, interspersed with longer intervals of sheer panic, knowing it's today I'm going to die.

I tug again, at least I'm turning his head, now we're heading back the way we came at speeds I've never gone, when suddenly the mustang gives an enormous buck. As its rear heels come up over its head I'm heading in the same direction, somersaulting through the air, landing with a crash on my back, knocking the wind out of me.

"You alright?" Billy's voice seems to come from far away. "Fuck, Thom. Go and get help…"

"I'm fine," I gasp on the whoosh of air leaving my lungs. "What about the horse?"

Billy puts his arm around me and helps me sit up. He does that thing all Navajo do, instead of pointing with his finger, he pouts his lips and I follow the direction he turns his face in. The fucking horse is grazing only a few yards away. At least it's not galloping across the plains with a rope that could get trapped around its feet.

Surprisingly Billy puts out his fist, I bump it with mine. "You can ride, White Boy."

Thom's shaking his head. "Lost the bet. Didn't even think you had the nerve to get on."

I know I'll feel the bruises later, but for now I'm grateful to be alive. For a moment, I thought I was dead.

I might not have broken the horse, but that day caused the first crack in the defences I'd put up between me and those I eventually came to see as my brethren. It also resulted in a warming of them to me. *Something in common.* Perhaps the 'white' boy wasn't so useless after all. Soon after I began kicking a football around with them, then was selected for the team.

As winter turned into spring, spring to summer and autumn came around once again, I began to feel this was my place. I even started to call it home.

Again I stop the bike, this time turning off the engine and dismounting, heading for the place I lived when I first arrived. A now neglected hogan, left for the elements to eventually destroy. I stand near, but don't go in through that door, which, like in all hogans, opens to the east to get the morning sun and good blessings. Inside is where twelve years ago, just two years after I'd arrived, my grandfather died, taking his last peaceful breath after a severe stroke had left him incapacitated. A merciful ending, as he wouldn't have wanted to live like that. In the way of my people, the hogan, having been a place of death, was vacated and thereafter left empty, now regarded as cursed or haunted.

After his death, my mother and grandmother moved closer to Window Rock, a new hogan built by myself and my uncles with the modern convenience of electricity. The small city is where I attended high school.

After paying respects to the memory of my grandfather, I return to my bike and head towards my mother's home. As I pull up outside, and switch off my engine, I sniff the air, smelling the unmistakable aroma of mutton and fried bread coming from inside. My taste buds salivate in expectation, my lips curve remembering when I lived here I'd longed instead for a Big Mac and fries. I dismount, take a step, then am stopped by a vibration.

At least we're in the vicinity of a cell tower now. "Yeah, Drummer. What's up?" I wave to my mom, who hearing my bike has appeared, indicating I'll be there in a moment.

"You know how long you're going to be gone?" Prez's voice booms in my ear.

"Jeez, Prez. I've just arrived. Not even said hello to my mom yet." My mom, who's not waited, and currently has her arms encircling my waist.

"Got things going on." I frown, not wanting to have to go back straight away.

"You need me?" I'm not surprised. Shit always seems to land on the club. Satan's Devils attract it like shit does flies.

"Nah. You're okay. Just need some info for now. Got a new club settin' up in our area. Chaos Riders. Check 'em out, will you?"

"Sure thing, Prez." I make a mental note to do just that. I'll need to find somewhere I can pick up wi-fi. "Anything else?"

"Not for now."

At last I'm putting my phone away, and swinging my mom around in my arms. *Home.*

CHAPTER 7

Mariana

I don't know what magic Tse has done to my car, but the next day it seems to run better than it has done in months. The engine turns over and catches straight away. Maybe my luck is turning.

I've just dropped Drew off at school, and now am making my way to the college where I'm getting close to completing my second year of studying for my associate's degree in Nursing. The one thing my mom did impress on me was making the most of the advantages living in the US gave me, and at the top of that list was education. Though it's been a struggle, supporting Drew and myself, and it's hard balancing the coursework with the jobs that I do, I'm determined to become qualified and do a worthwhile job, giving something back to my country. Drew's offered that after his birthday, he'll get a part-time job too. That should help. Eventually my plan is to work and hopefully complete my four-year degree after I've got a couple of years' experience under my belt. *Almost there.* Just another few months and I'll have my first qualification.

As I drive, I think about yesterday. I rarely take a day off, but persuaded by Drew to make time for myself, for the first time in ages I did something I'd long wanted to do. Until I strayed from the path and came face to face with that bear, I was enjoying the beauty of the canyon, which I'd wanted to explore for some time.

But the bear incident brought Tse to me. Last night I dreamed about my rescuer. The man so striking in looks, and so kind. If only I'd been free to indicate my interest in him. His card and number are stuck to the fridge in my trailer, and that's where they're going to stay. Though I'd love to, I won't contact him, won't do anything to encourage the mutual interest I'm sure I'd seen in his eyes. I won't even ring to say thank you, even though I know he did more than just swap out a broken bulb last night. A brake light working doesn't make a car run any better.

For a moment, I imagine what it would be like to have a relationship with a man such as him, or anyone for that matter. Someone who'd be there for me, someone to share things with. Since my mom had been taken away, I've had no one to lean on, no one to talk to. No one to share my hopes and fears with. Maybe that was why I'd been so open with Tse yesterday. He'd been easy to talk to. Drew's getting older now, but even so, there's only so much I can disclose to him. He's lost one parent; I don't like to worry him that he could lose me too. Unlike me, he doesn't have to fear exposure, he's a US citizen, with the birth certificate to prove it.

He's not stupid, that's why he was upset I was speaking to Tse yesterday. He keeps my secret, doesn't have friends over, doesn't talk to anyone about his illegal sister. Talks about his plans to sponsor me. But it's not just the money he'd need to be earning. What I haven't explained is that in order to apply for a green card, I'd have to enter the country legally. I'd have to get a visa to cross that border, and take the unlikely chance I'd be allowed back through. *It's safer to stay and take my chances.*

Life goes on, each twenty-four hour period the same. I work myself to the bone, study or do work experience during the day, fall into my bed each night exhausted. As days turn into weeks, my adventure in Sabino Canyon becomes just a distant memory. Even though I try to recall it, each day Tse's face fades in my mind.

"You look rough." Drew's critical eyes sweep over me.

I normally do when I've had little sleep, but last night was worse than normal. I had a dream, so vivid and real, my unconscious memory dredging up details I lose when I wake, however much I try to relive it. It was impossible to go back to sleep. What was it about Tse that my mind doesn't want to forget after all this time? I barely met the man, yet he haunts my nights. *Last night he was trying to tell me something, but I couldn't make out the words.*

"Coffee will sort me out." I fill the pot, glad water's coming out of the tap today, and wait for it to brew.

Drew's still watching me carefully. "I hate you having to push yourself the way that you do."

Putting on my brightest smile, I turn to him. "It's not for much longer, Drew. I'll be qualified soon, and will be able to take a nursing job. That will bring in much more money than I'm able to earn now. I won't be working eighteen-hour days anymore." My smile becomes genuine as I imagine the future I'm painting for myself.

"Long enough, sis. And what about when your DACA status runs out? What if they won't renew it?"

Pouring coffee into a cup, I wave him off. "I'll worry about that when the time comes." I might sound dismissive, but the truth is, I worry about that all the time. Waiting for my drink to cool, I gaze out of the window. This is the only home I can remember, I have a few shadowy recollections of the place where I spent my first four years, but that's all. I don't speak the language, don't know the people. If I was returned to Colombia, what the hell would I do? Would I still be able to be a nurse? Would the country of my birth reap the benefits of my education in North America? That seems crazy to me.

I shudder, and try to cover it up. I couldn't leave Drew, and certainly couldn't take him with me. My pulse races as I face my fears, and the coffee trembles in my cup. I make an effort to still my shaking hands. My back towards my brother, I breathe deeply, trying to get my mind on the day ahead, trying to force my ever-present anxiety into the background. *I can't let it show. Have to be strong for him.*

"Got football practice tonight, remember?" Drew reminds me.

"Mal dropping you off after?" The focus on everyday things helps bring me back to the here and now, *just take it day by day.* I keep my voice light.

"Yeah. You ready to go, Ma?"

I drain my cup and turn around with a cheery smile. "Let's get this day started, shall we?"

The dream from last night stays with me. Tse's face, so close, so detailed I felt I could reach out and touch it, his mouth opening and shutting as he spoke a warning. *Take care.* Why, after three weeks, should I still be thinking of him? Why that dream, why those words of caution? I'm always careful, I think as I drop Drew off. *Nothing unusual here.* I point my car towards the community college, and, as I normally do, drive carefully.

There's a traffic light ahead, it's just turned red. I slow, stopping well in time as I draw up to it. A few seconds while I wait, the signal obstinately refusing to change. Then suddenly my car's moving and my body tries to fly forward, violently halted by the seatbelt. *What the hell?* My chest hurts, my knees are pushed up against the steering wheel.

Someone's at my door, trying to open it. Stunned, I don't even try to help. Then it's open, and a stranger's reaching in, turning off my engine—*why hadn't I thought of that?*

"Are you alright?"

I can't answer, can't speak, just turn my eyes on him. I'm in shock, unable to understand what happened. A crowd has gathered. *Got to get out. Got to see what the damage is…*

As I go to move, the man places a hand on my shoulder. "Ambulance is coming. Stay there. You don't know how badly you're hurt."

I've got to get out and find out. Can't afford an ambulance. "I'm okay, just shocked." I find my voice at last. "I don't need medical help."

I fumble with the seatbelt fastening, managing to get it undone, then slide my legs out. Pulling myself up by the doorframe, I stand, leaning on the roof of the car while my shaking legs threaten to give out. It's then I look at the damage. My car's crumpled up, both rear wheels at odd angles. I know in a flash I'll never be driving it again. *I can't afford a new car.* Then I look at the one that's driven into me. The driver is out, his eyes shooting daggers in my direction, and he's gesticulating to the state trooper who's just arrived and got out of his vehicle.

It's then I notice the policeman's partner coming toward me. "Driver's licence?" he asks when he gets close.

Holding my painful chest, leaning into the car, I take out my purse and pass the document over. He peruses it, then glances up. "Mariana De Souza?"

I nod. Yeah, that's me.

"Can you tell me what happened?"

I wave back at the traffic light, now a few feet to my rear. "I was stopped on red, Officer. I wasn't looking behind me, I was concentrating on watching for the light to change. I knew nothing until that car ran straight into me."

His lips purse. He looks back at his colleague and shakes his head, then to me, he instructs, "Wait here."

Another police car has turned up. Two more patrol officers emerge. The four cops group together.

The man who helped me has slipped away. "Did anyone see what happened?" I ask, my voice trembling. *The cop didn't believe me.* That much is obvious. What did he think caused the accident? How could I be held responsible?

The crowd is dispersing, no one wants to be questioned. No one comes forward to support my account. But then, it's possible nobody saw anything. It happened so fast, after all.

I'm going to be late. I start taking my phone out of my purse to call my tutor, when the state trooper appears once again.

"I'm going to have to ask you to come to the station, Ms De Souza. There's some things we need to sort out."

"You're arresting me?" I squeak. *What? Why? How?*

He shakes his head. "We just need to question you further."

I feel faint, once again resting my weight on the roof. *Do they know I'm illegal? But I'm not, I've got the DACA papers.* "What about my car?"

"It will be towed."

Another thing I'll need to pay for.

I suppose I'm lucky he doesn't cuff me, but I'm led over to the patrol car, and made to sit in the back. He takes my purse off me, and places his hand on my head as I bend to get inside. I gasp as the movement hurts my ribs. Then I'm sitting behind a grill-like barrier separating me from the cops. When the door shuts, I notice it's got no handle on the inside.

The state troopers get in the front, the engine starts, and we drive off. They're not talking to me; they're discussing a ball game they watched last night. Laughing and joking while I'm hurting and scared to death. *What's going to happen to me?*

It doesn't get better. At the police station, they take my finger-prints, before escorting me to a cell. I'm left there. Alone. Worried out of my mind.

I didn't do anything wrong. It was the other driver's fault. He ran into me. Why have they brought me here? Why don't they believe my story? What other explanation could there be?

Tears, which have been threatening to fall for a while, now start streaming. To have a chance of permanent residence, I have to keep my record clean. *Have I been arrested? Will I be charged? Will it mean I'm deported? What's going to happen to Drew?*

The door opens. A dour looking woman waves me out. I'm taken to a room where a man is waiting. He's a doctor, he says, but I don't take much in. Simply let him examine me. "I doubt you've broken anything, but you hit the seatbelt with some force. There will be bruising and you'll be sore for a while."

He offers no sympathy, and neither does the female police officer. He makes some notes in a file, then I'm taken back to the cell again.

Why the waiting? Why can't they get on with it, whatever it is?

Drew. What will happen to Drew? What if I'm not there when he gets back from football? I haven't got my phone, I can't even let him know. *Last night's dream was an omen.*

I'm going to be deported. Sent to a country I have no knowledge of. *Will my father be waiting?*

Dread settles inside me as I sit alone, waiting for the unknown.

CHAPTER 8

Mouse

I couldn't tell Drummer how long I'd be away. I didn't know myself. Just as long as it takes for me to regain some perspective about my life. It's a chance to recharge my batteries, to reconnect with that part of me which calls to the wild and untamed land of my ancestors on my mother's side. Riding with the Satan's Devils satisfies the Anglo in my blood, being here quiets the Navajo essence flowing through my veins. I always end up grounded.

Immersed in my heritage, twenty-first century beliefs and teachings fall away as I'm drawn back in, listening and nodding without thinking to question it when my mother and grand-mother discuss the sighting of *yee naaldlooshii,* a skin-walker—a witch who takes on the form of an animal and who causes injury or death to their victim. Conversations abound as to who it could possibly be. I attend a Blessing ceremony given for one of my cousins who's pregnant. I ride, walk and simply let myself absorb the atmosphere. I have no desire to smoke a joint, or to touch a computer.

I don't spend time missing my brothers. They'll be there when I return, and if they needed me, I'd go back immediately. There's only one person who I seem unable to get out of my mind, and I think about her daily. When I'm enjoying my soli-tude, for some reason, memories of her come into my mind, and I find myself straining to recall every detail of her features. One puzzle I'm trying to solve is a way that we could explore what I'm certain is a mutual attraction between us. I'm having more difficulty keeping my promise to stay away than I'd have thought.

I wonder whether Mariana ever thinks of me. Ever remembers the firsts I gave her, the two different rides.

Last night I dreamed of her. It may have been the discussion about the skin-walker playing on my mind, or simply being enveloped by superstition, but I dreamed someone was after her. A shadowy figure who I couldn't bring into focus. All I could do was try to warn her, I'm not sure she heard. I woke with the sensation that she was in danger. I got up and stretched, and put it behind me. But I can't shake it off. *When I return to Tucson, I'll check up on her.* Yeah, I can do that.

I've spent the evening reliving old times with Billy. Thom, it seems, has got a good job for himself at the Navajo power station and is living in Page. Billy's stayed to look after his parents' horses and sheep. I meet his wife, a tiny woman who seems to rule the household, and their four children ranging in ages from ten to a babe in arms.

Halfway through the visit he opens yet another can of coke, I'm still drinking my second. "Your bike's a bit better than the one you started on," he observes.

I chuckle. "You could say that."

"Where the fuck did your grandfather get it from?"

"The scrap, I think." Which makes him laugh.

Yeah, that would have been believable. Grampa had known I was getting restless without some form of transport. He couldn't afford to buy me a car, so he picked up a heap of metal that was barely recognisable as a motorcycle. My eyes glaze as memories take me back.

"What the fuck is that, Gramps?"

He glares, but doesn't correct my language. "That, my boy, is your new way of getting around."

Throwing him a look as if he's crazy, I walk around the pile of junk, leaning heavily and precariously on its stand, looking like a breath of wind would topple it. I kick the two tires, bare in places, what remains has hardly any tread at all. "Looks more like a death trap."

"Just needs a bit of love and attention," the old man says. Then, putting his hand on my shoulder, he continues, "We'll do it together."

That's exactly what we did. New tires, brakes, exhaust, and we rebuilt the engine. At last it was finished, and I was able to ride. From the very first time I sat astride it, I was completely and utterly in love.

We hadn't bothered about the aesthetics, it still looked like a rat, but went like the wind.

"Thought I was going to come off, first time you took me on it." Billy looks over with a wide grin. "Thought you were going to pay me back for putting you on that horse."

The corners of my mouth turn up. "Thought about it," I admit, then smirk. "Especially when you screamed."

"Did not."

"Did."

His wife, who's nursing their youngest child, looks up. "You sound like a couple of kids." Her voice drips with amused scorn. One of the older children giggles. I enjoy the visit, enjoy hearing about Billy's life on the Rez, while he relishes in hearing about mine with the Devils. Sitting here I feel completely at home and relaxed. Life in Tucson seems a million miles away. *I'm not ready to go back yet.*

I promise to visit again soon, then take my leave of Billy and his family, and go back to my bike to ride home. While we used to be neighbours, when my mom and gramma moved, it put a fair distance between us.

A sudden gust of wind takes me unawares. My bike stays steady, but the strangeness of the breeze blowing up out of nowhere gets to me. Despite scoffing at myself, I look in my rearview mirror, half expecting to see a coyote lolloping after me. *Mouse, you've been listening to too many stories.* But still, as I ride on, I keep checking behind. What seems impossible in Tucson isn't inconceivable here.

Laughing at the feeling of relief I get when finally I draw up, unmolested by a skin-walker, outside the hogan, I put down the stand and am conscious of my phone vibrating in my pocket. *Trouble?* Could be.

"Mouse," I answer without thinking, expecting it to be Drummer.

"Er, I wanted to talk to Tse?"

"You got him." Hardly anyone apart from my family calls me by my government name. I grow cautious. "Who's this?"

"You might not remember me, but my name's Drew. Andrew De Souza. Mariana's brother."

Mariana. The girl I can't get out of my head. *The girl, last night, I dreamed about.* "What's happened?"

A noise which sounds suspiciously like a sob reaches my ear. "She's been arrested."

"What for?" I ask sharply, while clenching my fist. *Someone was after her. The authorities.* My dream had been right to warn me.

"I'm not sure, she rang me, but we didn't have long to talk. I didn't know who to call, but you'd left your number. The card was stuck to the fridge. Shit, Tse, I'm sorry. I just... There's no one. What should I do?"

"Slow down. Take a breath. What did they arrest her for?"

"She was stopped at a red light. Someone ran into her."

That isn't a crime. What's going on?

"Tse, I'm scared." His voice quivers.

Fuck. He would be. Sounds like the police could have used a trumped-up excuse to pick her up. "Have you got a lawyer?"

I know it's a stupid question as soon as I ask it. *He's a fifteen-year-old kid for fuck's sake.* But I still listen to the answer. "No."

"Any friends you can call to help? What about one of your teachers?"

Now there's a definite sob. "No. We never tell anyone our business. I wouldn't know who to trust."

He trusts me.

"I'm so scared she's going to be deported."

So am I. All my thoughts of the past few weeks assault me. The idea that I might have lost my chance to get to know Mariana better is chilling. Now that I *can't* go visit her, I realise how important seeing her again was to me. I don't understand it, but something in my blood, whether it's Anglo or Navajo, sees my strange yearning for her as significant. *She could be something to me.* But I won't get a chance to find out. Not if she's back in Colombia.

"You at home?" When I get the grunt in confirmation, I make a hasty decision. "I'm not in Tucson right now, but I'm going to come back, okay? Sit tight, we'll work it out." I try to sound confident, when inside I'm already worried this is likely to be one problem I can't find a solution to. "I'll be there by morning, okay?"

His exhaled breath, heavy with relief, shows I'm doing the right thing. Can't leave a boy that age to worry alone.

Mom's used to me being called away, so doesn't question or push me to provide a reason, only worried I'm making the three-hundred-mile journey at night. But there's an inexplicable sense of urgency driving me. Knowing the feeling eating at me would prevent me sleeping, I might as well use the night hours to get back to Tucson.

There's barely any traffic, and I make the trip in under seven hours, bypassing the Satan's Devils' compound and going directly to the trailer park where Drew and Mariana live. I don't think about removing my cut in my urgency to find out what's happening. During the journey, I've started to think Drew's right to be concerned. This could be the first step in Mariana being deported. What happens next might be down to me. There's little a fifteen-year-old boy with no support can do.

Trouble is, I've fuck all idea of where to start.

It's six am when I arrive. It's only when I approach the trailer I realise how tired I am. As I hear movement inside, I wipe my hand over my sore eyes. *I need coffee.* And, for the first time in weeks, I could do with a joint. The latter will have to wait until I return to the compound, I don't carry my gear with me.

"Tse. You came." There's such a look of relief on his face as he unlocks the padlock on the chain-link fence, that I suspect he thought I wouldn't.

I'm carrying my laptop that I got out of my saddle bag. I've had a hundred thoughts during the long journey. I'm a hacker. Why the fuck hadn't I given Mariana a new identity before now, legit paperwork, everything? But I'd thought she'd been safe, protected under the DACA program. Never did I consider she'd bring herself to the attention of the cops. *And I hadn't admitted I cared what happened to her.* Thought myself crazy for not being able to get her off my mind. I thought I was doing right by staying away.

"Have you heard anything more, Drew?"

"No. I don't know what to do, Tse." Poor lad is rubbing at his face, he sounds distraught. Like me he looks like he hasn't slept a wink.

I'm playing it by ear too. I frown. "If the police are holding her, then she might need a lawyer. First thing we can do is get down there, see if she's been charged and why they are keeping her."

"Do you know any lawyers?" he asks hopefully. I notice a little colour has come back into his cheeks, confirming I was right to drive through the night to be here.

I do know a lawyer. Whether she'd be able to help or not is another question. "Grab me a coffee, and I'll give someone a call in," I glance at my watch, "another hour or so."

In the meantime, I open my laptop and do some digging. A search on Mariana's name reveals a short newspaper report. I skim it, my brow creasing. "Drew. Mariana told you she was stopped at a red light?"

"She did."

That's not what the news says at all. He's clearly curious, so I turn the laptop so he can see it, then sit back and fold my arms, mentally going over what the article said.

Insurance Fraud

Todd Jenkins reports he was driving his Ford Explorer towards a green light this morning when the car in front of him, driven by Ms Mariana De Souza (20), slammed on the brakes, causing him to run into her.

Police have arrested Ms De Souza and are questioning her about a possible attempt to commit insurance fraud.

Short and sweet. Also, totally untrue. Might not have spent much time with her, but her number one priority was not to draw attention to herself and to obey every fucking rule of the road.

Drew turns his wide eyes toward me. Not for the first time, I notice he's got the same features and expression as his sister, and it strikes me how wrong it seems that he's a US citizen, and she might already be facing deportation. Splitting up families seems all wrong. *He's just a kid. He still needs her.*

"This is crazy." Drew looks back to the screen. "That's not Mariana. She'd never do something like that. Tse, she wouldn't." He looks like he's trying to convince me, as though I might think she's not worth saving if she'd commit a crime.

"I know," I reassure him quickly. "Last thing she'd want Something's off. If anyone's committing a fraud, it's this Todd Jenkins." *Who might be persuaded to tell the truth if my brothers and I paid him a visit.* But in the meantime, "I'll place that call now."

"Want some privacy?"

"Nah, stay put. Might need some info."

Dart, now the VP for San Diego, answers the phone in a sleepy voice. "Mouse?"

"Yeah. How you doing? How's Tyler?"

"Fine and fine. But you don't fuckin' ring at god-awful o'clock to shoot the shit. Whaddya want, Brother?"

"To talk to Alex." His wife's our new club lawyer. He'll not bother asking me why I want to speak with her. It's obvious, and not unusual for her to get a call early in the day.

There's a mumbling at the other end of the line, then Alex's voice. "What can I do for you, Mouse?"

After telling her all that I know, there's a moment of quiet. "You think this was a set up?"

I do. "Yes."

"By this Todd fella, or the cops?"

I hadn't thought of the latter. "Either is possible." We're in Arizona after all.

"Having DACA status, she's only safe if she doesn't get arrested for a felony."

"Is fraud a felony?"

There's a slight pause, the type which suggests what I'm going to hear next isn't good. "Could be," she says, quietly.

Fuck, that doesn't help.

"Look, I'll be honest, Mouse, I don't know much about immigration law. Just that it's a minefield. You need someone who knows their stuff. I can try to find a reputable person in Tucson, but it will cost."

I live at the club. Don't spend my money on much except my bike and computer. I don't even hesitate, don't have any second thoughts about my life savings going to help a stranger. "I'm good for that."

"Okay. Give me a chance to make some enquiries, alright?"

That's as much as I can ask. I thank her, and end the call.

Having an idea, I reach for the laptop again, checking where it said the incident took place. I sigh, it was never going to be easy. There are no red-light cameras left in Tucson, they've all been removed due to a vote by residents a few years ago. Now it seems I'll have to check any shops or businesses which could have CCTV cameras.

Drew's staring at me as if I can wave a magic wand and get answers. I wish that I could. All I can do is my best, and keep him busy. "Got our work cut out for us, kid."

CHAPTER 9

Mariana

They come to collect me again. This time, they put hand-cuffs on me. As I hold them out, my hands are shaking. I'm downright terrified. I don't know whether I'm going to be deported straight away or taken to an immigration centre. It's not anything that's happened to me before. I can't understand why I'm being treated like a criminal. *I've done nothing wrong.* How the hell did I, obediently stopped at a red light, break the law?

The police woman, a different one from the one who escorted me to the doctor, throws some words at me in Spanish. I just look at her, puzzled. Okay, I still understand a few words, but not when it's spoken so fast. *This is what it would be like in Colombia.* I feel tears start dropping from my eyes, unable to easily wipe them away as my hands are literally tied.

"I don't speak Spanish," I manage to say in little more than a whisper.

"Sure, you don't," she huffs, looking at me disbelievingly.

I'm taken to a room like the ones you see on TV. A table, some kind of recording device on it, two chairs either side. I'm pushed toward one of the chairs with its back to the wall and facing the door. The police woman folds her arms and stands against the wall. After a moment two men in plain clothes come in. They take a moment settling themselves, seeming to finish off a conversation they were having outside, and pulling papers together.

At last they sit down, look at me, and introduce themselves.

"Detective Daniels," one points to himself, then, moving his hand toward the other man, "Detective Geary." For a second I wonder whether I should introduce myself, but he continues almost without a pause. "So, Ms De Souza. You're an illegal immigrant, I see."

My indignation momentarily wins out over my fears. "I was brought here by my mother when I was four. I've got DACA status."

"At the moment, you have," Daniels agrees. "But that could change if you're convicted of a felony."

"But I haven't done anything." My voice isn't working too well. *Felony?* I cough to clear my throat. "I don't understand what you're talking about."

They exchange a look, then the second man speaks, tapping his forefinger on the folder in front of him. "I've a witness statement that states you were driving up to a green light, then suddenly slammed your brakes on so the car behind you was unable to stop."

My eyes widen. "That's not true." I look from one to the other. "I was stopped at a red light, as I told your colleague at the scene. The car behind rammed me. Surely there's something you could check?" I ask the latter hopefully.

"We've examined the scene. There's nothing to support your version of the story." This from Daniels.

Geary's looking at me with a tired expression on his face. "Why did you do it, Ms De Souza? Couldn't get a legal job? Needed the insurance money? Compensation for the injury your *accident* caused?" He must have noticed the way I'm sitting, breathing shallowly due to the pain in my chest. He'll have the doctor's report too.

"You're wrong," I object, trying to keep the quaver out of my voice. Hoping I sound indignant. "That story you've been told is completely wrong." But watching their faces, *they've already tried and convicted me. I bet their witness is white. Who is it? I didn't see anyone around until after the crash. It must be the other driver.* Thoughts are flitting around my head. There's something I should be doing, asking for. Mentally I try to get them to slow down so I can grasp hold of a notion and act on it. But along with trying to decide what to do, all I can think about is being convicted. I'd lose my DACA status. And of course, they've already found that out. My fingerprints would be on record with all my immigration status information. Is this something they've concocted to get an immigrant off the street?

I want to ask about Drew, want to tell them. But if I do, what happens to him? He'll get caught up in the system. *He's too young to look after himself.* I bite my lip. While I've still got a chance of getting out, I'll keep quiet about my brother. Don't want to lose him and not be able to get him back. *I hope he called the number I asked him to during our all too brief telephone conversation that they permitted.* But what would Tse care? I only met him the once. What could he do? I couldn't think of anyone else to get hold of.

"I want a lawyer." Suddenly I realise what I should have asked before. *It's what the people on TV do.* "I'm not saying anything else until my lawyer is here."

"Have you got a lawyer, Ms De Souza?"

I look down at my cuffed hands, feeling those tears running again. They have zero effect on the men seated opposite. In fact, they start gathering their papers together. "If you don't have a lawyer, then we'll have to get a public defender for you. That will take time. I doubt we'll be able to resume until the morning."

I've got to stay here? All night? What about Drew?

"Don't I get bail or something?"

Detective Daniels leans over the desk. "You haven't been charged yet. When we've completed our investigation, you will be. Then you'll go in front of a judge. But between you and me, you won't get bail. We'll argue an illegal immigrant is a flight risk."

"You're going to keep me locked up?" Now I'm croaking. This morning I left for college as normal. Everything the same as it usually was. Now I'm being held for a crime I didn't commit. My mind is whirling, unable to come to terms with it.

"That's the long and short of it," Detective Geary agrees, almost cheerily. "And if I were you, Ms De Souza, I'd start getting used to the idea that your days in the USA are numbered, and you probably won't see the country as a free woman again."

I'm led back to my cell, the door clanging behind me. I sit on the bunk and place my head in my hands. *You won't see the country as a free woman again.* This time, when the tears start, they don't stop. *Drew, oh Drew.* How many years would it be before I could see him? *How will he cope? Who's going to look after him?*

My position is hopeless. Unless I can get them to see I'm innocent, which they seem completely unwilling to do, I'm never going to be free again. I doubt if they care, DACA or not, one more illegal off the street probably pleases them.

Night falls. Lights are dimmed but not switched off. I lie down, my eyes open. Sobs are wracking my small frame. *What can I do? Will a court-appointed lawyer be of any help?* If he's one chosen by the police, I very much doubt it.

I'll never admit I'm guilty, because I'm not.

But that's what they try to persuade me to do the very next morning. "The position is this, Ms De Souza." My court-appointed lawyer breaks off and rubs his hand over his bald head. "We might be able to get a deal as it's your first offence.

Admit you're guilty, and you will be deported. Continue to protest your innocence, and if convicted, you'll serve time in jail. And then be deported. The outcome is the same, just depends whether you want to go to prison first or not."

My jaw drops. Admit to something I haven't done? The person who should be prosecuted is getting away scot-free, and with money from my insurance company. *It isn't fair!*

"I'm innocent," I tell him again, this time more forcefully.

"You have no way of proving it."

"It's my word against a white man's, I presume."

"If that's how you want to look at it, yes." He shrugs, as he doesn't even try to sugar-coat it.

What can I do? This lawyer isn't going to help me. From the way he keeps looking at his watch, he's got more important things to do. Other people he'd rather be representing and helping. Helping? He's been no help to me at all. Just emphasised I'll be deported, whatever I plead.

I've had no sleep, my heart's pounding to get blood around my veins, my pulse is racing. I've been stressed since yesterday morning, I can't cope. Can't think. *I just want to be home with Drew.* But the chances of that happening seem highly unlikely.

"Come on, Ms De Souza. See sense. Agree to plead guilty."

There's a commotion in the corridor outside. Footsteps, loud voices. I'm expecting no one, whoever it is won't have anything to do with me, but it's distracting. My lawyer looks annoyed at the interruption when he sees he's lost my attention.

"Ms De Souza. I haven't got all day. Make your decision…"

The door bursts open. A middle-aged woman wearing a smart pant suit pushes her way in, comes over to stand next to me and warns firmly, "Not one word, Ms De Souza." Then she speaks to a police officer standing in the doorway, after which she nods politely to the lawyer the court appointed for me. "Now, I'd like to speak to my client, alone. And please arrange to have the recording equipment switched off. Client/lawyer confidentiality."

I was recorded? Thank goodness I hadn't said a word to convict myself. Hadn't leaned towards a guilty plea, had I? No, I don't think I had. I look at her gratefully. *Has Drew managed to arrange this?* No, he wouldn't know how. *Tse? Has Tse come through? Or has Drew contacted someone else?*

While those thoughts were running through my head, the room was cleared, and I've been left alone with the newcomer. Her presence gives me a new worry. While I'm pleased she's here, immediately sensing someone is on my side, I have to be honest.

Drew's probably done what he can, but, "I can't afford to pay you," I say quietly, looking down, knowing she'll stand and leave. Perhaps Drew misled her, let her think we had money.

But she stays in place. "Don't worry about that. My fee's been taken care of. Just concentrate on us sorting out this mess and getting you walking out of here a free woman again."

I pull back, staring at her, wondering if she can be trusted. "Is that even possible?" And who's paying her?

"I can't say it won't be difficult, but that fiancé of yours is quite a persuasive young man. If there's evidence out there, he'll find it. I won't lie to you. You can't afford to lose your DACA status, though with the current political situation, you may lose it soon in any event. But for now, you've still got it. Which means you can't have a stain, or even the hint of one, on your record."

My fiancé? Who the hell...? But I don't contradict her. Just file it away as a puzzle to be solved later. If I said I had no man in my life, would she walk out the door thinking she wouldn't get paid after all?

"The detectives said I won't get bail."

"You've not yet been charged. Let's take it one step at a time, okay?" She pulls out a chair and sits down. "Take it from the top. I want to know everything."

Unlike the other lawyer, she doesn't look at her watch. I don't even see her eyes flick to the clock on the wall. It seems like we talk for hours. I tell her everything, about my mom, about how she was killed when she returned to Colombia, the threat that I feel includes me too.

"Your father. You think he would harm you?"

A fleeting memory of giggling as he tossed me in the air. *Do I really remember that, or was it just what Mom had told me?* Then the change, the violence. "He sees nothing wrong with forcing, *raping* women. My brother was a product of that. I've evaded him so long; he'll want me back. See me as nothing more than property. He may even force me to marry someone who'd be like him. He's got no compassion at all. He broke my arm just before Mom got me away."

"If you returned to Colombia, is there anyone you could stay with?"

"No. My grandmother on my mom's side died soon after she did. I think I've still got a grandfather on my father's side, but I wouldn't want to go to him. There's no one else. I was only four when I left." Sure, I played with the girl next door, but I can't even remember her name now. *Ann? Anna? Hannah?* Even if I could, you can't, as an adult, presume she would help based on a friendship that was between two little girls.

"So there's an asylum case we can put forward. Of course, it would be better if there were actual threats toward you that we could refer to."

Pursing my lips, I explain. "My mom had a cast iron case as was proved by events. And she wasn't listened to."

Carissa, as she's introduced herself, half smiles. "I know it's no comfort, Mariana, but that could help your case."

"Can I make a phone call?" I ask. "I want to check on my brother."

"Of course you do, but they won't allow that yet. I understand you used your one call to him yesterday? I will tell you this, he's in very good hands."

I hardly dare ask. "Who, who is looking after him?"

This time it's a full smile. "Why, that handsome young man of yours of course. Mr Williamson."

I'm no wiser. It could be Tse, I never learned his family name. It doesn't sound very Native American. But racking my brains, I don't know any of Drew's friends called Williamson either.

Chapter 10

Mouse

Alex came through. By mid-morning I had pledged a large portion of my savings and had engaged Carissa Beacham, an immigration lawyer with an apparently well-earned reputation.

I'm so far out of my depth, it's no joke. I watch Drew, aimlessly sprawled on the couch, his eyes fixed on a programme on TV he has no interest in. He's lost his mom, and now his sister. *He called me for help.* In doing that, he's somehow made me responsible for him. Like I had a fucking clue what to do with a fifteen-year-old boy. He'd been in no state to go to school, so I let him stay home. Until we have news, he's going to be in pieces.

What's worse is the phone call I've received from Drummer. He wants, *needs* me back at the club. I'm torn in two. My duty to my brothers, and my commitment to these people I've only just met.

I'm not in a much better state than Drew. Being here reminds me of Mariana, of her arms around me when I rode back with her on my bike, how I felt an immediate connection to her. *I should have explored it. Come back and seen her again.* Fuck knows, if I had, she might not have been in that place at that time. I'm swearing at myself now for not following up on that strange draw between us while I had the chance. *I'd thought the best thing I could do was stay away.* I thought she'd have forgotten all about me. But she asked Drew to call me. She must trust me enough to get her out of the bind she's in. *Can I do enough?* I'm far out of my comfort zone here.

"Come on." Standing, I jerk my chin toward Drew. He's already tall for his age and could pass for someone older.

He looks at me sullenly. "Where are you going? The lawyer might call…"

"She's got my cell," I remind him. *How do you deal with a fifteen-year-old who's lost his whole family?* My initial reaction is to treat him like a prospect, expecting my instructions to be obeyed. Then, grasping that approach would probably not work with a teenager, I untie my long hair, then smooth it back into a ponytail again with my hands. "I don't know about you, Drew, but I can't sit around here doing nothing. I need something to do. Something to help your sister."

His eyes sharpen with interest. "Like what?"

"We know there are no traffic cameras in the area, but there could be CCTV. I want to go down to that junction and see whether there are any businesses around. They might have security cameras which could have caught something, or hell, someone might have seen it for themselves." Something tells me the cops didn't do much investigating to find out the truth.

His whole face has brightened, then it falls. "I can't come along. Ma's car was totalled."

"I've got my bike." My head tilts in challenge.

He's on his feet, a tentative grin curling his mouth. "Ma might not like it."

"Mariana's got enough on her plate to worry about. She wouldn't want you to be left alone and brooding, and she knows I'm a safe rider. She'll understand." I'm crossing my fingers behind my back, while acknowledging Mariana might never get the chance to play mom with Drew again. He'll have to start making his own decisions. That thought's followed by the question of what the fuck do I do with him? There's no way I can walk out of his life, leaving him to fend for himself. *Call social services? Put him in the system? Roll the dice and hope he gets placed in a decent foster home?* As soon as the idea comes into my mind I dismiss it. *Can't do that now, at least not while we're still hoping his sister walks free.*

Knowing he's going to come with me, I open the door and step outside, nodding approvingly when he turns and locks it. Going to my Harley, I open the saddle bag and remove the little-used helmet that I carry with me in case I need to go to another state without warning. Unlike Arizona, Cali and Nevada both have helmet laws. Even in this state someone under the age of eighteen has to wear one. I hand it to him, and as I did with his sister, help him with the unfamiliar buckle.

"Lean with me, not against me. Don't fight the bike, okay?"

"I got this." He's back to sullen now.

"I'm sure you have," I mumble, as I get the bike off the stand. "There's grab handles, or just hold onto me, okay? Whatever makes you feel safe."

He climbs on behind me. He might be tall, but he's slender, hardly any different to taking his sister on the back. Starting the engine, I throw a look over my shoulder, his hands already holding on tight to the handles either side, his knuckles white. I'm hoping he's going to enjoy the ride, something to take his mind off Mariana if only for a few minutes.

I drive to the area where she had her accident, pulling up and parking at the curb, while looking around to see who might have seen something. There are a couple of closed businesses, and a furniture store. Two office blocks.

"Off," I tell Drew.

Like an ungainly calf he dismounts. Getting off with a more practised swing, I put his helmet back in my saddle bag.

"Where do we start?"

"We'll work down one side, then the other." But first I take out my phone and snap a few shots. One of the closed businesses has a security camera, and it's possible it's recording to keep the place secured.

After an hour, I feel like beating my head against a wall, and I think Drew feels much the same way. The newspaper report of Mariana being an illegal hasn't helped. I get the feeling a couple of people know more than they are telling, but aren't of a mind to assist us. Others, though, came running at the sound of the crash, but hadn't seen what had happened immediately prior. Unless Mariana has details of any witnesses, this morning's been a complete bust. *I need my full system to set up searches, try to access the security cameras.* I can do some stuff on my laptop, but not everything. But I can't abandon Drew and go back to the club. Not until I know what's happening with his sister.

Not even then, perhaps.

How the fuck have I found myself in the role of reluctant parent?

We're walking back to my bike, both of us disenchanted, when the phone rings. It's the lawyer.

"Tse Williamson."

"Mr Williamson. It's Carissa Beacham here. I've seen your fiancée."

"How's she holding up?" I'd claimed the relationship I had no right to, but thought it would make the lawyer think I was legit, and had reason to hand over my cash to her.

"Bewildered, worried. Look, Mr Williamson. I'm a lawyer, we represent the person we're supposed to in the best possible way that we can, it's not for us to consider whether they're guilty or innocent. But in Ms De Souza's case, my gut feeling is that she's telling the truth."

"That's good, isn't it? If she can convince you…"

She snorts a strangled laugh. "We're in Arizona, Mr Williamson. We might not have tented cities for immigrants anymore, but there's still some that wish that we had."

"Among the cops," I suggest, my teeth gnashing together.

"Could be what we're up against, yes."

"What do you suggest?"

A sigh, then, "You keep doing what you were suggesting. Seeing if we can prove her innocence, but..."

As her voice trails off, it doesn't take a genius to fill in the blanks. "She might get deported anyway now she's in their sights."

"Even her DACA status doesn't protect her. Could hold her until that runs out. A year or even more being held in an immigration centre isn't unknown."

Drew's only hearing one side of the conversation, but that's enough. His face is creasing with worry.

"You did the right thing engaging me, Mr Williamson. We won't lose sight of her now. She's not a statistic. I know how much she must mean to you."

"Can she get bail?"

"No. She'll be seen as a flight risk. Any bail set will be astronomical, if any is set at all. The price of someone's freedom will be sky high. She'll be going to court very shortly, and I have to be honest here, probably the best she can expect is to go to an immigration centre instead of going to jail. I'll stay in close contact, and let you know if she's going to be moved."

"And if I prove she wasn't the perpetrator?"

Her silence speaks volumes.

"She's not here illegally if she's got protected status," I try again.

"Technically that's true. But the times that we live in... I'll be in touch when I have more news."

"Any chance her brother can see her?" Drew needs to see his sister. Be reassured she's okay with his own eyes. But again, Carissa disappoints me.

"Not while the police have her, no. I'm sorry, Mr Williamson. I know how worried you must be about her. I wish I had better news for you."

Drew's looking hopeful. When I explain the side of the conversation he couldn't hear, he's gutted.

Realising how much he'll have been longing to see his sister, to reassure himself she's alright, I place my hand on his shoulder. "Look on the positive side. Mariana's got a good lawyer, and I, *we* won't be giving up."

He kicks at the curb, bites his lip in a way that reminds me of his sister, then shrugs. "What next?"

Next is getting him home. The bike doesn't allow for conversation, so I take Drew straight back to that sorry trailer, wondering how the fuck I can help this distraught lad. Once inside, I settle down on the couch and open my laptop. "Want pizza?"

He shrugs and throws himself down on the couch beside me, the thing lurches and groans under the sudden weight. I hold my breath wondering if I'll find myself on the floor, but it holds up. Just.

"Can't think about food, not when…"

"Gotta keep eating." When he gives a reluctant nod, I place the order. Having to pay extra, and by card in advance, to get it delivered to the park. I don't even blame them; this isn't a good area. Now food's been sorted, I start my investigating.

There's more than one Todd Jenkins in Tucson. I look back at the newspaper article. It had Mariana's age, not his, nor his make of car. I try to narrow it down as to area. *Where could he have been coming from?* I then do some searches to see whether he's done something like this before, but none of the people with that name appear to have put in insurance claims.

Mariana's insurance. I descend to the deep web, that place where establishments like banks hold records of accounts and account holders, no IP addresses to give shit away. Held securely, except from people like me, and…

"Drew? Mariana's insurance company. She got details anywhere?"

The sound of a scooter drawing up outside has me moving and looking out of the window. Our dinner has arrived. Drew's getting up to go get it. Guess he must have remembered he's hungry after all.

"In a box under my bed. She keeps stuff like that there," he replies, as he opens the door and disappears outside.

It takes less than a moment to find it. Another man might feel guilty going through someone else's personal documents, but as delving into other people's business is what I do for the club, remorse doesn't enter my head as I start to sort through. Drew's all important birth certificate is there, proving he's an American citizen. A couple of letters postmarked from Colombia that I put to one side, and there, her car insurance details. Thankfully she hasn't gone paperless.

I go back to my laptop, shake out my hands then my head when Drew waves me toward the second pizza, then put my fingers to the keys. *Christ, it would be better if I had all my equipment. I need to set programs running to break through the security shit. Gonna take far longer with just one laptop.*

"You got a computer, Drew?"

He disappears and reappears with an ancient laptop. *Beggars can't be choosers,* I remind myself, as I start up another search on it. Having done all I can, I open the second box and take out a slice.

"What are you doing, Tse?"

Seeing his interest isn't faked, I decide to come clean. "I'm trying to find the man who ran into Mariana's car. If it was an insurance scam, he'll have started a claim. It should be on her insurance records."

"How can you get into those?"

I tap my nose and grin. "Let's just say, I have ways. But got to let the computers do their stuff for the moment. Now, let's eat."

Automatically his hand starts putting his pizza to his mouth, his teeth tear on a mouthful, he chews then swallows, then repeats the process. His eyes fix on the numbers streaming over the two screens.

It's only belatedly I remember I should be doing that search Drummer asked me to do. Oh well, there'll be time to research the Chaos Riders later. For the first time in as long as I can remember, my brothers are taking second place.

CHAPTER 11

Mariana

Two days have passed. Yesterday I was accused of a crime I didn't commit. Today I'm taken again in handcuffs and shackled to the table where I first met Carissa. Each hour that passes makes me more frightened, scared on my own behalf and on Drew's. *What's going to happen to him?* Tse may be looking after him for now, as Carissa had assured me, but he wouldn't do that forever. No, there'll come a time when he'll go back to his own life, and deliver Drew into the system. Who knows where, or with whom, he might end up?

For now, I'm grateful both he and I have got Tse. Judging by the suits she wears, Carissa's fee won't be cheap. I'll never be able to afford it. *How will I ever repay him?* Then I realise I won't have the chance if I'm deported penniless to Colombia. *Will he stop paying her fee when he realises?*

The door opens and my lawyer comes in. I push back my straggly, greasy hair, I've been unable to wash it in here. I used to pride myself on my appearance, but already my skin feels oily and neglected. Raising my face, I look at hers, knowing immediately she isn't bringing good news.

Carissa sits down opposite, her eyes harden, and then she says, "You're going to be charged with insurance fraud. They're describing it as a felony. Not only, in their view, did you set it up as a deliberate attempt to defraud, you apparently caused serious injury to the person who crashed into your car."

But it was him who caused injury to *me*. My head's still hurting, and I know I've got whiplash as my neck has grown stiffer with each passing hour. I go to object; she raises her hands.

"If that was my only news, I'd be helping Tse get you a criminal defence lawyer. But I'm afraid that's not all we have to contend with." She places her briefcase on the desk and opens it. "Your fingerprints obviously exposed you as an illegal immigrant, currently with DACA status. The police have contacted ICE, and they have decided in the circumstances, and due to the crime you'll be charged with, that immigration enforcement action is necessary."

I feel her words like a physical blow. "But I didn't do anything," I protest, my hands covering my mouth. "I'm innocent. Surely I'll have my chance at proving it at a trial? I've a right to be here, for now, anyway. I've done everything I should."

"There won't be a trial," she replies grimly. "That's the bottom line, Mariana. I'm sorry, I could string you along, but there are other factors at play here. ICE will be arriving very shortly, and I suspect they'll take you into custody and send you to an immigration centre. I'm afraid being charged with a felony is as big a stain as being convicted."

"They can't," I squeak. *Deported back to Colombia? Leave Drew here?* "My brother… I'm responsible for him."

"Your brother is fifteen," she says bluntly, but not unsympathetically. "When babies are being pulled from their mothers' arms, why would the same people be worried about him?" The flash of her eyes shows she doesn't approve. But her hands are probably tied, and there's a limit to what she can do.

Oh Drew, I'm so sorry. She gives me a moment to process what she's told me. I'm an immigrant without legal status. My hands clench as I realise I'm helpless. There's no one to fight, or no one my protest would have any effect on. In a quiet, quavering voice, I ask, "What's going to happen to me?"

She puts her hands on the table, palms down. "You'll be taken to an immigration centre. The good news is you'll be able to have visitors, so your brother and fiancé can see you. At some point, maybe after months, you'll be taken in front of an immigration judge. He'll listen to your case, decide whether to grant you asylum, but I won't lie to you. Once the system gets hold of you, it's unlikely it will let you go. The outcome is you will probably be given a deportation order. You'll be sent back to Colombia."

To my violent father. Or death, or to be raped at the hands of a gang in the streets. I've always known it was possible, though inconceivable to my very American mind. I was brought up in the US. Even without my father waiting for me, the thought of being alone in a foreign country is terrifying.

My fingers squeeze into my palms again, as I try to force thoughts of a fate I can't even imagine out of my head. I focus on what I need to. "And Drew?"

"I'm hoping your fiancé will look after him. He could go with you, of course…"

"No. That's impossible." I don't want my father getting his hands on him. A twisted madman who killed our mother? Who knows what he'd do. *Those letters gave me a taste.*

"If I'm deported, will I be able to apply to come back?"

Her lips purse. "Not once you've been deported. Not with this charge hanging over your head."

"The charge they won't even try me for. No chance to prove my innocence."

"Even if you're proven innocent, if you're deported the judge will give you a time that needs to expire before you can reapply. That could be five, ten or twenty years."

Five years at the minimum?

Tears start to run down my face. She notices. "Ms De Souza, listen. I know some human rights activists. I'll enlist them on your case. It might mean you spend months, years in detention, but at least you'll be safe."

"I did nothing wrong," I repeat, aimlessly.

Her sympathetic glance doesn't help. Nothing can help. Not unless someone can magically change my birth certificate for me.

ICE officers come the next morning, uninterested in anything I have to say. They waste no time. Soon I find myself handcuffed in the back of a prison truck and being driven away. I have no idea where they're taking me, but do get an answer when I spy a sign on arrival. It appears my new home is to be the Service Processing Centre in Florence. I try to take comfort that I'm still in the same state.

Processing Centre. I'm processed alright. My personal possessions taken by the police are handed over to the people in charge, as are the clothes I had been wearing. I'm given a number and an orange prison jumpsuit. No belt, nothing that I could use to harm myself.

I'm allowed to shower before going to my new home, a windowless room with a bunk bed I'm sharing with a woman who knows no English.

I soon come to learn that while I've been convicted of no crime, being an immigrant is enough of an offence for them to treat me just like a prisoner. I might have lived in a tiny trailer but that doesn't stop me becoming claustrophobic shut up in that bleak cell, longing for daylight. But for that, it seems one hour a day will have to suffice, when we're allowed to go outside to stand around in a steel cage.

While there are many people who've been arrested at the border, and who haven't had a chance to learn the language, I soon find there are a few others like me. People raised from a young age in America. One woman who swears she was born here, and that she is an American citizen, but no one believes her. Although she'll tell anyone and everyone at every opportunity she was born and bred here, they are swayed by her Hispanic features and the colour of her skin. I gravitate toward her at meal times, both of us American down to the bone. But having heard her story, and having no reason to doubt her, I'm once again frightened for Drew. What if he were picked up, and no one believed him? Thought his birth certificate was fake? That's the thought that really scares me.

From the time my mother died I've been all I could for Drew, raised him like my child rather than my brother. Used to give him the last morsel of food off my plate, even if it meant I would go hungry. Bringing him up as an all-American boy, giving him every chance he could have. It's him I worry about more than myself.

"De Souza."

I turn around at my name, grateful they haven't called me by a number.

"You've got visitors," the guard says.

Oh, to see a familiar face. Expecting my lawyer, I nod, but ask to confirm, "Who?"

She consults a piece of paper. "Tse Williamson and Drew De Souza."

Drew can't be here. What if they lock him up? How will it affect him to see his sister in a prison uniform? I start to shake my head. *He's got to get away from here.*

"You can refuse to see them."

I've the option, but as I open my mouth to say the words, I can't get any refusal out. I know I'm weak, just wanting to see a familiar face. Wanting to see with my own eyes that Drew's okay. *Has he been eating? Who's feeding him? I left him no money…*

Oh God, it's just like on TV. I wait, shuffling my feet along with the other detainees who have visitors, until at last a buzzer sounds, the doors unlock, and then it's my turn to walk in to a room full of tables, one chair on one side, two on the other.

Drew stands as I walk toward him. Tse's hand shoots out and his eyes lock on his, and I hear his whispered word, "Sit."

A brief creasing of his eyes as though in pain, then the boy I wish I could put my arms around sits down, nodding at Tse. Tse's obviously tutored him. It makes me wonder whether he's visited his brothers in prison before. He's in a criminal gang after all, even though he denied it. His cut, I notice, isn't being worn today.

My eyes drink in Drew. He looks healthy, a little pale, but who wouldn't in this situation? His clothes are clean, and he's shaved those few skimpy whiskers I tease him about. But seeing him isn't enough. I need contact. Taking my seat, I reach my hand across the table. Drew grabs it and holds it fast. Until a guard walks by and coughs loudly, and reluctantly I pull mine back.

I don't know what to say. We've such a short time every moment is precious, every word spoken mustn't be wasted. There's too much I want to ask; I don't know what's most important. My mouth opens and shuts but there's a disconnect with my brain.

"I'm working to prove you are innocent." It's Tse who breaks the torturous silence. "Know where this Todd asshole lives, but I haven't caught him at home yet."

"Tse. It's useless. Even if you get him to retract his story, it won't help."

"How are you, Ma?" Drew suddenly finds his voice. "How are they treating you?" His voice breaks.

It kills me to know how much this is hurting him. I force a smile to my face. "Three meals a day. A bed. Yeah, a bed, Drew.

Better than sleeping on the sofa." I try to sound light-hearted, making the most of what I have here. The last thing I want is him worrying about me.

"I can't stay with Drew indefinitely," Tse says looking concerned.

"Of course you can't," I interrupt, trying to give Drew a confident look while wondering what the hell is going to happen to him. How can I arrange anything from here? Should I ask Tse to call social services? Is that me giving up? Risking losing Drew…

"I'm arranging for Drew to go and stay on the Rez, with my family." Tse's eyes rise in challenge as if I'm going to object. "He'll be able to go to school there, so he can continue his education."

"Same one as Tse went to," Drew butts in. They've obviously been speaking about it. Drew doesn't look worried, more interested it seems.

"I don't know about that," I start, then stop, realising there's no other option. How can I argue with the man who's proposing to care for my brother for me? *But a Navajo reservation?* "Will there…?" I want to ask if there would be issues, a white kid on a Native American reservation. My question fades as I don't want to insult Tse.

"Yeah." Again, it's Drew who answers, knowing me well and reading my mind. "Tse's told me what to expect. He's not sugar-coated it, Ma. But it's better than getting Social Services involved, or being homeless."

"Look at it as a life experience," Tse gives a quick smile to my brother who I realise seems to have grown up. His considered nod showing that. Then Tse looks at me. "Your neighbours tried to break into the trailer. They've heard you've been detained and expect you to be deported. If I hadn't been there…"

"Tse was great, Ma."

Tse brushes his comment away as though he'd done nothing at all. But when he speaks next, all my fears come back to me. "Seems your kindly neighbours think Drew's illegal." He presses his lips together, and now the reason for his suggestion becomes clear. "Don't want him mixed up in trouble. So I thought the best idea was to get him away. Spoken to my mom and she's looking forward to havin' him stay. Navajo like to adopt strays." His quick smile at Drew softens his words, then he focuses on me again. "Carissa Beacham couldn't give me any idea how long you'd be here."

She couldn't tell me either. "No news on a court case yet. But others I've spoken to have been waiting months."

Tse looks down at his hands with those long slim fingers I remember admiring before, in another lifetime it seems. We're all ignoring the elephant in the room, that apart from this facility, I might never set foot on American soil again.

"I'll arrange to have some funds put into your facility account. You can make phone calls, send letters." Tse seems to know more about how this works than I do. "It might make your life easier."

"Thank you." I'm in no position to refuse. "Tse, thank you for everything. You don't know me; I don't know you. Yet you're helping me, helping Drew." For some reason, I trust him. Then, I suppose, I've no one else even pretending to be in my corner.

Now it's Tse's strong warm hand that covers my own shaking one, and a quick grin flits over his face. "What else would I do for my fiancée?"

"Yeah, about that…" I've got to put a stop to this now. Him saying I'm his fiancée makes me think things I shouldn't be thinking. Not when the likelihood is that I'll soon be thousands of miles away.

"Listen, Mariana," he hisses. "You've got an American fiancé waiting for you, okay? Don't tell anyone any different. Every little thing might help."

My eyes widen. Here I am, a girl who's kept so far under the radar I've never dared have a boyfriend before. Now this handsome man is telling me he's my fiancé, and we've not even kissed. Let alone knowing anything about each other, except for a few basics.

Tse stares at me. When he sees I'm not going to voice an objection, he chuckles softly, lightening the mood. "I have threatened Drew with bodily injury, though, if he starts calling me Pa."

CHAPTER 12

Mouse

Drew keeps it together until we're in the truck that I borrowed from the Satan's Devils compound, and we've put a couple of miles between us and the detention centre. Then there's a loud sniff, followed by a couple of sobs, then more which just keep coming. Allowing him some dignity, I concentrate on the road ahead.

It hadn't taken me long to decide the safest place to take him. With nosy neighbours threatening to call the cops, I wanted him well away from that trailer park. Sure, he's got his birth certificate, and with my skills I can help him easily prove he was born in the States, but why put the boy through all that? Taking him out of his school and spiriting him away to the Rez, where no one would dream of looking for him, would be better. A phone call to my mother and it was arranged, it seems both she and Gramma wouldn't object to someone filling their empty nest, even just for a short time. Long term I've no idea what to do with him. But I've decided he's my responsibility. I can't abandon him, or make any permanent plans until we know what's going on with Mariana. I like the kid. And giving his sister peace of mind is the least I could do.

As Florence is between Tucson and the Rez, it makes sense to go straight there after visiting Mariana. Drummer wants me back at the compound, and I need to give some time to helping my brothers make sense of the shit that they, and by association I, am in. So I'm wasting no time, taking Drew there today.

Hoping that as the miles go by beneath us, he'll have time to pull himself together after seeing his sister, and start looking forward to what lies ahead.

While giving him time to process, I let my mind think about Mariana. I hadn't told her, but one of the security cameras revealed dividends. A clear view of her car properly stopped at a red light, the Ford ploughing straight into it. I'd shown it to Carissa, the lawyer, who'd taken it to the cops.

The assholes hadn't even arrested Jenkins, and had shrugged when Carissa suggested it had cleared her name, said the tape was too blurry to make out.

Pack of lies, but the truth is, Mariana's case is in the hands of the immigration authorities now. Her proof of innocence, or otherwise, has no bearing. The cops have washed their hands of her. The evidence I'd discovered would at the most mean she's deported without a criminal record, but it's apparently no argument against her being detained. Whether ICE picks you up or detains you is a lottery, Carissa had explained, and once they'd set their sights on you, it's almost impossible to secure a release.

But the lawyer is still working on it. Trying to get her hearing before a judge brought forward. If they leave it too long her DACA protection will run out, and who knows whether she'll be able to renew it? Even recipients on the outside, Carissa has confided, aren't registering again, fearing that giving the authorities updated details just makes it easier for them to be picked up off the street.

The only thing I can do is give Todd Jenkins my own form of retribution. Whatever Mariana says, I'll be delivering some punishment. He can't get away scot-free. If I get my way, he won't be getting any insurance money.

Drew's still sniffling, wiping his nose on his sleeve. Parental responsibility doesn't go so far as me calling him out on it, so I think about the reasons why Mariana can't go back to Colombia instead.

Those letters. Yeah, personal letters, but I'd read them, chills causing the hair on my arms to stand on end.

Dear Mariana

I arrived safely, but your father is as I remember him. In fact, he's worse. He's a powerful man now, he calls himself General and rules a corrupt empire. Do not on any account get in contact with him. Whatever happens, whether you hear from me again or not.

He's trying to find out your address. Mariana, I believe he has connections outside Colombia as well as within, men he can call on in the States. Whatever he does, I'm not going to be telling him where you are.

Keep safe, watch Drew for me. I can't tell you how much I love you and miss you. Kisses to you both. Stay safe.

Your loving mother

Dear Mariana,

Your father is getting worse. He was violent toward me last night. I only just managed to get out to post this letter.

He's desperate to find you. He still doesn't know where you are, and I'll go to my grave keeping it a secret.

Love and kisses to you and Drew

Your loving mother

Dear Mariana,

I'm writing this crying. My darling, I'm so sorry. He raped me last night, saw the caesarean scar from when I had Drew. He was going to kill me thinking I'd been unfaithful, I had to tell him he had a son.

He wants his son, Mariana. I wouldn't tell him where you are. I lied, gave a fake address in California. He may be able to check that out, if so, I doubt next time he'll hold back. He was so mad I kept Drew quiet. He wants you too, wants to use you to make a marriage that will benefit him.

Pray for me, Mariana. I'm praying for you and Drew. Know that I'll love you always.

Your loving mother.

The last letter is dated eight years ago, presumably just before her mother died. I need to get these letters to the lawyer, perhaps the thinly veiled threats about using Mariana as a pawn in a union she'd be forced into would help her case. It's all that I can hold on to.

The image of her in that detention centre, how pale she looked, how sunken her eyes were, plays on me as I drive. I drum my fingers against the steering wheel. I've visited brothers inside before, but they were doing their time for a crime they might have denied, but had committed. Mariana has done nothing wrong. What do they expect? A four-year-old kid to refuse to cross the border? It's the unfairness that gets to me. She should not be incarcerated. She should be here, with me. With her brother. Free to live the life she'd been brought up to expect.

"Can we stop, Tse?"

Turning, I notice Drew shifting uncomfortably in his seat. Intuiting the reason, I realise I could do with a break myself. Pulling off into a rest service area, I get out, stretch my long legs, cramped with the drive, then follow Drew into the bathroom. Coming out, I point toward the restaurant with a jerk of my head.

His eyes, tearless now but still red and puffy, light up. We go in, order, then sit to eat our burgers.

"Would you marry Ma?" Drew asks.

What the…? "I said we were engaged to see if that would carry any weight."

"But if you were married, you could sponsor her for a green card, couldn't you?"

"Drew, unless she's released, how are we going to get married?" I can't see ICE letting her marry an American citizen before she's deported. I haven't worried about having to do anything more than letting it hang as an intention, in case it could help.

"What if she's deported? Could you follow her, marry her, then bring her back?"

"Once she's deported, Drew, she might not be allowed to return. Married or not." His words make me consider the idea. *Would I go that far? Marry a girl I barely know?* While my cock thinks having her in my bed every night is a very attractive idea, it's the days I'm worried about. Sure, what I've seen of her I like, but fuck, I've only seen her twice. And once was her wearing orange.

While I go quiet, Drew fills the gap. "I'm leaving with her," he says, determined. "She's my sister, she's not going anywhere alone."

He hasn't seen his mother's letters. I'm certain. Otherwise he would know the danger she's in, and would have mentioned it. Instead his concern is about her being alone in a strange place. I'm not going to enlighten him; the boy doesn't deserve more worry on his plate. "Drew, there's a lot of water to flow under the bridge before we come to any decision like that."

Looking up, he seems older than his age when he presses again, "Will you at least think about marrying her, Tse? Once she's legal, you could get divorced."

"Whoa." I hold my hand up. "What you're suggesting is exactly what the authorities think happens. *If,* and it's a very big if, *if* I marry your sister it wouldn't have an expiration date." Not the way it works in my world. You don't make someone your old lady unless it's for keeps. Brothers would never agree to it.

I finish my plate, he clears his, then again catches my eye. "Wouldn't mind you being my brother, Tse. It would be cool."

I'm just about to blurt out I wouldn't mind being his, when I manage to stop myself. *Hey. My fake relationship with Mariana is to help her.* Don't want ideas of anything permanent to sneak up on me. For a start, she'd probably have a few objections of her own.

But if she was mine, I could imagine her under me, on top of me, bending over my bike.

I stand, abruptly, willing my cock to behave before I get a hard on in front of a teenager due to having inappropriate thoughts about his sister.

As expected, Drew starts to perk up, especially as he's now got food in his ever-hungry teenage stomach. This time I don't stop as I pass the Navajo Nation sign, just point it out to Drew. He immediately starts looking around eagerly as though he's going to spot Indians riding horses in full battle gear. As time passes, and all we see are a few produce stands, he closes his eyes and drifts off.

The Rez is exactly the same as when I left it a few days ago, but something inside me has changed. Instead of bringing me peace, it now does nothing to stop the thoughts churning in my head. The anger that rises at the thought of white men determining who has the right to live in this country that they all came to as immigrants in the first place. I wonder what the country would be like if my people had been successful in driving them out when they started their first colonies.

Would Natives have been better leaders? Nah, probably not. Tribes couldn't even band together to fight the white men. At the bottom of it, we're all human with the same frailties. All with the same strange desires—we each feel we were born to try to rule the world rather than just live in it.

That's why I joined the Satan's Devils. We live to a code, it's our own, not anyone else's. But anyone who steps on our toes, or tries to take anything from us, better watch out and be prepared for a whole load of pain. I suppose I'm not so far removed from either side of my ancestry when you get right down to it.

I park outside the hogan. Drew gets out, stretches and yawns, then reaches over the seat for his backpack of clothes, and I drag out his other box of belongings. He stands, his eyes taking in the hexagonal building built of logs in front of him. I'm half expecting him to turn around, put his pack back into the car, and demand to be taken back to Tucson. But the lad's made of stronger stuff.

"You know? The saguaro around Tucson always made me think of the old westerns. Now I'm going to be living in a tepee. With… Native Americans."

I smirk, realising he went PC at the last moment. "Hogan," I correct him, pointing at the structure he'll be calling home for the next few weeks. "Navajo don't live in tepees."

"Tse!"

I turn around still grinning, putting my arm around my mother. "This is Drew," I tell her, and to him I say, "And this is Lina, my mother."

She turns and looks at Drew who politely holds out his hand. After a quick glance at me she tells him, "Tse here was raised as an American, down in Tucson. He tell you that?" When Drew shakes his head, she continues. "He came here at sixteen, had his life turned on its head. Guess I know a thing or two about boys adapting to our way of life." When Drew grins as he's meant to, she grows serious. "I've heard about your sister, and that for the moment, you're all on your own. While you're here,

Drew, you're one of us. You need something explained? You just come and see me."

Drummer's been blowing up my phone, and I've got to return one of his calls soon. I'm eager to be off. I'd already explained to the kid I couldn't hang around. But something tells me he's more excited than uncertain. Part of my anxiety about him settling in fades. I check, though. "You okay with Mom, Drew?"

"Yeah."

"I'll take him up to the school, get him registered for while he's here."

"I'd like that." Drew nods. He would. Mariana's impressed upon him the importance of education. Never known a teenager so adamant on insisting on doing his homework on time.

"I'll be back next week to take you to see Mariana," I promise. A final hug for my mother. A back slap for Drew, and then, if only for a short while, I head back to resume my real life.

Not a moment too soon. My phone rings as I slide into the driver's seat.

"Drummer."

"Things are heatin' up here, Mouse. Need you back."

"I'm on my way. Just leavin' the Rez now."

"Good. See you in a few hours."

It's late evening when I arrive. A party's in full swing in the clubroom, but brothers with old ladies have already left. I ignore the bodies in various stages of their own porn shows, and without anyone taking any notice of me, go into my office. One by one I switch on the monitors, watching the screens all light up. Opening the drawer, I take out what I need to roll myself a joint then hold the flame of the lighter to the tip, leaning back in my black leather chair as I wait for everything to boot up. The familiar whirring of the fans in the computers providing the comforting music of home. I close my eyes, as I take my first real drag of my drug of choice I've not sampled for the past few weeks.

I expect to feel settled, but I don't. I take out my phone and check there's been no calls, half expecting Drew to want me to rescue him. Half hoping to hear from Mariana's lawyer with good news. Suddenly I feel like I've abandoned them both. *I'm doing my best. Can't do much more.*

Chaos Riders. I pull a piece of paper in front of me. Yeah, Chaos Riders. That's what Drummer wants me to investigate. I start tapping on the keys, and soon lose myself in the trail of names and faces.

After a tap on the door, my office door opens. "Mouse?"

"Prez." I thought he'd gone to bed.

Drummer steps in and takes one of the chairs opposite my desk. I start hoping he's not going to get into something detailed, after the day I've had. I'm drained. Seeing Mariana like that, a long drive, well, it's all caught up with me now. "What can I do for you, Prez?" My hands rub at my tired eyes.

"Want to know whether you got your head straightened out."

What can I tell him? That I'm engaged to be married without having brought it up to the club? To a girl I've not touched, yet alone kissed, and an illegal immigrant at that. Or that I'm now responsible for her brother? He'd probably tell me to leave it alone, it's none of my business, no reason for me to be involved. Probably the reason I'm not coming clean, there's no clear motive for anything that I've done. *Maybe I'm not telling him as I could be swayed by such advice.* Mariana and Drew don't need someone else to abandon them.

"I'm fine, Prez."

His steely eyes focus on me. "The fact you took so long to reply tells me you're not. Don't want to lose you, Mouse. You got anything on your mind, you talk to me, okay?"

"It's nothing that will affect the club," I reply.

Another sharp look. "Better not be. Got too much going on with the Chaos Riders and Rock going rogue."

"Rock's really betrayed us?" For an answer, he just nods. I stare at him, unable to process that Rock stole from the club and is now out bad. Seems a lot's happened while I've been away. "Well, let me know where I can help. Already started looking at the Chaos Riders." I inhale again, then blow smoke out.

It seems to be the signal for Drummer to leave.

The next morning, I try to get through to Drew to check on how he's doing, but the call never connects. It was optimistic anyway, the signal's not good there on the Rez. Still, he's got a good head on his shoulders, he'll get in touch if he needs me. I hear nothing from Carissa, but whether that's good or bad I have fuck all way of knowing.

My brothers greet me when they see that I'm back. If I'm slightly short when they ask how I've been doing, I turn away before I can see their expressions. I'm trying to give my all to them, but a big part of my mind is someplace else.

CHAPTER 13

Mouse

Mouse?” Again, it’s the prez interrupting me, making me start a bit guiltily as I was looking up immigration law and nothing to do with the club. I lower the lid of my laptop slightly, peering over the top. “Need me?”

“Got a name for you. Alexis Gardner. Got a handle, Hawk. Gone away on a three-year stint. ’Bout all the info I have.”

“I’ll get on it, Prez. Anything to do with that girl, Becca? Thought her family name was Gardner.” He’s staring at me, making me put my head to one side, and ask, “What?”

“Even when your head’s not completely here with us, nothing much passes you by, does it?”

I pick up the joint and hold it to the flame. “Listen and learn. People drop things. Puzzles fall into place.”

“And exactly what puzzle do you think you’ve solved, Mouse?” *None of my own.* I tap my nose. “Something’s going on, Prez. You’ve got a plan. But not my business to ask what.”

“You think?” Drummer scoffs. “Feels like I’m playin’ it by ear.”

I can understand that. As he gets up and goes, I call out, “I’m taking off for a couple of nights. Won’t be gone long, Drummer. Need to hit the Rez to sort something out.”

He narrows his eyes, opens his mouth, but just when I think this is the time he’s going to ask me to explain myself, he shrugs. “Keep your secrets if you want, Mouse. But I ain’t stupid. There’s something going on. I’ll leave you to figure out when you need your brothers at your back. Thing about brotherhood, Mouse, is you've got backup when you want it."

He closes the door behind him, leaving me to think over my problems. Can't see where he or anyone else could help.

I do a bit of digging on the name Drummer gave to me, set searches off to proceed while I'm gone, then set off to drive to the Rez. I'll spend the night there, and in the morning I'll be taking Drew to see Mariana. Fuck knows how much it will upset him to see her in orange again. He didn't cope well with it last time.

Drew's sporting a black eye, but he grins when he sees me. "The other asshole looks worse." He's so proud as he tells me, I suspect that he does.

I put my arm around his shoulders and lead him off to one side, indicating a fallen tree trunk which doubles as a seat. "Wanna tell me about it?"

"White boy, Navajo school," he replies succinctly.

Yeah, I can well remember that. "You doing okay?"

"They've moved me up a grade." He grins. Again, I'm not surprised. Navajo aren't stupid, far from it. Just don't think book learning will help them through life. He is probably more advanced than others his age. Now Drew's lips curve right up. "Got some good-looking chicks there, though."

Now I mock slap him around his head. "You're only fifteen."

His raised eyebrow makes me laugh. Yeah, he's got me there. Fifteen's when I lost my virginity. "Mom treating you okay?"

"Your mom and gramma are great. Make me eat everything though."

I suspect they do. Not a bad habit to get into. Night's falling, a rustle in the bushes behind me makes me shiver. Time for the skin-walkers to come out. Then I inwardly laugh. Dark doesn't bother me in Tucson, it's just here, on the Rez, where I can feel phantom eyes burning into my back. "Best get inside."

"What is it with that? Your mom always wants me in before dark. Is there a high crime rate or something?"

Something. He's an Anglo. We won't be sharing all our heritage with him, outsiders may scoff, but here things seem possible which wouldn't be understood anywhere else. While he's here, we'll keep him safe. Watch his back for things he isn't aware of.

We set off early the next morning for the detention centre, arriving in good time with relatively few delays. I lock my gun and both our phones in the truck, and then proceed to the entrance. I then have to submit to a full pat down before I'm allowed inside. Drew wanted to bring in some books for Mariana, but I explained we weren't allowed to carry anything in with us. Following my lead, Drew allows himself to be searched, copying my example as he did last time, holding his arms out wide, and making no protest.

I pass over my ID to be checked, explaining Drew, as a minor, is my responsibility. Then it's just a matter of waiting until we're called in.

We wait. There are several other visitors hanging around. One by one they disappear as they're summoned into the visiting room. Drew looks at me when Mariana's name's not called, and I start to wonder whether she doesn't want to see us. I've had brothers doing time who've preferred not to have contact with those outside. Places like this? There's no telling how it can affect a person.

When the room's empty except for us, and Drew's now fidgeting openly, a guard approaches, his white belly barely contained by his uniform shirt tucked into his trousers.

He consults a list. "You're here to see Mariana De Souza?"

"We are," I agree.

"She can't have visitors today." A plain statement of fact, ignoring the number of miles we've driven to get here.

Drew and I exchange glances. "Why the fuck not?"

"She's in solitary confinement."

"What the fuck for?" It takes every effort to force myself to stay still, and not advance on him. *Mariana in solitary?* I know enough about her to believe she'd follow every rule, going out of her way not to cause trouble. Something smells here, something I don't like.

He shrugs, completely unapologetic. "Nothing to do with me. I wouldn't know."

"Is there someone here who would know?" I'm trying to keep a tight rein on my temper.

"No one who'd tell you anything." The guard even seems happy.

"I'm her brother." Drew's bottom lip is trembling.

"I'm her fiancé," I back him up. "I want to know she's okay. I, *we*, have a right to know."

The guard shakes his head. "If there was anything wrong with her she'd be in the infirmary. It's not your right to know what she's done to get put in solitary. Both of you are out of luck. She'll probably soon be deported which is all to the good. Got too many of," he looks pointedly at Drew, "your sort in this country."

Now I see red. "Drew's a US Citizen. Mariana, *my fiancée*, who's never known another country but North America, is training to be a nurse to give something back to society. Looks like you're the sort we don't need in *my* country." I draw myself up to my full height, my dark hair flicking around me. "You proud of yourself? Keeping human beings who've done nothing wrong prisoner?"

My hands, twitching by my side, are already curled into fists. I'm not quite sure what would have happened if Drew hadn't grabbed my arm, reminding me this is not the time or place for violence. Getting locked up myself wouldn't help either Drew or Mariana.

"Come on, Tse. Let's go call Ms Beacham, the lawyer. Maybe she knows what's happening or at least can find out."

Yeah. Her lawyer should be able to find out. Having to be satisfied with tossing the guard my best sneer, I reluctantly turn, walk outside, and cross the parking lot to the truck. I slam the door shut, start the engine to get the air conditioning working, then grab my phone, impatiently drumming my fingers until it's answered.

"Carissa Beacham? Tse Williamson. We've got a problem. We couldn't see Mariana, she's in solitary." Drew's hanging onto my side of the conversation, the only part he can hear. "They wouldn't tell us anything, Carissa. Her brother and I are worried sick. Yeah, okay. I'll wait for your call." I replace the phone in my pocket.

I breathe out deeply, then turn to the teenager. "She's going to do what she can to find out what's going on."

I hesitate, waiting a moment before pulling away, my eyes going to the building in front of me. *Mariana's inside somewhere*. It's killing me not to know what's going on. If this was a normal prison, I might have ways of finding out, of finding someone we've got contact with on the inside. But here? For once I'm out of my depth. There's not enough data to go on. All I know is Mariana would have done her best not to do anything wrong. I doubt she'd even talk back. I work with facts, link them together, dig deeper. There's fuck all to go on here. No supposition, no comprehension. I'm frustrated as hell as there's nothing more I can do about it.

When Drew looks at me questioningly, I put the truck into drive. "Better get you back."

"I don't like leaving like this."

I know exactly how he feels. I give him the arguments I'm working through in my head. "Can't do any good here. Soon as we hear from Carissa and know what the fuck's going on, I'll bring you back, okay?"

Two days away from the club. Two days for absolutely nothing, except covering miles driving a cage across Arizona. I'm tired as shit after I drop Drew off at the Rez, and am now nearing Tucson. My phone starts blowing up when I'm turning up the track to the compound. Two, no, three missed calls. *Make that four.* I'm so close I don't bother to answer. I'll find out what's so urgent soon enough.

Parking the truck, I slide my cut on. *What the fuck?* Brothers are piling in, one word sounding from every direction. *Rock,* and that's being strangely coupled with the woman who's recently arrived on the compound, *Becca.* Fuck. I remember how I'd left those computers searching. *I should have been there in case they've found something Drummer needs to know.* I listen, absorbing what little information I can glean from their animated conversations. There appears to be a connection between the woman and our out-bad member. How the fuck does Becca know Rock? Data, or the lack of it, doesn't add up. That this is serious shit means I need to force worries about Mariana out of my mind, and focus on the club.

I'm surprised when I walk into church, the woman herself is sitting at the end of the table, Peg behind her cutting off her escape route. Still unable to get my mind totally off Mariana, I listen incredulously as it all comes out. How despite what we've all been led to believe, Rock's not a traitor who joined the Chaos Riders, *a club I should have been investigating,* to bring us down, but instead he's a fucking hero.

"Why the fuck didn't you tell us?" I yell as the details all come out.

Drummer shoots me a look as if to say I wasn't here anyway, but shakes a weary head as he points out, "Chaos had to believe Rock's story. It would only work if his old club, us, were out to kill him. Rock's life depends on his backstory holdin' up and nothing happenin' to make Chaos suspicious."

My hand unties and reties my hair as I listen to Becca's story with my jaw dropping open. How the sweet butt Jill found out the truth. She's always had her tongue hanging out for Rock, and now, it seems, she's set on locating him.

"She wouldn't know where the Riders have set up," Wraith suggests.

"Er," Becca's small voice and raised hand gets our attention. "Allie overheard Rock and the other prospect saying they were heading back to Long Horns. She told Jill."

For a second you could hear a pin drop.

Prez is looking at me. "Can she find it with that?"

I'm already tapping at the keys of my laptop, quickly unearthing the info I want. "There's a Long Horns out in the desert south of Tucson. An old ranch. If that's where they are, then yes. Clearly marked on the map. Even someone like Jill would be able to easily find it with a Google search."

Now Mariana has to be pushed to the back of my mind as I retreat to my office, digging to find anything I can on the Chaos Riders. It's not much. Except the club's got funding behind them. Abandoning their history, I look at the location where my brother Rock currently is. My gut feeling is that Becca's right, and he's in danger.

I turn to calling up the location of their clubhouse, and checking on Google View and the satellite images so we're equipped with as much information as possible and will know what we're heading into.

"Prez." His door is open so I walk right in, laying some print-outs in front of him.

"Mouse. Got something to help?"

I raise my chin. "That's the location of the old homestead. Got barns out back. But the rear is totally unprotected. No fencing that I could see."

Drummer takes out his phone and places a call. Within moments Peg's joined us. As sergeant-at-arms he'll need to be involved in the planning. Unfazed, I go through it all again.

Peg studies the photos and plans carefully, then looks up. "We attack front and back."

"Got the other chapters coming," Drum informs him.

Nodding, Peg taps on the clearest overhead satellite image. "We draw them out with Becca as the bait, go straight at the front. Get the other chapters circling behind them and flushing them out. They'll be caught between us."

"Pincer movement." Drummer's lips curve up. "Along the lines of what I was thinkin', Peg."

"You need me any more?"

"Nah, Mouse. Thanks."

It's not long afterwards that brothers from the other chapters start pouring in. I'll be fighting alongside these men tomorrow, so I stay in the clubroom to be sociable. Already adrenaline has started running through my veins, anticipation of the battle ahead, and the overriding need to bring Rock home. The thought crosses my mind that tomorrow may be the day that I die.

I know I have a reputation as a cold fish, almost robotically going about my tasks, more comfortable with the machines I spend my life with. I'm in a one-percenter club, living this life until the day I leave it, knowing I'm dancing with the devil, taunting him to take me. Normally it wouldn't bother me at all. Except now, I've got something to live for. People depending on me. I make a couple of phone calls to ensure everything's in place if I don't come back, then mentally try to prepare myself.

If it happens, so be it. Drew's in a safe place, Carissa's looking after Mariana's interests.

That I've taken on the sibling's burden without question surprises even me. I got myself mixed up in their mess. Could have walked away, no one would have blamed me, I only met the woman once. For once I'm invested in what happens in the human world, rather than binary code and machine language.

As I watch brothers from all chapters catching up, discussing the wrath they'll be raining down tomorrow, the Chaos Riders they'll be dispatching to Satan, I realise that while I have no fear of death, this time I want to come back. Want a chance. A chance with Mariana. *What would it be like if I really was engaged to her? Thinking of making her my old lady?* When she rode at my back, it was as though she'd been made to ride behind me. Only a few short hours that we had spent together, but it had felt right.

It's when I consider her being deported and – if she could evade her father – starting a new life, finding a man who wasn't me, my blood boils hot. Ask me and I couldn't explain it, but I'm feeling possessive. Over a woman I've barely met.

I don't know much about her.

But what I do, I like.

The next day I stand up beside my brothers as one by one we take all the Riders out. I might be a nerd, but I can shoot and kill as well as anyone else who wears the same patch. Rock, hell, Rock. *What the fuck have they done to him?* Beef's been shot, but he seems to be walking wounded. While the two injured men are taken back to the compound, I stay behind and do my share of moving bodies and cleaning up. For once my mind is quiet, focused on the task. When we ride away and Slick blows that shithole up, I'm happy to celebrate. *That's what we do to our enemies.*

I'm just frustrated I can't take the government on in the same way. Face it head on and fight. But no, I have to do what I can through the lawyer, and hope for the best. Used to being a man of action, a man able to find information where it's needed, it's hard to sit back and wait for someone else to pull it all together.

* * * *

"Tse?"

"Yeah. Hi, Carissa." I prop my phone between my ear and my shoulder as half my attention is on my computer screen.

"Got some info. Mariana's in solitary as you're aware. It looks like it might be they're preparing to move her to another detention centre."

"What the fuck? Why would they do that?"

"Who knows, Tse? But these things happen all the time. Why they do it, I don't know, but sometimes that's the reason for putting detainees in solitary. I'll keep on top of things and let you know as soon as I have anything else."

I swallow, not wanting to ask, but know I have to. "Could they be preparing to deport her?"

A pause, then, "I can't rule that out. But deportees are allowed to take a small suitcase with them. As her lawyer, I would have expected to have been asked to supply that. I haven't, so I assume moving her is more likely."

"Why move her?" I start to think of the logistics if she's moved out of state. "Drew and I want to visit. They know she's got family nearby. Or do the motherfuckers want her moved because of that? Punish her by keepin' her family from her?" ICE's intention seems to be to punish people for simply existing, or daring to cross into the US. I grow angry thinking none of this was Mariana's fault. She didn't ask to become an illegal alien. I shut my thoughts down when I remember Carissa's still on the line.

"Who knows, Tse. Who knows. But I promise, as soon as I hear anything, I'll be in touch."

Christ. The fucking government's holding all the cards on this one. I don't have one single hand to play. My muscles tighten, I work to unlock my jaw. *Nothing I can do.* Only more shit to worry about. That's getting me nowhere.

My attention is caught by information on the screen once again. *Work. Throw myself into it. Deal with other people's problems where I can help.* At least, for now. Let Carissa do what she does best and what I'm paying her for. She understands the system.

I open the office door, seeing immediately the woman I want to talk to. It's the first time I've spoken to her directly. She strikes me as timid as a mouse, an observation which almost makes me snort. But I force my features into a smile. Something tells me to tread carefully.

"Becca?"

As she swings around, there's trepidation written all over her face when she nods. Holding out my hand, I introduce myself. "Mouse. I'm the go-to computer guy around here. We've not been properly introduced." I wait for her acknowledgement, then continue. "If you've got a minute, Prez has asked me to do some investigatin' on your behalf. Find out what you're up against."

Examining her carefully, I can see she's been crying. Fuck, I'm an asshole. Of course she doesn't want to talk to me now. She'll be torn between our two injured brothers. Now's bad timing, she'll want to be with Rock, and also must be worried as hell about Beef who's taken her under his wing. But I do need information only she can supply.

As she wipes away tears, my eyes soften with compassion. "Hey, I know you're worried about Beef. But darlin', he'll be fine. I'm certain. Come in and let's discuss your situation. Take your mind off everything that's happening. Unless you'd rather be with Rock?"

Her dismissive shake of her head when I mention Rock's name surprises me, but as usual, I'm focused on data and pulling puzzle pieces together. I'd also spoken the truth. Both men are in good hands, her brooding on their condition won't help them recover. I'm confident they'll do that by themselves. Both strong, determined brothers. Then I feel guilty, of course she'll want to be with her man. My needs will have to wait.

But she follows me into my office. I'm an unfeeling bastard, so again I check. "You sure you're okay not being with Rock?"

She gives me a sharp look. "Have you spoken to Rock?"

"Nah. Not since he's regained consciousness." A burst of guilt floods over me. Sometimes I'm so taken up with getting the facts, I forget to consider feelings. *This can wait.* Cognisant I'm using her situation to take my mind off the helplessness I feel about Mariana's, I offer once more. "But did you want to wait to go through this? You've probably got things to talk about with him."

It's the tone of her voice when she tells me she and Rock have said all they needed to say, which makes me look at her strangely. *Something's happened there.* Or perhaps Becca's feelings were one-sided, and she's been rebuffed. If so, she's taken it to heart, indicating she's more concerned about Beef who's taken a turn for the worse and been rushed to the hospital. I hadn't known that. I wonder briefly what could have happened, then dismiss it. *He'll be in the right place.* I'm worried about Beef myself, we all are. But as I can't offer medical help, there's nothing I can do for him.

"Tell me about Hawk," I start, wanting to know about the man she was, is, married to. The man who left her to be neglected and abused by the Chaos Riders.

Unsurprisingly, before she tells me much, we're joined by Drummer. Prez will want to know about any possible threat to the club. I'm soon absorbed and disgusted as Becca goes through what happened to her. Prez and I exchange a few glances accompanied by shakes of our heads. For the first time this morning, the horror she's lived through pulls my head completely away from my own problems.

Hawk's in prison now. But he'll be out. Possibly sooner than his three-year sentence suggests. "I'll look into when he's eligible for parole."

Becca takes in a sharp breath, seems she thought she'd have the full three years to get shot of him.

We question her further, but apart from finding out Hawk's a pastor with a violent streak, she doesn't know anything about the secret life he's been living. Her first impulse is to run, but a girl like her has got no chance on her own. When I offer to look into her getting a divorce, becoming legally separated from him, I end up nodding when Drummer promises she'll be free of the man who trapped her into a marriage she didn't want. I exchange a look with Prez. A look which says, a man like that? If we have to, we'll kill him.

Drummer's phone pings. When he reads the text, he gives what for him is a broad smile. "Beef's come through surgery. The doctors think his prognosis is good."

Rolling my head back on my shoulders, I let out a breath. *My brother's going to be fine.* It's only at that point I admit there was a moment there when I was worried he wouldn't make it.

As Becca and Drummer leave to go to the hospital, I promise to keep digging. The story she told me makes me eager to help. If I can't do anything for Mariana, I'll focus on finding the information to help another woman.

CHAPTER 14

Mariana

When Drew and Tse visited last week, saying goodbye tore me in two and I lost it. I returned to my prison cell and collapsed on my bed, tears flooding from my eyes as my hands thumped the hard pillow, cursing the world for letting me end up like this. It's so unfair. All I had to do to keep my DACA status was to abide by every law, which I did. Every action, every thought, taking into account the rights and wrongs of what I should be doing. I even sent Tse away because of his connection to an outlaw motorcycle club, not allowing myself to see him again or know whether we'd have a chance to start a relationship.

Now, through no fault of my own, the authorities think I'm a criminal. *What could I have done differently?* Except not be in that place at that time.

I constantly go back to that morning, running the events over and over in my head. Knowing the crash had been out of my control. Hating the man who set me up and lied about it. *Has he any idea of the landslide of repercussions his actions have caused?* Separating me from the only family I have, and who depends on me.

Drew. A man/boy who'd be lost and adrift if it wasn't for Tse. But why has Tse taken my brother under his wing? Given him shelter? Making sure he's looked after? It's not that I'm not grateful, there aren't enough thanks in the world to give him. But I'm bewildered about the Native American who always seems to be rescuing me. Only this time, he can't protect me from the bear that's intent on killing me.

Lying in my cot, I'm certain death or worse is waiting for me should I return to Colombia. From my mother's brief correspondence with me, I know my father's in a position to be able to find out anything with his network of connections. He'll probably be aware I'm there as soon as I step over the border. *He wanted me back.* He'll take his revenge on me for returning, and for keeping his son away from him. The son he didn't know he had, but found out about when he saw the scar my mother got from birthing him. The son he'll probably want to mould into his own image. I can't let that happen to Drew. But am I strong enough to fight him?

"*¿Estás bien?*"

I'm crying again. The woman I'm sharing with is kneeling beside me, her eyes shining with sympathy. She speaks no English, I know hardly any Spanish, but understand enough to realise she's asking me if I'm okay. I'm about as far from that as I could be, and doubt I'll ever be right again. I don't have the words to explain, even in the English she wouldn't understand, so I just pat her hand, sit up, and attempt to dry my tears on the scratchy sheet.

She'll be going through her own hell. Separated from her family too, perhaps? I've no way of knowing, no way of communicating. *This is what it will be like in Colombia.* A stranger in the country of my birth. A land so alien to me, the States is all I've ever known.

Knowing my distress is upsetting her, I try to pull myself together. Her features now relax, and relieved I've stopped my tears, my cellmate goes back to what she was doing. My angst isn't unusual here. Cries and wails continue through the night as people try to come to terms with being caught up in a relentless machine that treats us little better than animals. I swear the guards don't even see me as human. I've no rights, no dignity. All taken away when Todd Jenkins rammed into me.

Each day is the same. I long for that one hour of sunlight when we're taken outside, raising my head to the sun, soaking up the rays. My misery so great, I don't share it with anyone else. Staying on my own, like so many others here. Knowing our fate is already determined, just waiting for the executioner's axe to fall.

I know Carissa, my lawyer, will be doing her best, but it's hopeless. Even when I go before a judge, I'll just be a number, another illegal to be deported. Another DACA recipient who mucked up and got charged with committing a felony. One strike and you're out. You don't even need to be found guilty.

"Hey, you." I look around to see a guard using his finger to beckon to me. I walk across. Something about him seems off, and I'm glad there's a chain-link fence between us. "You and me, later, okay? I can make your life more comfortable here."

As his hand briefly covers his groin, I have no doubt what he's asking. Using one of the few Spanish phrases I know, I respond, "*No entiendo.*" Hoping if I pretend I don't know what he's asking, he'll leave me alone.

Instead he leers, then shrugs. "Don't need to speak English, darling. Don't need to speak at all. I can use that mouth for other things."

I keep my face blank as though I can't understand him. When he saunters off, I shudder, my heart racing. I've heard rumours of what goes on, but with my other worries I thought they were exaggerated, and naively I thought it wouldn't happen to me. *What the hell do I do?* Can the guard make good on his threat?

Not if you don't let him catch you alone. Moving away from the fence, I place myself in the middle of the women. It becomes my practice to do the same at meal times, avoiding being in a corner by myself, keeping my head down, not wanting to draw attention.

That night, in bed, I'm still shaken. Yeah, we're animals. For the guards' entertainment. I'm scared stiff, wondering if I'll be able to prevent having something taken by force that I've not had the chance to give willingly. I've never dated, never been out with a man. I'm chilled by the thought my virginity could be taken by force. The guards are clever; they'll make sure no one believed me.

My real fears of the possibility of being raped lead my thoughts to the man who says he's my fiancé. For a moment, I allow myself to wonder what it would be like if that was true. From what I've seen of him, from how he is with Drew, there's no one I've met I'd like better. My situation pushes me into admissions I wouldn't otherwise have considered. As I lie there in the dead of the night, I know I can't allow anyone to steal my virginity from me, not when the only man I've liked and wanted to give it to is Tse.

Crazy, crazy thoughts. I barely know him.

But that doesn't seem to matter. *I want him.*

Another rush of sadness when I realise what I want is not what I'm going to get. I'll be thousands of miles away, while he'll be here, living his life.

My nerves are on edge. The next day, completely wound up, I keep jumping as I hear heavy footsteps approaching. But as the hours pass and I remain unmolested, I start to think it was all a bad joke. A guard taunting an inmate. I grow angry instead, how dare they toy with us in such ways?

Trying to put the unpleasant incident behind me, I count off the days until the next visit when Tse has promised he'll be returning with Drew. I long to see his friendly face and that of my brother. As much as any mother, I worry about Drew constantly. *Is he eating enough? Is he keeping up with his school-*

work? How is he getting on in such an alien environment? Is he holding his own, being bullied? The worst thought I have is that he'll be upset, lonely, and missing our home. *All I want is for him to be happy.*

Two nights before they are due to visit, a guard comes to fetch me, indicating I should leave my cell. I look at her suspiciously.

"Where are you taking me?"

She's six feet tall, muscular. Her face wearing that grim expression all the correction officers seem to adopt. "It doesn't matter where. Just come with me."

I don't like this. But what can I do? I've no rights here. I can't protest. *It could be something good. My lawyer might have come to visit me.* Or, *it might be the worst. Tonight, I may get deported.* But I haven't yet been before a judge, they can't just do that, can they? What do I know? Everything that's happened recently has been out of my control, why should this be any different?

I follow the prison guard. She stops, unlocks a door, then leads me down a different corridor. It's quieter here. Dismal. Closed doors to either side. She stops in front of one that's open, steps back, and waves me inside. The door slams shut behind me, the bolt ominously clanging.

I'm in a cell with an uncomfortable looking cot, a basin and a toilet with no lid. I've seen enough TV to realise I've probably been put in solitary. *But why?* Had my cellmate complained I was crying too much? That would be unfair, she wasn't unknown for tears herself. Surely that's not it. *Why am I here?*

Sitting on the bed, I wipe away fresh tears. It's the shame of not knowing, of not being able to understand. I'm being punished for a crime I didn't do. But no one cares, do they?

Eventually the bolt sounds again, and two men enter. One is the guard who called me over to the fence. One look at his face and it's clear he's come to collect. *Oh God. No.*

Holding my hands up in front of me, I inch backward, my progress halted by the low bed. "What do you want with me?" My voice sounds weak.

"I think you know exactly what I want, *puta*."

I might not know many Spanish words, but I know that. "I'm no whore," I spit out, as forcefully as I can, but manage little more than a squeak.

He shrugs, and his hands go to his belt. "Whatever. You'll be giving it up."

He's going to force me. No. No, he's not. I'm not giving in. I ignore the man standing outside the door, presumably on guard in case anyone comes along. *I can't let him do this. It's not his to take.*

Belt undone, he starts to unzip his fly. "On the bed, *puta*. Make this easy on yourself."

That word again. It makes me see red. Going on the offensive I fly at him, my nails raking down his face leaving marks, blood welling in their wake.

"Bitch!" he shouts, and backhands me, sending me flying.

My eyes open and horrified, I put my hand to my lip that's already swelling. Pulling it away, my own blood shines red on my fingers.

"Shit." The other man looks into the room. "Bert, you shouldn't have done that."

With a hand to his bleeding face, Bert steps out into the corridor where they have a whispered conversation, grunts and growls showing they're not too pleased with the situation, while I sit wondering what they're going to do next, my heart pounding, pulse racing. *I'll fight again.* I'd rather die than be raped.

After their altercation, the one not named Bert steps in, his face glowing red. "You fucking fell, got it? Anyone asks, you're a fucking clumsy bitch and you slipped and fell, okay?"

I'll make sure to tell my lawyer and Tse the truth. Exactly who hurt me.

Suddenly one corner of his mouth turns up. "If you'd done what we said? You'd be back in your cell after a good fucking. You've gone and attacked a guard now, so now you're gonna have to stay in solitary. Serves you right. Fucking bitch."

I was protecting myself. I can't stay here. Tse and Drew are visiting the day after next. "How long?" There's no point in protesting, I can see that.

"Two weeks," the guard proclaims, unsympathetically.

Again, my hand goes to my sore mouth, this time to cover my gasp. "I've got visitors…"

"Ain't gonna be no visits for you." He steps out, pulling the door closed as he goes. I can just make out the words, "Come on, Bert, better get those scratches disinfected," before it slams shut completely.

Two weeks. Two weeks on my own. No visits to look forward to. No answers to my questions about Drew. Just alone with my terror that these two men are going to come back.

"Noooooooooooooo!" I scream.

CHAPTER 15

Mouse

Being unable to see Mariana plays on my mind, and so does my responsibility for her brother. Part of me worries it was wrong to leave him as I did, but what else could I have done? I admit it was a knee-jerk reaction to have him someplace safe, but I'm concerned about him. Selfishly, I'd like him closer. He's the only one who knows what we're fighting, as I still haven't let my brothers in on my problem.

Would they care? It's hard to know if they'd be concerned about an illegal immigrant. They'd have my back, but hers? Would they understand why I'm so committed to Mariana, when I barely know her? Being unable to explain my feelings to myself, I can't find the words to confide in my brothers.

I'm frustrated when Drew's obviously out of the range of a cell tower. I call a number of times to check he's okay, but the call never gets through. I'm beyond relieved when he does eventually answer. Our subsequent conversation reassuring me that apart from being worried sick about his sister, he seems to have adapted to life on the Rez better than I had done when I'd first arrived all those years ago. I suppose I was reluctant to see it as anything other than an unwelcome change to my all-American boy's life in Tucson, and still reeling from the death of my father. Drew is treating it more like a temporary adventure. Still hanging on to the hope that Mariana will walk free again, and that he'll return to live with his sister.

Having never been responsible for a kid, I find I'm choosing my words carefully, not giving him false hope, but downplaying my own fears about why his sister's being kept in solitary. I don't tell him Carissa's assumption that they might be about to move her.

Ending the call with the promise I'll tell him the moment I hear anything, I take a long drag on my joint, but even my drug of choice doesn't do much to relax me.

There's a knock, I call out "Enter", and in steps Rock with Becca. The two seem to have made up whatever their difference was, and now are never far from each other. My eyes fall on their joined hands, jealous, knowing I'd give a lot to be able to hold onto Mariana's.

I raise my chin at my brother, but my eyes focus on his woman. "Just the person I wanted to see." I've been doing some digging while finding out all I could about her ex-husband. What I found was an interesting anomaly. I give them the details; Rock takes them to Drummer.

When my phone rings, I'm back to worrying about my own problems again.

"Tse. They're moving Mariana."

Moving her? My mind leaps to the worst. "Deporting her?"

"No, not yet," Carissa assures me hurriedly. "Moving her to another facility. This one's in California."

"What the hell for?" I ask, while thinking how difficult that's going to make it to visit her. "Can I see her before she goes?"

"You won't be able to see her; these things move fast. It could simply be the immigration judge has too heavy a workload in Florence. Might be able to get her higher up the list somewhere else." Carissa sounds resigned. I don't know what to think. Again, I realise how out of my comfort zone I am.

"Do you know where, exactly?"

"Not yet. Soon as I know I'll tell you."

"Can you see her?"

There's a sigh. "Look, Tse. There's no point until we know when her hearing is. I've got all the information I need. I'm aware how much this is costing you. I don't want to run up a high bill if we don't have to. This could take months; I know some people have waited years before having their day in court."

She's right. The money I have is fast dwindling. I don't want to run out.

"As her lawyer, they'll tell me, eventually. I know it's hard, but be patient, Tse. There's only one way to play this game, and that's their way."

That's the bit I don't like. Satan's Devils buck the system; we don't go along with it. I'm tied up in knots as there's nothing I can do. I can't remember ever feeling this helpless. Nothing I research brings me comfort, innocent people get deported every day. I've even read cases where bona fide American citizens have been caught up in the system and sent to a country they've no connection to, then have to fight for the right to return. What chance has Mariana got? Angrily picking up my joint I light it again, inhaling deeply, blowing out the fragrant smoke into the room. Right now my mind's like the air surrounding me. I haven't the foggiest idea what to do.

Deciding to let Carissa work on the legal side, I start researching in another direction, deeper than I've done before, working late into the night, trying once again to get background on Mariana's father. I set up searches and wait for the results, delving into systems I shouldn't have access to. It's surprisingly hard to find any information at all.

The next morning, I'm back at it again when I'm interrupted. *A bomb on the compound?*

I spring into action, helping where I can best. First, I need to check the security tapes to find if anyone got access to the compound, then when Slick finds a bomb in a car at the auto-shop, I'm looking into the fucker who brought it in.

We know how the explosive was brought onto the compound. But what we can't do is stop the bomb going off. Now I've another brother fighting for his life in the hospital. I haven't time to give another thought to what might happen when Mariana returns to Colombia. Retribution for whatever fate awaits my brother trumps concerns about Mariana for now. My first task is to discover who planted the bomb.

I do. He's made it easy for me, it just involves tracing a VIN. Bo Brayden. Stupid asshole, bought the car that he planted the bomb in. We get him easily enough, and dispatch him with as much pain as trying to kill one of our own warrants.

Crisis somewhat dealt with, except that Slick hasn't woken up, the next morning I'm free to research Mariana's father all over again, when my phone rings.

"Drew." I'm pleased to hear from him. "How's it going?"

"Good. Woo hoo!"

Woo hoo? "Where are you, Drew?" I ask, suspicions running through my head.

"In a jeep, crossing the Rez. Bit bumpy." Well, that explains the excited shout. With everything going on, the boy deserves to have a diversion. My lips curve as I ask, "You havin' fun?"

"Yeah. Yesterday your uncle took me hunting. Taught me to use a bow and arrow. A *real* bow and arrow."

Now I'm grinning, knowing exactly which uncle he means. Normally he uses a gun, but he's an archery ace. "Who you with now, and where are you going?"

"What? I lost you there for a moment."

"What are you doing today?" I repeat.

"Learning to ride."

At least they're keeping him amused. I'm grateful to my family. "Yeah? Who with?"

"Billy."

I'm on my feet, my chair's fallen over backwards. Long-ago memories of Billy putting me on an untamed horse flooding back into my head. "Drew," I growl quickly. "Do not, I repeat, do not get on any horse Billy gives you. Drew? Drew? For fuck's sake. Drew!"

The signal's gone. My warning unheard. The boy I'm responsible for is heading off with a man who thinks learning to ride means seeing how long you can stay on. Visions of Drew in the hospital with broken bones flash in front of my eyes. "Damn it!" I yell, throwing my phone at the door.

The door which is opening. Prez's reactions are fast and he catches the phone with a two-handed catch.

"Whoa there, Brother. What the fuck is up?"

My breath is coming in spurts. "I've got to go, Prez." I've got to get to Drew. Give him a few words of advice he obviously needs. That's if I find him in one piece.

"Sit the fuck down, Mouse."

Drummer's roar has me planting my ass back in the chair. He stands, his arms folded, his steely eyes on mine. "I've given you more than enough leeway. Now you're gonna tell me what the fuck's going on."

I stay silent. How can I explain I'm riled up because of a woman I hardly know, and her brother who I feel it's my responsibility to protect?

"Well?" he snarls.

"Nothing to do with the club, Prez."

"That so? That's what you might think. But you're not here for your brothers, even when you're on the compound." I start to protest; he stops me with a raised hand. "Oh, you do everything we fuckin' ask for, can't fault you on that. But you're distracted, your mind's someplace else."

He's right. I gaze down at my hands solidly planted on the desk. "Need to take off again, Prez."

"Sort of gathered that." Now Drummer kicks out a chair and sits down. His hardened gaze burns into me until I look up and meet his eyes. "Brother. What you do," he waves his hands at the monitors, "couldn't ask you to do more. We need something? You pull out all the stops to find it for us. We need you to fight beside your brothers? You do it. You give your fuckin' all to this club."

Embarrassed, I resume looking at my hands again.

"You got a problem?" he continues. "Don't like being shut out. Ain't nothing you can't bring to the table. You've given a lot. Time you spend in here? You work as hard, if not harder than any of the other assholes hanging around. You need something? We'll be right behind you."

"Prez," I start, wondering why there's a pricking at the back of my eyes. "It's not that I want to keep you out, it's more that I don't know what the fuck needs doing."

He raises his chin. "When you figure it out, come to me, okay? Every man who sits around that table will be there at your back." Shaking his head, he sighs. "Club's more than one person, Mouse. Ever thought we could help figure out what needs to be done? Don't shut us out, Brother."

Gradually I begin to nod. Perhaps it will soon be time to come clean. "Let me go now, do what I need to, okay? I'll be at the end of the phone." Or when I can pick up messages at least. "When I return, when I know more. Then we'll sit down."

He purses his lips, his brow furrows, then he shakes his head. "One last time, Mouse. Then you will tell me what's got you twisted in knots. This time I know it's got fuck all to do with you needing to go off on a vision quest or such."

"One last time," I agree.

He stands, leaning on the back of the chair to push it tidily back against the desk, then turns and opens the door. Before he leaves, he mumbles something under his breath. Something I manage to make out. "There's a fuckin' woman at the bottom of this, sure as fuck of that."

I stare hard at his back. Not saying a word. But he's got it in one. I wonder how he'll react when he finds out he's speaking about the woman I claimed as my fiancée.

I take a moment to finish my joint while thinking over what Drummer said. Some of my research showed me my brothers could prove useful. But I'd have to ask them to do something way outside of their comfort zone. It's something to think on, though. For when I return.

Closing down the systems I don't need to keep running, I switch off the monitors, then walk out through the clubhouse. Apart from Diva, one of the sweet butts cleaning down the bar, the room is empty. No chance for goodbyes. *No questions to answer.* How I like it.

I can't take a club truck without knowing how long I'll be gone. So I stuff what I can into my saddle bags, then get on my bike. With one last lingering look over my shoulder, I start the long ride back to the Rez.

<h1 style="text-align:center">Chapter 16</h1>

Mouse

I'm anxious to get back to the place I used to call home. Anxious to see Drew, a need to talk to someone about Mariana, someone who shares my fears and knows what I'm going through. It's not fair to place all that on a fifteen-year-old's shoulders, but the thought of just being with her kin, sharing his burden, shines like a beacon to me.

When I stop for gas I check my phone, no one's called to tell me Drew's lying dead or dying from falling off a horse, so at least I'm expecting to find him alive. Unlike Billy who won't have much longer to live if he's endangered him in any way.

It's into the evening by the time I arrive and pull up outside the hogan. Unusually, the sound of my engine doesn't draw anyone out. But as I shut it down with a sense of uneasiness and pocket the key, I don't have to look hard to find the reason why. Loud shouts of laughter are ringing out from inside. My gramma, my mom, Drew's voice, and a couple of my uncles too.

I grin, the kid's alive. In good spirits too by the sounds of it. I was going to have a chat with him tonight, guess if he's having fun, I'll leave it until the morning.

First person I see on entering is that fucker Billy. I pause to clout him around the back of his head.

He turns fast, his hand rubbing his skull, his eyes blazing. "What the fuck?"

"You take my boy riding?" I growl.

"Yeah. He's a natural." Billy's shaking his head as though trying to shrug off the pain. I barely touched him. He's putting it all on.

"A natural? What fuckin' unbroken beast did you put him on to prove that?"

Billy smirks. "Actually, the same paint horse as I put you on." As my eyes widen, he continues. "Gelded now of course. Tame as a fuckin' lamb. I looked after the kid for you."

Hmm. Sounds like he might have done just that. That mustang must be twenty years old now, must have calmed over the years.

"Tse!" Drew's on his feet. Well, fuck me, he looks pleased to see me. *He'll probably think I've got news of Mariana.* "I got an A in computer science." I'm pleased as fuck at his grade, and also that's what he was bursting to tell me.

Mom gets me a plate of stew, and as I sit cross-legged on the floor to eat it, I know coming here was the right thing to do. If I can't be watching out for Mariana, having eyes on her brother will have to suffice. Both of us can support each other.

In the morning Drew's getting ready as usual, but I stop him. "Need a word."

"You want me to skip school?"

It's not that I do, but that I think he needs to. We've got things to talk about. I'm relying on the fact he's got an old head on young shoulders. "Yeah." I wave him through the doorway. I shiver, the weather's cooler here than in Tucson, but not as cold as some parts of the Rez. "Let's take a walk."

His eyes crease, but he raises and dips his chin. "You want to talk about Mariana."

It's obvious, so I don't reply. "No beating around the bush. I don't think there's a chance of anything else. Got to deal with the fact she's going to be deported."

Suddenly his hand's on my arm, his eyes flaring. "Don't say that, Tse. Please don't say that. There's got to be a chance."

"Worst-case scenario." I give him that. I lean my back against a tree. "But we've got to be prepared for it."

"What does that mean?" He's paled.

"She stays out of the US for at least five years before she can apply to come back."

"I'll go with her," he offers without hesitation. "She can't go back on her own."

Raising my head, my eyes focus on his. "You'll stay here. Complete your education."

"She can't go alone."

"She won't be." It's now I take a deep breath and jump into the unknown, the decision I know is the only one I can make. Would have preferred more time to date her, get to know her, but I know I don't want her with anyone else. That's enough to base a relationship on, isn't it? Under the circumstances. "I'll go with her. Marry her."

His eyes widen. "You'd do that?" Suddenly he's almost bouncing with excitement. "If she's married to a US citizen, she can get a green card, can't she?"

I hate to dampen his spirits. "It's not as easy as that. Married or not, if she's deported, the five-year limit will apply." Could be ten or twenty years. I force my mind away from what I'd be giving up. We'll have to prove it's not a marriage of convenience. *Remembering the feeling of her behind me on my bike, consummating the marriage would not be a problem. I'm offering up my life here. To a woman I don't know.* I don't even know what she'd think of my proposal. Would she want to shackle herself to me?

"Thing is, Drew. If she leaves under a deportation order, it will be harder for her to return. Much as I hate to say it, if she leaves voluntarily and pays her own way, that would go in her favour."

He stills. "Voluntary deportation? That's what you're suggesting? That she agrees to leave."

"I'd be with her," I remind him. The vision of riding away from my club is painful, but I couldn't stand the thought of her being alone. I'd survive. We both would. Five years isn't so bad. It could be an adventure. *Or not.*

He kicks a stone on the ground, and then another. Finally, he looks up. "That's saying she's got to give up. Isn't it better for her to fight while she's still here? There's such a risk. Even with you. If she returns to Colombia…"

"What do you want me to say, Drew?" I suddenly round on him. "That everything's going to turn out right? What have we got left to fight with?"

Now this young kid's up in my face. "With everything we've fucking got," he shouts. "She's innocent, she committed no crime. We should prove that. And find reasons why she can't return and fight for asylum. There's things we can do, Tse." He turns away, then swings back. "Take me back to Tucson. If you won't do it, I fucking will. We're talking about my sister's life here, her happiness. I'm not going to give up on that. I *need* her. She's been my mom for the past six years. I'm not going to let you take her away from me. There must be something we can do."

He's challenging me. My eyes flare. I open my mouth but nothing comes out. Instead I start questioning myself. *What have I been doing? I've given a lawyer all my savings, but what have I actually done? Looked for information from behind my computer screen, hoping to find the answers there. Perhaps I should have been doing more. Questioning Todd Jenkins for a start, getting him to tell the truth, not giving up when I hadn't been able to find him at home. Going back time after time until*

I'd seen him face to face. That's what my brothers would have done. Not taking no for an answer. And doing more to find out what Mariana would be heading back into. I might be paying the lawyer, but I've given her nothing to fight with.

It's taken a fifteen-year-old boy to show me by doing what I thought was right, handling my problems alone, I may be wrong. Drummer's voice echoes in my head. *Every man who sits around that table would be there at your back.* Perhaps it is time to involve them.

Drew's staring at me as though he can see wheels turning in my head. "I've researched Colombia. It would be a nightmare for my sister. Two years' military service is mandatory once someone leaves high school, I don't know if she'd have to do that. She'll need to pay taxes on anything earned in or out of the country. Which means she could be liable for back tax on every-thing she's earned in the US. She wouldn't be able to pay it. She doesn't speak the language or know anything about the country. And on top of all that, she'd have to stay out of the way of our father."

"I hear you. And I suppose she hasn't got a passport."

"Or identity card." He kicks another stone. "Just her birth certificate back at the trailer."

I don't waste another moment coming to a decision.

"*We* are going back to Tucson," I announce, my tone set. "Go pack your things, Drew, or the essential stuff which will go in the saddle bags. Anything else we can collect later."

Hopeful eyes are turned to me. "We're going to fight?"

I look around the Rez, my Navajo blood stirring within me. "Yes, Drew." My voice is full of determination. "We're going to fight."

A seven-hour bike ride as a pillion passenger who's not used to riding has to be tough, but though Drew rubs his ass at the extra stops I put in, not once does he complain. With the breaks for him to stretch and fill his teenage stomach a few times, we don't arrive on the compound until after midnight. I take him straight up to my room where he again demonstrates his young years by falling fast asleep as soon as his head hits the pillow. While I lie awake, wondering how I'm going to explain him, and everything else, to Drummer and my brothers in the morning.

"I can't believe I'm on a biker compound," Drew says through a yawn as he walks out of my bathroom. "Ma would have a fit if she knew."

I bet he's right on that. "She'll know soon enough." I reach over the bed and grabbing my jeans, slide into them.

He walks to the door and looks out at the balcony and the view beyond. "Not quite what I expected."

"It was an old vacation resort that burned up," I explain before disappearing into the bathroom myself, "club bought it cheap and rebuilt it."

"Wow."

"Come on." Drew's gone outside and is leaning on the balcony when I come out, having showered and shaved in minutes. I'm as prepared as I can be for the day ahead.

Drew's gazing around, his eyes wide, taking in his new surroundings, as we walk down to the clubhouse. Last night when he arrived it had been dark, now he can see it in all its glory. He pauses for a moment to admire all the Harleys parked up before following me into the clubroom, his nose twitching as he smells bacon. Rolling my eyes, I lead him straight to the source.

He stops dead when he comes face to face with Peg, Blade, Wraith, Dollar and Bullet, and takes a sideways step to move behind me when, almost as one, they put down their forks.

Blade lifts his knife, points it at Drew, and growls, "Who the fuck is this, Mouse?"

I knew it was coming. "Friend of mine, I'll explain later. Need to have a chat with Drummer first. Kid wants some food."

"How old are you, kid?"

A timid voice from behind me responds. "Er, fifteen."

His tender age seems to relax them, but as I wave Drew forward to take a seat, he appears tentative as he sits down.

Sam's eyes travel over him, then she smiles, puts together a plate and brings it over. "What's your name?"

"Drew."

"Well, Drew. If you're a friend of Mouse, you're welcome. Hey, guys. Introduce yourselves. Make the kid feel at home." Her tone is pleasant, the glare she gives my brothers is almost as scary as her old man's.

Knowing my brothers are understandably suspicious of strangers, and the trouble they may bring along with them, seeing Wraith shaking his head at Sam, I do the introductions for them. "Wraith here is our VP, Blade our enforcer, the bearded one's Peg, our sergeant-at-arms, and that's Dollar who looks after our money."

"Pleased to meet you." Drew's voice is respectful, but cautious. He gets a couple of chin lifts in return, but not from everyone.

Blade's studying him carefully. "You in trouble?" he asks, bluntly.

"No, he's not." I speak for him. "But he's my responsibility, so don't any of you assholes go upsetting him."

Eyes widen at that. Wraith gives me a considering glance. "He the reason you've been absent so much lately?"

"Part of it." I hope my concise answer will stop the questions. Turning to Drew, I point to his plate. "Get that inside you, then we'll go meet the prez."

He eats, but more cautiously than I've seen him before, each mouthful accompanied by nervous glances toward the men sitting around the table. I take my own plate from Sam with thanks, and start on the eggs and bacon. Joker and Lady appear, arms around each other. Drew looks from them to the others, his jaw dropping open. Inwardly I smile, yeah, we're a slightly different type of MC, an all-inclusive club. I note Joker and Lady seem so wrapped up in each other, they're paying no attention to the newcomer in their midst.

"How's Beef?" I ask.

Wraith stares, then sighs. "Oh, fuck. Forgot you missed that. Fucker almost died the day you left. Took a sudden downturn. That he survived is a fuckin' miracle. He's on the mend now."

I stopped eating while Wraith was explaining, guilt washing over me that I'd left my brother behind without a thought. *He could have died.*

Bullet's glaring at me. "I hope now you're back, and you seem to have brought your issues with you, that you've pulled your head out of your ass."

"I have. Gonna need your help, Brothers." I look around at each of them. "Want to run it by Prez first though." That I have 'pulled my head out of my ass', as Bullet so eloquently put it, is all down to the boy by my side, the youth with the now clean plate in front of him. "Prez around?"

At their nods, and Wraith's head jerk in the direction of Prez's office, I pick up Drew's plate and mine, and put them in the dishwasher. "Come on, Drew." *Time to face the music.*

Chapter 17

Mouse

With Drew sitting beside me, I tell Drummer the full story. From the first time I met Mariana to now. It's hard to read the expression on his face, difficult to know what he's thinking. His lack of reaction makes it easier to explain. Whatever he may say to me later, in front of Drew, at least, he's giving away nothing. When I've completed the story, he takes out his phone and sends a quick text.

Seconds later, Truck appears. "Prospect. Can you take young Drew here under your wing for a while?"

As any prospect should, Truck agrees without asking any questions. "Sure thing, Prez."

When Drew looks at me, I give him a look of encouragement. "I'll catch up with you soon," I reassure him.

When the door's closed behind them, Drummer sits back and folds his arms over his chest. "I take it this Mariana means something to you?"

I don't immediately answer, looking down at my hands. After a few seconds have passed, I look up. "It's stupid, crazy, Prez. But yeah, I care for her. A lot."

"Enough that you'd claim her? Marry her?"

That's what I told him. "Yeah."

"Are you sayin' that just to get her legal? 'Cause you're going to face one fuck of a lot of suspicion. You'll have to make it appear genuine." His face grows grim. "I don't give a damn about citizen laws, but that's not going to be easy."

"If you think it would be a fake marriage, then that's what everyone else would. Prez, I haven't even asked her yet. She might say no. I've told her she's my fiancée. Not even had a chance to question what she thinks about that."

"You talked yourself into this marriage thing as a way to try to save her? Get her a fuckin' green card?"

I'm quiet for a moment. There could be a bit of that in there. I shrug. But how can I admit there's a lot more to it than that? That already, she means something to me.

"Let's pick this apart. Her mother was killed by her father when she was sent back to Colombia. I want to know all we can about this man. What have you found out, Mouse?"

Pinching the bridge of my nose, I tell him, "Not a lot. He's supposed to be a general in their army, but I'm having no luck finding his service record. From what Mariana's said, he's a violent man. And vindictive, with what happened to her mother. I found letters, Prez. Letters from her mother that backed up her story. I've got a feeling about her father. There's a reason I can't find him."

"Have you asked Devil?" My eyes sharpen. I hadn't thought of that. "It's a long shot, but he might have heard something."

Devil owns a security firm in London, works internationally, and we came across him when he was a consultant to the feds. He's got fingers in a lot of pies and has been a good friend to the club in return for our services.

"I'll get on to him," Drummer offers. "Just give me all the info you've found about this General De Souza. If there's something we can dig up on him, might strengthen her reason to seek asylum."

"What about Todd Jenkins? Reckon we can get him to come clean?"

"Think you'll have no end of volunteers to try." Drummer sits forward. "Problem is, we can threaten, but can't leave a mark on him. Police wouldn't believe an admission of guilt if it looked like it was beaten out of him."

I frown. "Could we bribe him?"

"How much money would it take for a man to voluntarily put himself inside?"

It's a good question. More than I've got. My account's being drained by Mariana's lawyer. I shake my head.

"Have you thought about getting her fake papers?"

"I have. Should have done that from the fuckin' start. Thing is, I don't think she'd have taken them. She was doing every-thing right. Respected that, you know? That's why I stayed clear. Knew it would do her no good to be associated with us." I shake my head. "She's training to be a nurse, Drummer. Too many people know about her status. She'd have to move elsewhere and start all over again if she had a new name."

His fingers drum on the table. A sure sign he's thinking. "If she hadn't, through no fault of her own, got into a situation that put her DACA status in jeopardy by being charged with a felony, she'd still be here and workin' toward her goals. If she'd kept her nose clean for another six years, her brother would have been able to sponsor her. But now the system's got hold of her, it's not going to be easy to get her out of its clutches. What does her lawyer say?"

"Summed it up in about the same way."

"Mouse, you spend your time with computers. Perhaps you don't mix with humans enough. You say none of the CCTV cameras were pointed at the junction? No fuckin' need to stop there, Mouse. Your computers can't help you all the time. Some of those stores were open when the collision happened. Have you thought about putting a leaflet up to see whether anyone saw anything?"

Of course I hadn't. I just went to my go to. Technology. "You think that might work?"

"No fuckin' idea, Brother. But what would it hurt to try?"

Nothing at all. Just a trip back to the stores. "As soon as Mariana's out of solitary I need to go and see her again."

"Expected that. I don't like hearin' what happened there. Something's not right. Heard stuff about those detention centres, shit I don't like." Drummer's eyes darken. "You're her lifeline while she's in there, Mouse. Go as often as you can. And Drew? You brought him back here for a reason."

"I like the kid, Drummer. He's been forced to grow up fast. I feel responsible for him. Didn't like leaving him on the Rez. It was a fun time, but he stays any longer? He's going to get shit thrown at him. Doesn't deserve that along with losing his sister. It would be better for him to go back to his old school."

"Took a likin' to him myself. Carried himself well while he was in here. Polite, respectful. Probably used to keeping his head down. He can stay. Prospect can give him a ride to school if there's times you can't take him. How old is he again?"

"He'll be sixteen in a couple of months."

Drummer nods, then gives a half-smile. "In Arizona he can get his driver's permit already, only needs to be fifteen and a half. Eligible now. He'll have to have someone over twenty-one driving with him for six months, but helping him learn to handle a car might be a better use of the prospect's time than just acting as a taxi service."

I sit back. I hadn't thought of that. Buy him a car… I grin, fuck, kid's not even mine and he's already becoming expensive. "Great idea, Prez. And getting a car will help take his mind off his troubles."

"A bit of independence always helps," Prez agrees. "Only thing is, he'll have to have a legal guardian go with him to get his permit." My face falls. Prez notices. "Fuckin' world we live in, parents being torn away from kids. Bet there's an expedited way for someone awaiting deportation to sign their child over.

Must happen often, especially where there's a risk to the parent returning to their home country. Documented kids probably better off livin' here."

"You could well be right, Prez. I'll get hold of the lawyer. See if Mariana can sign something."

His face grows grim and his lips press together. "Just think about it carefully, Mouse. Make sure this is a step you want to be taking. If Mariana stays in detention, or fuck, is deported, you'll have responsibility for him until he's eighteen. Can't decide it's not what you want later."

It might fuck up my plans to go with her if that happens, but I'll take that step when it comes. Apart from that, "I'm already responsible for him, Prez." There's no way I'm walking away from the boy.

One of his close scrutinising looks, then he raises his chin. "We'll bring this to the table later. Now scat. You've got a car to buy."

I laugh out loud as I leave Prez's office. I find Drew at the pool table playing with Truck. I wait until their game's finished. The prospect's won, but the result doesn't surprise me.

Drew looks at me anxiously. I smile, and slap his back. "You're fine. You're staying."

"Mouse?"

"Yeah, Sam?"

"I take it Drew's going to be here a spell?" At my nod, she continues, "Viper's just finished two new blocs. If you don't mind moving, you could take one of them. One suite for you, one for the kid."

I hadn't considered living arrangements. Brushing my hands through my hair, I don't take long to consider it. "I don't mind moving, Sam. That's a great idea." I like the kid, but not so much I want to keep sharing a bed with him.

Truck's putting away the pool sticks. "Guess that's my afternoon sorted," he grumbles, but there's a twinkle in his eye as in that roundabout way he offers his help.

In the end, Truck and Drew move my shit as I go to compose and print the leaflets Prez suggested, then take them into town and visit the stores. All are happy to display them after a few dollars change hands.

That night, Prez calls the brothers into church.

"As you might have noticed, Mouse is back with us." There are a few chuckles and comments at that. "He's at last come to his senses and is ready to ask for help."

"Got cowboys attacking the reservation?" Joker puts in. They're all well aware I go back to the Rez.

"Don't see how you could help if we had," I reply drily, "if anyone's a bunch of cowboys, you lot are."

Blade points his knife toward me. "Careful, Brother. It's you that wants help."

But most of the others are laughing. Drummer shouts for quiet, then points at me. "Fill 'em in, Mouse."

Where do I start? "I met a woman…"

"Knew it!" Viper and Rock bump fists across the table, then hold out their hands, and money's passed down the table to them.

"Called that!" Blade turns to Dollar, who shrugs and gets out his wallet.

"Always a fuckin' bitch at the bottom of it," Shooter observes.

"Nothing wrong with that." Peg's comment is echoed by Wraith, Heart, Bullet, Viper, and Rock. Even the prez is nodding while the single men look on incredulously.

"So who do we need to kill?" Road asks sounding resigned.

Drummer bangs the gavel, then growls, "Can we get fuckin' started? Want to get a bit further than hearin' Mouse has got himself a woman."

"Is she a Mac or a PC?" Shooter enquires. Drum gets him to shut his mouth fast with one look.

It was quite amusing, even my lips quirked. "Neither, she's flesh and blood."

"Need some tips on what to do?" Bullet raises his hands, making a circle with his forefinger and thumb with one, and using a finger of the other, makes a show of pushing it in and out of the ring he's formed. "Part A goes into part B just like this."

I sigh. "If I do, I'll come and find you, Brother." In truth, their assholery is touching. It's their way of showing they care.

At last they quiet down, and I'm allowed to tell my story which is basically a repeat of what I told Drummer earlier.

Heart raises his eyes. "Get me the names of the cops who arrested her. I'll run them past Marc, see what she knows. Could be ones who are overeager to get immigrants off the streets."

That's something I hadn't thought of. I raise my chin in thanks.

Blade's knife stops spinning when it's pointing toward me. "I'll come with you to visit the motherfucker who rammed her."

Peg's fast to raise his hand. "Me too." He starts flexing his muscles.

"Need to use persuasion, not force," Drummer reminds them as he did me. He runs his hands down his beard, then suggests, "Maybe he was mistaken? Maybe he was going too fast, she stopped when he thought she was going to cross. Yeah, yeah, Mouse, I know that wasn't the way of it, but it would enable him to save face."

"Want me to see what funds we can free up?"

Prez stares at Dollar for a moment. "Don't want to pay the asshole if we don't have to, but if it comes to that, could be useful." Then he looks at me. "Movin' this along, I've put a call in to get Devil to contact me. I'll let you know when he does."

Wraith's staring at me, his head slightly tilted. "You really ready to marry a woman you've only seen a couple of times, and one of those behind bars?"

I purse my lips, breathe in through my nose, then let the air out on a sigh. "I would have gone back the first time, 'cept for her need to be squeaky clean. You know what the cops think of us." I don't need to explain. "So I kept away, but kept thinkin' about her. Couldn't get her off my mind. Truth, Brothers? That's why I spent time on the Rez, tryin' to get my head straight. She'd ridden on the back of my bike, kinda felt right havin' her there."

"She feel the same about you?" Viper asks.

"Haven't had a chance to ask her," I admit.

"You claimin' her, Brother?" Peg asks.

I look around the table. Wraith had eyes only for Sophie from the moment he met her. Drummer, the man known for tapping everything in sight, only had to meet Sam once to be a goner. Peg himself met Darcy by the side of the road and was immediately smitten. Heart, well, it might have taken him a little longer, but then the circumstances were different for him. Slick, too, he claimed his old lady fast, though it took longer for them to make it together. Rock wouldn't have gone out on a limb for Becca if there hadn't been anything there. There are no looks of derision coming my way from the men with old ladies, it's only those who haven't met their one yet who don't understand.

Clearing my throat, I say the words, "I'm claimin' her."

Prez gives a sharp nod. That seems to have come as no surprise. "Well, let's help our brother get his woman home. By whatever means we can."

"Breaking into a prison, Prez. We've not done that before."

"Let's hope it doesn't come to that, Blade."

CHAPTER 18

Mouse

Mariana should be out of solitary by now, that's what Carissa told me when I called. She still doesn't know the reason she was removed from the general population, but Drummer's comment about it worries me, and I'm determined to find out. Today we're going to visit her.

Drew's waiting by the side of my bike, bouncing on his feet in anticipation of seeing his sister again.

"Sorry, Wraith wanted a word." I go to the saddle bag and take out a helmet and pass it to him.

His hands don't move to take it. When I lift my eyebrow he shrugs. "Don't need to wear one in Arizona."

"Wrong, kid. You're not eighteen. Anyway, I'm responsible for you." I hope I'm not going to regret that when I see his sullen look. I've started the process to make it legal with Carissa, she's going to prepare a document for me and Mariana to sign.

Straddling the bike, I walk it forward to give him room to get on. While I was doing so, he's at last put on the helmet and has it buckled up. At my nod, he climbs up behind me. The winter day's chilly, but at least it's not raining. I grin to myself. If Mariana signs that document, soon Drew will be driving us there himself. I've already got Blade looking for a car for him. A good runner, but cheap and easy to learn on. Not that the kid knows that yet. Didn't want to get his hopes up until everything's in place.

We drive up to the facility. Drew's not the only one excited to see Mariana. Now I've claimed her in front of my brothers, I've got to start getting her onside with the idea. Somehow my brain has accepted *she's mine*. And I'll be fucked if that doesn't sit easy.

We again go through security which makes me feel more like I'm entering as an inmate than a visitor, and I feel ill at ease as if somehow they're going to lock me up. I eye the door behind me as though checking my escape route as we wait in line.

The same guard that was here last time is on visitor duty once again. I suppose I stand out, a Native American with a Hispanic boy, but he recognises me, and walks up with that sneer which I assume is habitual. Idly I notice he's got marks healing on his face as though somebody scratched him. I can't summon up any sympathy.

"You come to visit Mariana De Souza?"

His tone annoys me, but I tamp down my irritation, suspecting full well things can be taken out on the inmates. I content myself with a simple, "We are."

He snorts and shakes his head. "Well, you've had a wasted journey. She's not here."

What? My heart leaps. Drew turns to me with hope in his eyes.

He might be a boy almost grown into a man, but I don't object when he takes my hand and grasps it firmly. I can feel him shaking as he asks, "She's been released?"

"Nah," the guard informs us with something akin to glee in his voice. "Transferred to another facility."

What? I step forward, trying not to appear menacing, but failing. Carissa did suggest that was going to happen, but why wasn't she, and we, told? "Where is she?" comes out as a snarl.

"How would I know? We just stop them from getting out. ICE deals with everything else."

Now it's Drew holding onto me firmly, holding me back. The guard's moving closer as if he's longing for me to take a swing at him. I notice another guard coming up to cover his back.

It's hard, but I resist my impulse to attack, knowing I'd only end up behind bars. "Let's get out of here," I snarl, turning and dragging Drew with me.

Collecting my phone, I don't bother putting it away. As soon as we're clear of the building, I call Carissa.

"What do you mean you didn't fuckin' know? Surely her lawyer should have been informed?"

"No, I don't have a fuckin' clue when. Just that she isn't here now. Or that's what they're saying. Can you find out what the fuck's going on?"

I end the call quickly, hoping she's more successful at getting answers than me.

"Could she already have been deported?" Drew's in pieces. I'm trying to keep it together for him, when all I want to do is lash out at something. *I've got to man up. Be the adult here.*

Deported? *I fucking hope not.* The cloudy sky above reflects what I'm feeling, as if the sun's gone from my life. *I never had her. I already miss her.* I've got to be fucking strong for Drew.

"I don't think so." I try to sound convincing as in my head I go back over what Carissa told me. "She should have her day in immigration court before being sent out of the country. Carissa hasn't received word to bring any of her personal possessions in either. I also think they need time to get her a Colombian passport. She hasn't got one."

Drew confirms what I already know. "No. Just her birth certificate. That might be all she needs."

"And that's back at the trailer and we haven't been asked for it." I'm grasping at straws. "Don't think it happens this fast." But

I won't be satisfied until Carissa gets back to me with some answers. *Where the fuck are you, Mariana?*

All the way back to the compound I'm thinking of how I can find out where they've taken her. The dark web is like a home to me, government systems not so much. *I need help with this one.*

Leaving Drew with Sophie, who, after a quick explanation, and by a rise and dip of her head, assures me she's got him covered, I retreat to my office, calculate the time, and place a call to an international number.

"Cara. It's Mouse." Cara can get into systems I can't. Face it, she can get into anything.

"What do you need, Mouse?" It's early morning there, but she sounds wide awake.

Quickly I explain my problem, concluding with, "I need to know where Mariana's been moved to."

Cara's quiet for a moment. "Mouse, you know I'd help you. But Nijad would have my hide if he knew I was hacking into US government systems." She breaks off and gives one of her tinkling laughs, "Mind you, he'd tie me to a spanking bench and flog me. Might be worth it." She's quiet again, presumably considering whether the crime is worth the punishment. Then resumes, "What will you do with the information?"

"Go and see her," I respond without thought.

"If you haven't been told officially, how will you explain how you came by the knowledge? Mouse, we've worked together for a long time. I can hear you're personally invested in this. God knows I've got sympathy for Mariana, I know what it's like to be locked up and kept away from the man you want. But everything you and I do is under the radar. On this occasion, I'm not going to help, because all you're going to do is give us away."

I fill my cheeks with air, then let it out. She's right. I'd go off half-cocked demanding to see her. Getting myself arrested for hacking won't help Mariana at all.

"Mouse, can I give you some advice?"

"Of course."

"From what you've told me, I'd say she's going to be deported. That's what you've got to plan for. Fight to try to prevent it, sure. But prepare for the worst. Look into what you can do, what happens when she is."

"She'd be headin' for some bad shit in Colombia."

"Then focus on that. Don't think you can stop the train that's in motion now."

A few pleasantries, a half-hearted enquiry about her family, then I end the call. Cara's right. If Mariana is released, that's all I want. But if she's deported, I don't want to be blindsided. Devil's information on her father is becoming critical.

Rolling a joint, I pull my laptop toward me, and open the programs which will take me into the murky depths of the internet. What I find out at first is very much what I expected from hearing Mariana's story, when I at last hit a database with some information on it.

There's not a lot I can find on a current service record for a General De Souza. A Raphael De Souza joined the National Army for his mandatory military service, the timing fits. There was a short break in his service record, it seems he tried to make it work in the civilian world, and married young during this gap. Shortly after Mariana would have been born, it seems he re-enlisted.

He clearly showed aptitude from the start, moving up the ranks fairly quickly. Some of his service record is redacted, making me suspicious. That he was chosen to train with the US military is a matter of record. He received recognition for his prowess in the counter-insurgency campaign. After that he did a short spell in what's described as comprehensive reparation for victims of conflict. *So after making their lives hell, he's now one of the good guys?* I shake my head. *Leopards don't change their spots*. Neither do soldiers who've got a taste for violence, rape and abuse. Then the records stop. There's nothing more, the trail goes cold. No discharge mentioned, no further promotion. No death recorded. Zilch.

Picking up my joint, I relight it, the tip flaring as it meets the flame. I've got to prove she's at risk if she returns. Something, anything. The man I'm seeking is metaphorically in the wind.

Her mother. But that quickly turns up another dead end. Mariana's convinced her father killed her, but officially it was put down as an untargeted gang rape and murder. It doesn't seem the police even investigated.

When my phone starts vibrating, I'm so engrossed in the information on the screen, it takes me a second to respond.

"Carissa."

"Mr Williamson. I've got news."

I fill the pause. "Good? Bad?"

She draws in a breath. "She's been relocated to a detention centre in Los Angeles."

"Okay." I draw out the word.

"It's not good news, Mr Williamson. It doesn't have a particularly good reputation. The better news is that as an immigration attorney, and this is federal law, I'm licensed to practice in any state. So I can continue with the case. But obviously, my costs will increase. Travelling to Los Angeles means I'll be spending more hours on this one."

I suck in air, thinking of my depleting bank balance again. But I don't hesitate. "Whatever it takes."

"I'm glad you feel that way, Mr Williamson. She needs legal representation. Else she'll be just like the rest, left with a court-appointed lawyer, or none at all."

I read between the lines. Whatever goes on in that facility, if they know Mariana's got a proper lawyer, then maybe that will afford her some protection.

"Whatever it takes," I repeat, before ending the call.

I'm sitting with my head in my hands when my door opens. It's Prez. Dragging my palms down my face, I fill him in on what I've just learned.

He sits, folding his arms across his chest. "You did right claimin' her. She's club property now. That means she belongs to the club. And we take care of our own. You need funds? Speak to Dollar."

I take a deep breath. While claiming her had been premature and probably a heat of the moment impulsive decision, I hadn't realised the ramifications. "That's not why…"

"I know it isn't. You might work in the background, Mouse, but you do one fuck of a lot for this club. Do your share like all the brothers. Without the shit you dig up, we'd be walking into situations blind." Unfolding his arms, he sits forward. "You go above and beyond using that clever head on your shoulders. If you hadn't dug up those plans for Becca's ex's church, we wouldn't have been able to get the Herreras off our backs. Hell, we might be in a war with them now."

My shoulders rise and fall as I shrug off his comment. "Just like digging deep, that's all." It's a game to me, nothing like work.

"No one else has that logical mind, Mouse. We rely on you. Time for you to rely on us." He settles back again. "Now, what's your next step?"

That's easy. "Now I know where Mariana is, I need to see her."

"The boy will want to go too." I'm aware of that. But there are things I need to say to her in private. I open my mouth to speak, but he's read my mind and gets in first. "Leave it with me. I've got an idea."

When I emerge from my cave, as normal, I blink a few times to get used to the bright light. When I can focus again, I see

Blade talking to a very animated Drew. On seeing me, the enforcer raises his chin. I take it as an invitation to join them.

Drew's about jumping on the spot. "You really going to buy me a car, Mouse? Help me get my permit?"

I mock glare at Blade who shrugs. "You told me to look out for one and that's what I've done. How the fuck was I to know you hadn't told the kid yet?"

Sighing, I wave off his apology. "Was going to speak to you, Drew, but with everything else…"

"'S'all right, Tse. I'm just lost for words you're going to do something like that."

"So you're up for it? Tomorrow? He's not going to hang onto it after that. There's a couple more people interested."

"Whoa, Blade. Hold up. Drew. Mariana's been moved to Los Angeles. I'm going to try to see her tomorrow." I look from one to the other, my hands gesturing I don't know what to do.

The kid looks undecided, then says with a resigned sigh, "I'll come to see Mariana."

Blade lays it on thick, and it's then the penny drops. *Prez has set this up.* "Fuckin' shame. Honda Civic. Good little runner, good bodywork too. And it's not a bad price. Next person to see it will probably jump at it." He looks down at his feet, then back up as he adds shrewdly, "Got an ace sound system." Yeah, that will tempt Drew. "Ah, well. Something else will come along." But the way he says it, it doesn't sound like he believes it. Neither is the pat on Drew's shoulder very convincing.

Drew's face has fallen.

It's my turn to step in. "Hey, Mariana would understand. To be honest, Drew, in order to get your permit, I'll need to be your legal guardian. I'm hoping the lawyer has got the paperwork ready for Mariana to sign, need a discussion with her about making it official. Long as you don't mind me being your guardian, that is." I belatedly realise he might want a say in it.

"Shit, no!" he exclaims, back to grinning again, and I wonder if I need to caution him about his language. Don't think his sister would be too impressed if he starts copying how we talk here. *Perhaps being a guardian isn't going to be easy.* "Mouse, sorry, Tse. I'd be proud if you'd take official responsibility for me."

I notice him stumble over my name, so I place my hand on his shoulder. "Call me whatever feels easiest, Drew. I answer to both. If you want to go and see the car Blade has found, I'll explain it all to your sister." It's the rest of what I've got to tell her which will probably be harder.

Twin expressions of disappointment and excitement seem to war for first place. Then he turns to Blade, enthusiasm for putting his first step on the road to independence seeming to win out. "Thanks. I can't wait to see the car you've picked out." Then he spies the girl who he's become friendly with, it's not surprising, she's the closest to his age being just a year older, and calls out, "Hey, Jayden. Guess what?"

As he goes over to talk to her, Blade and I raise our hands and bump fists.

CHAPTER 19

Mariana

My relief at finally being released from solitary confinement—which coincided with the evidence of the blow to my face fading to nothing—is short lived. Initially I was just grateful I wouldn't have to lie awake waiting for a key to turn in the lock and the guard returning to molest me. He never did, but my fear didn't leave me all the same. But instead of taking me back to join the general population and my original cell, they handcuff me, and I'm taken outside to a large truck. There's already a number of other people inside, most looking as puzzled as me.

I swing around to the female guard who accompanies me. Terror making it hard to speak. "Am I being deported?" I ask. *Is this it? Being taken away without the chance to say goodbye to Drew, or Tse? Will I find myself sleeping in Colombia tonight?*

My guard clearly has no concerns, or opinion on my future. "ICE wants you in the transport. That's all I know."

"Don't you care?" I ask, without expecting an answer. "I've committed no crime. I've lived all my life in the US." But my voice trails off at the set expression on her face. One which suggests she's seen and heard it all before.

Her hand on my back encourages me to move. I glance around, taking what I fear is my last sight of Arizona. *Perhaps I'll see the last view of the States as I fly over in a plane.* My gut rolls, and I swallow down bile. *This can't be happening.* My quick look has shown me armed guards standing around, there's no way of escape. No option but to climb the few steps up into the transport, feeling unstoppable tears rolling down my face.

Cuffs snap around my ankles, they're fastened to a bolt on the floor. I'm being treated as if I'd committed murder, and not as if, by no fault of my own, I happened to reside in a country where I hadn't been born.

A couple of others enter after me, looking equally bemused, then the doors are closed with loud bangs. Voices shout outside, then the truck lurches forward, throwing me against the person at my side.

"Where are we going?" I ask, but if my companions understand me, no one answers. It seems they're as much in the dark as I am. So I continue asking questions in my head. *Does my lawyer know? Does Tse? Drew?*

There are windows, but placed up high, just enough to let light in, but there's no way to see out.

The journey seems to take forever. I equally want it to end and don't. I'm terrified our destination will be an airport. *Where else would they be taking me?*

No one speaks. It's clear we're all caught up in our own misery. Time drags. The truck progresses on. Eventually it starts making turns, then slows, and then arrives at what I suspect is the journey's end. Confirmed when the doors open and the guards undo the chains.

Almost the last in, I'm one of the first out. Hardly daring to look, I stare at the ground, so it's my senses which first alert me. There's no sound of planes taking off or landing, no smell of gasoline in the air. Nothing to suggest it's an airport. My sense of relief is immense, and now using my eyes, I realise where I've been brought. Apart from the layout, the institutional smell, the way we're treated as we're hustled into the building, it's evident this is a different Service Processing Centre.

I can't understand why I've been moved, scared nobody knows where I am. A chilling thought strikes me as I wonder whether this is only a short reprieve. Maybe I've simply come somewhere where the deportation process can be speeded up.

Does my lawyer know where they've brought me?

As I'm taken through the booking procedure, unnecessarily and intimately searched, then taken to yet another cell—this one I'll be sharing with three other women—I find breathing becomes difficult. When I walk through the door my steps are uneven, when I throw myself down on the only free bunk, I'm shaking.

What if no one knows anything? What if I'm abandoned? Alone? What if I'm sent back to Colombia and no one knows where I am? *Except for my father who's certain to find me.*

Trying to force myself to calm down, I start to concentrate on taking deep breaths in and out. It's up to me to do something. *Ring my lawyer. Talk to Tse.*

But that's not easy. Yes, I'm allowed to call my lawyer, but I haven't got her number. I had it in Florence, but the things I had there weren't brought with me. I haven't a clue what Tse's is either. And while Tse put money into a facility account, has that been transferred with me?

So many thoughts flying through my head. I pick one to ask. "Will anyone be able to know where I am?" My eyes plead with my jailers. *Am I lost somewhere in the system?*

When I start shaking again, at last a guard takes pity on me and deigns to answer my question. "If you've got a lawyer, then yes, they'll be able to find out where you are."

If. I know why she qualified it. So many people around me haven't. "Where am I?"

Los Angeles comes the answer. *So far away.* I haven't even been out of Arizona before. A wild laugh escapes my lips. *I'd dreamed of being able to bring Drew to Disneyland. Never expected to come to LA as a prisoner.*

I try to console myself with the knowledge Carissa will get the information if she asks, that I haven't disappeared never to see a friendly face again, but it's hard. I don't eat, can't sleep. I spend all my time worrying.

The first day passes slowly, with no contact. I might be in a different city, a different state, but life's much the same here as it was in Florence. It's the second morning something changes, when I hear I've got a visitor.

Carissa. It must be Carissa. Now perhaps I can get some answers. It's the not knowing that's destroying me.

But when I'm taken into the visiting room, across the table I'm pointed to, I don't see Carissa. I see Tse. My first feeling is relief. *He knows where I am.* The second is panic, and that drives the first words to come out of my mouth.

No greeting at all, just, "Where's Drew?"

Tse smiles, and glances up at the clock. "Right now he's looking at a car with one of my brothers."

Okay. *What? Looking at a car is more important than me?*

"Hey, I can see your mind working. We've got things to catch up on, things I need to explain. There's not much time. Drew's fine, okay? Let's get that sorted now." He seems to wait for my nod, then carries on. "What about you? How are you doing?"

"I just want to breathe fresh air, Tse. I'm suffocating in here." I hadn't meant for it to come out. I meant to stay strong and would have in front of my brother. But seeing Tse, it all comes out. How I want to be able to walk out of here with him.

"I know, darlin', I know." Tse's voice reflects my pain. His hands flutter on the table as if he wants to be doing something. I zip my mouth to stop further complaints coming out, he doesn't deserve to hear them. I'm not in here because of anything he's done, I'm just envying the fact he's free.

He's watching me closely. I wonder whether he's seeing the weight I've lost, how my hair has lost its shine.

I wait for him to comment, he doesn't. Instead he says something I don't expect. "I've brought Drew to live with me."

"I thought you lived on the biker compound." My eyes open wide.

He holds up his hand. "Going to the Rez was always temporary. And the compound isn't what you're imagining. Lots of the brothers have ol' ladies and kids, it's mostly got a family vibe. When it hasn't, I'll make sure Drew's well out of the way. He's got his own suite, Mariana, bathroom all to himself. Kid's loving it."

My eyes open wider. *I'm sure he is.*

Tse continues, "I, or one of my brothers, am making sure he gets to school. It's better for him there. Though he loved his time on the Rez, it was strange for him. I wanted him close to me. He wanted to come today, Mariana, I assure you, but I found something to distract him. I needed to talk to you about some stuff, and it's better if it's just between us."

I still can't get my head around my brother living on an outlaw biker compound. But at least Tse's looking out for him. Whatever arrangements he makes for Drew, I'm in no position to object.

"First," he takes a piece of paper out of his pocket and unfolds it. A guard comes over, checks what's on it, and nods. Tse takes it back, but pauses before passing it to me.

I take a second to read it, my jaw dropping open as I do. It's a legal document which will enable my lawyer to get Tse appointed as Drew's legal guardian.

"He doesn't need you. He's got me," I tell him fiercely.

With compassion in his eyes, Tse starts to explain. "This doesn't mean anything, Mariana, but it will make things easier for Drew. He can get his driver's permit…"

"He, we, can't afford a car," I hiss. It's out of the question. Especially as mine was wrecked. *Not that I'm ever likely to be driving in Arizona again.*

"I can. I'm buying him one. Just a little run-around that he can use to get to school and back. I, and my brothers, will be his accompanying drivers until he's been driving six months."

"I can't ask you to do that." I'm torn. It should have been my job. Drew would be over the moon to learn to drive. Should I hold him back? Is it fair? Just because I'm incarcerated doesn't mean his life should come to a halt too. *I don't want to sign; it feels like I'm abandoning my brother.* Then I look at Tse's intense face, and realise I can do nothing for my brother from here. Can't keep or get him out of trouble. *Perhaps I'm lucky Tse is offering to take him on.*

"You're not asking." Tse's brow creases. "Look, Mariana, I know it's hard for you, fuck knows how difficult it is for you in here. But the uncertainty's killing Drew too. This gives him something to look forward to. Doesn't mean he cares about you less, but it's not good for the kid to be constantly worrying. That's partly why I've got him back to familiarity, and going back to his old school. And why I've taken him to the compound instead of leaving him on the Rez."

He's making me feel selfish. But *I'm* the one who should be teaching Drew to drive. Not anyone else. I'm not even certain what I feel about his version of normality for my little brother. *A compound?*

Now he smooths out the paper again. "No one can help Drew get a permit unless someone's made his legal guardian. Signing this assigns those rights to me."

I'm really trying hard to process all this. "Have you thought this through? It's not only getting his driver's permit. People will be looking to you as the one responsible for him."

He taps the paper. "I don't know how long you'll be in here, Mariana. I know as a kid younger than Drew, you were abandoned and forgotten by the system, but what if someone starts asking questions about your brother? I don't want to see him put in the system."

I don't want to sign him away like you'd part with an unwanted pet. This seems wrong. "Is this all I need to do?"

"You sign, Carissa will sort out the legal details. It's not something that's unheard of in here."

No, it's probably not. I've met a number of women who've been separated from their children.

What's best for Drew? That's what I've got to think of. I can't see any other option; all I've got is Tse. I feel rushed, pressured, but Tse is right. A teacher or social worker might start interfering. I suppose I'd rather he was with this man sitting opposite me than with anyone else. There are tears in my eyes as I find my answer. "I'll sign."

Tse signals the guard who, when asked, produces a pen. When Tse mentions something to him, he nods. After I sign Drew away, the guard witnesses my signature, then takes his pen and moves back to his position. Tears blur my eyes as I look up. "Take care of him for me, Tse?"

Compassion shines out from his. "I promise I will."

"Do you know why I was moved?" I'm not sure I want to know the answer. Perhaps I should have asked, *how close am I to being deported?*

"Carissa's got some ideas. None bad. Judge might have a lighter caseload here. And the sooner we get you in front of a judge, sooner we can get your case heard."

"How long might that be?" There's people who've been here months. One, that I know of, over a year. From Tse's headshake, I know he can't tell me. Nobody can.

"Mariana. You've got people on your side working to get you released."

"You and Carissa. Yes."

He smiles. "Not just me. All my brothers too. And we've got a security consultant trying to dig up dirt on your father."

Now it's my turn to frown. Why would his club help me? I make that my next question. His answer takes my breath away.

"Because I claimed you."

"*Claimed* me?"

He raises his chin and looks straight into my eyes. "Good as a marriage in my world. But we'll do that as well. Soon as you get out of here, you and I are getting hitched."

"*Tse!*" I hiss loudly, drawing a few looks. "Don't be stupid. The likely way I'm getting out is on a one-way flight to Colombia."

"Then I'll follow you."

Shaking my head, I explain. "It's not easy, and probably not possible for me to get a green card even if I marry you. I might never be able to come back. Even if I have a sham of a wedding and am married to a US citizen."

He rears back, then leans forward, his words spoken so softly I have to strain to hear. "Who says it will be a sham?" Then he sits straight again, one brow raised as if challenging me.

"You don't know me, I don't know you..."

"I know enough to make a commitment to you in front of my brothers." His hands smooth back his hair. "See, Mariana, I figure getting horny at the thought of someone is a very good place to start."

He gets horny thinking of me? My face glows. "I don't think that's all that matters, Tse. There's got to be more than that."

He folds his arms, places them on the table and leans on them. "I came running to help you when Drew called. I've organised a top fuckin' lawyer for you. I'm lookin' after your brother. I'm visiting you in these damn places. Would I do that if I didn't care for you?"

His words pull me up. He's right. Since my mom was deported, no one's ever watched out for me in the way he has.

Seeing he's made me think, he resumes, "I've never done anything like this before. Never felt I wanted to. Never cared enough."

He cares, but whenever I thought about doing the impossible, being able to date and marry a man, I always thought it would be for love.

"Is that a good enough basis for marriage?"

"Mariana," he growls. "That night I rode away from you, have you any fuckin' idea how hard it was for me to not come back? The only reason I stayed away was out of respect for your wishes, that I didn't want to expose you to any risk." He huffs. "Not that it did any good in the end."

He's right. It didn't. Where would we be now if I had let him into my life? My voice is soft, and croaks, as I admit, "And I wanted you to come back." I had. My dreams had been filled with longing for the mysterious man who'd come into my life.

He sits back as though he's won a victory. "So we're just cutting out the stuff in between."

Could he be right? "Do you really think this has any chance of working?"

"If we both put the effort in, yes, it does."

A bell rings. It's the end of our visit. I don't want him to go. *But is that just because he's a friendly face? Or is there really more between us?*

I stand with the rest of the inmates, say a quick and inadequate goodbye. Then take leave of *my fiancé*. The man who says he's claimed me in front of his club.

CHAPTER 20

Mouse

"That the right house?"

Answering Blade, I tell him, "Yeah."

"Lights are on. Looks like someone's home." Peg's eyes are fixed on the one storey in front of us.

Blade grins evilly. "What we waiting for, then?"

I roll my eyes. "His wife to leave for work." She works nights. I've already found that out.

"There's movement," Peg announces.

We all freeze. The front door opens, and out walks a woman. From the casually yelled 'goodbye' over her shoulder, I take it that's the wife we've been waiting for.

We stay in place while the woman backs a car out of the garage, and then for a moment longer when she drives off. As her taillights disappear into the distance, the three of us straighten and move out from the bushes behind which we've been crouched.

Blade takes the lead, I don't argue. Drummer was right, I tend to fight my battles from behind a desk rather than face to face. Not that I can't hold my own if I need to, but the enforcer's more used to this shit. I stand back as he knocks on the door.

Heavy footsteps reach us, then it's opened by a man with a large paunch. His eyes narrow suspiciously.

"Mr Jenkins?"

"Who wants to know?"

Well, in my mind that confirms it. If he wasn't, he'd have said upfront.

"Need to talk with you."

"I'm busy." As he goes to shut the door, Blade's steel toe-capped boot prevents it closing. He pushes inside, forcing Jenkins to step back. Peg and I follow, Peg turning to close the door.

"Who are you? What do you want?" Jenkins' eyes flicker between us, and sweat starts to appear on his brow. "I'd like you to leave before I call the cops."

"Now, now," Blade starts, his voice sounding amused. "Why would you do that when we've just popped around for a friendly chat."

"I've got no money."

The enforcer's head shakes. "Not here for cash or to steal shit. Just want a conversation like I said."

Jenkins' eyes narrow. "Don't know what we have to talk about. But you can say what you need to, then get out."

While our target's been talking, Peg's been circling around to his back. Now his big meaty arms have Jenkins' pinned. "Search him." Peg jerks his chin to me.

Jenkins is kicking, trying to get free, but the sergeant-at-arms has got him in a firm hold. I find a gun tucked into his waistband, and relieve him of it fast. While I've been occupied, Blade's taken out a knife. One of his favourites by the look of it. Jenkins stills when it's laid against his cheek.

"That your wife who just left?" Blade casually asks.

"Yeah." The whites of the man's eyes are clearly visible. "She'll be back in a minute. She'll call the cops."

"You're lying." Blade angles the flat of the blade, and slides it down Jenkins' face to his throat.

"She's gone to work," he squeals as he corrects himself.

"Better." Blade grins. It's that evil one again. "Now my brother here wants to have a discussion with you. You're going to listen, then do what we need done. You hear me? You do it right, then you'll not see us again. Do anything else, and I'll slice you into fuckin' pieces."

Peg asks nonchalantly, "Gonna cut his dick off, like you did to that other asshole?"

"Could be a possibility," Blade replies thoughtfully. "Didn't take long for him to bleed out."

"Screaming the whole time," Peg adds. "Looked fuckin' painful to me."

If Jenkins looked worried earlier, he seems terrified now. I know Blade and Peg aren't kidding, I've watched the enforcer's handiwork before, and the sergeant-at-arms can have useful ideas of his own. Jenkins can't know they're telling the truth, but in his position, I wouldn't want to put it to the test.

"What do you want me to do?" Jenkins' eyes flick between us.

"You crashed into a car a few weeks back. Rammed it. On purpose. Put the blame on the woman driver."

"It was her fault," he protests. "Bitch stopped in front of me deliberately."

I glare at him, but keep to my script. "Need you to go to the police and change your story."

"Change my fucking story? What I said was the truth. Fucking bitch could have killed me. Got a neck brace I'm still wearing for whiplash."

"You're not wearing it now," Peg observes. And fuck me, when I look around, I see it conveniently placed by the front door.

"So you're running an insurance scam." Blade's almost looking impressed. Until that knife's lowered and in a flash has cut the button off his fly.

Jenkins struggles, but Peg's holding him tight. "I can't contradict my story," he shouts. "Fuckin' cops would arrest me instead."

"You can change it. Say it was a blur when you first spoke to them. The light was just changing, you thought she'd be going across, so you accelerated to get through after her, but she stopped on amber. You couldn't brake in time."

"Then they'd have me for intending to run a red light."

"You'll have to attend a traffic school, but that's surely better than having your cock sliced off."

"They could take my licence."

"First offence? Maybe a thirty-day suspension." See? I've looked it all up. I doubt the cops would do much about it. In their view, his wrongdoing allowed them to catch an illegal immigrant. I don't give a damn, as long as those charges are dropped. "Of course, there's no evidence. Just your word. Probably tell you, you should have come forward earlier, but with your *injury* they'll understand you were confused."

Blade turns around and shows him the back of his cut. "You know who we are."

"Satan's Devils. I can fucking read. I don't understand why the fuck this matters to you."

"That's none of your business. But if you don't do what we say, we will be back."

Have we scared him enough?

"If I do…"

"You won't hear or see from us again."

"I'll know when you've done it." I will, with Marcia's help. She can point me to the police database where the report of his changed statement will be recorded.

"You've got one day," Blade suddenly snaps. "Tomorrow. If you don't, we will be back."

I can't tell by his face whether he'll do it or not. As we leave the house, my gut tells me he won't. When Peg raises his eyebrows, I know he's thinking the same thing. Man's faking a neck injury to get a good insurance pay out. Going to take more than one visit, I expect.

Blade pauses by his bike. "Thought he'd piss himself at least," he tells us, morosely.

"Man did worse than that," Peg huffs. "You weren't standing behind him." He takes in a deep breath as though he needs it. "Crapped himself. Didn't either of you two assholes smell it?"

"There was something rank." I glance at the enforcer. "Just thought Blade had farted."

I get a shove which puts me off-balance, and I stumble a few steps before righting myself.

"How did it go?" Drummer's standing at the bar with his arm around Sam as we walk back into the clubhouse. I shrug. *Who can tell?*

"Mouse!" Drew comes over. "I can't thank you enough."

I slap him on the back. I've barely seen him since Blade drove the car back earlier. He's been down at the auto-shop just sitting in the car, listening to music, some modern crap I've been told.

"Sound system's as loud as fuckin' shit," Road grumbles as he walks past. *Hmm. Seems his fifteen-year-old musical taste isn't appreciated by everyone.* I grin after my brother as he walks away. His comment was said good-naturedly.

Apart from the audio and speakers which are obviously in good working order, Blade's pretty sure it's mechanically sound, he's given it the once over himself.

Raising my chin toward Mariana's brother, I tell him, "Just keep studying and doing the practice tests to make sure you're going to pass your written exam. Once you've done that, we'll go get your learner's permit."

"I will, Mouse."

Good to see the kid enthusiastic about something. Seeing the enforcer walking in, he makes a beeline for him, probably to ask him something else about his damn car. Shaking my head, I grin, grab a soda from Paige who's bartender for the night, then go to my office. After taking a swig from the bottle and wiping my hand over the back of my mouth, I sit back. Have we done enough to make Jenkins change his story?

The importance of whether we have or not diminishes the next morning when I get a call from an unknown number.

"Yeah?"

"Er, is this the person who placed the leaflet about the recent collision?"

I sit up straight. "Certainly is."

"I saw it. Saw what happened. Poor girl was stopped; a man drove straight into her. I do hope she's okay."

"Ma'am, she's really not." She's not injured, or wasn't badly enough for the cops to delay calling in ICE. "Look, can we meet to discuss this?" A voice on the phone is one thing, I need to pin this person down, check whether she'd be a credible witness.

"Don't see why not. If we can meet somewhere public. I don't know who I'm talking to."

"My name's Tse Williamson. And that would be fine with me. Name the time and place."

She names a coffee shop, and a time which is just half an hour away. I can make it if I push it. Ending the call, I race through the clubhouse, not stopping even when Wraith calls my name. I'm on my bike and flying out of the compound before I start processing the ramifications. *This could be just what we were looking for.* I try not to get my hopes up, but it's hard not to feel optimistic. *Just once, just fucking once, could things go Mariana's way?*

The coffee shop isn't crowded, and there's only one woman sitting on her own. I go to the counter and order a drink, saying my name loudly. Having to spell it out for the girl to write on the cup. When I turn around, the woman in the corner raises her hand. Making a quick perusal, I walk over. *She's white, not young, but not too old to be unreliable. Well dressed.* She'd tick many boxes. Approaching the table, I hold out my hand. "Tse Williamson."

"Martha Schmitt."

My name is called from behind me. I go back to collect the drink I didn't really want, then return to the table and sit down. "Ma'am, thank you for meeting me. Can you remember what you saw that day?"

"Sure can. Such a loud crash. I was waiting for a friend to finish purchasing something, looking out of the window wondering whether there was going to be a storm. Saw the light turn red and a car pull up and stop. Suddenly another car came up out of the blue, didn't look like he even slowed down."

"You didn't say anything to the police who turned up?"

She shakes her head. "No. Why should I? Enough people went running over, I thought one of them would have said something. My friend was ready to leave, so I left. Thought nothing more about it until I saw your leaflet."

"Ms Schmitt. The man who drove the other car, he lied and said the light was green, and that the car in front stopped suddenly."

Adamantly she shakes her head. "Not what I saw."

"My fiancée, well, she's been charged with a felony. Insurance fraud, the cops believe."

"Oh my." Her eyes go wide. "They've charged the wrong person. Why didn't they believe your fiancée? Surely she must have protested her innocence?"

This is the hard part. But if she later finds out the truth and doesn't like it, she might refuse to make a statement. "Ms Schmitt, my fiancée came to the US as a child when she was four years old. The US is all she's ever known. She's studying to become a nurse."

Her eyes have narrowed as she quickly puts two and two together. "She's here illegally?"

"She's one of the Dreamers."

She humphs, but waves at me to continue.

"Dreamers can't be charged with a felony. If they are, they lose that protection. Cops picked her up, ran her fingerprints and called in ICE. She's now in a detention centre waiting to be deported."

"Well, I can't really help with that. Don't agree with all these people coming into our country. She'll have to go back to her own."

I blink slowly. It's just as I had feared. "Her father raped her mother before she escaped. My fiancée's got a brother who was born in Arizona. Their mother got deported when he was nine, was killed by her father almost as soon as she got home. Mariana, my fiancée, has been responsible for the kid for six years. Been a mother to him. If she's deported, kid will have lost his only family."

"Well, that's just a shame. But the authorities will look after him."

"Authorities did fuck all when they took her mother. Left a fourteen-year-old girl to look after her young brother. No one went to check on them. Forgot they existed. She kept them together when no one else cared. I'm the boy's legal guardian now that she's imprisoned. He's devastated at losing the sister who's been like a parent to him."

"Look, I'm sure all that was a mistake." She starts to shift as though uncomfortable. "I don't see how I can help you, I'm sorry. But I've no time for anyone who comes here illegally."

I narrow my eyes. "Your family, Ma'am. Or your husband's? Schmitt, did you say your name was? You descendants of Germans?"

"Austrians," she corrects. "My late husband's relatives came from Austria."

"And your own?"

Her hands flutter. "Ireland. But way back then you didn't need to prove anything."

"But your ancestors reaped the benefits of living in the US?"

"And we've given back. We've all paid taxes."

"So does Mariana. And if she can complete her education, she'll be a nurse."

Now she brightens as if she can prove something. "Don't like foreign nurses. Can't understand a word they say."

"Mariana speaks nothing but English, and has done so all her life." I sigh, hoping to find something to get through to her. "If she's sent back to Colombia, she'll be in a country she's never known, unable to speak the language. What if you were sent back to Ireland?"

"Ireland's a lovely place."

It probably is, now. "But what if it was a time when the troubles were still going on? The IRA bombings and killings. And if everyone around you spoke Gaelic." I raise my hands. "I don't see how I can convince you, but I'm not asking you to do anything wrong. All I'm asking is that you tell the truth."

Her head tilts to one side, and her brow creases. Suddenly she gives a startled laugh. "You are, aren't you?" Her frown deepens. "You marrying this girl so she can get her green card?"

"No, Ma'am, I'm not. I'm marrying her because I love her." My lips curl. Somehow that's right. Sounds stupid, but she's found herself a place in my heart. The more I try to make it a reality, the more I know I want her with me for the rest of my life.

She looks at me sharply, then smiles. "She must be one special lady."

"She is."

CHAPTER 21

Mariana

"Come on. You've got a visitor."

It's not visiting time. Wary, remembering the last time I was taken away from the rest of the inmates, I move slowly to my feet, putting down the book I was reading. The female guard gestures at me impatiently. There's nothing else I can do but follow her.

I still haven't got my bearings here yet, but I know I'm not being taken to the room where I met Tse, instead I'm taken down different corridors. A door is opened, and I'm pushed inside. There's a table and two chairs, one placed either side of the desk.

Wrapping my arms around myself, I stay on my feet, scared, not knowing who's going to come in.

It's not long before I hear the tapping of high heels coming down the corridor. *That's not one of the guards, they don't wear shoes like that.* My eyes firmly fixed on the door, I watch the handle turning, then raise my eyes to the person who's just walked in.

"Carissa," I exclaim, as relief washes over me. Tears prick at the back of my eyes. Much as I like seeing Tse, if anyone, it's her who's got any chance of getting me out of here. I examine her face. *Has she news? And if she has, is it good or bad?*

"Mariana." She smiles her pleasant smile, waving me to the seat behind the desk, then takes the one with her back facing the door for herself. As she sits down, I try to read her face, but it's impossible. I doubt I'd want to play poker with her.

Preparing myself for more stuff I don't want to hear, I take a deep breath. "Is there anything new? Do you know why I was moved?"

"To answer your second question, no, Mariana. But it's possible the judge's workload isn't so heavy here."

"I thought I was going to be deported." The memory of how I felt makes me shudder.

"You shouldn't be deported until you've been in front of the judge," she reassures me. "But I'm here today to tell you something positive at least."

My ears prick up. *Am I going to be released? What's her version of good news?*

Still smiling, she at last enlightens me, "The charges against you have been dropped. A credible witness came forward and corroborated your version of the story."

It takes me a moment. Then I'm smiling as broadly as her, my facial muscles feeling awkward for being unused to that expression for so long. "Then they can't hold me. Am I free?"

Her head tilts to one side and her lips narrow. "I'm afraid not, Mariana. You're in the system now. But the fact the charges have been dropped and there's no longer a suspicion you've committed a felony, will go in your favour."

Anger rushes through me. Leaning forward, I hiss, "I've done nothing wrong. I'm missing college. My brother needs me. How the hell can they hold me?" I wipe my hands over my leaking eyes, feeling my cheeks burning red. "I was brought to the US because my mother's life was in danger, and she thought mine was too. I've never known anything else. Colombia isn't my country, the US is. I'm training to be a nurse…"

"Whoa." Carissa holds up her hand. "I know that, and that's what we'll tell the judge when you're brought before him. You're in the DACA program, that should count for something."

I notice she uses the word 'should' a lot. It doesn't fill me with confidence. "Have you any idea of when my hearing will be? Is there no way of getting me released in the meantime?"

She clasps her hands on the table and looks down at them, sighs, then meets my eyes. "The immigration system is a mess. Too many people to process, too few judges. You're one of the lucky ones in that your fiancé is paying me to represent you. But there's no way of telling how long it will be before your case is heard. I'm sorry, Mariana. Sorry you've been caught up in the system for no fault of your own."

"It was only a matter of time," I mumble.

"What's that?"

I stand. "I've lived here for sixteen years; I contribute by paying my taxes. I'm working to become a nurse. I live in a nation of immigrants. I'm taking nothing, never had anything given to me, but because I wasn't like my brother, born in the US, everyone wants to get rid of me. Why should the country of my birth want me? I don't even speak the language. The only thing I have to offer is the benefit of the education I gained in the US."

"And that's what we can explain to the judge."

When I eventually get a hearing. Something I both look forward to and dread. But from the conversations I've had with other inmates, it could be weeks, months or even years.

I'm taken back to my cell where I lower my head into my hands and once again give into tears. I'm in utter despair. It's even worse now my name's been cleared and everyone knows I'm not guilty of a crime. The fact seems to be that it makes no difference; I've been caught up in a net. I don't even hold out hope it might sway the judge. He'll be following his instructions to process people as fast as he can and deport them. With such a heavy workload, what time can he spare on each case?

Oh, I suspect, *hope,* some judges are fair. But being human, some will just go through the motions. Who's going to criticise them? Public opinion is against illegal immigrants, and like it or not, that description applies to me.

My days are regimented. Lights on, lights off at set times. In between I eat mechanically, only the thought of how much Drew needs me, making me fuel my body. I don't mingle, there's no point talking with people in the same position as me, it just re-emphasises my position. I spend my days lying on my bunk, wishing things could be different. At night, I don't sleep. I don't dare hope I'll ever be walking the streets of Arizona again, ever feel like a free US citizen. Although I might not have the papers to show it, how can I regard myself as anything else? I'm as much American as anyone. It's all I've ever known.

When Tse visits next, he brings Drew with him. While I'm happy for Drew, his delight in the Honda Civic Tse bought him, his joy at driving to school—albeit someone has to be with him—and being on the path to having his independence only depresses me more. *I* should be with him. *I* should be the one helping him learn to drive, helping him with his homework. That my *fiancé* is his legal guardian now hits me hard. Oh, I can't fault Tse for anything he's doing. If he wasn't looking after Drew, my brother might already have been kicked out of the trailer and be living on the streets, or in a foster family who might mistreat him.

That man and boy have developed a good relationship is easy to see. Drew looks up to Tse, admires him. Tse's fond of him too, ruffling his hair, *touching* him, when I can't.

As Drew prattles on about everything he's been doing, talking to fill the silence when I've got nothing to say, I see Tse's eyes examining me. Dark depths staring into mine, making me shift uncomfortably, knowing I'm hiding nothing from him.

The next visit, Tse comes alone.

"Where's Drew?"

He inhales deeply, then says slowly, "It's not good for him seeing you like this, Mariana. He hides it well, but the last visit upset him."

"You're keeping my brother from me?" The first emotion that's not despair hits me for the first time in weeks. "You can't do that. He's my brother, not yours."

"He's a fifteen-year-old kid, Mariana. It's killing him that you're not there. But last week you couldn't even speak to him. He's got to go on with his life. Who the fuck knows how long you'll be here?" He sweeps his hair back from his face. "Look, darlin', I hate seeing you like this. You look like you're giving up, when you've just got to keep fighting. I'm doing everything I can to get you out, but I can't influence the timetable. Just hang on in there, okay?"

I shouldn't take my misery out on him, he's done everything he can for me, and more. I know he was behind clearing my name. But I snap. "Giving up? You have no idea what it's like in here. It's like waiting on death row for the sentence to be carried out." I puff air into my cheeks, then blow it out. "Don't bother coming any more, Tse. I won't see you. And you can forget this relationship you've been talking about. I don't want a fiancé, and even if I get out, I won't marry you. Got it?"

My heart speeds up with every hateful word I'm snarling across the table. "I don't want to be hitched to a criminal. I don't want to commit to living with you. I don't even like you. *I hate you!*"

Tse's face softens, rather than hardens at my words.

"Get out. *Get out now.* I never want to see you again. Got it?"

My voice rises, the guard comes across. "I want to go back," I tell him. He nods, seeing my visitor is upsetting me, well, it's probably the other way around. But knowing that doesn't stop me walking away, leaving Tse sitting with such a look of compassion on his face, I feel emotion welling inside me, but haven't a clue what it is.

With tears streaming uncontrollably down my cheeks I'm taken back to the prison ward.

In my cell, I throw myself onto my bunk, and cry inconsolably. I really don't know why I sent my lifeline away. Tse's the man I fantasise about, but now he must hate me. But I can't allow myself to think of a man with whom I've got no future. The longer I'm here, the more I'm convinced, the US has already washed its hands of me.

CHAPTER 22

Mouse

It broke my fucking heart to see Mariana so beaten down. I didn't get angry or riled when she was spewing those words at me, words which tried to dismiss me from her life. It was why I hadn't taken Drew with me, last time I'd visited I could already see she'd given up hope.

I've done one thing for her, got her record clean. The reason for her arrest doesn't exist now. But I'm too aware that they won't just set her free. Now they've got hold of her, she'll be processed like everyone else. All I can do is to keep trying, digging up evidence that might help her.

Which would be easier if I could find a General De Souza in the military database in Colombia. The fact I can't worries me. The lack of data is annoying. Could he be in intelligence? His records are hidden deep where even I can't find him? Or had he been lying to her mom, claiming a rank he'd never ascended to? All I've got to go on is the information in her mother's letters.

A reminder goes off on my watch. Standing up, brushing back my hair in frustration, I walk to the room a couple of doors down from mine and enter the meeting room where we hold church.

I take my seat, my laptop in front of me in case I need to look anything up, and prepare to sit through another meeting. It's business as usual, not much on the agenda that's any different. No one gunning for us.

Joker raises his hand. "I'm not happy with the surface of the kids' playground. Can it be replaced with something softer in case they fall?"

Lady's nodding. The pair make me smile. Hell, who'd expect them to end up with a daughter? Well, she's technically Joker's niece, but they're both acting the part of her dad. Going through a proper adoption. Surprised us all when they brought her back to the compound a couple of weeks ago.

Viper puts his head in his hands, then looks at Drummer. "Prez. We're working construction on that mall. Ain't got time to keep doing shit here."

Prez's eyes narrow, then he grimaces. "You're right, Viper. Joker, you've raised a good point. Be good to have a place where babies can crawl and play, and where Grunt doesn't shit." He throws a pointed look at Joker. "You want it done? Why don't you look into it?"

Joker glances at Viper, who nods. "Sure, just didn't want to step on Viper or Bullet's toes."

"We're good," Bullet replies.

Beef raises his hand. "Can I suggest you have a separate meeting to discuss kids? I prefer the topics of killing and blowing up shit."

My lips curve up. You can tell by his face that he's joking. It's just good to have our brother with us and fully recovered after being so close to meeting the grim reaper a few months back.

"Mouse. How's your ol' lady doing?"

Prez's direct question has me off-balance. I close my laptop, sit back in my chair, and sigh. These are my brothers; now I've brought them in on my problems, I don't mind sharing. "She's refusing to see me or the kid now. She's given up, Prez. It could be months before she has a hearing, and she's not hopeful of the outcome of that."

"Meanwhile you're trapped in a relationship that's going nowhere." Wraith sounds sympathetic.

"Good one," chuckles Blade. "Our Mouse has been trapped." When no one laughs, he continues, "Mouse trap. Get it?"

Everyone ignores him, well, except Prez who sends him a glare, before turning more compassionate eyes on me. "No one would think worse of you if you stepped away, Mouse."

"Don't want to do that, Prez." The more Mariana's pushing me away, the more I want to stay close to her. *She's mine.* We'll be together one way or another. *Even if I have to follow her to Colombia.*

"The car's perked Drew up. Like the kid myself," Blade throws in, redeeming himself.

He's right. It has.

Something occurs to me. "Anyone got any objections to Drew being here? It could be for longer than I expected."

"You're his legal guardian now, aren't you? Making him your responsibility makes him ours too." I hadn't thought of it that way. I raise my chin in thanks toward Prez. "Okay, if there's no other business, let's wrap this up. Mouse, can you spare a minute?"

"Sure, Prez." As the other brothers make their way to the bar, I follow him into his office. It isn't empty as I'd expected, there's a man sitting there. A man with an ugly jagged scar running down his face.

"Devil," I exclaim, stepping forward and holding out my hand. There've been a couple of times the Satan's Devils and Grade A Security have worked together for our mutual benefit.

His fingers wrap around mine. "Good to see you, Mouse."

"You on the clock?" Drummer asks. "Or would you like a drink?"

The Englishman attempts a smile, but as only one side of his mouth turns up, it's not very effective. "Knowing the quality of the whisky you keep behind your desk, Drum, I'll gladly take a dram."

As Drummer pours two shots—he doesn't bother asking me—I take a seat, waiting while Devil smacks his lips in appreciation.

"Have you got any information?" I ask, impatiently. The fact I'm in this meeting means Devil may have answers for me.

He parks himself in the chair by my side, and rather than answering mine, poses a question of his own. "You get very far tracking down De Souza?"

"The father? No. His military records just seem to end for no reason. I passed everything on that I found. I got no further than that."

The only corner of his mouth which can move, nudges higher. "I thought not." He takes another sip of his drink. "He's an interesting character. Or perhaps, I should say, one that very many people are interested in."

I raise an eyebrow, and jerk my chin toward my prez. "And?" I prompt.

"He was in the army, never made it above sergeant before he got a dishonourable discharge. But he likes to play the soldier, so he's given the title General to himself."

Drummer leans his elbows on the desk. "Dishonourable discharge? I thought any behaviour of the type leading to that kind of expulsion would have been encouraged. Wasn't the army responsible for genocide?"

"Not when you get three members of your own team murdered. And in particularly nasty ways. And when several leads pointed to you being responsible, their deaths being to your benefit."

"What did he do after that?" Understand the history, join the dots, know the man.

"Well, he was no boy scout. Joined a gang, rose up the ranks." He pauses to pass his now empty shot glass back to the prez. Drummer refills it. "You know my interest in slave trafficking? Well, he's come up quite a lot."

"So why did you have to search for him, if you already know the name?"

"Ah, because that's not the name he's known for." He nods at me. "Already made some useful progress, with the history you've passed to me through Drummer, we were able to follow the trail. You started from the beginning, we were able to start at the end and work back. I had a hunch, it paid off. The name we had was *El Procurador*, The Procurer."

Prez sharpens his eyes. "Procurer of what? Or don't I want to know?"

Devil raises and lowers his shoulders. "Whatever you want to get a hold of. Guns, drugs, slaves. And on the latter, he's not too concerned whether it's women or children for sex, or men to work your fields. Pay the right price, he can get whatever you want." As my eyebrows rise, he adds, "Heavy artillery if you're looking for it."

"Jesus," Drummer exclaims.

"Yeah. That about sums it up. We knew what they called him, but not who he was or where he came from. When Mouse got me looking for a General De Souza, I tracked down what we knew of him. It was the key to us putting two and two together. Thanks to your man here, his identity is now known."

I seem to be floating above this conversation. Hearing it, but not participating. I knew it would be bad if Mariana was deported, but just how bad, I'd had no idea. "I've got to get this information to her lawyer." Suddenly I'm spurred into action. As I start rising to my feet, Devil puts his hand on my arm.

"Not so fast, Mouse. We've got to think carefully how we handle this new intelligence, and how it affects Mariana. This knowledge is critical to taking him down, and we need to have time to do that. We can't have it discussed in an open court."

"You're worried that once he knows you've learned the connection, he'll disappear?" Prez's eyebrows rise.

Devil nods. "Seems a fair bet he'd reinvent himself again."

They're not worried about my woman. "Mariana will be in danger if she returns…"

The security consultant, or whatever he regards himself as, sighs. "It's not her who he wants. It's the boy."

"Drew? Why?"

"It's all supposition on my part, Mouse. But I've been finding things out and adding them up." He glances at me, I nod. *Data. Joining it all up.* "He was injured before he was discharged. Nasty injury, especially for a man. Medical records show he's infertile."

"So," it starts to make sense. "He finds out he has a son he never thought he had and wants him to groom."

"That's my view. With no chance of having any other children, Drew's the only male bloodline he has left." Devil waits for a moment for that to sink in. "Seems like his wife, Mariana's mother, kept her mouth shut as to where her two children were. But there's a price on Mariana's head. He's had people looking for years. Luckily his contacts in the States aren't that strong or haven't much reach. So far, they've been unable to find her."

The news makes me suck in a breath. "If she's sent back…"

Devil's face grows grim. "His network is far more extensive in Colombia. Government officials in his pay. He'll know she's back as soon as she steps in the country. Probably even before that, if her name appears on any deportee list that will need to be cleared by their immigration, or any application for her to get a Colombian passport or visa."

"He'll want to use her to get Drew to go to him. If he thinks he can persuade her," I shake my head, "he's got no idea about her at all."

"If he gets his hands on her, he'll use her as an inducement in some way or another." Devil seems unaffected that we're discussing the fate of the woman I've promised to marry. "If Drew knew she was being harmed, I doubt he could keep away."

"Drew's not going anywhere," I tell him forcefully, clenching my hands. "And neither is Mariana. With this information, there must be some way to keep her Stateside."

"Are there plans to take The Procurer out?" Drum steps in, a warning look in my direction.

"We know *who* he is, but not where he holes up," Devil explains.

A really bad feeling starts growing inside me. "If Mariana returns to Colombia, he'll know, and he'll take her." I stand so fast my chair rocks backwards and falls with a crash. "You bastard," I roar, leaning over Devil and getting into his face. "You're going to fuckin' use her, aren't you?"

See? I can put information together too. *Of course, that's their plan.*

"Sit down, Brother," Drum says sharply, then turns to Devil. "If that's what you intend to do, I like it as little as Mouse does. Haven't met her myself, but from what Mouse has said, she's young, innocent, and not equipped to be an international spy."

Devil shrugs. "She won't go without backup. Remember the GPS locator we used for Sam…?"

Drummer humphs loudly. "Like that worked well, I can't forget we almost lost her, Devil. I recall you and I havin' words about that."

Instead of being cowed, Devil leans forward, and his eyes find mine. "Chances are she'll be deported, Mouse. If we get her onside, we can make sure she's protected."

"Chances are if she's got a credible reason to be afraid of returning, the judge will let her stay," I fire back. "I'm telling her lawyer."

"And put yourself in the sights of the CIA?" Devil challenges. "You'll be blowing up a plan we, *they've* been working on for years. You'll gain nothing from that."

I'm thinking fast. "How about keeping Mariana here and using a decoy instead? Someone who's trained and can deal with this shit."

"You're missing the fact that no matter what you say she could be deported. Her mother lost her plea for asylum and was sent back to a bloody rapist. Haven't got much sway over what the judge determines or what mood he's in on the day. Isn't it better to have her onside so she can help us?"

Again I stand, this time placing my hands flat on the table. "And you're talking about the woman I've claimed. The woman I want to be my wife. What do you expect me to fuckin' do? Live apart? Go make a life for myself in Colombia? Once she's deported, she can't come back for five years at least."

Drum raises his eyebrows at Devil. "Man means what he says, Devil. He's serious about the girl. I can't lose him from the club. Don't know what you have to do to get her out of this mess, but I say, you fix it. Don't like putting bitches in danger. Mouse has given you enough, the identity of this Procurer you've been seeking. You owe him for that."

"She can't do it, Devil." For the second time, I find myself planting my ass in the chair. "She's been living on her nerves all her life, I want her to feel easier, not make things worse. The life's already gone out of her." I want her here with me, so I can start building her back up. Taking away that fear she's lived with for years. "I know her. Any suggestion of her coming face to face with the man who killed her mother, she'll completely shatter. My assessment? Too risky. Unless you don't give a damn. One more immigrant out of the country and what's the value of one life?"

"You look here," Devil snarls, taking me by surprise. "I'm not from the US. Don't give a damn about your immigration policies. Don't give one fuck whether she stays here in a house with a picket fence or not. What I do care about is the hundreds of people separated from their families and turned into slaves, I do care about people being killed by others equipping their private armies, and the amount of drugs on the streets. You say she's worth more than that?"

"That's what he's saying," Drummer points out. "You caught me in this trap once before, Devil. Yeah, so that turned out right in the end, but it could have gone south. Find another way, Devil. If you want to help Mouse, get a statement from the CIA to confirm there's a credible threat to Mariana if she returns, help her to stay. But if you want to rely on me and my help in the future, do not set her up."

Devil shoots him a look which speaks volumes, but doesn't offer any commitment one way or the other.

CHAPTER 23

Mariana

Was I *wrong to refuse to see Drew or Tse?* I turn the question over and over in my mind, changing my view on the answer as many times as I ask myself. The reasoning that I was right comes back to me time after time. If I'm never going to see them again, better get used to it sooner rather than later. If all I have to rely on is myself, best I start now.

I'm depressed, and it doesn't take the time I've been studying as a nurse to understand that. Then again, most of the people around me are all trying to come to terms with their likely fate. That the system's not letting me go even now that I've been proved innocent seems to have sealed my future. This country, the home I've only ever known, is determined to get rid of me.

Apart from Tse and his people, apart from the blacks who were brought here as slaves, everyone in the States is an immigrant or a relatively recent descendant of one. Do they have less compassion due to that fact, that they don't want anyone else to enjoy the advantages they had? Is it because my features are Hispanic, my skin not white, that they want me to leave?

"Your lawyer's here."

Without enthusiasm, I get up from the table where I was sitting wallowing in misery, and follow the guard. I can't get excited, having resigned myself to months of staying here, then a one-way ticket to a place I don't want to go.

"Mariana."

Today Carissa's there before me. She stands as I go to the chair opposite hers, then sits and pulls a folder toward her. Opening it, she peruses a document, while I'm getting myself settled.

"I've got some news." She takes off her glasses. "Your immigration hearing will be happening soon."

Is that good news? I hold out little hope that a judge would be sympathetic. For an answer, I shrug. But curiosity does push me to ask, "When?"

"Your initial hearing will take place in a couple of days. That will only take a quarter of an hour. It's just a formality. Your individual hearing is scheduled for next week. They'll firm up the date nearer the time. Most immigration hearings are completed in under three hours, unless people have lawyers speaking on their behalf. This far out, it's still too early to give an exact time and day. If the judge gets a lengthy case, it could be pushed back."

The judge probably hears so many sob stories, mine will barely register. Even if I'm luckier than most, having someone to represent me. At least I speak the language. Like a native. What a joke. I speak US English, I can barely introduce myself in Spanish. *How will I cope when I'm deported? Do they speak any English there? Where am I supposed to go? Or do?* The thought of getting off the plane in a foreign country, alone with no money, no idea of the culture or customs, terrifies me.

"Have you spoken to Tse?" I suddenly find myself asking. "Does he know?" *Whether he does or doesn't, there's probably little he can do.*

"I have updated him, yes." She seems to want to say more, but as she removes her glasses once again, and looks at me searchingly, she shuts her mouth, shuffles papers, then brightens. "Well, I'll be working on your case and the submission I'll be making on your behalf."

I bite my lip. "If they decide to deport me, how long…"

Her mouth purses. "Let's hope it doesn't come to that."

"How long?" I insist, making my voice firmer.

"As soon as they can arrange a charter plane," she gives in and tells me. "Tse will be bringing a bag you can take with you. But only as a last resort. I'll be doing everything I can for you to be permitted to stay." I stare down at my hands as she continues, "Your fiancé will be arranging to cover the cost of your flight. That you've paid for your own deportation will count for you if you ever return legally to the States. Otherwise the outstanding bill will be just one more obstacle to get over."

She's holding out a glimmer of hope for a time in the future when I'll be free to come back.

"Is that a possibility?" I perk up. "Could I return?"

She sighs. "The judge will determine how long before you can apply for a green card. I'm assuming if you get married, Tse will be able to sponsor you, otherwise your brother once he's turned twenty-one."

Though it will be almost six years before Drew can help, and I don't want to force Tse into a relationship that however much he says he wants, I think is crazy. A *wonderful dream*. But impractical. "I won't be able to return for five years in any event." *Five years*. My eyes close. That seems like a lifetime.

"That's the minimum. It could be ten or twenty. Depends on the judge."

I'm only twenty. I could live the same number of years in exile, I think, as she reminds me how long I could be gone. There's no guarantee I could ever come back.

Carissa gives me a moment, then stands. "I'll be with you when your case is heard. I'll be doing everything I can to persuade the judge to allow you to stay. You're not facing this alone, Mariana. Tse will be there, of course."

"It's a public hearing?"

A nod. Then a spoken, "Yes."

It's no better knowing that my time in the immigration processing centre is coming to an end. If I was more hopeful of the outcome, I'd be ecstatic. As it is, each time I feel the slight optimism that I might be going home with Drew, I tamp that notion straight down, knowing if I build myself up, the disappointment would crush me.

Trying to keep any thought in my head is like trying to catch a particular fish from a shoal with my bare hands. As soon as I think of something I need to decide on, another idea enters and pushes it away. Until finally, exhausted, I give up thinking at all, and end up staring at the ceiling, my brain numb. Then the worrying starts all over again as I've made no plans, have no clue what to do after I arrive, as I expect is inevitable, in Colombia.

What happens? Do they just point you in the direction of the airport and leave you to get on with your new life? Is there any support mechanism at all?

It won't come to that. I won't be deported. I most likely will be.

As Carissa has pre-warned me, a short initial hearing takes place after a couple of days. Then nothing more until I get my time in front of the judge.

It's a bit like waiting for the guillotine to fall. You get to the point where you know it's coming, can't evade it, Christ, you can't ignore it, but there's part of you that wants to get out of the way. When a guard comes to get me one morning, I know there's something different. I'm given the clothes that so long ago I arrived in. They hang off me now as I've lost so much weight. *Detention centre for dieting, must recommend it.* It doesn't have anything else going for it.

There's a truck waiting, I step inside, once again handcuffed and chained to the floor. Windows again high so I can't see out of them. There's half a dozen people with me. They speak Spanish, I don't understand it.

A trickle of excitement bubbles in me even while I try to suppress it, the thought that I could be heading for my freedom. The idea that Tse might be there. Drew? No, I doubt Tse would have brought him, just in case it doesn't go my way. But Carissa, Carissa seems to know her stuff. *When I'm free, I'll have to find some way of paying Tse back, her fees must have cost him a fortune.* My foot's tapping impatiently, just wanting to get there, get this done and over with. *There's a chance I'll be able to go home.* Just the idea has my heart singing.

It's stupid, pointless, but every mile of the way to the courthouse, I'm getting my hopes up and can't push them away. The threat of Colombia seems to recede as surely the judge will see my home, my rightful place is here?

There's a turn that unbalances me as though the truck's gone around a sharp corner, then shortly after, it pulls to a stop. I eye my companions, they look resigned, maybe their cases aren't as strong as my own, maybe they were caught crossing the border. Maybe they haven't got anyone to represent them. I might be a hateful person, but I'm thinking if the judge turns them down, he's more likely to let one through. *Please let that one be me.*

The doors open.

Wait. What?

Sounds of engines fill the air, and it's not LA traffic. Those sounds are from planes taking off and landing. *I've been brought to an airport.*

Calm, calm your breathing, Mariana. Maybe the courthouse is nearby. But the embryonic thought doesn't get the chance to take hold when we descend from the truck and are led to a terminal. I may never have seen the outside of a courthouse before, but I'm certain it wouldn't look anything like this.

The guard practices his Spanish on me, I shake my head and he repeats it in English. "No bag?"

My voice so weak, he leans forward to hear me. "My lawyer was bringing it to the courthouse. I'm supposed to be there, not here. My immigration hearing…"

"You're right where you're supposed to be, Miss. You're going back to your own country."

"But my country is here."

"Ha. What they all say, isn't it, Tom?" One of the other guards laughs and not in a nice way. This is the one who pushes at my shoulder. "This way."

My hands are still handcuffed, but that doesn't stop me. All my life I've done what I'm supposed to, so afraid of otherwise drawing attention to myself. But my one thought today is to get the time in court that I deserve. I turn and run…

I fall flat on my face as a massive bolt of pain jars me, my arms twitch and I can't stop them. Gasping air into my lungs I try to get them working again. *I've been tasered.*

"I advise you not to try that again," the guard tells me without any sympathy. "Now get up and follow the rest."

I have no idea how long it normally takes to get through an airport even when you're travelling to somewhere you want to go; I've never experienced it. Here, we're led to a room and kept hanging around, but I don't mind waiting. *Somebody's got to realise their mistake.* I've been put on the wrong transport. Or perhaps it had been done on purpose, my case not worthy of a determination by the judge in person. Eventually we're on the move again, and being loaded on to a small charter plane, and my hand is handcuffed to the arm rest.

There's no entertainment, nothing the TV had prepared me for. Just a utilitarian flight to a country I've never seen, never wondered about and never researched. I've no love or fond memories of the place of my birth.

I want the flight to last forever, I don't want it to end. I want it to turn around and take me back to Los Angeles.

What lies in store for me? I've no plans, no idea what to do. The one thing I won't do is make any attempt to contact my father. He is not a good man.

An announcement in English and Spanish, and a change in engine noise and air pressure signal we must be landing. I look out on an alien landscape, then move my head so instead I'm staring down at my hands. Burying my head in the sand like an ostrich. If I ignore it, it can't be happening.

But it is. A bumpy landing. It's raining, hard from what I can see. *I don't even know what city we've come to.* What's underneath me doesn't look like it would qualify as a big town, but not having bothered to learn anything about the country, I don't know if they have skyscrapers, or even the low-rise buildings like in Tucson. This is certainly not like a large American airport. There's no bus from the plane to the rundown looking terminal. We're walked across the tarmac into what's little more than a ramshackle shed. There's a desk where we stand in line.

I'm at the back. Everyone's speaking in Spanish, and I keep wiping the tears from my eyes. It's not home, it's foreign. Even the air smells different. If I was on vacation it might be exciting, but I'm not, and instead it's terrifying.

"I don't like this," I overhear one of the guards saying.

My ears prick up as his companion replies, "Pilot told us he had to divert the plane due to a traffic control hitch in Bogotá. But I agree, soon as we get off the ground and back to civilisation again, I'll feel easier."

"Sent us to the back of beyond. Just look at this place."

"Soon as the line moves through, we'll be back on the plane. Can't be quick enough for me."

My intrigue is piqued by their conversation and that we've arrived at a different airport, though why should it worry me where I am? I'm standing on Colombian soil, and I'd have no sense of coming home, whether I was here or in a big city.

There's a heated conversation going on in Spanish at the desk in front of me. Suddenly a man turns and glares at the US guards. "We need bus to Bogotá. Not good you bringing us here."

The guard shrugs as though it's none of his business. The men behind the desk ignore everything that's going on. There are a couple of Colombian guards who openly show their interest in the man who's spoken, their hands resting on their guns. He throws up his hands and backs down.

"Señorita De Souza," a man announces as at last I get to the front of the short queue. A process of elimination, I suspect, as I'm the only ill-fated passenger left.

"That's me," I say, timidly.

He spurts a string of words so fast I can't make out any of them.

"I don't speak Spanish. *Yo no hablo Español*," I add in case he doesn't speak English.

But he does. It seems, surprisingly well. "Your work permit and identity card are here, Miss De Souza. And so is your ride."

My ride? Does he mean the bus like the others were asking about? Is there somewhere I'll be staying? A hostel perhaps? For the first time in hours the future doesn't look quite so bleak. If I've got a work permit, maybe there's a job lined up too.

I start to open my mouth to ask him, when the rugged looking man standing behind him steps up. Opening his wallet, he takes out a wad of cash and hands a large stack of notes over to the man who gave me my papers.

Then the man who'd passed over the money looks at me scornfully, clearly having overheard. "You don't speak Spanish?"

I shake my head, taking an instant dislike at the sight of him.

"Your father will be disappointed. But perhaps it won't matter. I doubt he needs you for conversation."

CHAPTER 24

Mouse

I was lost, adrift, before I found my place with the Satan's Devils. Brought up as an all-American boy, then taken to embrace my Navajo heritage, feeling like I had been torn apart, ending up neither one thing nor the other.

To my counterparts at college I was a Native American, to the people on the Rez, I was a white man.

That bike I'd restored so lovingly opened up a new life. Having got a scholarship from the Rez, I'd returned to Tucson to attend college, going back to the place that I'd known, immediately thinking I'd feel at home. But my years on the Rez had changed me, I wasn't the same person who'd left. I made friends, or rather, acquaintances, as I was out of touch with the life they'd been living. The music, culture, drinking and parties, a far cry from life on the Rez. Starting to prefer my own company, I kept to myself. There were two things I enjoyed far more than socialising: losing myself in code, and riding that rat bike.

I'd been out riding one spring morning, no real destination in mind, when a kid in a souped-up Chevrolet overtook me at speed, cutting in front of me to avoid a group of bikers coming in the other direction riding two up. I had to act fast to avoid him clipping my front tire, braking too quickly and swerving, resulting in me laying my bike down by the side of the road.

As the car disappears into the distance, I lie there, gingerly flexing my muscles and limbs, cataloguing possible injuries. I realise with relief I've done no serious damage, and recovering from being winded, I start to sit up.

"You okay, man?" a gruff voice sounds from above me. Shielding my eyes from the glare of the sun, I look up into concerned eyes, and for the first time notice a group of bikers surrounding me.

You don't live in Tucson without hearing about the Satan's Devils, a notorious motorcycle gang who've got a nasty reputation. Fuck. I'd gone for a pleasant ride, a chance to clear my head, and karma's biting me hard. First that fucking car, now who knows what the fuck is going to happen to me. Was I on their turf? Shouldn't I have been? As all manner of thoughts cross my mind after I've seen the patch on the leather jackets they all wear, I realise I haven't answered the question, when I hear another man say:

"He seems out of it. Think we should call him an ambulance?"

I snap out of it fast, pulling myself into a sitting position. "I'm fine. Bruised, scuffed. But I'll be alright. Just needed a minute."

One of them has picked up my bike, and has it leaning on its stand. "Got some scrapes on your ride, man. Shit. Fender's bent, and has gone into your tire."

Fuck! As I go to stand up, I gratefully take the hand held out to assist me. Brushing sand off my jacket and jeans, I go to examine my bike. Yeah. Cosmetic damage, that doesn't bother me much as the bodywork wasn't that good as it was. But as the biker had said, the tire is a mess.

"I can take it back to our shop, get it fixed up for you."

Their shop?

"Yeah, Blade. Get a prospect here with the crash truck."

I eye the half-dozen men standing around me. A couple have lit cigarettes. They look rough, tough. Would they steal my bike?

It's not worth much, except to me, but apart from my computers, it's about all that I've got.

"Thank you, but I'll get it sorted." How the fuck, I've no idea. It's not able to be ridden and I'm certainly not a member of the AAA.

The man with the gruff voice looks at me shrewdly. "The name's Drummer," he informs me. "I'm the club's president. I know the rep we've got, but we do run an auto-shop for citizens. It's Blade here's baby."

"Tse," I automatically respond.

The man who's been eyeing my bike nods over. "You can't ride it. I've got a tire in stock that will sort you, won't take long. Won't be pretty, but will get you mobile."

It's tempting, but still I have doubts which are clearly visible.

"That kid in the Chevy, well, it was his fault. But he swerved because of us."

"Drummer." I use his name for the first time, not knowing at that time just how much he, and the rest of the men, would come to mean to me. "Not your business, you were just riding on the road."

"Can't leave a fellow biker stranded," he insists.

Giving in, simply because it was easier to say yes than argue, I wait until their crash truck arrives, then travel back sitting alongside a man who simply has the word Prospect on the back of his vest.

Their auto-shop is on their compound. As we drive in, my eyes open in wonder. I remember this being a vacation resort, though the name escapes me now. I hadn't realised who'd bought it up after the fire destroyed it. At the gate, there's no immediate evidence of a fire now, just a spanking new garage, and further up, buildings which look like they've been rebuilt or restored. But beyond that there are burned-out shells. Still working on it, I suppose.

They're efficient. Have my bike downloaded and jacked up fast. I wince as Blade pulls out the fender, but at least the tire's free and can be removed. A new one is wheeled out quickly.

I'm leaning against a workbench. I'd assumed the president would probably have better things to do, but he comes and stands next to me, and his eyes watch Blade working.

"So, Tse. Nice bike."

I huff. It was before it got smashed. "I restored it a few years back."

"Good work," *Blade shouts out.* "Nice. Shame it got scratched up."

I shrug. Things get broke, get fixed. "I'll just have to work on the paintwork again."

"You got anywhere to do it?"

I live in a one-room apartment without a yard. Perhaps it will wait until I visit the Rez. Fuck, I'll hate riding around on my baby looking like that. The shake of my head gives Drummer the answer.

"You're welcome to work on it here."

His offer takes me by surprise. As I turn to him with my eyes wide open, I start re-examining my impressions of the Satan's Devils. "That's great, man, I may well take you up on that."

That's how it starts. A week or so later, while I am respraying the paintwork, Blade is swearing about the shop's computer system going down. I handle that shit fast. He's picked up a virus, I restore the lost files.

Blade is a strange man, mostly serious. When I learn he's the club enforcer, I'm not surprised. Working alongside him, I suppose we share a few tales.

"Hey, Tse, you back again?"

"Viper, yeah." *I grin at him.* "Not for much longer, it's almost done now."

"Looks like fuckin' new."

I preen at the compliment. Yeah, it's turned out better than ever. Helps when you've got the right equipment, and access to spare parts.

"Guess you won't be seeing so much of me." *If I sound disappointed, I am. I've met a number of the men, and get on with them all. I've begun to enjoy the camaraderie, the good-natured jabs, and seeing the relationship between them. I'm an outsider looking in, but I envy what they have.*

Wraith, who I've learned is the VP, is watching me carefully. Then he says something I don't expect. "Always looking for good prospects."

That night, I spend time reviewing the future I thought I'd seen in front of me. A job working with computers. Maybe eventually my own business. A corporate life. But is that for me? The white side says it's right and proper, and what I should do. But the side that lived on the Rez chimes in that I wouldn't be able to bear the restrictions.

Maybe I'm throwing away my education, but armed with my degree, I join the Satan's Devils. And I never look back.

Especially today.

"Mariana's had her initial hearing," Carissa updated me earlier. As she'd expected it had only taken fifteen minutes, so she'd warned me it wasn't worth me going along. That they'd schedule another was, as the lawyer had advised me, a foregone conclusion. "Her full immigration hearing is on Tuesday," I update my brothers in church. "I'll be going down to LA."

Prez stares that steely stare. "What are her chances?"

"Good, I think, Prez. It's a public hearing, but Devil's been in touch with the lawyer. She's going to ask that part of the hearing is conducted in private. She's got a sealed envelope to give to the judge. I don't know what's in it, but assume it will state her special circumstances, and that she should be granted asylum to stay in the US."

"Yeah, Devil said he was going to do something."

"You gonna be bringing her home, Brother?"

I fucking hope so, I think as I answer Blade. "In most cases, Carissa's said, the judge will give an oral decision. But he could wait to give a written one, if he wants to take longer to consider. She may have to stay locked up until he comes to a conclusion."

Blade's considering something. "I can't understand it. Drew and Mariana are brother and sister. Got the same Mom and Dad. But he's an American, she's an illegal even though she's lived almost all her life here. Where's the fuckin' sense in that? Should keep blood together."

At times I don't understand it myself. "Place where you're born determines your nationality, Brother." I purse my lips and sigh. "I can only hope the judge thinks the same way as you."

"Be hard sitting through that, Brother. Don't want you there on your own. I could do with a trip to LA."

My eyes shoot to Prez. I didn't expect to have company. But if it goes south, it would be good to have support with me. "I won't be riding," I warn him. "Just in case, I've got to take a bag of stuff down for Mariana." It was hell packing and preparing for something I hoped would never happen. I had to involve Drew, returning to that trailer to pick up some mementoes and photos as well as clothes. He was brave, but the implications hit him hard too.

Blade's brow is creasing; he wipes his hand down his face. "Reckon you could do with your brothers with you, Mouse. I don't mind tagging along. Get Matt to come along with the crash truck."

"Good idea, Blade." Drummer nods.

"I could do with a ride," Viper holds his hand up.

This brotherhood, men jumping in to give moral support as well as physical, is the reason I joined the MC. A slight uneasiness washes over me as I wonder whether they think the immigration case will fail.

But that's washed away when Dollar snaps his fingers. "I'll come with too. Want to see this woman who Mouse has claimed."

Nosy fuckers. When Marvel says that's a good fucking point and he's up for it as well, the corners of my mouth turn up.

That's how I find myself riding to Los Angeles with my brothers, in formation, two up. When we pass a lone biker coming our way on the opposite side of the road, my mind flits back to that day I'd been the lone rider, and how the Satan's Devils had stopped. I've never regretted my decision to join them. Not once.

If I'd been travelling alone, I'd have worried the whole journey. With my brothers at my side I feel invincible. *We're going to win today. Mariana will be coming home.* As the bike rumbles and growls beneath me, I feel ghost arms holding my back. I can't fucking wait for Mariana's flesh and blood ones to be around me.

We arrive, park up. Our cuts safely stored in our saddle bags as they have been since we left our territory, the prospect instructed to watch over the bikes. I go inside, taking my place next to my brothers at the back of the courthouse.

Carissa's sitting at a table, a mound of paperwork in front of her. Someone who I assume is an ICE official, similarly equipped, is close by.

My leg bounces in anticipation, longing to see Mariana again. My eyes are on the door I'm expecting her to come through. Glancing at my watch, I see it's close to two pm. *She should be here any minute.* I then run my eyes over the men seated around me, Prez, Blade, Viper, Marvel and Dollar, wondering what they'll make of the woman I've claimed. Hoping they take to her as much as I do.

A door opens, and a man steps in, followed by another who seems overeager, and we're given the instruction to rise until the first man takes a seat in the middle of the bench. Then, like him, we sit.

The judge, as that's who he must be, raises an eyebrow at Carissa. "Your client hasn't turned up."

Carissa stands. "Your Honour. ICE is transporting her from the processing centre. Any delay is on their part, and not hers."

"We can proceed in her absence as you're here to present her case."

I grit my teeth. From his attitude, I don't think he's taking this seriously. It's Mariana's future at stake, surely she should be present to take part in the proceedings.

I feel a brief touch to my leg. It's Drummer reminding me to keep quiet.

"I'd prefer to give her a few more minutes," Carissa says firmly.

The judge looks at the ICE representative. "Could you please find out what the delay is?"

The man from ICE gets up and disappears out of the court-room.

I start fidgeting. Fucking ICE can't even get their detainee to the courtroom on time. No wonder immigration is in such a mess.

Minutes tick by. The judge looks impatient. Then, eventually, the ICE representative returns. He approaches the bench. There's an exclamation from the man sitting behind it, then he waves Carissa over. A heated conversation ensues, but one carried out in low voices. Then the judge stands and indicates to his clerk. As the judge, Carissa and the ICE man disappear, the clerk announces we should all stay seated.

"What the fuck's going on?" I snarl at Drummer, while in my head running over all the reasons why Mariana hasn't appeared.

She could have been hurt, the truck bringing her here could have crashed… My leg bounces, and I can't keep it still.

"Don't get yourself worked up. They could have got caught in traffic."

But I don't like it. Something awakens inside me, a premonition that there's something very wrong.

"Perhaps she escaped," Blade suggests from my other side.

Yeah, right. I don't deign to reply.

Without my laptop, my hands have nothing to do, I clasp and unclasp them in my lap. If I had it with me, I could at least look up traffic hold-ups.

It's about half an hour that we sit with nothing happening. At last the clerk is summoned, then reappears. He stands and says loudly, "Court adjourned."

What the fuck?

"Why?" I call out, but my cry's answered only by its own echoes from the empty courtroom.

I'm stunned. I've hoped for the best, prepared for the worst, but expected to know the outcome today. I'm reeling as though I've taken a blow to the head, not able to process that the case isn't proceeding, and I won't be seeing Mariana this afternoon. For a moment, I just sit there, wanting to wake up from this nightmare. I dreamed of taking Mariana home with me. Now I don't know what the fuck is going on.

Behind my monitors I'm in control. I can't cope without data, without something to process about what's happening.

Carissa comes out from the judge's chambers, and stomps over to us. "Outside," she instructs, "and I'll tell you what's going on." Her face is red, her body tense. Whatever she's got to tell us isn't going to be good.

"Okay," she starts when we're gathered around her. "Mariana's been deported."

What? "That can't be right," I snap.

She glares at me and continues. "The judge is furious that the decision was made without his input. I demanded he get the plane turned back. There's a precedent for that, the case happened a while ago. When I reminded him of it, he did indeed try to do so."

Mariana's on her way back? "Did he stop it?"

Carissa puffs her glowing cheeks and blows the air out. "No. It had already landed." She looks at me. "I don't like it, Tse. Something's wrong. When he demanded the guards find Mariana and put her back on the plane, they said they couldn't do that. The plane apparently had to divert to a provincial airport as there was a problem with air traffic control in the capital. They turned it around pretty damn quickly, it's already preparing for takeoff."

"But the guards are still there—they could search for her."

"They could. But she had transport arranged for her."

"She couldn't, she doesn't..." *Oh fuck!* My eyes find Drummer's. He's already taking out his phone.

He moves away a discreet distance, but we all hear him when he roars, "*Devil!*", even if we don't hear the rest.

"I take it you've got suspicions," Carissa sharply observes.

"Her father," I explain quickly.

It's not long before Drummer comes back, his eyes darkened, his face set. "Devil's onto it," he says succinctly.

Carissa looks from me to him, then at the men surrounding us. "I've not been in this situation before, but there's nothing I can do here. I'll return to my office and see if there's any legal ball I can start rolling." Her eyes meet mine once again. "I'm sorry, Tse, but now she's been deported, it's unlikely she'll be allowed back. Christ, nothing was done properly. The judge wasn't able to determine how long she had to stay away. This whole thing's a mess."

"Why did it happen, Carissa? Why?"

Her eyes narrow. "A mix-up, the detention centre says. She was put in the truck with the deportees early this morning, instead of in the one to bring her to court."

Drummer's hand on my arm stops me saying anything. There was no mix-up. I'm certain of that. Devil has to be behind it. And his days walking the earth are now numbered.

"I'll be in touch, Tse." Carissa looks so defeated as she walks away, I can't apportion any blame to her.

CHAPTER 25

Mariana

The man has my arm held in a death grip. He must be near six feet tall, heavily built at that. There's no way I can shake him loose. As soon as he mentioned my father, I tried to run, but he moved too fast. Now, as I'm being forcibly marched through the tiny airport and out into the heavy rain, I consider my options.

I've papers, but no money. No place to go. My brain's numb as I try to process how quickly I've been removed from everything I've ever known. Even if I got away from him, what would I do? He works for my father. I'm not stupid, he clearly had a hand in bringing me here.

I'm exhausted, tired of fighting enemies too strong for me. It's easier just to give in and go where this man wants me to go.

I can't remember my father other than that he was a man who shouted a lot. A man who hit my mother. *Hit me.* Could he have changed in the intervening years? Could he really want to nurture a meaningful relationship with me? Somehow I doubt it.

As I get into the car, I automatically fasten the seatbelt, and let fate do with me what it wants. I'm glad I never allowed myself to believe a future with Tse was realistic, he's lost to me now. I'll never see him nor my brother again. But at least I met Tse, know enough that he's a good man, and he'll do the best he can to look after Drew. I have to believe that, can't allow myself to think he'd do my brother wrong.

How will Drew take it when he hears I've been deported? A tear runs down my cheek as I realise I won't ever see my brother again. *Ma,* he used to call me, joked that he looked on me as his mom. Well, I certainly looked out for him like any mother would have done. *He's got no one now. No one other than Tse.*

I'm grateful now that Tse bought him that car, if Drew hadn't had to have a guardian's approval, I would never have signed that form, and Drew would have no one. Yes, Tse must honour his commitment to him, to me. *He will, won't he?* I regret my words the last time I saw him. I told him I hated him. I lied.

My concern about my brother overrides any apprehension I have about my own fate. As we drive through unfamiliar scenery, the wipers constantly sweeping large drops of rain off the windshield, I look out with no interest on the country I've been shunted off to. The man beside me is silent, I'm glad, I don't want to engage in conversation.

All my hopes and dreams for my future are gone. What could Colombia offer me? A home with a man who killed my mother? *What does he want with me?* That's the conundrum. Why would he want his daughter when he had no feelings at all for his wife?

At last the rain begins to ease, and the sun bravely tries to shine weak rays, but hardly seems to brighten anything up. The ground has become hilly, and now we start to climb. There are mountains around us, trees and lush greenery unlike the dry desert surrounding Tucson. The very difference makes me homesick all over again. *This isn't my home. It's not where I'm meant to be.*

I should be thinking positively, not drowning in despair. But I'm so scared, I feel like I've been beaten into the ground. A fish out of water, unable to breathe air. Since the moment the police arrested me I've had no say or control in my fate.

We're coming up to a fortress, or that's how it appears. High walls, a barred gate, a castle-like building inside. There's a man on the walls, he's got a rifle slung over his shoulder. *Who is my father? Does he work here?*

The gates are opened. The car pulls in and parks. The driver gets out, comes around and opens my door. I'm not waiting for him to be polite, just terrified of stepping out.

"Come."

Another few seconds, then I take a deep breath. My legs are shaking when I put my weight on them. I wrap my arms around my waist as I look at the oppressive building in front of me. *It looks like a prison.* One from which there's no hope of escape.

Inside, I soon find, it's lavishly furnished, as though someone very rich lives here.

My escort nods to a heavily armed man in jeans and tee who's appeared. I rack my brains as I look at him, comparing him with the vision of my father I try to conjure up. But his features have been lost in the depths of time. Rationally I realise sixteen years have passed, and this man's too young to be my parent.

He takes up a position next to an enormous fireplace as the man who brought me here leaves.

The door opens again, causing my eyes to look across expectantly. A woman comes in carrying a tray, and places it in front of me. There's coffee and cakes on it. Automatically I thank her, but have no desire to eat or drink.

An ornate clock with a swinging pendulum loudly ticks off the minutes. I watch as though hypnotised as the weight veers back and forth. It's half an hour later, the untouched coffee now cold, that I hear loud, uneven footsteps from the hallway.

The guard, who's obviously been assigned to watch over me, stands straighter. I hold my breath. A man enters. He looks to be in his forties which makes him the right age, he's got a scar on his face, and walks with a heavy limp. His eyes are hooded, his lips thin, his features sharp. He's not handsome, but there's something there that reminds me of Drew. I think this could be my father.

The man whose hands are red with the blood of my mother. I shudder. Something breaks inside me, and my strength returns. *I refuse to be cowed.*

"*Déjanos!*" he snaps.

The guard almost salutes, and replies, "*Sí, General.*"

When we're alone, the newcomer approaches. "*Mariana, mi hija. Bienvenido.*"

I stay seated. I get his gist, but respond to make it clear, "I don't speak Spanish."

His eyes rise, and he spits out, "A *la mierda tu madre*! Your mother never taught you?"

I shrug. "She wanted me to fit in in America." I notice him looking me over, I do the same to him. "You are my father, I presume."

He startles, as if it hadn't occurred to him I wouldn't know him. "I am." He limps over and sits down on the couch opposite, the low coffee table in between us. Still his eyes are taking me in. "You need feeding up."

"I've been in a detention centre for a few months. I wouldn't look my best," I snap at him.

He sits forward, his eyes blazing. "Let's get things straight right now. I demand respect."

"People earn respect." I don't know why I'm challenging him. *For Christ's sake, this man murdered my mother. He could do the same to me.* But he wants me for a purpose, I'm certain. There's something about the way he's assessing me. He didn't bring me here just to kill me. What would be the benefit of that?

"I don't think you know who you're talking to. I am General De Souza. *El Procurador.* People fear me with good reason." He swipes his hand through the air. "I could snuff you out just like that."

It must be that I feel I've lost everything, that I've nothing to live for, as his comment doesn't worry me. Other people might show they're afraid of him, I refuse to show fear. "Just tell me why you've brought me here. Now I'm in Colombia, I'll need to figure stuff out. So let's get this over with, then I'd like to go to a city and try to get on with my new life." I sound far braver than I feel, but he's rubbing me the wrong way.

As if he realises confrontation isn't the best way to get through to me, he raises his chin, and his voice is less gruff when he speaks next. "You are my daughter, Mariana. Where else would you be but with me? My home is comfortable and you are welcome here. You will stay with me until I, we, decide what's best for you."

I haven't had a parent decide anything for me in a very long time. Inappropriate things come into my head, like asking why he killed my mother, why he raped her and forced her to leave. *Why he broke a four-year-old's arm.* I force those questions and my anger down.

Instead, I indicate our surroundings. "You were a corporal in the army when I was a baby. How did you get to be a general, and I presume this is all yours?"

"All mine." His lips curl in a self-satisfied grin. "And I'm *the* General, not a general. Let's say I saw a need for things to be supplied, and filled it."

"Things…?"

Again, his hand moves through the air in a downwards direction. "No need to discuss business now. Not when I'm getting to know the daughter I haven't seen for so long. You'll find everything out in good time."

Now why does that sound more like a threat than a promise? I shiver.

He notices. "You're cold? Our climate must be a little cooler than what you're used to. Your clothes, perhaps you'd prefer to change into something warmer? I have a room prepared, clothes in different sizes." He breaks off, and for a moment a look comes over his face which is almost of regret. "You are my daughter, Mariana, yet I know nothing of you. Not even how tall you've grown."

If you hadn't been such a cruel man, my mother wouldn't have left taking me with her.

"If there's a room prepared, I'd like to go to it." *And be done with this painful interview.* I raise my eyes to his face, firmly meeting his gaze. Knowing I've got to portray myself as a strong independent woman from the United States of America, and not some pawn he can play with. *Except I never was, and never will be, an American.*

He chuckles. It's rather an unpleasant sound, one you could imagine him making when he takes an enemy down.

"Alright, Mariana. I'll get you taken to your room. You can rest until dinner. You'll be escorted down."

A strange choice of words, but as I just want to get away from the company of this murderer, who I suspect has more than the death of my mother at his door, I go with it. I stand. He gets up himself, going to the fireplace and pressing a bell.

The man who'd been in the room earlier reappears. A quick exchange of Spanish, which I take is my father issuing instructions. Confirmed when the man reopens the door, holds it ajar and steps back to allow me to pass.

Before I go through, my father's final words reach me. "Later, Mariana. We'll continue getting to know each other later."

I shiver again. Then I am led up a marble staircase. On the landing, there's a full-length portrait of my father. *Pompous ass.* Then I'm led on, down a corridor which looks filled with antiques, and finally another door is opened. The man steps back, waving me inside.

That I hear a key turning in the lock is disturbing. Quickly I turn. No, I wasn't mistaken. I've been locked in.

Looking around, I survey the room I've been given. There's a large bed in the middle, a satin cover on it. The curtains to the large windows match. The furniture is elaborate, nothing like the functional type I've been used to. In fact, my whole trailer would fit in here and then some. An open door leads to a bathroom, a luxurious tub with massage jets, and a large walk-in shower. Various toiletries have been provided, more expensive looking than I could ever afford.

I stay standing, then turn in a circle, my mind whirling. Finally deciding, though this might be nicer, the fact there's a key between me and freedom means I'm secured as much as I was in the detention centre. The only difference being, there, at least, I knew why.

CHAPTER 26

Mouse

What the fuck has Devil done," I scream into Drummer's face. "What has he done, Prez?"

"Step back, Mouse," Drummer rasps. "Calm yourself down. You're in no state to help Mariana."

But I don't move. "Help her? How can I fuckin' help her? She's in fuckin' Colombia!" My hands rake through my hair. When I snarl my fingers on a tangle, I just rip strands out, ignoring the pain.

"Will you fuckin' let me talk to you?" Prez pushes his chest against mine. We stand head to toe. "If you give me a minute, I can tell you what Devil said."

"Come on, Mouse." Now it's Blade trying to talk me off the ledge. "You think we're going to desert your ol' lady? Turn around and go home? Ain't you been a brother long enough to know we don't walk away from shit like this."

"For fuck's sake, Blade. She's in *Colombia.*"

But Blade's watching Drummer carefully. "Listen to Prez, Mouse."

"Not discussin' it here," Drummer says, looking around the courthouse. Yeah, we've found a quiet corner, but could be overheard. "Come outside, Brothers. Let's find some space."

We walk past the bikes Matt's still guarding. There's some sort of park opposite, so we head that way. My feet step in front of each other automatically, my brain seems to have shut down. *I've lost her. I'll go after her. Don't know where she's fuckin' gone.*

Drummer leads us to a clearing, and doesn't keep us waiting. "Devil had nothing to do with this."

"Like fuck," I spit out in disgust.

"Mouse," Drummer warns again, this time his voice, as well as his eyes, steely. "I'm warning you. We're not abandoning Mariana, but if you can't reel it in, I'm sending you home."

Not abandoning her?

He waits, until I even my breathing and stop clenching my hands. "I've known Devil for a while, as have all of you. You particularly, Mouse. You know what he works on. He can be a bastard, but if he was using Mariana, he'd make sure she had a wire. He wouldn't send her in unprotected."

"He left Sam," I remind him.

As Viper growls from behind, Prez's face tightens. "She had a GPS implant. Not his fault they found it."

"Prez," Viper starts.

"No, Viper. We've no time to rehash history. But think, Mouse. If Devil was using Mariana to bring The Procurer down, she'd be wired up, and he'd be close by. Fact is, he's nearer to us, in San Diego. He wants to bring The Procurer down, not send another victim to him."

Victim. "I've got to get to her, Drummer." Don't know how the fuck I'll manage it, but I've got to do it.

I expect him to talk me down, instead he's nodding. "You're not going alone, Brother."

Blade, Viper, Marvel and Dollar all look at each other, then they shrug. "Presume we're going along," Blade suggests.

Drummer glances at them quickly. "Volunteers only. But yes. Look. Devil's willin' to put a team of mercenaries together to deal with this fucker The Procurer once and for all."

"Mercenaries?" Viper raises his eyebrows. "Not sanctioned?"

"Not officially, no. Wouldn't look good if the US launched an attack on a Colombian citizen."

"But the government wants him brought down?" I ask.

"That seems the way of it."

"Haven't got a passport," Marvel observes. "With my record, I couldn't get one."

"I suspect Devil will organise a private plane, private charter. They won't want to leave a footprint. And I doubt many of us have them."

I nod at Prez, I certainly haven't got a passport. Nothing stopping me, just never travelled out of the States.

There's something bothering me. "Look, Mariana's mine. This sounds risky. Don't want anyone putting themselves at risk. You get Devil to take me, Prez, the rest of you go home. Fuck, man, you've got your baby due shortly."

His piercing stare is on me again. "I'm the prez of the Satan's Devils, Mouse. What the fuck do you think comes first?"

"Club's not at risk, Prez."

"It is." It's Viper who's contradicting me. "You claimed the woman, that makes her ours. Ours to protect."

"I can't ask…"

"You didn't," Blade interrupts. "We've got your back, Mouse. Just like you've had ours when we needed you."

"Now hold your horses, everyone. There's just one snag." Prez tugs on his beard, his eyes, softening now, focus on me. "Need you doing what you do best, Mouse. We need to find the lair. At the moment Devil's working blind. He's prepared to share all his info with you. He's talking to Emir Kadar to sanction Cara to help you."

I blink rapidly. From the way Drummer has been speaking, I assumed we'd shortly be in the air on our way to find her. My thoughts of racing to Colombia immediately to start tracking her down start dissipating. *We need data.* I turn away, and look out over the well-maintained park, barely seeing it. Slowly I unclench my hands. I've been wrong to blame Devil. There's no benefit to him if Mariana has disappeared into thin air. It's my job now to find her.

Over my shoulder I say, "Need to get back to the compound, Prez." My laptop's not powerful enough for all the searches I want to start. I'll need to contact Cara. She's married into the ruling sheikh of Amahad's family. Her hacking into government systems is curtailed as there could be fallback on that country if it was ever discovered, as shown by her reluctance to hack into the ICE database for me. But Colombia? Surely Emir Kadar would allow that. With Cara's skill and our combined contacts on the deep web, hopefully we'll be able to flush The Procurer out.

As the adrenaline rush starts to fade when my body realises this is no time for action, my brain kicks into gear. My skills are all that can help Mariana now.

Blade stubs out his cigarette on his boot, then steps to the nearest bin and drops it into it. "We going home or what?" He's watching my face, giving a slight nod when he sees I'm now more focused.

"Yeah, we're going." Prez slaps me on the back, then we're walking back to the bikes, mounting up, and riding back to Tucson.

All the way I push the memory of Mariana riding behind me out of my head, remembering I'd had hopes she'd be returning with me. Instead everything got fucked up, and she's in the worst place she could be. *Hang on, Mariana. I'm coming for you.*

On my return, I grab a plate of food from the kitchen, then go straight into my cave, light a joint then start thinking. *How do you find a drug baron, gun running, slave trafficking mastermind in South America?* I'd searched his real name before, now I start looking for anything under his handle.

My phone rings. "Cara. Has…"

"Devil's been talking to me. I've got the go ahead from Kadar." She laughs. "He says he owes you one for taking Rais down a peg or two."

Yeah, after a bizarre combination of events, Satan's Devils ended up going to Kadar's extravagant wedding in the Arab state of Amahad. Flying in a private jet, we got away without passports then too. It still amazes me that we were rubbing shoulders with the world's politicians, royalty and film stars. There were celebrations for people of all types, and we gravitated to the less civilised desert sheikhs, interested in the tribespeople's entertainment. I took part in the bareback riding, and to Sheikh Rais's disgust, came in first, beating his best rider. They hadn't thought anyone from the US could ride without the support of a western saddle, but they hadn't reckoned on a Native American. Even in the circumstances, her reminder makes me smile. And if that means her brother-in-law, Kadar, thinks he's in debt to me, so much the better.

"I've notified my contacts," Cara continues.

"That's great." Cara's a world-renowned hacker and moves in circles even I can't get into. "Thank you, Cara."

I hear an intake of breath. "We'll find her, Mouse."

"We will," I say firmly. I can't think of the alternative.

As I end the call, my door opens. "Mouse?"

I replace my joint in the ashtray. This is going to be a difficult conversation. "I've just come back from football practice. Drummer said I should talk to you. Mariana…"

"Come in, sit down, Drew," I say wearily. I knew this conversation was coming, yet am completely unprepared for it. Seems that piece of paper I signed so he could have a car has more ramifications now than I ever imagined. I'm not going to abdicate the responsibility I've taken on. I'm his guardian in the eyes of the law, and with Mariana out of the country, the only person he has. Instead of keeping the desk between us, I rise, going to the chair next to his.

Splaying my legs, I place my elbows on my knees, and clasping my hands, rest my chin on them. I try not to let my voice crack, as I begin. "Mariana's been deported."

He'd have known something was wrong when we didn't bring her back with us. "She can appeal. That can take months, Mouse. I've been looking it up…"

"Drew," I say firmly, "She didn't appear in court. It's not a deportation order we're up against. She's gone, Drew." Yeah, my voice breaks, even though I wanted to remain strong. "She's already in Colombia."

Suddenly it's not a fifteen-year-old boy trying to be a man in front of me. His upper lip trembles, his face pales, then he launches himself at me, tears flooding from his eyes. His fists hitting my cut, but without any force to them. My arms go around him as he sobs into my chest.

"No, Mouse. It's not true. Mouse, tell me you're wrong. Tell me, tell me."

But I can't do that. With tears sliding down my own face, all I can do is hold him. My anger of earlier, my resolve to concentrate my efforts on finding her, all slip away as I let another emotion consume me. As my own tears mingle with his, I'm holding onto him as tight as he's holding me.

We stay like that for a few minutes. Gradually his sobs start to abate, and my tears stop flowing. When I'm at last able to speak, I make us both a promise. "I'll bring her home, Drew. I'll find her, I promise you." I don't mention Devil's involvement, or the danger I might be putting myself and my club in. He doesn't need to know that. He just needs to know I'll save his sister, or die trying. She's under my skin, and in my heart though I couldn't explain how she got there. This kid in my arms? He's become important to me too.

"What's going to happen to me, Mouse?" Hiccups punctuate his sentence.

Pushing him away, I hold him at arm's length, and wait until he raises his face. "I'm your guardian while Mariana's not here, Drew. You're staying here. With me. With my brothers. You're my responsibility now, okay? Not going to abandon you."

His head tilts, his watery eyes fix on mine. "Why, Mouse?"

"Why?" I try a smile; I think it works. "Because not only do I like your sister, I seem to like you too. Even if you can be an asshole at times."

His lips curl slightly. A moment passes. Then he frowns. "You are going to find her, aren't you?"

"I'm going to find her." As I confirm it, I'm hoping I'm making a promise I'll be able to keep.

I know there are a number of people trying to find this particular needle in a haystack. Cara and I speak frequently, so I know effort isn't a problem, but getting results is. When Devil shows his face on the compound, I resist the urge to punch him, knowing deep down he wasn't responsible for her disappearance, but needing someone to blame. But as he outlines the plans in place for when we do have a destination, I know I need to keep him onside. He's got men on standby, a plane at his disposal. Everything ready for when I've done my job.

But each day when nothing turns up is another disappointment. I resent anything taking me away from my office, even church. Tonight I'm listening as Dollar runs through his mundane update, trying to ignore the laptop in front of me, my fingers twitching to lift the lid and keep searching.

Viper's talking about progress at building the mall, Shooter, working with him and Bullet, is apparently showing promise. Paladin confirms there have been no further threats toward Jayden. Blah blah blah. Nothing to distract me from the matter which consumes me.

"Mouse?" Prez catches my attention. "Progress?"

I shake my head. If there had been, I would have told him. But I do have something to ask. "Prez. When we know the location, Devil assures me we're going to move fast." I wait until he dips his chin in agreement. I pause before continuing, while I don't like to think about it, I've got to face facts. What I'll be heading into will be dangerous. My voice drops slightly as I make my request. "I'm Drew's guardian. I want to know someone will be looking out for him if something happens to me."

Peg leans forward and looks down the table, his eyes flaring. "You even have to ask, Mouse? How long you been a fuckin' member?" His head moves side to side. "Kid's yours, that makes him ours. He'll have a home here, and all the brothers watchin' out for him. Nothing can happen to change that."

Blade's knife is pointing at me. "Think all that weed's gone to your head, Brother. Agree with Peg, wonder why you'd doubt it."

I hadn't wanted to assume. Needed to hear them say it. I sit back, my mind eased. Then at last the meeting's over, and I can get back to doing what I do best. Seeking out fragments of information and sewing it together.

Chapter 27

Mariana

That first night, as my father had led me to expect, I was collected from my room, and taken to the large dining room for an elaborate dinner. The food was probably excellent, but I couldn't taste a single morsel, my hand automatically moving my fork to my mouth where I chewed without thinking. I ate the minimum, just enough to keep me alive. I could still have been eating the bland food of the detention centre for all it was exciting my taste buds.

I was on edge, nervous. Concentrating on trying to stop myself shaking as my father, sitting at the head of a large dining table, introduced the men around me. They were his lieutenants. No other women were in the room. I felt I was invading their masculine environment.

Nothing was said, no expression sent my way, to make me feel welcome.

My mind grew no easier over the next few days. I watched, listened and tried to learn. One thing that became obvious, the only females I saw were servants. If any of my father's men were married, their wives remained out of sight. It made me feel this was less of a family home and more like a garrison.

Though the lock remained on my bedroom door, I couldn't say I was badly treated. I'd been taken on a restricted tour of the house and grounds, though some parts were clearly out of bounds. I was provided with books, and there was a television in my room transmitting programmes in Spanish. But although I requested it, I was allowed no access to a phone, computer or tablet. I was unable to contact the outside world.

As the days pass, I become frustrated, wondering at my role and why my father had me brought here. Apart from the obligatory evening meals, I rarely see him. When I'm sitting amongst his intimidating men, I don't feel able to question him. I remain in ignorance as to why I'm here, kept captive in a gilded cage. Physically I want for nothing, mentally I remain disturbed and worried.

What must Drew be thinking? Is he still with Tse? He's only a year older than I was when our mother disappeared, which makes me recall how I'd felt abandoned, even if she had no choice in the matter. *Is that what he's thinking? How is he coping?* I remember the emotions I'd gone through, upset to lose my mom, lost without her, deep concern how I could cope alone with the added responsibility for a nine-year-old boy. I'd been angry too, venting my fury against the system, and I have to admit, against my mother for leaving me, even while it hadn't been her choice.

Is Drew angry at me? How's he dealing with not knowing where I am? He must be crazy with worry. I pray Tse is looking out for him.

It's becoming hard to even evoke memories of what life was like before I was incarcerated. Living in that trailer with my brother, not many creature comforts, but we were happy enough, we were family. It's like it was another lifetime, so long ago. I've forgotten what it's like to live my life a free woman. Now I've exchanged one prison for another.

I've been here a week when my father sends me a summons. Lieutenant Rojas, who always seems to sit beside me at dinner, comes to collect me. On our way downstairs, he tries to make small talk, but I don't respond. I'm not here to make friends. I'm here to seek out any weak spots, to find a way of escape.

I can't return to the US, I've accepted that. But although I could continue to live a life of relative luxury here—if I could ignore the locked door—nothing my father has done or said has made me even begin to trust him. The other option, though, that's equally unattractive. Even if I did escape, I'd be penniless and homeless in a strange country.

I've been expecting to be called to see him. Why bring me here if he doesn't make time for me at all? Perhaps today I'll find out what my father wants with me. Whatever it is, I have my suspicions I'm not going to like it.

"Thank you, Miguel." My father nods at Lieutenant Rojas as he escorts me into the room. Out of all his men, I notice Lieutenant Rojas is the only one he calls by his first name.

As Miguel leaves the room, my father beckons me over. "Mariana, come sit, please." He takes a place on the opposite couch, unbuttoning his expensive jacket as he does so. He indicates the ever-present coffee pot; I shake my head. "How are you settling in? Are you comfortable?"

I raise my eyes to the ceiling then back down, refusing to be cowed by the man who sired me. "As I spend my time locked in my room, which, I admit, is comfortable enough, I haven't had a chance to settle in. I don't appreciate being kept like a prisoner."

His brows knit together. "This is a compound for my men, Mariana. I admit I'm very possessive of my daughter, particularly as I haven't been able to feature in your life. The actions I take are to keep you safe. I wouldn't want you to be taken advantage of. You do not understand our ways."

"You have so little control over your men that they would act inappropriately?" I ask, incredulously, scorn dripping from my voice.

A sharp look toward me. When he speaks, he sounds terse. "You have grown up in the United States. You have picked up their ways. Your manners, the brazen way you address me and my men, may lead to a misunderstanding."

"You mean I shouldn't speak at dinner?" It's true, questions I've asked have gone unanswered.

"You should try to be polite. In Colombia, we do not place elbows on the table, or eat with our hands." His head is shaking. "I can't believe your mother didn't even show you how to use a knife as well as a fork."

I bark a laugh. I'd noticed the strange way they use utensils even to eat fruit, where I just pick an apple up in my hands. "You're seriously criticising me for that? What do you expect, *Father*? When I've been taken away from everything I've ever known? Expect me to know your ways and how you want me to behave?" I shake my head, exasperated.

He suddenly stands, walks to the fireplace and faces it. His hands are clenched tight at his sides. His whole body seems to be battling with rage. As I watch, his shoulders slowly relax. Turning, he comes back. He now has a smile on his face. It looks fake.

"I could have given you a wonderful life. Instead your mother took you away. Brought you up in poverty in a land that wasn't your own. You, and your brother, should have been here with me. You'd have lived in luxury, never wanted for anything. Yes, I could have given you all that and more. Now I want to make up for it." He pauses and looks pained. "What I regret most is not knowing your brother. My son. You must miss him dreadfully."

I keep my face impassive. I don't want to give him any weapon he might turn against me. I certainly don't want to talk about Drew.

The pause stretches out. I wonder if he's going to push me to answer. But when he speaks next, he changes the subject. "I can understand you are frustrated not having your freedom here.

And that you will need time to learn our ways and about this beautiful country. Your home country, Mariana. I have asked Miguel to take you out and show you some of the countryside. There's a lovely village up in the mountains. It's small, but the people are so friendly. You'll love it, Mariana. You're going to love Colombia when you become accustomed to it."

I might, if I was here as a visitor. But I doubt I'll ever prefer the lush green that I see every day from my window to the beauty I find in the desert in Tucson.

"Your happiness is important to me, Mariana. Will you go with Miguel and enjoy the beauty this part of Colombia has to offer?"

I don't trust him. Don't believe a word that he says. This is the man who broke a young child's arm, and who raped and killed my mother. I can't see how he could have changed. There's nothing attractive about the thought of spending time with Miguel. Like the other men, he's battle scarred and not only looks, but acts scary. The suggestion of a day in his company makes me shudder. On the upside, I'd get to know my surroundings. Might even have a chance of escape. *Find one of the villagers willing to hide me? Or at least find a way to get a message to Drew?* A very slim chance, but a chance I could take.

If I refuse, what would happen? Though my impulse is to object, I'm sensible enough to pick my battles with my father. I don't want to cross him before there's something worth fighting about.

"Okay," I reluctantly agree.

After nodding his acknowledgement of my capitulation, he reaches for a folder, and takes out a piece of paper, saying enthusiastically. "I know how much you'll be missing Andrew. So, let's invite him for a visit."

My eyes narrow. *Why does Drew interest him so much?* As he holds out the paper, I automatically take it. My jaw drops as I realise what it is. A letter he's written, in my name, and obviously wants me to send it to Drew. My eyes narrow as I read it.

Dearest brother,

I wanted to write as soon as I could to reassure you that I'm in Colombia and I'm safe. Not only that, but I'm with our papa. Mama misled us about him. He's not a cruel man at all, he's been nothing but kind to me, and I could want for nothing in his home. He's done very well for himself and has created a business empire. His house and compound are beautiful, nestling under the mountains.

He wants to meet you, and I'm longing to see you myself. Papa's offered to pay for you to come for a visit. You can stay as long as you want. Please do come, as you know, I can't return to the States, so this is the only way I can see you.

Your loving sister
Mariana

"No." I hand the letter back. "I don't know why you're so anxious to see the son you've never met, but I don't trust you. I'm not bringing Drew here."

"I want my son!" he thunders, his fist hitting the table. "You will sign this. And give me his address so I can send it."

At least *he doesn't know where Drew is.* He might be a kingpin here, but his reach clearly doesn't extend to the US. *Thank goodness.*

"No," I repeat. His anger is making me uneasy, but instead of making me want to appease him, I vow instead to forfeit anything, even my life, rather than enticing Drew into his clutches.

Once again his hands clench, and I flinch, wondering whether I'm going to feel those fists hit me. Whatever he does,

I'm not going to give Drew away. I watch, nervously, but slowly the tension begins to leave him once more.

He stretches his fingers, looking down at them, then clasps his hands together. "Miguel will be waiting for you outside, Mariana. He'll give you time to prepare for your outing. Go, have a pleasant day, enjoy yourself. I'll see you at dinner." He picks up the envelope and letter and hands it over once again. "Take this, think on it. Think how wonderful it will be to see your brother. You can post it today; Miguel will show you where to send it."

The trip's today? Rather than arguing, I take the paper and blank envelope. My initial reaction is to tear it up, but instead of that, I hold it tight, a plan forming in my mind. A little burn of excitement inside.

When I step out of the door, Miguel is indeed waiting. He grins a slimy grin. "Are you looking forward to your excursion, Mariana?"

I'm not, except for the opportunity it provides. But I don't want to be rude to him. An escape might be helped if I have my father's men on my side. "It's good of you to give up your time, Lieutenant."

His grin broadens. "Miguel, please, Mariana. I think we're going to be friends."

I can do friendly, if it's going to help me get away. In other circumstances, I'd run a mile from such a man. There's a vibe I don't like coming from him.

"I'll take you to your room, then come back in half an hour."

As soon as the door's closed *and locked* behind me, I open the desk drawer and find a pen. There's also paper, but no envelopes. But my father had supplied that for me. Quickly I scrawl a letter of my own.

Dear Drew

I haven't got much time, so must make this quick. By now you'll know I was deported without a hearing. On arriving in Colombia our father's men picked me up and brought me to his compound. He's a rich and powerful man now, and I hate to think how he got that way.

Stay away from anything to do with him, Drew. On no account must you come to visit. No matter what you hear from me. I wouldn't put it past him to forge my signature. I'm a prisoner here, but I'm being well treated. Don't worry about me. Take care of yourself.

Love you forever

Ma xxx

I put the letter in the envelope, seal it, then write the trailer park address on it. Even if Drew's still staying with Tse, hopefully he'll think to check the mail. Apart from putting 'Satan's Devils Compound, Tucson, Arizona,' which I suspect has less chance of getting to its destination, I've no other ideas on how to get a letter to him. Then I quickly change into a pair of jeans and a warm sweater, putting the letter in my back pocket.

Grabbing a jacket, thinking it could be cooler in the mountains, I've finished just in time as Miguel knocks at the door.

"So, are you ready to do some exploring?" He's casually dressed. A light linen button-up shirt over a pair of jeans, and, like me, he's carrying a jacket.

"I could do with getting out of this place," I respond, truthfully. Unable to say I'm thrilled about a day in his company. My answer seems to suffice.

I thought it would be nearer, our destination is a two-hour drive away. The journey takes us through gently rising gloriously green woodland. As we get higher, the gaps in the forest begin to show stunning views. If I was on vacation, I'd be snapping pictures. If I still had my phone, that is. Which reminds me I'm allowed no communication device. Speaking to Drew, checking he's okay, would be easy if I had. The thought makes me frown.

"My company isn't that distasteful to you, is it?" Miguel chooses that moment to turn around and notices my expression.

"What do you know, Miguel? Why does my father want me?" I ask questions of my own rather than answering his. It's not like I could be truthful. "He doesn't know me."

"Perhaps he wants to get to know you."

"Man like him? If he had more regard for family, my mother wouldn't have left him."

Miguel cocks his head to one side. "Do you ever think you only heard her story? That he might have one of his own? That it wasn't just one-sided?"

Holding out my left arm in front of me, I spit back, "The arm broken by him when I was a child tells its own tale."

"An accident. The truth warped by your mother," he snaps back. "You were a child, Mariana, your memories shaped by what you were told. Your father is a good man, give him a chance and get to know him."

"Oh, I remember it clearly. You don't forget a bone snapping and the pain, even when you're young." I'm angry. I hadn't needed my mom to remind me. I recall it well enough myself. The only thing I can't recall is what he thought I'd done to deserve it.

He doesn't have an immediate comeback. For a few miles we drive in silence. I'm hoping it will continue that way, but then he starts speaking again. "Your father's older and wiser now, you need to understand the pressure he, *we*, were under back in those days. We were fighting for peace in our own country. Atrocities committed on either side. You had to become a certain person to deal with that. Now peace has come, that can all be put behind us. Your father has changed,

Mariana. Give him a chance to prove it. All he wants is his family to be reunited again."

I don't reply. It would be easy to be taken in by his words, yet I've seen my father struggling to control his temper. It would be a very long time, during which hell would probably freeze over, before I'd trust the man.

Miguel leaves me to my thoughts, concentrating on driving. After a few more miles, he points to a sign. "Not far now."

Although I'm not in the mood for sightseeing, even I have to admit to the charm of the beautiful mountain village we're approaching, taking in the sights as we arrive. Brightly coloured buildings surround a cobbled square, more cobblestone streets leading off of it. With the sun shining down, illuminating the painted houses, I'm enchanted. It wouldn't be a hardship to explore the little craft shops.

We've had a car following us from the compound. When we park at the side of a road, it draws up behind us. Two armed guards get out, and as Miguel opens the door for me, they come and flank us. I study the reactions of the people around us. Some, who look like tourists going about their business, seem unaffected, but several who I assume are residents look wary. At least one abruptly closes up shop. Guessing the men with us haven't got a good reputation, it confirms I'm right to be suspicious about Miguel's defence of my father.

The people in the craft shops that remain open are friendly enough. I've no money, and no reason to buy anything, but it is nice to be out and have some semblance of normality for the first time in months. Not eager to return too quickly to my father's residence, I feign an interest. There's a pretty scarf on a stand outside the shop, I pick it up to examine it.

"You like that?"

I shrug. "I have no money."

"I'll buy it for you."

I look at him in scorn. "You have no reason to buy me a gift, and I have no reason to accept," I tell him, wanting to preserve the boundary between us. "You say my father wants to get to know me? Well, I'm used to being an independent woman, now I've not got a cent to my name."

"Cents wouldn't do you much good here, woman." He reaches into his pocket and extracts some notes, then presses them into my hand. "Here's some pesos. Don't worry, I wouldn't want you to think I was being kind. I'll get your father to reimburse me."

Little things like walking into a shop and buying things denied to me for so long stop me from arguing. "Thank you." I take the money, pick up the scarf I pretended had caught my eye, then step into the cute little shop, coming out a few seconds later with my purchase in my hand, and change in my pocket.

Slowly we edge our way around the colourful displays. I'm keeping my eye out for anything resembling a post office, but nowhere has a post box outside. Reluctantly, I'm going to have to ask my companion.

"Miguel. My father wanted me to write to Drew. I've got a letter to post. Where do I send it?" I ask nonchalantly, trying to contain the excitement that I'll be able to get my letter and warning to Drew, while kidding them I'm sending the draft my father wanted sent.

"That shop there. She'll sort you out." I glance in the direction he's pointing.

"Um, how do you say I'd like to post a letter in Spanish?"

"I'll come in with you." He sounds decisive.

I don't want him to see the address on the envelope. "No, if this is going to be my home, I've got to learn to do things myself."

His look now is approving. *"Deseo publicar una carta."*

I thank him and go into the shop he's directed me to. When I repeat the words he told me, the woman nods her head. I pass over the envelope and the money. Pleasant smiles are exchanged, and I'm back out on the street, my heart leaping at the thought my letter will reach Drew and warn him.

Feeling lighter as though I've rid myself of a burden, I resolve to enjoy the time I'm in the fresh air, even if it means I have to ignore the three armed men with me. After some more time just walking around, Miguel takes me into a little café. The two guards wait outside. I have coffee and some sort of cake. He tries to engage me in conversation. While I'm not abrupt, neither am I forthcoming. He's not here as my friend, he's one of my father's men. Despite my hopes earlier, there's no way of slipping away and seeking help. Miguel's my jailer, as much here as when he locks my bedroom door at the compound. I trust him as much as my father, and that means I don't trust him at all.

I sense Miguel would show an interest in me if I allowed it. There's something about the way he keeps accidentally touching my hand, or when he stands just a little too close. His nearness makes my skin crawl; *I don't like him.* His mouth opens and the right words come out, but there's an air about him that suggests he's cut from the same cloth as my father.

The slight liberties he takes worry me, and make me think of Tse. If Tse was my companion, I'd lean into his touches, welcome them. The fleeting thought of the man I'm unlikely ever to see again brings a wave of sadness. *He said he'd come with me.* But he's got no way of finding me. I turn away before Miguel can question the tears that come to my eyes, as I allow myself to realise how much I miss Tse.

When we exit the cafe, Miguel asks one of the others a question in rapid fire Spanish. For a reply, the guard touches his pocket. For some reason he seems to look smug.

Then we're back in the car, and now descending the mountain, retracing our path. On the journey back, Miguel doesn't try to make conversation.

CHAPTER 28

Mouse

Yeah?" Having been interrupted I take the opportunity to take out my stash and papers and start rolling again. My brow creases as I observe my unusual visitor. Prospects know better than to interrupt me while I'm working. My interest is piqued as I suspect he's got a good reason.

Matt shifts on his feet. "Thought I ought to let you know. I picked Drew up from school today. He asked to go back to the trailer park, seems a book he needed was there."

I nod. All good so far.

What Matt says next has the hairs on the back of my neck pricking. "Fuckin' trailer was a wreck. Someone had been through it, and through it good."

"Neighbours?" It wouldn't surprise me. The people who live there are as poor as shit, and an abandoned trailer fair game. Couldn't even blame them.

"Nah. TV was smashed. Thieves would have taken it. I reckon someone was trying to find something. Info where Drew had gone, perhaps?"

Narrowing my eyes, I consider the prospect. He's a smart one. He's not been involved in our discussions, and only brothers know Mariana's father wants to get his hands on Drew. Seems we might have brought the fight Stateside.

"Drew okay?" I ask.

"Yes, and…" Matt looks like he hasn't quite finished, but he pinches his nose. "He was upset, obviously. Took some time pokin' around. Found the fuckin' textbook he was after—one of the only things not destroyed. We went to the manager's office to see if anyone saw anything. Of course they didn't. There were a couple pieces of mail waiting there. One a bill, and one which upset him. Think you need to talk to him, Mouse. Oh, and the manager said someone had been hangin' around the park. A Hispanic, but he couldn't give a better description. He couldn't say it was him who wrecked the trailer. Oh, and I secured it as best I could."

Wondering what could have caused Drew to become more distressed than the destruction of his home, I start to stand. Matt holds up his hand. "When we left the trailer park, I noticed we'd picked up a tail. I stopped that damn car, changed places with Drew. Took some evasive actions and managed to lose whoever it was."

Now it's me that's troubled. "You did good, Prospect." When it comes to deciding whether to patch him in, he'll get my vote. "When you stopped to take over the driving, he approach you?"

"Nah, stayed well back. I had my gun handy in case. Looked to me like he wanted to find where we were heading, rather than wanting a confrontation on the street."

I purse my lips, thinking. First thing to do is to make sure the kid's okay. Then I'll need to bring Drummer in on this. Hopefully, Matt's right and he lost the tail. If not, trouble might be brewing.

Without having to say the words, Matt knows he's dismissed. I follow him out to see what state Drew's in, concerned today's events might have disturbed him. But that's one thing I needn't have worried about, and my lips curl slightly when I see Drew standing by the bar, his arms gesticulating wildly, an audience around him.

"Then Matt slammed on the brakes and cornered fast. Damn, didn't know my car could move like that. Went around it on two wheels. Whoever was after us couldn't keep up." He pauses for breath. "Matt took us off in a different direction, moving like a racing driver. Pretty sure we lost him."

Well, great. The whole club knows. Drummer's standing in the entrance to the kitchen, he looks over, meeting my eye. "Mouse, Drew. My office. Now." As he stomps past me he pauses. "We need the prospect?"

"Nah. He's already briefed me."

Drummer goes behind his desk. "So, someone's on the lookout for you, Drew, or perhaps Mariana's the target if they don't know what's happened to her. Let's go through the obvious first. D'you know if your sister owed money? Left a bill unpaid?"

Drew shakes his head adamantly. "Ma never wanted to draw any attention to herself. All the utilities were prepaid. Even the trailer rent's paid up until the end of next month. She never borrowed money."

Prez presses his lips together. As he goes to question Drew again, I stop him. "Matt tells me you got a letter that put you in a bit of a state. Care to tell us what it was?"

As an answer, he reaches into his pocket and passes it over. "It's from, or supposed to be from, Mariana."

Taking it, I slide the paper out of the envelope. "You think it's not?" As I read it, at first it seems like an excited letter from a sister who's reunited with her father. A relative her opinions seem to have done a one-eighty of. Credible, perhaps. She could hardly remember her days in Colombia, relying on her mom's word about why she left. After I read it, I pass it to Drummer.

If Devil hadn't warned us this Procurer fucker was after his son, we might have taken it at face value. But armed with that information, the letter sounds wrong.

"It's the signature," Drew interrupts my thoughts and Drummer's perusal. "She's Ma to me, not Mariana. She'd never sign a letter anything else. And we only ever called Mom, Mom. And Father wasn't even Dad, let alone Papa. Mariana wouldn't change that. Not when she's addressing me. Someone else wrote it. Had to have done."

"It says she wants you to visit, to get to know your father," Drummer sums up. His eyes flick to mine.

Drew's eyes fill with tears. "Mariana would never have told anyone where I was living." His excitement at the car chase seems to have faded. "If my father forged the letter, he also got my address out of her." His gaze meets mine. "What if they've hurt her, Mouse? What if I'd been at the trailer…"

"They trashed the trailer, presumably looking for clues as to where Drew is. It would have been obvious no one's living there now," I inform Drummer, the piece of the puzzle he doesn't yet know. Then I fix my gaze on Drew, and place my hand on his shoulder, my fingers squeezing momentarily. "You weren't there. I'm not going to let anything happen to you."

Prez pulls his shoulders back and fixes his stare on the kid. "*We*," he corrects, pointing at me. "Mouse is your legal guardian. That makes you part of the club. One of ours. And we protect our own. Matt did good getting you out of there today. No one's going to take you and force you to do something you don't want to. Not when every man in this club is at your back."

Drew's eyes widen. His stunned expression making me remember all he's ever had to rely on before was Mariana. He looks overcome for a moment. All he can stammer out is, "Thanks, Drummer."

"As for your sister," Prez continues as though he hadn't spoken. "She was probably tricked in some way. Don't worry yourself too much. My bet is that your father will try to use her to tempt you to Colombia." Now he lightens his voice. "I hear fried chicken's on the menu. After the excitement you're probably hungry. Why not go and get something to eat?"

I almost laugh when Drew licks his lips. Yeah, Prez understands how to distract a teenage boy.

"I'll be there in a minute." My words echo Drummer's. Subtle instruction to leave us alone.

When the door has closed behind him, I turn over the envelope I hold in my hands. "They might have fucked up, Prez. There's a postmark on it. Bit indistinct, but I'll see what I can do to sharpen it up."

"Won't give us a precise location, but the area could be a start." Prez strokes his beard, I give him time. He stands, his body flanked by the large Satan's Devils flag which hangs behind his desk. "Liaise with Devil, will you?" His comment is unnecessary. That was the first thing I was going to do.

Drummer paces, then halts. "I'm going to speak to Matt. See if he's certain he lost him."

"Prospect seemed pretty certain he had."

"Nevertheless, got to beef up security, Mouse. Don't want any fucker getting near the compound."

"What about Drew going to school? He'll be vulnerable. They could snatch him off the campus."

Suddenly Drummer swings around and leans his hands on the desk. "Don't like not knowing where and when they are going to hit. If there's just one, or more. Could Mariana's father have contacts he can call on? If he's working with the Herreras, we could have trouble on our hands."

The Herreras are the crime family in Tucson, with links to Los Zetas, the cartel. Prez has made a good point. If they're in bed with *El Procurador*, we could be in a heap of trouble.

"I'll speak to Devil. He might know if there's any connection. I'll also do some diggin' myself."

"If they're not, and we've got a lone fucker or two trying to get their hands on the boy? I don't like letting shit just happen. I like to be in the driver's seat. Kid's reliable, seen that already.

Your woman brought him up right. All the shit that's gone down? He's handled it. We get him covered, then let them approach him. We'll bring 'em back here and get them to give us some info."

Closing my eyes, I picture what Prez is suggesting. Snapping them open, I reply, "Don't like putting the kid in danger. But it could help get information on the precise location Mariana's being held." The postmark could help some, but not the detail. I've enough confidence in my brothers that they'll make any man we capture speak.

"Find out what we might be up against, Mouse. But if we can rule out them getting help from the Herreras, that's the course of action I'd prefer. Fuck with them, before they fuck with us. And Drew? That kid doesn't go off the compound unless we've got brothers as well as a prospect with him."

I'm calm until I enter my office and shut the door. Then I kick over both of the chairs in front of me. My chest is heaving, my warrior blood warring with the white man inside, telling me instead to keep calm, to do my job. Do what I can to find her and trust that Drummer's instinct is right, that she was tricked in some way. The alternative that she was tortured is too terrible to consider. In frustration, I pull the tie holding my hair back, allowing my long hair to flow free. Shaking with frustration that I don't have an enemy in front of me.

What did they do to Mariana to get her to betray Drew's address? Nah, Mouse, don't go there. Focus.

Mariana had nothing except her purse with her when she was arrested, Drew brought nothing but clothes and what few bits a teenage boy thought he needed. My suspicions are there's probably a wealth of information stored in that trailer. Reports, letters, shit that would divulge all manner of information, such as the school he attends. Maybe the football club he goes to.

Maybe more, I don't know. I doubt if the kid does either, moms take care of that shit.

Mariana wouldn't have willingly given him away. Even Drew knows that. I know it intuitively. She was scared to go back, I don't for one second believe that her father's turned loving. The shit we've dug up on him points to him being anything but. Mariana's only a means for him to get hold of his son.

Is she hurt? My palms grasp either side of my head as I try to suppress my roar of frustration. *I don't know what's happening to her.* Even whether she's still alive.

I inhale a deep breath and hold it, then slowly let it out. And repeat. My heart rate starts to return to normal, my brain begins to work. Going around the other side of my desk, I sink into my seat and pick up the phone while simultaneously getting a search running.

Devil agrees to investigate any of *El Procurador*'s links to the US. I can't blame him for not immediately knowing, but I just wish we had some answers for once. The next couple of hours I spend trawling the darkest depths of the web, but nowhere can I find a link between Los Zetas, the Herreras, and *El Procurador*. In truth, I hadn't expected to find one, suspecting it more likely they're in competition with each other. I hardly expect cartels to meet up and exchange working practices. But Drummer was right to ask me to make sure. We need to know what we're up against, and if we can't find that, at least who we're not. If the crime family or the cartel had their sights on Drew it would be a different ball game. Hopefully we're only dealing with a couple of men.

Just as I've reached that conclusion, whoever it is is acting alone, Devil calls back to tell me he's found the same. His contacts in the CIA and FBI were unable to find anything that showed Los Zetas or the Herreras were linked with *El Procurador*.

When I tell him we're planning to use Drew as bait, he wants to be involved. Prez won't mind the invitation I extended for him to come to the compound, he's been here often enough before.

After I've updated Drummer with Devil's involvement he calls an emergency church for that evening. Having sharpened up everything on the envelope, I now know it was posted from Villavicencio, the capital of the Meta department. It doesn't narrow anything down, being a huge area of over thirty-three thousand square miles. By the time I've looked everything up and am thoroughly despondent, members are passing my door heading into church. I go to join them.

Having flown up from San Diego, Devil's already arrived and has taken the spare seat that's been placed alongside Joker. Prez starts the meeting. When the scarred man waggles his fingers, Drummer nods for him to speak.

"I suspect Mariana's been tricked," he addresses himself to me. "It's notoriously difficult to send a letter in Colombia, let alone one going to a foreign country. It's not unheard of to be asked to provide two forms of identity for the slightest thing. If she wrote to Drew, she'd need help sending the letter. It's not a case of putting it in a post box. In fact, there are virtually none of those at all."

"So she trusted the wrong person? Her letter was intercepted?"

"That makes sense to me. She'll want to contact Drew, to let him know what's going on and where she is. She obviously can't get access to a phone, so maybe tried snail mail instead."

"Or," I put in. "She could have been tortured."

No one contradicts me. We can't rule it out.

"*El Procurador* seems fixated on finding his son. I may know the reason for that." Devil's got everyone's attention. "He's visited a specialist. Seems he's being treated for cancer. It may have reminded him of his mortality."

"Dying?" I ask, hopefully.

"Seems not," the man from England replies, his accent sounding odd around our table. "It's in an early stage and odds are it's treatable, but it may make grooming his son, presumably to take over, more of a priority. He won't want to waste time that, if the treatment doesn't work, he may not have."

"Can we track him from his medical records?" I ask. I hadn't found those.

"No. He went to Bogotá, the capital of Colombia. Received treatment and listed his hotel address as his residence."

Rapping the gavel, Drummer takes the floor, and updates everyone on the man, or men, who were following Drew, and the proposed plan to turn the tables on them.

Dollar removes his glasses and polishes them on his shirt. "Have you considered they might be plain old debt collectors?"

I raise my chin. "Unlikely. Why trash the TV and not take it? And Drew seems pretty certain it's not, and I believe him. Mariana did everything by the book. Never took out loans or bought things on credit."

"I'm taking this seriously." Devil leans forward with his elbows on the table. "It's worth a shot. If they are *El Procurador*'s men, they may have information we can squeeze out of them." One side of his face turns up, I suspect the other would, but the scar keeps it in place. "I'd prefer the Satan's Devils handled it, and not just because you've got what they want. Nowadays the FBI has to be more, shall we say, circumspect, on how they get information."

A chuckle goes around the table.

"There won't be much left," Drummer promises.

No, there won't. That's my kid they're after. *My kid?* It's at that point I realise just exactly how much I'm invested in

Mariana's brother, as well as the woman herself. It prompts me to say, "The priority is keeping Drew safe."

"We'll all be there, Brother," Drummer promises with a snarl. His expression questioning why I should think anything less.

Receiving chin lifts from all my brothers, silent promises of support, I start to feel more positive. *We will pull this off.* "When?"

"That's the six-million-dollar question. Sorry, Brothers, but we'll have to give Drew a tail from now on, not knowing when or where they'll try to take him. We don't change anything, don't want to draw suspicion. Prospect will drive with him as normal. No extra shit like escorting him to the door."

I frown, thinking. "He's got football practice, hasn't he? If they're watching him, I reckon that's when they'll try to take him. Less people around than when school lets out."

"Good point, Mouse. That's when I'd make a move. Normally he gets collected, but he's unprotected while he's there. Tomorrow we'll keep out of sight, but we'll be there in force." Prez breaks off, his gaze landing one by one on his men. "All of us."

Now he's the focus of nods of agreement.

There's a flicker of excitement inside me. Of course, this could all be for nothing, but at least we're doing something positive when we get down to thrashing out a plan.

It's toward the end of the meeting when I realise Paladin's been particularly quiet. Drummer raises the gavel to bang it, when our youngest member speaks. "Prez?"

Putting down the gavel again, Prez nods his permission to speak. "What is it?"

Paladin's lips press together, then relax. "I know you haven't found a link with the Herreras. Worries me there might still be one. This *Procurador* fucker might be able to call on favours, even though they're not known for working together. I'm worried about them finding out Drew's on the compound, coming to get him. And taking Jayden too."

"Bit of a stretch there, Brother," Peg scoffs.

Slick, though, is sitting forward. "Hold it right there, Peg. Don't dismiss it lightly. We all know it's only a matter of time before the Herreras come to collect. I, for one, don't want Jayden here if they decide to do so."

The Herreras had been the ones responsible for grooming and raping Jayden two years earlier when she was just fourteen. The men who took part all died at the hands of the Satan's Devils, with the then head of the family's blessing. Old Leonardo Herrera hadn't wanted the crime family to be involved with a child grooming ring. But Leonardo's gone now, and the new head, Javier, has let it be known he wants revenge. We've been given the nod he wants to get his hands on Jayden, take something valuable from us. We're determined that won't happen.

Prez pulls at his beard. "It's the 'don't knows' that concern me. We know someone's coming for the boy, we're already providing cover for Jayden. That's stretching us thin. Jayden's carrying on as normal, going to school, isn't she, Slick?"

"We're doing what we can to keep Jayden safe, Prez. Paladin's her shadow the whole time. Anywhere she fuckin' goes. Takes her to school and back. When she goes out with her friends to the mall or movies." Slick looks worried. Jayden's his pregnant wife Ella's young sister.

Joker grins. "That's what you want to do, isn't it, Paladin? Not let her out of your sight?"

"No, it's not," Paladin snarls at Joker. "Girl's got a right to live a normal life. Think she's getting sick of the sight of me. It's not like we're allowed to be boyfriend and girlfriend. I'm spending all my time watching her, making no other contribution to the club except for the few hours when she's in school."

Slick passes his hand over his bald head. "Jayden's starting to rebel. She likes Paladin's company, sure, but is becoming suffocated. If it's not him, it's another brother keeping an eye on her." He pauses, looks around the table. "I'm grateful for the help. But I worry it's only a matter of time before she, or we, slip up. Don't want to risk leaving her exposed, not when we know the Herreras have the hots for her. If we're going to be protecting Drew too, I agree with you, Prez, could be consuming too much manpower."

Prez pauses before answering Slick, then sighs. "I see your point, Slick, Paladin. I don't trust the Herreras as far as I could fuckin' throw them. We know they've set their sights on taking Jayden."

"Then I want to take her away," Paladin states firmly. "Like we've talked about before. If there's a sniff of trouble, I want to act before it becomes a bad fuckin' smell." Paladin looks eager. Though he was instructed to be hands-off, since the night we rescued Jayden from the fuckers who were raping her and brought her back to the compound, he and the girl have been inseparable. It was how he got his handle, she'd looked at him as though he were her knight in shining armour. The feeling appears to be mutual, wherever she goes, he'll be determined to go too. But not as her club appointed shadow. Once he's away from the compound, they'll both believe the shackles have been removed. But the kid's sixteen now, perhaps it's time. Although where Slick and Ella are concerned, it will be hard to see her as anything but a little girl.

Slick leans forward, his head hitting the table, before he straightens back up. "Much as I hate to say it, I agree with Paladin. Kid's got no chance of a normal life here in Tucson. That's what I'll have to discuss with Ella. You've already agreed with Hellfire, Prez, that if it came to it, they could both go to Colorado. At least there she can act like a teenage girl and not be followed wherever she goes."

"Hellfire's happy," Prez agrees. "Paladin could transfer as a full member, and Hellfire will let Jayden stay with him and his wife."

Seeing Slick watching me, I mouth, *I'm sorry*. It's my fault I might have put the Satan's Devils back on the Herreras' radar. Knowing how I feel about Drew, I can well understand why he wants his wife's young sister to be safe.

Paladin's stare goes to the prez, then to Slick. Slick takes a deep breath. "I'll speak to Ella." His shoulders slump, suggesting that's one conversation he's not looking forward to.

Again Prez raises the gavel, but before he brings it down, he says, "I think it's for the best, Slick. Don't want anyone to sneak up behind us while we're focused on protecting Mouse's kid."

Chapter 29

Mariana

oping I'd slipped the woman sufficient money to more than cover the mailing charges, I was optimistic my letter, with the warning, was now on its way to Drew. When time for dinner approaches, and there's a rapping against my door, I open it to find, as expected, my escort waiting to walk me down to dinner. Tonight I have a spring in my step as I descend the stairs, believing I've got one over on my father. *He wanted me to write to Drew, and I did.* Just didn't extend the invitation he wanted.

I enter the dining room as usual, walking to the seat that I habitually take. As I sit and pull the chair into the table, I'm aware there's a difference about the atmosphere. Feeling eyes burning into me, I look up to see my father's lieutenants are openly smirking. A cold feeling settles inside of me. *What's going on?*

When I glance toward him, my father smiles back, reaches over and pats my hand. From anyone else it would seem a friendly gesture, but I feel like a mouse being pawed by a cat. He's never shown any outward sign of affection before.

"Did you enjoy your day with Miguel, Mariana?" he asks as the first course is set down in front of us.

As his men start dipping spoons into soup, and everything gets back to normal, I question whether I'd been imagining things. I decide to act normally, while staying on my guard. "I enjoyed getting out into the country," I reply, honestly.

Miguel, sitting next to me, leans closer. "We had a lovely time, didn't we?" Without waiting for my response, he grins widely at my father, letting me see his yellowed teeth. I shudder, there's something about this man I really don't like. It's not just his looks. He tries to be pleasant, but my gut tells me it goes no deeper than the surface.

My father's smile broadens. "That's so good to hear. Mariana, I don't know if you realise it, but Miguel, here, is my second-in-command. I trust him."

I nod, not knowing how I'm supposed to respond. The first course is over, the second placed in front of me. I toy with it, knowing I need to fuel my body, but having no appetite in this place. Or, not in this company. When I eventually decide to tackle it, my father glares at me when I put my fork in my right hand. I narrow my eyes in response, and continue eating as I always have done. *I'm not Colombian, and he's not going to change me.*

As I've done every night, once the dessert course is over, I push out my chair, signalling I want someone to take me back to my room. Tonight, no one stands in preparation to escort me.

"Stay seated, please, Mariana. I wish to talk to you," my father says, his hand again snaking out over mine. "Please be patient while I finish my coffee."

With no other option, I settle back again. Coughing when he lights a cigar and puffs smoke into my face. On my other side, Miguel does the same.

I notice I'm now getting snide glances from the men sitting around the table, it dawns on me they all know something I'm not party to. It's unnerving, I don't like it. *Something's going on.* Something I have strong suspicions that I'm not going to like.

I've nothing to do, nothing to occupy my hands. I clasp them in front of me on the table, staring at them. Being kept incarcerated as an illegal immigrant took all the fight out of me, at the mercy of the machinery that rolled on mercilessly. It had made me depressed, I had nothing to fight, no one would listen. Authority on the side of the system and not me.

Here I'm a prisoner with no means of escape, but instead of retreating into the dark depths of my mind, I'm determined to fight. Whatever plans they've got for me, I'll protest. I won't willingly do whatever my father wants me to. If he thinks he's got an obedient daughter, he's soon going to find out differently. My backbone imperceptibly straightens. *I won't give in. Won't give up. Somehow I'll find a way out of here.*

At last the cigars are extinguished, stubs lying dead in ashtrays. My father stands. It's a sign for the others. When he indicates I'm to accompany him, I get to my feet and exit the dining room.

"This way."

With his hand on my arm, I'm led in a different direction and into a room far more utilitarian than the luxury I've seen so far. My father goes to seat himself behind a desk. Miguel, who's accompanied us, leans against a table to the side. I'm directed to a chair in front of the man who sired me.

"I have to thank you, Mariana, for making it easy."

Immediately I know I've made a mistake. My blood runs cold through my veins.

"You took the bait. Oh, you think you're so clever. But we retrieved this." He opens a drawer and slides something out, pushing it over in front of me. *My letter to Drew.* "But don't worry, your brother will get a letter. The one I wrote instead. He'll know his sister hasn't forgotten him."

My eyes widen, and I swallow a couple of times. "How?" I croak out.

Miguel crosses his arms. "The shopkeeper had already been warned. My man retrieved the letter while we were in the café. Child's play." His casual tone makes me want to hit him.

"You threatened the woman?"

"Come now, Mariana. What must you think of me?" My father shakes his head. "There was a reward offered, a nice one. Large enough for us not to worry she would give anything away. There's one happy woman in the village tonight. She earned herself a fortune."

Proving I'm a bad judge of character. "Drew won't believe it, if you sent that letter you tried to make me sign. He knows what you are," I tell him bluntly.

There's that chilling smile again. "Oh, that doesn't matter. We know where *Andrew* lives." He taps the address on the envelope.

But he doesn't. *He's with Tse, isn't he?* Or is my brother alone and unprotected? Not wanting to give any suggestion that I'm not expecting Drew to be living at the trailer park, or that when they find him gone, I'll know where he is, I put my hands over my face, partly to hide my expression, and partly to remonstrate with myself that while I thought I was being clever, I'd fallen into their trap. *How could I have been so stupid?*

When I feel composed, I look up. "He won't come."

"He won't have a choice," Miguel speaks for the first time. "If he thinks you are in danger, he'll come."

He might try. I wouldn't put it past him. A teenage boy over-confident in his abilities to deal with men. *Tse won't let him.*

"I don't know why you're so interested in a boy you've never met. Never knew existed," I say with spirit. "Leave him alone. He's getting a good education and has the chance of a good life in the States. If you care for him as a father, you'll know he's in the best place. He's an American citizen."

Leaning on his desk, my father snarls, "He's my son. He should be with me. He's my heir." He waves his hand around him. "Everything I have built up will be his one day. He deserves to learn of his heritage."

My eyes widen, then I scoff. "Drew wouldn't want to be involved in anything you're offering."

Miguel steps forward, leans his hands on my father's desk and turns his head in my direction. He laughs. "A fifteen-year-old boy? We've got things to tempt him. Women who'd do anything for him, and who he can do anything to. Alcohol, drugs, money. Yeah, what kid would turn down all that?"

The picture he's painting is shocking. My mouth opens and shuts, then I spit out, "Drew wouldn't be tempted. He's a good kid."

My father snorts. "He's my son. My blood. He'll take after me."

I feel faint, the Drew I know wouldn't be bribed by such disgusting things, would he? I've never seen a sign of the cruelty inherent in my father.

"He'll be a prince in my kingdom. Wealth beyond his wildest dreams, anything will be his for the asking. He was born to this role; he'll take to it."

He's placing doubts in my mind. But if I can speak to the boy that I raised, maybe I can convince him to refuse temptation. I won't allow him to accept the degeneracy that's on offer. I purse my lips as my thoughts firm up. *I can make Drew see reason.*

"Now, dear daughter. You've fulfilled your purpose. I *will* have Andrew here, and I *will* groom him as my successor. A few days enjoying the good life, and he'll forget all about you and his American ways."

He won't, will he? Of course he won't. I lean forwards. "You don't know him like I do. He's a good kid. He won't be taken in by you, or what you're offering. When I speak to him, I'll tell him exactly the type of person you are."

"Which is why," Miguel interjects, "you won't be allowed anywhere near him."

"I'm afraid," my father puts in, "your time of enjoying my hospitality here is coming to an end."

Are they going to kill me? My jaw drops open in horror.

"I had several ideas what to do with you. You see, I hate any commodity being wasted. Don't try to appeal to me. I never wanted a daughter, thought you were a waste of space from the moment you came out of your mother's womb. But now you're grown, I may be able to make use of you."

My determination not to give into him is hard to maintain. But I don't plead, I don't beg. Even if I did, I'd be wasting my breath. All I can do is go with the flow, and hope there's an opportunity for escape. At least a chance to see Drew and warn him.

His fingers tap on the desk. "I had several ideas what to do with you, but Miguel here, well, I have a lot of respect for him. He offered to take you off my hands, and as my thanks to him, I'm inclined to accept."

"I'm not something you can hand over to anyone you want." My cheeks redden with anger.

Still tapping the desk, he looks across to Miguel. "Show her the hospitality we offer to *putas* like her," my father suggests. "I think she's gotten too used to the accommodation we provided up to now."

I focus on one word. The word the guard at the detention centre had used. The word that upsets me so much, being so far from the truth. "I'm no whore." My cheeks blaze, my eyes go wide as I wonder exactly what they intend to do.

My outburst lands me a sharp look from my father. Then he bursts out laughing. "Don't tell me you're a virgin?" When I don't reply, he reads the answer on my face, and laughs. "Oh, this is priceless. Miguel might give you more to think about."

Miguel nods vigorously, a lecherous leer on his face. "Oh, I know exactly what I'm going to do with her. That's she's untouched? Yes, that gives me more ideas. I've got a few ways to make her start thinking about changing her behaviour and learning respect."

They then have an exchange in rapid fire Spanish which I'm unable to understand. I try to sit tall, lock my shoulders in place, determined not to show my fear. Detention in the US broke me; I was fighting an impossible enemy with no face. Here I'm determined to survive. Breaking me is exactly what they intend, and whatever they do, I'm not going to give my father that satisfaction.

When I'm told to stand, I do, my head held high. I spare one look of disdain for the man whose genes I carry, then follow Miguel out of the room.

From what they'd said, I wasn't expecting them to take me upstairs to the bedroom I'd been staying in up to now. No, it would be somewhere far less comfortable. *As long as it's not in Miguel's bed,* I shudder at the thought as I'm led across the elegant entrance hall. *Could I remain aloof if he raped me? Took what I wasn't prepared to give?* Remembering the damage I'd done to the guard's face, I'm determined I won't give in easily.

His hand on my shoulder brings me to a halt in front of a curtain. He pulls it back, exposing a doorway. From his pocket, he takes out a key and opens it. There are stone steps leading down. The elaborate decoration of the house hasn't extended to here; the walls are plain brick. The stairs bare. Wherever they lead to, it doesn't look inviting.

CHAPTER 30

Mouse

Everyone in position?" Drummer's voice sounds loud in my ear. He made Devil get transmitter/receiver devices that fit into your ear and which we're now all wearing.

One by one my brothers respond. I keep my eyes fixed on Drew, my heart warming and my doubts somewhat assuaged by the thought of the amount of backup I've got. Not wearing our cuts, we're scattered around various parts of the football field. All entrances are covered. The changing rooms too, Joker having volunteered to dress up as a janitor.

Blade's at my back, Sam and Sophie sitting beside us. We look like any other parents come to watch their kid practise. Which is what I feel like. *Drew's mine.*

Drew makes a good run, I zip my mouth closed, cheering on a random boy who's just tackled him, not wanting to draw attention to myself, or who I'm there for.

Drew goes to sit on the bench and a teammate takes his place. Drummer's sitting right behind him. *He's safe.*

My leg keeps bouncing as my eyes constantly search left and right, trying to spy any suspicious characters. I want, need, Drew to be approached. I want those men taken. Then we can question them, hopefully being able to follow a chain which will give away Mariana's location. Or at least her father's, but I know she'll be with him. My gut churns as I think he might have already hurt her. *He's using her as bait for Drew. Until he's got the boy, he has to keep her safe. Doesn't he?*

"We'll get them, Mouse," Blade reassures me out of the side of his mouth. "When the kids are packing up, that's when they'll make their approach." We've discussed it. They wouldn't snatch him off the field. "Don't draw attention to yourself. We'll all saunter down as though we're just picking up our kids from practice."

I might not have been at the sharp end as much as others, but I'm not going to do anything to jeopardise our mission. *My mission. To save my kid.* "I won't fuck up, Blade," I answer through gritted teeth.

"He's yours, Brother. Time for holdin' back is now. Later, when we've got them at the compound. That's the time you can let loose."

My eyes widen slightly. "You'll let me lead?"

The enforcer raises his hands. "All yours, Brother."

Half my mind's concentrating on what's going on, the other half is planning what I'm going to do if, as we suspect, the man, or men will attempt to snatch Drew this evening. Yeah, I've got some ideas about making them talk. As I sit, my native blood races.

On the field Drew scores a touchdown. I'm about to leap up when Blade's arm shoots across me. "Chill," he reminds me.

It's hard. I can see the kid's got talent, and I want to cheer him. *Next time,* I tell myself. *There'll be a next time.*

Then practice is over. The coach calls the teams together, stands talking to them for a while. I notice him slapping Drew on the back, probably to congratulate him. *Kid's done well.* I'll be telling him that myself.

"We're on," Blade whispers, standing up and stretching to get the kinks out of his back.

I'm on my feet too. Ah, there's Lady. He's started down. Viper and Bullet have appeared as well. Closer to the boys, following them as they make their way to the changing rooms, are Wraith, Peg and Dollar. Heart and the rest will be waiting out front, just looking like dads come to collect their sons. Beef, Rock, Shooter and Marvel will be hidden at the edge of the parking lot.

Drew emerges from the changing room and goes out to where the cars are waiting just like I told him. He takes out his phone, looks at it, then around at the parked cars as if not seeing who he's looking for. He does good, he walks a little distance away from the others as though to get some privacy, still looking at that darn phone.

I send him a quick text.

Got you covered.

I see him give a quick smile, but never once does he raise his head trying to find us. *Kid trusts us.* One by one the other kids get into cars. The parking lot starts to empty.

What's that? I nudge Blade. A car with its engine idling draws closer to Drew.

Walk back towards the entrance.

Immediately Drew obeys my text. I don't want him to be grabbed and tossed into that vehicle. The distance increases between the car and my ward. Out of the corner of my eye I see Marvel, Rock and Beef approaching from the rear. Shooter's veered off to meet Heart, and they're heading for the side of the car. I nod to Blade. We start moving to position ourselves on the passenger side, and I check to make sure Drummer and Wraith have the front. Unseen by the few remaining kids waiting with the coach, Prez has his gun in his hand and is pointing it at the windshield.

Heart wrenches open the door, his own gun pointing inside. I pull the passenger door more or less at the same time.

Two Hispanic faces look at us in dismay.

"What are you doing?" one says, while the other swears in Spanish.

"Out," I tell them, gesturing with my gun.

"We're here to pick up my nephew."

"Oh?" I ask conversationally. "Which one would he be then?"

His eyes flick to Drew, then past him. He points... to a kid who at that moment starts waving at another car which has just arrived.

"Seems *your nephew* doesn't need a ride after all. So we've got time for a conversation. Out." I wave my gun again; Blade having positioned his body to prevent anyone seeing it.

At that point the crash truck draws up alongside. Our operation proceeds to go down like a knife through butter. Without anyone else having seen, we've got them zip tied and in the back, fast. Protests coming out of their mouth, but duct tape soon quiets them.

As Matt and Peg zoom out of the car park, Blade tilts his head to one side. "Sure that's them, Brother?"

"I'm sure." There's no doubt in my mind. They were targeting Drew. If we hadn't been here, they could easily have snatched him.

"Just got to get them to admit it." Blade, like me, is staring after the truck.

Yeah. We have. I might have an idea how to do it. Slapping him on the back, I tell him, "Don't start without me." Then I go to my bike. There's a quick detour I want to make before I go back to the compound, it won't take long.

I've seen the store in passing before. A quick word with the assistant and I have what I need, and head home. Parking in my usual spot, I don't go straight to the storeroom, knowing my brothers will have the two men ready and waiting. They'll give me the time I need, Blade's giving me the lead, and we all know anticipation is all part of the preparation. The longer they're kept stewing, the more worried they'll be.

In my suite, I take down the trunk from the top of the wardrobe, brushing the dust off the top. A treasure trove of memories. Reverently reaching in, I take out my grandfather's centuries old flint knife, handed down from generation to generation.

As a youth, I'd been fascinated.

Wide-eyed I stare at the blade my grandfather's holding. "Would it have killed the Spanish? Or the white settlers?"

A gnarled hand ruffles my hair. "Probably more likely used as a hunting knife, my boy."

He was probably right. But it's a wicked-looking knife, and the two Hispanics wouldn't know the history. If it truly hasn't been used in anger before, it's probably going to be now.

I pull out my grandfather's buckskin trousers, fringes down the sides, the ones he would wear at pow-wows. Together with the knife he'd passed them down to me, a reminder of my Navajo heritage. On his deathbed he'd also given me the right to use his face paint patterns and colours.

I stand, moving to the mirror, and bring out the bag of shit I'd purchased. Again my victims aren't going to know the difference between stage face paint and the dyes traditionally used, made from animal, vegetable and minerals. I've bought four colours, the ones that represent our four sacred mountains; blue, white, yellow and black. I grin at myself, then start painting the bottom half of my face yellow. The colour that denotes the heroism of the wearer, which shows he's prepared to fight to the death. In this case, their deaths, not mine. I harden my features, preparing myself. Vowing that before they take their last breaths, they'll be telling me all their secrets. Yellow also reflects the intelligence of the wearer. I'll take my brain over theirs any day.

Removing my shirt, I smother my hands with the black, and press them to my naked chest leaving two hand prints. Though it's not made from powdered charred wood and black earth, I am hoping the markings will still channel energy to me, the wearer.

With the other colours, I paint symbols my grandfather used to wear. Opening my mind to memories as I do so, letting my white blood drain from me.

Paint on, I brush out my long straight black hair, then pull it together at the top of my scalp, twisting it four times, then folding it the same number. Reaching for a strand of the white wool I also purchased, I fasten it into a bun which stands erect from the top of my head. As I prepare my hair in the traditional style, I find myself mellowing. To the Navajo the process is a form of prayer, of meditation. Calm I might be, but that just equates to being more controlled in my quest to harm those who would hurt one of mine.

Remembering once more who I'll be facing, with a smirk, I find a loose eagle's feather in the trunk, and secure it in the top of *tsiiyéél*, the hairstyle unique to the Navajo.

I breathe deep, standing tall. Channelling my inner warrior.

Slipping the knife into my belt, leaving my chest naked, I exit my suite. *Time to get some answers.*

I skirt the clubroom taking a direct route to the storage room. On my way, I pass Drew. He's walking with Matt, talking animatedly, and with some actions, describing the touchdowns he scored.

As I pass, his jaw drops at the sight of me. "Mouse? You look like a Red Indian." Then his face falls, and he hurriedly corrects himself, "You look like, you look…"

"It's alright, Drew." I grin as I pass him. Seems like I'm making the effect I was aiming for.

I push the soundproofed door to the storage room open. Outside there was silence, in here, there's a buzz of conversation. It dies down as I enter.

"Fuckin' hell. It's Chief." Joker's staring at me, nudging Lady on the arm so he turns around, fixing his eyes on me too.

Seeing the two bodies strung up in front of me, I scowl, my expression while not aimed at them is enough to make my brothers part, leaving the way clear so I can get to my targets.

Blade looks me over from head to toe, a grin slowly forming on his face. It's the one he wears when he's anticipating pleasure in the form of blood and torture. He gives me a nod, and steps back. "Over to you, *Chief.*"

Throwing him a quick look that tells him he'll pay for that later, I stalk towards the men hanging by their arms from the overhead beam. My brothers are practiced at this, strung up precisely so their toes only just touch the ground. They'll be feeling the strain on their shoulders already.

They were protesting as I walked in. Their voices quiet as I approach. Two pairs of eyes seem to bulge out of their sockets as they look around the leather clad men, and then back to me.

"We weren't doing anything," one of them says.

"Names," I snap. Not wanting to keep thinking of them as number one and number two.

"Why?"

"So I know what to write on your grave." I'm standing my full height, my *tsiiyéél* giving me another couple of inches. My voice is deep, a hint of a Navajo accent.

Blade growls when they don't immediately answer. It prompts a response from the first one.

"I'm Castro. This is Rodriguez."

I step up. Castro is shorter than me by about a foot. Even strung up I can reach his head easily. I take the flint knife out of my belt, noticing Blade's eyes flaring with interest. I take hold of Castro's thick curly hair, bunching it in my hand and pulling it back from his forehead.

"Hey," Blade's voice is full of wonder. "You gonna scalp him, Chief? Thought you only did that when they're dead."

"That's more common," I say coldly, my voice devoid of any emotion. "Yet quite effective alive, don't you think?"

Castro's eyes are flickering wildly. Rolling up as though to look at my knife, then into my face to see whether I'm serious.

While a lot of North American tribes used to practice the art on their enemies, it wasn't particularly followed by either Apache or Navajo. In fact, the South Americans would be more familiar with the practice. Mexicans were paid for each scalp of an Apache they collected. But a history lesson isn't what I'm about here.

Without speaking, I press the tip of the blade in just above Castro's hairline, and trace it lightly in a semi-circle around where I would make my first cut, should I want to do so.

Castro squeals like a stuck pig. *Fuck.* If that's his reaction and I haven't done anything, what's he going to do if I really start to sever his scalp?

"Heads bleed really badly, Chief."

"You've got the tarp down," I reply to Blade. My eyes never moving from my victim. "Now, tell me what you wanted with my boy."

"Your boy?"

The sharp tip of the flint presses in. "Andrew De Souza. And don't think you can kid me into believing you weren't there for him. Won't work. Lie and I'll start cutting."

Castro shuts his mouth, and closes his eyes, seeming to wait for me to begin.

"May I?" Blade steps up alongside, pulling out one of his knives, and waving it at Rodriguez. "You could teach me a thing or two, Chief. Never scalped a man before. This blade do the job?"

I feel my lips twitch, momentarily it's hard to maintain my warrior expression as I look at his knife and give what I hope is a serious and considered nod. Fuck knows whether it would work. The enforcer would know better than me. I notice the room has gone silent, brothers pushing closer to watch. *As if I really know what I'm doing.* All my knowledge comes from playing with the boys on the Rez, kids messing about. But I think there's some truth in the playacting we'd done.

"You gonna tell me who paid you? Who you were working for?"

"Tell him," Rodriguez cries out. Seems he's more afraid of Blade than Castro is of me. Well, I don't blame him. When Blade wears his enforcer's face, there's not an ounce of compassion in him.

Castro tries to pull back, but I've got a firm grip on his hair. "Don't say anything," he calls out. "Remember what will happen to us."

"Chief?" I suppress a smile, realising Drummer's tagged the handle too, and hope it's only temporary. "They're both illegal. We've taken their documents. Reckon they'll be sneaking back over the border."

"Going back to your master? Like whipped dogs?" I snarl at Castro. While he doesn't answer, the spark in his eye tells me I'm right.

"You work for *El Procurador*," Blade tells them. Then gives a sideways glance to me. "We know that answer, Chief. Now, how do I do this?" The enforcer might be using a conversational tone, but when Rodriguez squeaks I realise Blade has pressed the tip of his knife into his skin.

I take over again. "I want to know where *El Procurador* holes up. Tell me and maybe you'll keep your scalps."

Castro spits in my face. I wipe it away with the hand holding the knife. Yellow paint comes off with it. As I stare at the colour on my hand, seeing it gives me strength.

My captive answers, "He'll do worse than that."

"Worse?" Blade asks casually. "Does anyone survive a scalping, Chief?"

"Not very often. It's rare."

As an acrid smell fills the air, Blade looks down. "Fuckin' pissed himself." He glares at Rodriguez as though offended. Then again to me, "You'll have to talk me through this."

There's no way I can suppress my quick grin in his direction, but it's off my face when I tighten my grip on Castro's hair, and speak directly to him. "Let's get this done. Any time you want me to stop, Castro. Just give me the answers I want." I nod at Blade, seeing I've got his attention. "Press in until you're slicing through skin, then draw your blade in a semi-circular cut, holding the knife slightly sideways so you're separating the scalp from the skull."

"Castro," Rodriguez whines. He kicks out at Blade with his legs, spurring my victim to start fighting too. Brothers step up and quickly have them contained and held steady.

Both our knives are bloody as we cut deep into and under the skin. Rodriguez is crying, then he's screaming.

"What next?" Blade has to raise his voice so I can hear him over the din.

"Now do the same to the other side." I use the flint knife, wondering whether it's ever been used for a job such as this before.

"Done, next?" A glance at Blade's face shows he's grinning widely, not paying attention to Rodriguez's cries.

"Next you take a good hold on the hair, and pull." I tighten my grip as I'm talking, wondering whether I've got the guts to do this, then remember Mariana, and my promise to her and her brother. That I'd get her back, and keep Drew safe.

"Don't do it! Please God, stop. I'll tell you." It's Rodriguez who screams out, which doesn't surprise me.

"All the details. Location. Manpower. Access." Drummer snaps the words out as he steps up beside me, meeting my eyes and sheepishly grinning as he brandishes paper and pen.

"At least record this shit," I suggest, showing my disdain for the old-fashioned approach.

Wraith holds up his phone. "On it, Brother."

After a while Castro joins in, driven to correct some of Rodriguez's assumptions. To my amusement they almost have an argument about the best access routes. Seems now they've started they can't tell us enough. At last their voices fade. They've given us everything. Even down to the fact they knew Drew was *El Procurador*'s son, and how important he was to him.

Blade looks at me. "Gonna let me have some fun now?"

"Hold on a moment, Blade. I've got one more thing to ask." Drummer stands with his arms folded, his pen and paper put down. "The Herreras. You got links to them?"

Castro and Rodriguez glance at each other, then must realise their only chance is not holding back. "*El Procurador* pulled in some favours. Herreras let us use their route to get us over the border."

"And what favour did *El Procurador* promise them?"

"Something to do with a motorcycle club."

Drummer questions them again, but they don't know any more. They're grunts. They probably wouldn't have been privy to much more than that. I exchange a quick look with Drummer. Maybe Paladin was right to be worried. Can't take the chance.

Then Blade brings my attention back to what we're here for, when he whines, "Now, please, Chief?"

I harden my heart, blacken my soul, and tell him, "Yes."

The scalp has been loosened, with the hair held firmly and yanked hard, the circle of flesh is torn from the skull. In truth, both Blade and I have only gone for a circle of about five inches in diameter, but enough to scar them for life.

I hold my trophy in front of Castro, tears of pain are streaming down his cheeks. Blade does the same to Rodriguez who throws up, my brother having jumped back to avoid the vomit.

"What do you want to do with them, Chief? If we let them go, they'll talk."

They're would-be kidnappers. Paid to take a teenager out of his country and deliver him to a man known for his cruelty. If I let them go, word will reach Mariana's father. He might even take out his rage on her. Certainly send others to take Drew. Killing them would give us more time.

As if he knows my decision has been made, Drummer places his hand on my shoulder. Blade glances over and raises his chin, I interpret this time he means for me to follow his lead. I'm just a few seconds behind and cutting Castro's throat as the blood spatter from Rodriguez mingles with the paint on my body.

"I'll get the prospects to clean up."

"I'll supervise," Peg suggests.

"Chief. Suggest you go get showered." Blade's chuckling as the blood trickles down my bare chest. I glare, noticing there's not a spot on him.

The metallic smell of the blood, the air tinged with acrid fumes from the urine and vomit, turns my stomach. I need to get out of here. Not the first man I've killed, but the first I've tortured. Now it's done, I know I'll have to find a way to live with myself. *Didn't know I had it in me. Did what I had to, to save Mariana.* My brothers seem to know I need space as once again they part to allow me to get out. In the fresh air, I lean over, my hands on my knees, taking deep breaths. It doesn't help.

Moving out of sight behind the storage room, I let the bile and vomit spew from my mouth, vaguely aware of another man joining me doing the same.

When at last my gut is empty, I stand, wiping my mouth. Blade's alongside me, a handkerchief in his hand dabbing at his lips. He catches my eye. One corner of his mouth turns up, and he shakes his head. "That was some sick shit in there, Brother. Remind me never to upset you. Fuck knows what other things you've got up your sleeve."

That it gets to him too, for some reason makes me feel better. I straighten, look up at the cloudless sky, and feel my lips curving. Preparing to leave, I slap him on the back. "Pray you never find out, Brother."

I start to turn away when he stops me. "Just one question, Chief. What are you going to do with your trophies?"

When I cock my eye at him, his face almost splits in half. "The scalps. You going to dry and frame them or something? Isn't that what you Indians do?"

I shove him in the chest, but that doesn't stop his laughing. I push him again. Each time he rocks back on his heels, still chuckling. It's not long before I'm joining in.

CHAPTER 31

Mariana

I estimate it's been about a week since Miguel led me along a dark, dismal passageway, through a larger room almost devoid of furniture, then down another equally depressing corridor, but it's easy to lose sense of time, and it feels so much longer.

Eyes widening in disbelief and horror as he led me into a larger area, past cage like cells to each side occupied by women and young girls, several little more than children. Weeping and wailing came from some, in other cells they sat quiet, looking resigned. A couple of the women looked catatonic, one rocking back and forth on her heels. In each cell were two dirty mattresses and a bucket in the corner. It smelt of fear, of human waste and dampness. I could see moisture dripping down the walls. This place wasn't healthy, the women held for no good reason.

As I lie on the filthy mattress that has become mine, in a cell I have the privilege of not having to share, I think back to the first day I was brought here. Miguel's explanation, delivered in a business-like tone, had chilled me then, the memory now is no less frightening.

"For most, this is only a temporary stop off. They'll be sold as slaves and shipped out soon. Your father is a brilliant man; he knows how to make extra income on top of the slave fee. You'll see in time."

He'd stopped in front of an empty cell and had pushed me inside. I tried to hold onto the bars to stop myself being thrown in, but his fist to my back had me off-balance and I stumbled, falling to my knees. The door slammed shut behind me, the iron clang causing a ring to echo around.

"I haven't quite decided yet what to do with you. I could use more, shall we say, personal methods to break you? Hmm. Are you worth the bother, I wonder? Maybe if I leave you here, you'll be begging to come to me. We'll see. Just understand, your father has washed his hands of you. Your fate is mine to determine. There's no one here you can appeal to."

I didn't turn to look at him, didn't give him the satisfaction of seeing my fear. When cooped up in that detention centre I thought I had known what hopelessness was, but at least there I had the hope that eventually I'd be free, even if it wasn't in a country of my choice. Now any chance of a future where I'm able to live a life of my choice is fast disappearing like light down a tunnel.

He'd walked away to the symphony of cries and wailing around me, pleas that rang out unanswered. I'd always known my father was evil. It was at that point I realised how malevolent and vengeful he really is. *And I've put Drew in his sights. How could I have been so damn stupid?* My only excuse that I've never come up against men like this before, so manipulative, so powerful. So immoral.

A week or so I've been in this filthy place. I'd found it difficult to eat in my father's presence, but at least what was put in front of me was gourmet food. Here it's barely edible, just a substance to keep the women, of whom I'm now one of their number, alive, and just barely.

There's a number of different languages spoken, some speak English. There's another American woman, who was snatched off the street. She's in the cell a few doors down from me, our only communication is a few sentences we can call out. I'd spoken to her when I heard her crying fruitlessly for help in

English. She'd come to Colombia backpacking, wanting to explore this beautiful country, believing the worst of its troubles behind it now. She found she was mistaken when she'd been seized. She didn't think it was by *El Procurador's* men, as she didn't even need the Spanish she could speak, money changing hands showed she'd been quickly sold on. That's when she ended up here.

There's a regular change in women. My English-speaking friend went after a few days. Some women stayed a night, some had been here longer than I.

Fear taints the atmosphere, horror at the current situation, terror at what may lie ahead. It's hard not to be affected. While I may not understand all the languages, sounds of distress are universal. I try to stay strong. Try to keep the fight within me. But it's hard.

Occasionally men come into the cells and rape the women. I tried to turn away when one used a pretty young girl next door. He was hurting her, hammering into her tiny body. Her screams annoyed him, so he clamped a hand over her mouth. Her eyes had turned my way, full of pleading. Tears rolled down my face, I was unable to help, my own cries begging him to stop were ineffectual. Her fear, her pain, her utter desolation when he at last got off. Presumably because I'm my father's daughter, they leave me alone. *For now.*

The next day they come for me. I don't know what to expect, don't like to think what might lie ahead as an armed guard waves me out and another steps into line behind me. I'm taken back to the room I walked through before on my way to the corridor of locked up women.

Miguel's standing in the middle of the room, he smiles when he sees me. "Ah, Señorita De Souza. Mariana. I'm so pleased to see you again."

I deign not to answer. If I'd ever wanted to be polite, my manners have been knocked out of me by the way I've been treated.

His nose wrinkles. "A shower first, I think. And a change of clothes. Then we'll talk." He nods to my guards. One takes my arm and leads me off to a short hallway. There's a bathroom without a lock on it. Set out inside is a towel, shampoo and soap. A pile of fresh clothing is laid on a chair.

I could refuse. Where would that get me? Would they force me into the shower themselves? The idea of clean water, clean clothes is sufficient to tempt me. With one eye on the lockless door, I strip quickly and jump under the water, relishing the feeling of being able to get clean again. I waste no time, I soon have my hair and body washed and dried, though my hair is left damp and hanging.

There's a pair of jeans and a tee shirt, fairly plain, but fresh. I dress quickly, still worrying about being disturbed. *What happens now?*

"Ah, that's better." Miguel nods approvingly as I walk back to join him. "Now you're going to find out how brilliant your father is. How he gets double profits on the slaves he sells."

Am I to be sold as a slave?

"You're lucky. You'll get to go back to the US," he continues.

For a moment, my heart leaps. *I'm going home?* Then doubt fills me. *How could I go back if my father's bringing Drew here?* I could never desert him. *But he's an American citizen. Maybe I could get the authorities involved. Tse could help me…* Then I think about myself. It's a trick, it has to be. They wouldn't be letting me go that easily.

Seeing the doubt on my face, he smiles in what is probably supposed to be a reassuring way. "Yes, back to the United States, Mariana. I'll be accompanying you to the border."

I'm suspicious. "How will I cross it?"

He laughs. "Oh, we've got a route in, don't worry your pretty little head about that, *querida*. We'll get you in."

"Why are you letting me go home?" There's something decidedly wrong with this scenario.

Now he shrugs. "Your father and you haven't exactly got on. You've been corrupted by the Americans, not good material for a Colombian wife. He'll have his son, and be rid of a troublesome daughter."

It still doesn't add up. But I can fight for Drew. Tse will fight with me. While I want to stay here and be with my brother, we'd both end up trapped. If they're taking me back to the States, perhaps that's for the best. I know I don't have a choice, so rather than protesting, maybe it's best to go along with it.

"When are we going?" I don't want to stay in Colombia any longer than I have to.

"Soon. Very soon." His face grows serious as he nods at a man off to one side. A man I can't see clearly, though he seems to be carrying something in his hands. "We just need you to do something for us first."

My misgivings grow. What could they possibly want from me? "If you're bringing Drew here, I want to stay and see him." It dawns on me I've been imprisoned a week, and a lot might have happened in that time. "Is he already here? Can I talk to him?"

"Whether he is or not is nothing to do with you."

Perhaps they haven't got to him. Maybe if I go back, I can find him and stop him. Get Tse to protect him...

The man behind me comes into sight, he's carrying a tub in his hands. Miguel takes it from him and brings it over. "All you've got to do is swallow these, *querida*. Then I'll take you over the border."

As I stare at the tub full of latex bundles, I might not have come across them before, but I read the news enough to know exactly what they are. I shudder, my eyes open wide, my body starts to sweat. "No." There's no way on earth I'll be helping them smuggle drugs over the border.

Miguel waves the box in front of me. "A little uncomfortable, I admit. But it will soon be over, and you'll be free. Well, as long as you stay away from immigration, and don't bring any attention to us if we're stopped."

"I won't smuggle drugs for you."

"Then you won't be going home," he threatens.

"No." I won't do this. Whatever that stuff is, there are enough drug problems in the US without me adding to it. However much he emphasises the incentive. Trying to summon up every argument, I suggest, "One of them might burst…"

"It might," he says, unsympathetically. "Which would be a shame, but we'd still have the rest."

"I could *die*." I'm feeling nauseous at just the thought.

"You could," he replies conversationally. "But we'd still have the drugs."

"Does my father know?" I know he's a monster, I know we'd never have a father/daughter relationship. But still…

"It was his idea." Miguel's dismissiveness takes my last hope away.

"No," I say, again.

But they're ready for that. Miguel moves quickly, his hands on my face, his thumbs either side of my jaw, stopping me from closing my mouth. The other man steps forward, placing a contraption in between my teeth, turning a screw to force my mouth wider. Miguel steps back, and takes something off a table.

"This will make it easier." He squirts a liquid down the back of my throat which I can immediately feel going numb. "It's an anaesthetic, and there's oil in it. It will be easier for you to swallow these down."

I try to shake my head, but I can't spit, can't do anything. Miguel stands and watches, his hand goes to his crotch. "You know, looking like that? It's hard for me to resist putting my cock in there."

If it was possible to be more horrified, his threat would do it.

"Tell you what, I'll remove the dental gag so you can swallow. But if you refuse, it's going back on. I, and the guards, will all mouth fuck you."

"Why stop there?" the other man mumbles, his mouth opening to show what teeth he has are yellowed and rotten. I keep my eyes above his groin, not wanting to imagine what diseases he harbours down there.

"You going to be a good girl?" Miguel asks, casually. His expectant expression shows he really doesn't mind one way or the other.

"Nice tits." His companion palms my breast, squeezing it so tightly it brings tears to my eyes. "Shame to take the gag off and waste it."

"Last chance." Miguel's hands start going to his fly. "*Querida*, I really don't mind how we do it. There are benefits for me if you continue to refuse."

A glance shows the other man already has his dick in his hands. He's looking eager. *I can't, I just can't.* They'll find some way to force me.

"How many men using that mouth will it take to convince you, *querida*? I've got a compound full of volunteers…"

I don't know what sign to give. A nod? Would that encourage him or correctly inform him I'll swallow the damn things rather than be molested? A shake? Would he think I meant I was refusing to do what he wants? In the end, I settle for as loud a sound as I can make with my mouth open. "Ahhhh."

His hand settles on my head and ruffles my hair as he unscrews the gag. "Good girl. But a little disappointing."

There must be a hundred filled condoms in that tub. Miguel first drops them into a bucket of water, picking up the ones that float. A couple have sunk. "See," he murmurs, "how good I am to you. If they don't float, they're not properly packed."

I'm blown away by his concern.

As he approaches me with the first one in his hands, I panic, knowing I can't do this. It's too big to swallow… I have trouble even getting tablets down. His fingers push it in, I gag, spitting it out. Ready for me he catches it, pushes it back, this time forcing my mouth closed and pinching my nose at the same time. My cheeks burn as I struggle to breathe. *I have to swallow.* I can't.

"Swallow, *puta*. Or I'll give you something else to swallow. Something that might slip down more easily."

My nostrils try to suck in air. I don't want to, but his threat has me trying to work my thankfully numb throat. The oil probably does smooth the way, at last the filled latex has gone down.

Miguel grins. "Now that wasn't so hard, was it?"

I turn away, gagging, feeling a lump in my chest.

"Don't you dare throw up, *puta*." His tone is warning. After no more than a second, his hand's there with the next one.

I think I'm going slightly insane. Each one I swallow gets easier, my brain sees each as another nail in my coffin. I'm filled with fear, in my mind I feel them burst and start leaking, poison leaching out into my veins. One by one he passes them to me. After I've had as many as I think I can possibly take, I squeeze my lips together shaking my head.

"Oh, we're only half way through. Open up." His hand comes menacingly close to my jaw.

With a whimper, I part my mouth once again. *America. I'm going back to America.* I'll find Tse, hopefully Drew… *I can do this.*

As if he can read my mind, his hand hovers before putting the next packet of drugs in my mouth. "Of course, you won't be going back to your old life. You, my dear Mariana, will be sold as a slave. Someone as pretty as you will attract good money, your virginity will mean top dollar for us. You see what I told you? Double profits. First from the drugs, then from selling you. Excellent plan, you have to agree." His chest puffs in conceit.

My plans to save Drew shatter. *Me? A slave?* I stare, open mouthed. Trying to envisage such a future. Realising the reference to my looks and my untouched status means he's omitted a word. *Sex. Sex slave.* I can't even imagine what depravities a woman whose man feels he owns her could put her through. Hell, sex. I've seen enough of that these past few days. The face of the woman in the cell next to me will always haunt me, and the knowledge that these men see nothing wrong in taking and using women as they want.

His lips are still curved; he gives me time to process what's going through my head. *What the hell can I do? I've got a stomach full of drugs.* For a moment, I hope I really can feel one bursting. The future he's painting is beyond bleak. *I'd rather die. You'll be back in the US.* I try to think positively to stop myself just giving up. *There I might have a chance of escape.*

"Open now. I've been counting. Sixty down, sixty to go. Come on, I haven't got all day. Our transport is waiting."

"No. No more." If at the end of all this I'll be facing a fate worse than death, I'll refuse to cooperate anymore.

"Yes. You will. We'll get a tidy sum for you. You told your father you were untouched. First the money from the drugs, then the fee for a virgin slave. I was never going to rape you. Your purity has far greater value. But I could still mouth fuck you. Don't think I won't."

My stomach feels too full. The anaesthetic is wearing off and my throat feels bruised and sore. My body drips with sweat, my head pounds, and I'm trembling. "Please, no…" I start to beg. "No more. I can't…"

"You really are a stuck up *puta*, aren't you?" Miguel looks amused as he exchanges a glance with the other man. "You think you've got a choice?" Then he snaps, "Hold her."

Chapter 32

Mouse

My hair once more tied back in a ponytail held by my usual leather thong, my skin clean of paint and blood, I join my brothers around the table.

"Ch…" Shooter opens his mouth.

I point my index finger at him. "You can stop that shit right there."

A cough brings my attention to the prez who seems to be trying to smother a laugh. I glare at him, but it does no good. "Think you picked up a new handle." He chuckles.

"Fuck me, Chief. You scared the shit out of me." Road's sitting back, his arms folded. "Channelled your inner Indian, I see."

"Native American," I snarl. Now I'm pointing at him. "I might have developed a fondness for scalping. I suggest you don't push me."

"Can I see it?" Blade asks. Holding out his hand. I know what he's asking for. Taking my now cleaned knife out of my belt, I slide it across the table. "Nice." He feels the edge. "This a real scalping knife?"

"All purpose," I explain. "My people made such weapons out of whatever they could find that they could sharpen. Flint works well."

"Old?"

"The blade, yes. A few hundred years. Probably had a new handle or two in that time."

"Okay. Now we've discussed scalpin' implements, can we get down to business?" Yeah, that's the prez. He will allow us a few minutes, but then remind us why we're there. "You got any more you want to say, or can I call in Devil?"

"Yeah." Slick raises his hand, "Paladin and I have had a discussion with Ella and Jayden." He breaks off, his head shaking as if he hardly wants to get his next words out. "They reluctantly agreed it's safer for Jayden to leave."

I notice Paladin is nodding. I'm surprised he doesn't look as ecstatic as I'd expected him to. While here, he had to wait until Jayden was eighteen, but the age of consent is a year earlier in Colorado. Got to admire the kid for biding his time and waiting. I expect there were a few bets placed that he'd break and move on to someone else. There's no doubt in my mind that he hasn't.

"I'll speak to Hellfire," Drummer starts with a nod. "Can't argue with the decision you've come to."

"Hey, does that mean Paladin can claim her in a few months?" Marvel looks like he's going to fist bump the man beside him, but Paladin ignores him, his eyes shoot to Slick's instead.

Drummer is the one who answers. "The fuckin' age of consent isn't why she's going to Colorado. Hellfire and his wife have a family house. Think their kids have grown and left home now, but they'll know what a teenager needs. Paladin will bunk down in their clubhouse." His glare stops any further comment like Marvel's being raised. "Red's got a rep as a manwhore. Lost is still finding his way. Snatcher, well, is Snatcher. Hellfire's the best to give her a new home. I, for one, am grateful to Paladin." After the prez gives his quick assessment of the presidents of the other chapters, a summation no one would be able to object to, his focus is on the young member. "Will be sorry to lose you, Brother. There'll always be a seat for you around the table."

Again Slick raises his hand. "It's not going to be easy for Jayden. Having Paladin with her, as her friend? Well, that might help her adjust. Paladin knows my feelin's."

He doesn't have to say more. I reckon he's put the fear of God in the lad if he oversteps.

"Okay, we sort out the official transfer details later. Don't like losing a member, but we've been prepared for this. Now, let's get Devil in here and back to Mouse's problem. And remember. Devil doesn't need details on how we've learned what we have."

Because it could incriminate us. Devil will be well aware there're two less people walking the earth right now, but he won't want to know the details.

That's confirmed when he walks in and takes the spare seat. Even before he sits, he looks pointedly around. "You've got info. I don't want to hear anything about how you obtained it. Rumour, I'm putting it down to."

Prez shoots his handwritten notes down the table. Not going far enough, Viper gives it a helping hand, the paper passes from brother to brother until it's in Devil's hands. The unscarred side of his face curves. "Christ! You've hit the bloody mother lode. Not bad for a bunch of amateur arseholes."

Blade passes my knife back, grabs his own, spins it and stops it when it's pointing at the Englishman. "I object to the use of the word 'amateur'," he says in all seriousness.

Devil shakes his head as chuckles go around. He holds up his hand. "Your show, Drummer. But I think we need to start planning. Mouse," he waves toward me.

"Chief," Shooter interrupts.

I leap out of my chair, the knife Blade passed back in my hand, and I'm around behind Shooter before he knows what's happening. I tangle my hand in his hair, and pull his head back…

"Shooter! You'd fuckin' deserve it. But I ain't getting blood on this floor. Too damn hard to get off. Mouse. Sit the fuck down."

"Has he pissed himself?" Rock inquires.

"'Course I haven't fucking…"

"*Shut up!*" Prez yells. Then his voice goes back to normal volume. "Devil, excuse this bunch of *arseholes*." His use of the English word and the emphasis he puts on it has us in stitches again. Until we catch sight of his face. Suddenly I find I'm far more interested in what Devil, sitting at the other end of the table, has to say.

Devil continues as though such an interruption is normal in his life. "I've got a team ready to go, Drummer. Twelve men. And a plane. You know who's coming with?"

"There'll be six of us. Mouse, obviously. Myself. Blade, Viper, Marvel and Dollar." Prez looks around at each of the men named. They're all nodding their heads, fulfilling the promise they made to me in Los Angeles. I'm filled with emotion for my brothers.

Truth is, taking a life like I had, had caused me some regret. I'd stood in the shower watching another man's blood run down the drain, wondering what I'd turned into. Coming into church, my doubts had been swept away by the jokes and now the commitment of the men around me.

Rock's putting up his hand, Beef, after a silent exchange between them, raises his too. "Want us?" they both offer at once.

Prez goes to answer, but Devil gets in first. "Eighteen ought to be plenty."

A plan had been formulating in my head. "Devil, Prez. Mind if I say something?"

Prez opens his hands wide, Devil just dips his head. "The way they were describing the compound. It sounds hard to get out of, but not necessarily to get into. The security seems to be on the inside to prevent escape. They're relying on their location and secrecy to guard the compound. Sure, there's an armed guard on the wall by the gate, but that sounds about all."

"Mouse has got a point," Devil agrees. "Don't want to underestimate *El Procurador*, but it could be his men are more warders than fighters. More used to controlling women they hold there, than heading off a direct attack."

"As you say," Prez's eyes have narrowed, "but we can't afford to miscalculate. Our information could be misleading."

Devil nods, then focuses on me. "You were saying, Mouse?"

He's right, I haven't finished. "I've got an idea about how we can deal with the numbers."

Even those not going lean forward interested and let me proceed without interruption while I explain what's on my mind. When I finish, Prez nods approvingly. "We'll reassess when we get there. But I like it. I like it a lot." He breaks off, an unusual smile comes to his face. "If it works, Mouse, think you might be stuck with a new handle."

"Chief! Fuckin' called it."

It's only Peg's firm hand holding my arm that keeps me in my seat. And Shooter's scalp in place.

After the meeting, I go to find Drew. He's retreated to his suite next to mine, and is sprawled out on the bed doing his homework. He looks up, his face worried, when he sees me leaning against the door frame.

"Shouldn't you be in bed?" I ask. It's going on eleven o'clock.

He shoots me a look only a teenager can master, then jerks his chin down to his work. "Need to hand this in tomorrow."

Can't fault him for his diligence. "When you're finished…"

"I am." He puts down his pen. "Just been checking it over."

"Need a word." Walking across, I move some papers out of the way, and sit down on the bed, cross-legged.

"Yeah, I'm sorry."

"Sorry?"

He's mumbling, looking down. "What I called you. Didn't mean to be disrespectful."

I snort, realising he's referring to when he'd seen me going down to the storeroom earlier. "Hey, Buddy. That was the effect I was going for, okay? You've spent time on the Rez. You know today's Navajo aren't any different from anyone else. But sometimes it can be effective to pretend. To fulfil another's expectation. To play on their fears. You with me?"

"Did it work?" he asks eagerly. "What about the men who tried to take me?"

"Yeah, it did." I grin. "Questioned them. Got answers. Sent them on their way." I don't add they've been dispatched with a one-way ticket to meet Satan.

His eyes widen. "Fucking pussies. They gave all the info up? Just because you had war paint on?"

I punch his arm lightly. "Worked on the white folks, didn't it? Scared the shit out of the settlers when they saw us all dressed up."

He giggles, like he's meant to.

I chuckle too, then grow serious. "You okay, Drew? After today?" I worry he might have been scared and that being in danger might have scarred him.

"Fuck, yeah, Mouse. With all the brothers there? I knew nothing could go wrong. You all had my back."

Not for the first time, I worry about him starting swearing, but don't have it in me to admonish him now. I give him a nod, then tell him, "We think we know where Mariana is… Drew! Sit down. Whatever you're thinkin', forget it. There is no way on this earth you're comin' along. Okay?" I wipe my hand back through my hair in exasperation. "We didn't keep you safe today, just to lose you tomorrow."

"Is that when you're going?"

With a jerk of my head, I confirm it.

He stares at me. An expression so fierce, any of my ancestors would be proud of it. He looks like he's going to beg to come along. I'm starting to compose arguments in my head why he shouldn't, when he surprises me. "Just promise me you'll bring her back, Mouse. If I can't come with you, I want to know I can trust you."

"Drew. If I can't bring her back, it will be because I've died trying." It's true. I'll give my life for hers, die before I give up. The thought doesn't worry me. The brothers coming with me will be of the same mind, which means we won't fail. There's too much to lose. For all of us.

In the morning, he says goodbye like a man. A handshake, a brotherly hug, a slap on my leather. I step back, holding him at arm's length, ignoring his watery eyes. "I'll bring her back," I make the promise again. "I'll be in touch as soon as we've got news."

"Don't worry, Drew. Cell reception might be non-existent where we're going," Drummer has the forethought to add. "Just because we can't call, doesn't mean we haven't been successful."

Drawing his shoulders back, Drew raises his chin at the prez.

I nod at Truck, who jerks his head in understanding. Kid doesn't know it, but I made a phone call to Jacob earlier. While we're gone, the prospect will take him to see the horses. I thought doing something different, riding and perhaps helping the old man like I used to do, might take his mind off what's going on. Things which are out of his control.

Knowing I can't do any more, anxious to get where I'm going, I go to my bike. Minutes later we're riding in formation out of the compound.

When we arrive at the private airport just outside Tucson, Devil's already waiting by a hangar. We ride our bikes in and park where directed. Then, placing my cut in my saddle bag, I hoist my duffle over my shoulder. Guns, ammunition, knives. Including, for good luck, my ancient flint knife. I've a yearning to save it for Mariana's father.

It quickly becomes clear most of the mercenaries are English, their accents sounding odd to my ears. But everyone quiets as Devil starts talking.

"I've got autos and semis on the plane," he informs us. "If anyone's short or something else takes their fancy." Blade's eyes light up at his suggestion, then the Englishman continues, "Two of my lads, Jones and Wessler, are snipers. There's a couple of others not bad at a distance. Should help put your plan in action, Mouse."

I nod. Seems he's taking my suggestions seriously. As I follow my brothers up the ramp, I'm in a state of disbelief at the turn life is taking. I'm a computer nerd, I'm not someone who mocks my own heritage by dressing up, I don't scalp people, I don't draw up battle plans. And I certainly don't fly thousands of miles to rescue a woman I've met on the outside just the once. Added to that, I'm going with the determination to bring her back and make her my wife.

Dropped down a rabbit hole? A sink hole, perhaps. But hey, maybe there's more to life than being stuck behind a computer. Which reminds me… Opening my duffle I take out then pass around the maps and Google Earth images I'd printed out. Every man takes a copy and starts to study them.

The men indicated as Jones and Wessler start an animated discussion, presumably deciding the best places where they can set up.

For a private jet this doesn't have much going for it. A utilitarian troop transporter from the look of it. I catch Viper's eye. He'd envisaged a pretty steward handing out champagne. He gives a self-deprecating grin back. Well, last time—and the first time for most of us—we flew in the Emir of Amahad's private jet when we attended his wedding. VIP treatment the whole way. I can well understand Viper's disappointment. Me? I just hope this thing will fly, and that the engines are better maintained than the inside.

Take-off is smooth, and soon we're in the air. Devil doesn't give us a chance to relax, gathering his team, and us, around him.

Without introduction, he waves his hand in my direction. "Mouse. Want to let my guys in on your idea?"

A computer nerd detailing a battle plan? Yeah. That makes sense. I clear my throat. "There's eighteen of us, we think probably double or more of them. Seems the maximum could be fifty, but that's unlikely as not all the men are often there at the same time. But we're going to be outnumbered. If we storm the compound, then they've got the upper hand." I wait for the nods of assent. Seems everyone's with me so far. I unfold one of the photos of where we're heading. "What we've got to do is deplete their numbers." I point to a weakness in the defence. "My proposal is that a raiding party goes in here. Makes a disturbance, gets attention, then gets out of there fast."

"Raiding party?" One of Devil's guys raises an eyebrow.

Marvel nudges my arm. "Get on with it, Chief." He smirks.

I ignore them. "The men inside will give chase; another team will be waiting to finish them off. In the meantime, we make a simultaneous… attack…," I'm now choosing my words carefully, "on another part of the compound. Here, I'd suggest." Again I move my finger on the paper. "Also here, if we can."

"Six on one team, two others of five." Devil joins in. "Three to get their attention, the others waiting to finish them off. That leaves our snipers to pick anyone else who escapes. Don't want them to regroup and catch us from the back. Mouse's plan means they won't know how many they're up against, and which direction the next salvo is coming from."

"Causing confusion. I like it." The mercenary whose name appears to be Carter gives a wicked grin.

It's the way the Navajo raiding parties worked. Get the enemy confused, chasing their tails. Small groups of Navajo took out much larger enemies. If it was successful for them, can't see why it wouldn't work for us.

"Once we've decimated their numbers," it's Devil's show now, "we join up and approach the main building, entering here and here." Now it's him pointing to the entrances, front and back.

"Need any survivors?" Wessler asks, his tone indicating he doesn't care one way or the other.

"I want them all dead." I've no doubt about that.

Devil sends me a quick look. "If we can capture *El Procurador*, all well and good. But the team's safety, and that of Mouse's woman, comes first. Shoot to kill."

"I want to find Mariana." That's my sole aim.

"Yeah. Once inside, Drummer, your boys can focus on finding the woman while we try to take *El Procurador*."

The rest of the journey is spent fine tuning our approach, with Devil assigning us to teams. As there's six of us, Satan's Devils will be sticking together. It makes sense. We know each other's strengths and weaknesses. Blade, myself and Marvel are all the fastest sprinters, so we'll be the ones going inside first. When we've picked up pursuers, Drummer, Viper and Dollar will be waiting to take them out.

How Devil arranged it, I've no idea. But we land in Colombia at a private landing strip where transport is waiting. It's a four-hour journey to our destination. In the trucks, we're mostly silent, all thinking our own thoughts. I've checked my guns and ammunition, and go over the plan again in my head.

At least after the initial forays, I'll be searching for Mariana. Where is she likely to be held? Is her father treating her like a treasured daughter? Will I find her in the main house? There's no way of knowing.

As if he's reading my mind, Drummer leans over. "*El Procurador* is the key, Mouse. Get to him and make him talk. Your ol' lady might even be with him."

"Yeah. Got your scalping knife, Chief?"

I shoot Blade a disdainful look, not bothering to again tell him my knife is multi-purpose. Perfectly good enough to do the job of cutting throats. I'm glad I brought it with me, somehow hoping it will be a conduit to the spirits of my ancestors, and bring me good luck. Today I'm not the man who sits behind the computer, I'm on the front line. Gradually I feel the white in me fading, my warrior side coming to the fore. *Mariana.* My muscles start to tense in anticipation, my back becomes straighter. *Hold on, Mariana. I'm coming for you.* The thought of what I'll do when I find her, of bringing her home, I push to the back of my mind. *No room for distraction. Just focus on the task.*

The last time I saw her, she said she hated me. I'd put that to the back of my mind. But now I feel so close to rescuing her, it worries me. *She hadn't meant it, had she? It was only something flung at me out of her own desperation. Wasn't it?* If not, I've fuck all chance of making her my old lady. *Shit. Worry about that later.* For now, I have to concentrate on fulfilling my promise to Drew to bring his sister home.

Once again everyone's fallen silent.

When the trucks halt, it's a trek across open country. Devil's mapped out a path which takes us through forest then along a tree line. Eventually the compound comes in sight. Drummer leads our team to the prearranged location, then we wait.

We're going on a timed entry. Drummer studies his phone. "Going in five."

In my head I'm going through the countdown, and then Blade, Marvel and I are off.

We're the first to attack. Getting over the wall proves easy. Silently we approach the first guard. Blade slices his throat, then throws a grenade. A few shots give away the position of our attack, then we're running back fast, sprinting to get away.

Shots fire around us, but none hit. As expected, a few guards flood out to our point of entry. Drummer, Viper and Dollar have our backs and take them out.

Now there's firing the other side of the compound. Some guards look panicked, and start to run towards that sound. We make our second approach; I shoot one in the back with no remorse.

They turn. We run. Drummer and the others again do their stuff. A third approach and we find no one, though there's still sporadic firing from the other side of the compound.

"Let's get into the house," Drummer suggests. "Devil's got the others distracted."

"They might have retreated inside," Viper inserts.

"Yeah, so take care, Brothers."

Inching around the building, using the brickwork to protect us, we approach the rear entrance. Yup, a couple of their soldiers are guarding it, but we're fast and take them out. A back corridor, a door leading downwards. We ignore it for now, and carry on into the house.

Devil's men have entered. A quick nod shows he's taken the rest of the men guarding the exterior out. The only casualty is the man called Carter, and that's just a graze to his arm. He seems more annoyed than incapacitated. Slowly we clear all the downstairs rooms. There are some women looking scared in the kitchen.

Questioning them in quickly spoken Spanish, Devil discovers they haven't seen the woman who had been living in the house for a while. Whether they're lying, he can't tell. We lock them in the pantry. From the sight of them they won't be a threat, but we're not taking any chances.

There are two floors above us. Shouts of 'clear' come from each room.

Satisfied, when apart from the kitchen staff, and of course, us, the house seems devoid of life, Devil swears when he can find no trace of *El Procurador*, or his lieutenants. I'm devastated that Mariana can't be found.

"The door. There's a basement," I remind Drummer.

"Could be *El Procurador*'s escape route," Devil suggests. "Carry on searching," he says to his team. "They might have a priest hole or something."

As Drummer looks at him in confusion, Devil explains. "Old houses in England have hidden spaces where priests used to hole up when the Protestants were killing Catholics. Hard to find, but that's the type of shit we're looking for." His men, mostly British, all nod. One starts moving a tapestry, one pushes at a wardrobe to see if it will slide. "I know he's here, somewhere." Devil looks disgusted.

"Could blow this house up," Viper suggests.

"Not with Mariana in it," I spit out.

"We're wasting time. Let's explore the basement."

We're used to sound proofed doors and walls; it comes in useful in our storeroom. But I didn't expect to hear what I do when we carefully open the door to the basement. As soon as we do, cries and loud howls of distress reach us.

"Fuck!" Drummer looks at us, then says quickly, "Proceed quietly, Brothers. If it's soundproofed down here, they might not have had warning of what's happening up above. Blade, if we can take them out without shooting…"

The enforcer's knife is already in his hands.

The first two guards go down easily. They're standing, smoking, laughing at a woman being raped. Her eyes widen when they see me, but that's all the warning the rapist gets before I cut his throat.

"*Gracias. Gracias,*" the woman cries as I roll the body off her. I hold a finger to my lips. Through her tears, she nods.

We proceed past cells which are more like cages. I check every one, but see no sign of Mariana. *Where the fuck is she?* But seeing, and smelling, this environment, I become more and more certain we're looking in the wrong place. Even a bastard like Mariana's father wouldn't treat his daughter like this.

"Women and children to be trafficked," Drummer says out of the side of his mouth. He's probably right, but for now we can do nothing for them.

Then we're edging onwards, but come across no more guards. Presumably it doesn't take too many to keep the women secure when they're locked up.

We come to another door. There's a woman crying out inside. *In English.* Mariana? I put my shaking hand on the latch and open it, Drummer right at my back. My gun ready to fire, I don't allow myself to take in more than the man with his hand on my woman's face, and another standing grinning to the side.

"I said, no interruptions!"

Fuck me, intent on what they're doing, they haven't noticed us. A quick shot and the man watching goes down. A bullet's too good for the man touching my future wife. Before my target has hit the ground, Drummer's weapon's pointing at Mariana's tormentor. Blade's fast, intuitively knowing I'll want payback for this one, he's disarmed him and fastened his hands behind his back with a zip tie.

Once the room's secured, I take my first look at Mariana. As soon as she sees me, she starts screaming.

CHAPTER 33

Mariana

My stomach already feels full to bursting, yet apparently, my torture's only half way done. I try to fight Miguel, but the next drug filled condom goes down when he holds my nose, forcing me to open my mouth. If his count was right, that's number sixty-one. Only, *only*, fifty-nine more to go. I don't think I'm going to survive this. The thought of the alien substance inside me makes me feel ill. My belly wasn't meant to hold latex and whatever drugs he's forcing me to swallow.

I want to die. I'm sure I'll get my wish granted. Surely what he's doing is killing me? And even if he gets me over the border, what if I'm caught? Caught smuggling drugs into the US? What fate is worse? Being sold to a cruel pervert, or being taken into custody? Becoming a statistic, proof people like me can't be trusted—being deported and coming back carrying drugs. What a cliché.

My protests are in vain. Miguel's got no sympathy. Instead, the opposite, seeming to delight in my distress.

I don't hear the door opening. My first warning is a loud shot, and in my peripheral vision, seeing Miguel's helper going down. It happens so quickly, one second Miguel is there, the next men are surrounding him.

Then my eyes fall on the tall man who's entered, recognising him in a flash. It takes my brain a moment to process that he's not a vision I've summoned up. *Tse's here.* He's really here. He's come to save me.

A scream comes out of my mouth, and then another. I'm struggling, fighting the bindings that hold me secure. A knife flicks in his hand, and then I'm free. He tries to hold me; all I do is flail with my arms.

"Get them out of me!" I scream loudly. "*Get them out of me!*" His strong arms come around me, but I try to push him away. "Tse! Get them out!"

"Shush, shush." He tries to calm me, his eyes going dark as he takes in the bowl of un-swallowed latex wrappers and immediately knows what's going on. "Shush. Tell me, how many have you taken?"

"None. I took none. He forced me…"

"Shush, darlin', shush. I know that. How fuckin' many?"

"Sixty-one!" I'm screeching again. He lets go of me, and my arms wrap around my stomach. "Tse, help me, please."

"Jesus." A new voice, another man entering. He looks at me, and at the bowl. Tse turns to look at him, a helpless expression on his face. "This changes our plans."

"*El Procurador?*" another man asks.

"Can't find him, Drummer. But we're still looking. Who's this?"

They're after my father? I'm sobbing, scared stiff. Worried now Tse has found me, I'll die anyway if one of the condoms bursts. But I raise a shaking hand and point to my tormentor. "He's Miguel Rojas, he's one of my father's lieutenants."

"Do you know where your father is?" The scary looking man with a scar running across his face turns his attention to me, startling me into giving him an answer.

"No. He gave me to him." I nod toward Miguel. "He's his second-in-command."

The scarred man nods. "How many lieutenants has he got?"

Miguel roars, but he's restrained tightly, and doesn't alter my response. "Three more."

"They're somewhere in this fucking house." The man turns to the heavily armed men who've followed him in. "Take this Rojas and get some answers."

I'm still trembling, my breathing shallow and fast, but something eases inside me when Miguel's taken out of my sight. When the scarred man takes a step toward me, panic rises again, and I step back, coming up against Tse's hard body. Now I take comfort from the warmth behind me.

Only one side of his face moves, as he attempts to smile. "My name's Devil," he says softly. "No need to worry, Mariana. You're going to be okay."

"They forced me to swallow…" Even my voice shakes.

"I know. But they won't be hurting anyone again. This will soon be over, Mariana. Tse's with you now, and he won't let anyone harm you."

"What do we do, Devil?" Tse's rich voice booms out, and this time, when his arms come around me, I lean back. His hands start smoothing up and down my biceps, such a gentle touch. It immediately soothes me. *I trust him. He won't let me die.*

Devil purses his lips, then looks directly at me. "Can't go back until those drugs are out."

The stroking of Tse's fingers is having a calming effect. "How long, how long will it take?"

"We need to find some laxatives, and then nature will just have to do its job."

Again I shudder, but a reassuring voice speaks into my ear. "It will be alright, Mariana. I promise you. It will be alright, and soon you'll be coming home with me. Back to Arizona. Back to Drew."

Home. Arizona. My brother.

Without turning I ask, "Promise?"

When he does, the force in his voice makes me start to believe him. Another man enters, a bundle of keys being twirled in his hand, blood oozing down his other arm but it doesn't seem to bother him. Devil turns toward him.

"Want us to start freeing the women, now?"

"You're sure the upstairs is cleared?"

"We've gone over the dining room thoroughly. No routes in or out except the main door. I suggest we put them in there." His face contorts as though in pain. "Got to be better than where they are now."

I'm horrified that in my distress I'd forgotten the women who were locked up.

"See if you can get the kitchen staff to get them some decent food. Water too. I suspect they could do with both."

"They'll want baths, showers…"

Devil nods. "That will have to wait until we're certain no one else is here. Don't want anyone to be taken hostage and used for bargaining." Then to his man, he says, "Thanks, Carter. Yeah, do that. I'll come see what's what. See if there's medical attention they need which you can provide."

"I'll do what I can," his man, Carter, agrees.

There's been a group of men chatting in the corner, as Devil disappears after Carter, they now approach. Tse briefly squeezes me, as though giving me support.

The man in the lead holds out his hand. "Drummer. I'm the President of the Satan's Devils." I shake it. "Tse's boss?"

He grins. "Suppose that I am. This here's Viper." He begins to introduce the men at his side. "Blade, Marvel and Dollar."

There're a few 'pleased to meet you's' which seem incongruous given the circumstances.

"My brothers," Tse whispers in my ear. "Your family too now, darlin'." For the first time, I turn and face him, my head tilted in question. "Sweetheart, told you I was claimin' you. Marryin' you. That hasn't changed. And doing that means you come under the protection of the club. My brothers have come here for you."

"That's right, sweetheart," the man introduced as Viper confirms. "You belong to Mouse, you're one of us."

"Mouse?"

The corners of Tse's mouth turn up. "Road name," he explains.

"Or Chief," the man called Marvel mutters under his breath.

A man less like a mouse I couldn't imagine. "Tse, *Mouse…* We need to talk."

"Nah. Know what you're thinking. But you're mine, and Drew too."

Christ. I've been so caught up in myself, I haven't asked about Drew. "How is he, Tse? My father was going to bring him here…"

"Don't you worry about your brother," his president interrupts. "Kid's fine. Yeah, your father tried, but we intercepted the fuckers he sent. That's how we knew where to find you. Drew's having a good time on the compound. He's a good kid, Mariana. You've done well with him."

I go to answer, but at that moment, Devil walks back into the room. He comes straight toward me. "Carter had this in his first aid pack. Seems he likes to be prepared for all eventualities." He hands a packet to me.

I immediately see what it is. "How long until it works?"

"Possibly thirty minutes, maybe not for a few hours. It's sodium phosphate."

"Is it safe?"

I don't miss the slight tic by the side of Devil's eye before he responds to Tse. "She'd have been given it had they got her to the States."

"Doesn't answer my question, Devil," Tse growls.

"Just tell me, Devil. Please," I put in. It's my body after all.

He frowns, then admits, "Some laxatives can cause the latex to be compromised. But this is a saline solution, and I'm confident it will work."

"She's not taking it. We'll wait it out."

I swing around so I'm face to chest with Tse—I'd forgotten just how tall he is. "Tse. I've got a belly full of drugs which is driving me out of my mind. One could break any minute. I'm freaking out here. I'd rather take my chance and get them out of my system. As Devil said, I'd have been given laxatives anyway."

His dark eyes stare into mine. Then he raises his chin fractionally. "Your body, your call."

"One thing, Mariana." As I turn back to face Devil again, I notice he's now looking apologetic. "You're going to have to count them as they come out. Got to know you've got them all."

My face scrunches in disgust. Isn't it bad enough they're inside me? Now I've got to examine my shit.

"Babe, I've got you." I'm back in Tse's arms, and he's comforting me as he would a child.

As Drummer steps up with a mug of water he's scrounged from somewhere, and I'm swallowing what I hope is the correct dosage down, the man with blood now drying on his arm returns.

"Devil. We've found *El Procurador*'s fucking lieutenants. You were right. Dimensions didn't seem to match up. Found a secret room under the floorboards. Just like a priest hole."

Priest hole?

"I'll explain later," says Tse quietly.

Then my brain processes that my father's men have been found. "My father?" *Is he dead?* That would be the best news I could be told. He deserves it. He's traded in misery far too long.

Devil cocks his eyebrow as though seconding my question.

"He's escaped, Devil. Sorry. Seems he thought one man had more chance on his own. Went through a secret passage and locked a steel door behind him, trapping his men on the other side. He's in the wind."

"I want this place torn apart," Devil growls. "Paperwork, computers. Mouse, can you help?"

"As long as Mariana's by my side I will."

I'm shocked when Devil turns to me. "We'll find him, Mariana. I promise you that. We *will* find him."

The house is a hive of activity. A couple of men are trying to sort out the women. From what I hear they're getting information which will help reunite them with their families if they have them. Others are pulling out drawers and going through desks, putting aside paperwork which presumably they'll take with them.

Though I'm following Tse, I hesitate on the threshold of my father's office, still feeling his presence here. Tse comes back when he sees I'm standing at the door, holding out his hand.

"He's not here. He's gone."

I shiver, again wrapping my arms around me. "I hate him, Tse. I thought I did before, but having met him? He's more evil than I could ever imagine."

He nods, tugging me to him, and resting his chin on the top of my head. We stand like that for a few moments. He's giving me comfort, and I'm taking it. Enjoying just being held in his arms, the feeling I've longed for, but never thought I'd get to experience.

After a moment, he draws back, takes my hand and leads me over to the desk. "Sit with me while I get down to work."

I take the chair I last sat in opposite my father. This time I'm watching Tse as he fires up the computer and starts doing stuff, his long lean fingers racing over the keys. His brow creases, then relaxes, a small smile forms, then he's back to frowning again. I don't need to see what's on the screen, I can tell by his expressions if he's having success or not.

One of the maids enters the room with a tray of coffees. She's escorted by one of Devil's men. He raises his chin toward us. "I watched her make it."

They're being so cautious, it's reassuring.

Still Tse taps on. Again we're interrupted with a plate full of sandwiches. Tse stops me with a shake of his head. "Wait until…"

I nod quickly. I don't want to discuss my bowel movements, and neither have I any desire to chase the drug filled condoms with food. I'm not in the slightest bit hungry. *There's no room in my stomach.*

As Tse takes a break to eat, I nod at the computer. "Are you getting anywhere?"

Tse grins widely. "Yeah. Fucker kept all his details on here. The computer's not connected to the internet, so he thought he was secure to record all his shit. I've got his pipelines and every-thing. Devil will be able to destroy him."

"Good." The news makes me very happy. I watch Tse eat, licking mayonnaise off his fingers. Taking huge bites in a manner that reminds me of Drew. It strikes me there's so much I don't know about him. I've never seen him consume anything before. All I know is that he's done everything he can to help me. To save me.

"Tse. What's going to happen to me?"

He swallows his mouthful, washing it down with fresh coffee. "I told you. You're coming home. Devil's got a private plane, and transport to get there. We'll land in Arizona and you'll come back to the compound."

"I'm still an illegal."

His eyes narrow. "Forget about that for a moment. We'll deal with it, okay? You'll be safe with the Satan's Devils, with your brother. And I'll look after you."

"I'm not your responsibility, Tse." How could I be? This man with the striking good looks could have any woman. Why would he want me, and the baggage I'm carrying?

His hand snakes over the table and grabs mine. "What part of 'you're my woman' did you not get? I haven't been able to get you out of my mind since the first day I met you. Not going to let you get away."

"That sounds creepy," I warn him, my voice going low. "You don't know me."

"Then let's get to know each other. Not going to pressure you, babe. But think about this. Being married means I can sponsor you for a green card."

"I can't force you into a relationship just for that."

"Force *me*?" He huffs a laugh. "Just then you were implying it was the other way around."

"A marriage would have to be real."

"You're seriously saying it wouldn't be?" His eyes become heated. They stare into mine, then move down, focusing on my breasts before moving back up. "Wouldn't be any hardship for me, darlin'." Where my thoughts go must be written on my face. Immediately he stands, comes around, and crouches in front of me, taking both my hands in his. "What's up?"

My voice is little more than a whisper. "They raped the women. One in the cell next to me. She was hurting, screaming..."

My hands are shaking; he squeezes them gently. "I'd never force you, Mariana. Never do anything you didn't want. You believe me, don't you?"

Right now I don't know what I believe. Worse, my stomach clenches. For a moment there our discussion had distracted me. I'd forgotten what was going to come next. A bout of gas has me wrapping my arms around me, then cramps have me doubled over.

Tse's up off his chair, food forgotten, and around my side. "Is it time?"

"Yes. Hurry."

There's a bathroom next door, plastic has been set up ready. "I'll be right outside."

His words are probably meant to be reassuring, but I cringe with embarrassment.

CHAPTER 34

Mouse

If I could go through this for her, I would. The noises she's making that she's trying to suppress make it sound like she's in terrible pain in there, but I can't open the door. She'd die of mortification, I know that. The way her face reddened when she had to explain she was ready showed me how humiliating she found the situation. I don't give a damn whether she thinks it's disgusting or not. I just want her body rid of those fucking drugs. I won't breathe easy until they're all out.

I suppose I did seem a bit creepy when I announced I was marrying her. Having been kidnapped *right under the noses of ICE* and her father on the loose, she's got a credible reason to seek asylum, and with me sponsoring her for a green card… There must be a way to keep her in the US. I'll ask Devil to help. Some of the information I collected will stop a lot of misery for many. Even if *El Procurador* tries to set up another operation, all the routes and connections he's using now will be useless. His border crossing points, the people who take bribes from him. That's just some of the information I've extracted. It was down to Mariana being kidnapped that Devil will have the means to put an end to his operation. Surely he owes us, and her, something in return.

"Mouse. I take it…?"

Drummer gestures to the closed door I'm standing outside. With a glance at it, I move away a few steps.

"Fuckin' scared. What if one of those things breaks? What if…?"

"Mouse. All we can do is hope it doesn't. Hate to say this, but people are used as mules every day. Some volunteer because they're attracted by the money. Sure, occasionally it doesn't work out and they die, but if that happened in the majority of cases, it wouldn't be as common as it is, or worth trying to smuggle drugs that way."

He's right. But just because the odds are on her side, doesn't mean she won't be one of the unlucky ones.

Pinching the bridge of my nose, I tell him, "Can't lose her, Drum."

His mouth curves in amusement. "From what I picked up, she hasn't exactly agreed to your claimin'."

"It's her best option." I'm certain of that.

"And yours?" His smile disappears.

I point to the office where I've been working. "I don't even know how long we were in there, Prez. It worked though. Her and I. Was easy, wasn't awkward. I can't explain it, but we fit."

I'm subjected to the full stare from those steely eyes, then he pats my arm. "Hope it works out for you. When you know, you know."

"Tse?"

I'm immediately outside the bathroom. "Mariana? Can I come in?"

A panicked, "No."

"Are you alright?"

"I, er, I think so. I don't know what to do with… And there's only sixty."

"I'll go get Devil," Drummer tells me, then goes off.

"Hold on a minute, Mariana."

"I'm going nowhere," she scoffs.

Loud footsteps sound on the stairs. "Devil, she wants to know what she does now. And there's only sixty."

Devil slaps my back. "Mariana, can you hear me?"

"Yes."

"Do you know how many there were in all?"

"A hundred and twenty," she calls back.

"Well, you or that fucker miscounted. There were sixty left, so they've all come out. Just leave them, open the door, and Mouse will take you to get showered."

"I... I...leave them?"

"Yeah."

The door opens, Mariana quickly pulls it to behind her. She's pale, but there's now a spark in her eyes which wasn't there before. I let her lead me up to the bedroom she'd been using. She has a quick shower, and then reappears in clean clothes that had been left there. She looks beautiful, and is smiling.

"Never appreciated fresh water so much before." Her head tilts to one side. "Wasn't able to think beyond those drugs being inside me. In there," she points back to the shower, "I realised I haven't thanked you. I can't believe you're here. Can't believe that you came." Her teeth worry her lip. "Last time I saw you, I said I hated you."

That has been playing on my mind. It seems it has on hers too. Realising I don't want to hear the wrong answer, but knowing I have to ask, "Do you?"

"God, no!" she exclaims.

I can't resist. I go over, lean down and breathe in the scent of her hair. "You smell nice." Out of the corner of my eye I notice a mirror, and notice too, what a good couple we make. Both with similar colouring. Placing my arm around her shoulder, I half turn her. "We look good together, darlin'."

Her reflection is still nibbling her lip. "Looks can be deceiving."

"Not in this case," I murmur, encouraging her around once again. "I want to kiss you, you going to let me?" I give her fair warning.

Her brow creases, her eyes widen, then her head dips up and down in a tentative yes.

I lower my head. My lips move across hers. A chaste kiss. *I want more.* "Open for me."

Her mouth opens fractionally. Gently, hesitantly, I increase the pressure, my tongue meeting hers, slowly sliding together. She tastes of peppermint from toothpaste. I keep my touch light, gentle, non-invasive. My cock jerks to life and I move my hips back so she's unaware of it.

Her hands grasp my arms; she's not pulling away. I hold myself back, aware I mustn't pressure her. When I end the kiss, it's too soon for me, and I hope, her.

There's a dazed look on her face. Wonderingly she places her fingertips to her mouth. Then she says something I didn't expect. "I've never been kissed before, Tse."

"Never?"

She shrugs. "I was too busy looking after Drew. Too worried about doing something that would expose us. I couldn't risk someone reporting me, so I never got close. Never dated."

"You're a virgin?" I hadn't expected it. Nor the burst of primeval pride which swells inside me, along with the knowledge I've got to take this slow. But *fuck me*, I'm going to be the first man who'll have her. Again her teeth worry her lip, and she looks down. "Hey," I place my finger under her chin. When she looks up, I softly brush my lips against hers again. "You're mine," I tell her, knowing I'm repeating myself, and will continue until she gets that into her head. "But we're going to take this as slowly as you want. Just understand, we'll be together. Facing whatever life brings, side by side."

Her shoulders tense, and I'm worried she's traumatised by the women she saw being taken forcibly. Fuck, if she's no experience, and that was her first exposure… I've got to slow this to a crawl. But when she speaks, it's to name another worry. "What if I'm deported again?"

"What if a fuck load of things, darlin'. Don't borrow any more trouble until we get out of the spot we're currently in."

Her eyes darken, and I hate that I reminded her we're not home and dry yet.

"Yo, Mouse?" Blade's loud voice comes up the stairs.

"Come on," I hold out my hand, pleased when she takes it. "Let's go down, see what's going on." Then I shout, "We're coming!"

Blade's halfway up the stairs. His eyes flare appreciatively when he sees the woman by my side, his stare lingering a little too long for my liking.

"Blade," I growl, warningly.

"What?" Acting innocent, he holds out his hands. "Just thinking how well she scrubs up."

"She's mine."

There's a startled laugh at my side. "You going to piss on me next?"

Leaning down, I speak into her ear, loud enough for Blade to hear. "Might have to with these assholes around."

We reach the bottom of the grand stairway, to find Devil holding court. He motions for us to join the throng standing around him.

"Right. Now we're all here. Mariana, are you feeling alright?"

She shrinks into my side as though unsure of being the centre of attention, but speaks up for herself. "My stomach feels a bit sore, but I'm fine. Just glad it's over."

It won't be over until we're out of Colombia and on our way home, I think to myself.

"We going to burn this bitch down?" Viper calls out.

"The house," I reassure her quickly. "He's talking about the house."

Devil looks at Mariana. "This could be yours, if your father made no other plans."

"Burn it," she replies forcefully. "I want nothing to do with him, or anything here."

Devil scrunches the side of his face which moves. "We found a huge store of cocaine and heroin. If you're certain, Mariana, then I agree. We set fire to it."

"I can do that," Wessler offers. "Brought explosives and a timer with me just in case."

"How soon can we get out of here?" Drummer asks, with a glance toward me. Like me, he's probably getting twitchy that we're not on home turf. I remember how pregnant Sam is. Drum's got every reason to want to go home.

"Soon as the explosives are set. You got everything you needed, Mouse?"

"Yeah. Sent it all up to the cloud, Devil. Encrypted of course."

"What's going to happen to the women?" Mariana asks.

"Already sorted. We transported them to the nearest hospital. Authorities will take it from there."

They've done a lot. But then, waiting for the laxatives to work had given them enough time.

Wessler sets about his task. I wonder if he's as efficient as Slick, but he seems to be. It's not long before we're getting into the trucks, and starting our first leg of the journey to go home.

Rolling my head back I inhale deeply, then let my breath out on a sigh, unable to resist squeezing Mariana's fingers. Home. With my ol' lady. As the truck bumps across the uneven road, I close my eyes, imagining the feeling of her riding behind me, her hands tight around my waist. Her wearing my property patch. Opening my eyes a fraction, I peer at her. *Yeah. This feels right.*

She dozes, her head on my shoulder, my arm holding her securely. As she drifts into a deeper sleep, she emits little snuffling sounds. She's probably catching up on many long nights when she remained on guard. I frown as I remember *El Procurador's* man, who I'd seen with my own eyes openly raping that woman. Mariana must have lived with the worry it might happen to her. *Had they touched her? They hadn't raped her, but could have…* My blood boils, but I won't ask her. Eventually she'll tell me all the horrors she's been through, and we'll work our way through them together. Now she's sleeping so soundly, I know her body trusts me, it's just her mind that needs to catch up.

Marvel's turned to stare at me. "She lost it, and I'm not surprised, when we first found her. But she's pulled herself together now."

I kiss the top of her head, even that doesn't disturb her. "She's got backbone," I answer him quietly. "Never had anyone to lean on."

He examines me for a moment, then nods. "She's got a good one in you, Brother. You'll be her rock from now on."

I'll try.

"So," starts Blade. "We going to change your handle?"

I start to sit up, Mariana objects with a moan, so I settle back and make do with a fierce whisper. "One mention of Chief and I'll gut you with your own fuckin' knife."

Unrepentant, he grins. "Thought you were going to scalp me."

"I'll do that first."

"Want to wake Sleeping Beauty, Mouse? Airport's ahead."

I act on Prez's suggestion. I'm learning shit about my woman all the time. She wakes up grumpy. Her indignant face has me grinning, then when she remembers where she is, she looks sheepish seeing my brothers looking on.

The plane's there ready and waiting. I get out, lift Mariana down. Once she's standing I raise my arms, stretch, then place my hands in the middle of my back and arch my spine. The truck was cramped for a man of my height.

I smile down at Mariana, and see the exact moment the bullet hits her. Her mouth opens in an O, then, without a sound, she falls to the ground.

For a second I'm frozen, unable to comprehend what I've seen. Then I fall to the ground beside her, conscious that both my brothers and the mercenaries have formed a circle around us, Devil shouting orders, returning fire going in the direction he's yelled out.

Then he and Drummer drop down beside me. "How bad?" Devil snaps.

My hand goes to the pulse in her neck. "She's breathing." *Thank fuck.*

Devil and Drummer turn her over as I rake my hands through my hair, feeling so fucking useless. I work with data, don't know shit about anything medical.

"It took her in the top of her leg. Bullet's still in there," Prez announces steadily, keeping calm while I'm losing my shit.

Mariana groans, her eyes finding mine, but they're unfocused.

"I've got you," I tell her, trying to pull myself together. She needs me to be strong.

"Mouse, lift her carefully and take her to the plane. We've got your back, Brother."

My hands flail in the air. "Should we move her?"

Devil's eyes snap to mine. "Can't stay here, Mouse. Who knows who's out there? *El Procurador* will be behind it. It's his country, he must have more men on his side. And he's had plenty of time to arrange an ambush. We've got to get out of here now, while the plane can still fly."

"Was it hit?"

"Not yet," he replies grimly.

Blood loss or shock, I don't know which, but she's lost consciousness. Carefully picking up Mariana's limp body, I move as fast as I can toward the plane, Viper, Dollar, Marvel, Blade and Drummer surrounding us on all sides. Blood's flowing down my arms, and looking back, there's a huge puddle on the ground.

She's bleeding out. In my fucking arms. I never got to tell her I love her. Love? Yeah, that's right. How the fuck it happened I don't know, but the woman I've barely seen has got under my skin and into my heart, and I'm only fucking realising it when she's dying. She trapped me from the moment I first saw her facing up to that bear. I loved her before I even spoke to her.

I should have realised we were still in danger. Got too fucking complacent.

You can't leave me now. Not like this. Not when we were so close.

CHAPTER 35

Mouse

ay her down here," Devil instructs, quickly grabbing a blanket and throwing it on the floor. "Carter? Leave Wessler. He can sort himself out. I want you looking at her."

Carter nods, throwing an impatient glance at Wessler who's cleaning his own wound, then wrapping a bandage around it. He must have taken a bullet too and I hadn't noticed. Carter drops down to Mariana's side, feeling for her pulse just like I did. "Pulse is weak, Devil. Get this bird in the air now."

"You a medic?" I ask, hoping he is. I don't know what the fuck to do.

"Yeah," he replies offhandedly, his concentration on Mariana. "Mason! Get the first aid kit."

First aid? She looks beyond that. *Why aren't they better equipped?* But the big duffle Mason drops down beside him looks like it holds a lot. I can only hope there's something to help her in there. Christ, that blood… there's so much of it.

"Buckle up, we're taking off."

I glare at Devil, he doesn't tell me to take a seat. Nothing is going to make me leave Mariana, not even for a second. Plane crashes? I'll take my chances. Carter stays where he is too. He's grabbed a towel and is holding it to Mariana's leg. It becomes red fast.

It's a six-hour flight, give or take. Six hours. Unless Carter can work magic, even with my lack of medical knowledge I can see she won't last that long.

At last the plane levels off. "Cruising altitude," the pilot says.

"Right. Let's see what we're dealing with."

I growl, I don't like Carter's hands on my woman, especially not when he starts slicing off her clothes.

"Got a tranquilliser dart with your fucking name on it," Carter snarls, throwing me a glare of his own. "Either fucking help or keep clear. I'm doing my best to save her here."

He raises her eyelids, whether he's satisfied or not I can't tell. "I've got to try to slow the bleeding." He sounds grim. "Can we get this seat moved to give me more room?"

A couple of his teammates step up. Apparently, the inside of the plane can be rearranged depending on cargo. A few bolts undone, and at last he's got space to work.

My eyes narrow. "You know what you're doing?" I ask. "Wouldn't it be better to wait until we land?"

He closes his eyes as though summoning up patience. "Nothing I'd like better, man. But if I leave her like this, she'll die. Use my limited skills to help her? Well, she'll have a chance."

Devil appears, and kneels beside us. "I'll help. What do you need?"

"A bottle of whisky," Carter drools.

Devil slaps his back. "After," he promises.

Drummer's behind me, his hand on my shoulder. There for support, but probably also to hold me back should the need arise. Carter slips on latex gloves, then gets out a pair of forceps and disinfects them. He then does the same to a pair of scissors.

"Devil, get the flashlight and illuminate this area. I need more light."

"Are you going to anaesthetise her?"

Carter shakes his head. "She's not going to feel anything, Mouse. She's out of it. Just monitor her, will you? Let me know if anything changes."

I raise an eyebrow.

"Her pulse, breathing. Tell me if she seems to feel cold or clammy."

Ah. I place my fingers against her neck. He nods.

"Right, I'm not removing the bullet, could do more damage taking the fucker out. It's nicked the femoral artery, not much I can do but make sure fibres are removed then I'm going to try to slow the bleeding. Looks like a fairly small calibre, that's one thing at least."

I watch as he starts with the forceps, pulling away the strands of her jeans which had been caught up with the bullet. He then uses a sterile fluid to wash out the wound. A dusting of what he says is an antibiotic powder, then he's pulling the wound together and holding gauze over the top. Gauze that gets soaked pretty quickly. Devil's there with a bag, and he drops it in it, replacing it with fresh gauze. After he's gone through three soaked pads, I'm starting to lose hope that she's going to make it.

I catch his eye. He's looking at me, assessing. After a moment he asks, "Do you know her blood type?"

I barely know her name. There's so much I don't know about her. I stroke back the hair from her face, now oh so pale. "No fuckin' idea. Her pulse is getting weaker."

"What blood group are you?"

"O neg. Why?"

Carter's face lights up. "You are what's known as a universal donor. You're not averse to needles, are you?"

Hate the fucking things. That's why I've got no tattoos. "Again, why?"

"Blood transfusion."

Give my blood to her? I'd do a fuck more than that to save her. "Where do you want me?"

He removes a length of tube and a couple of catheters from that magic bag. Takes a moment to find a vein on her, then I look away as he first disinfects then sticks a needle into my arm. But he's professional about it, and it's not long before blood starts draining from my body into hers.

It's probably psychological, but I soon feel faint.

"Shit, Brother, I'm O positive. I can't fuckin' help. Would if I could." Weakly I nod at Blade.

"I can't either," says Marvel.

"Nor me." Fuck me, Viper and Marvel sound disappointed.

"I'm not," says Dollar.

Word goes around the plane. Another man, Kleinman, says that he's O negative too.

At the news Carter gives a wide grin. "Against the bloody odds, but good news. Thanks, Kleinman."

I notice Carter's watching both me and Mariana carefully, and the tube lying between us. My blood leaving my body and hopefully giving a chance of life to hers.

"Her blood loss is slowing down." He still sounds grim. She's lost an awful lot of blood. *Too much?* I've no idea what eight pints looks like. Drop a pint of milk and it looks like a whole cow's exploded.

"Okay." Carter's leaning over me. "That's it for you now. Be careful standing, Mouse. You might feel dizzy. Stay sitting down." I want to protest; she can have all I've fuckin' got. I can't let her die. But he gives me no chance, having already removed the catheter and slapping a band-aid over where it was. "Kleinman?"

Drummer helps me stand, as Kleinman takes my place. I do feel dizzy, but feel Carter should have let me give more.

"Let me do it again," I suggest.

"No, Brother," Drummer says firmly. "You need to look after yourself as well. Not going to be any good to anyone if you collapse."

I feel so useless. Marvel appears with a bar of chocolate; I stuff it down without tasting it. The plane drones on, time seems to move slowly.

Devil appears from the front of the plane. "I've arranged for an ambulance to meet us."

My shoulders slump. "Devil, she's a deported immigrant. They find out…"

"Mouse. Do you trust me?"

After thinking for a moment, I decide he's never appeared untrustworthy. Fighting by our sides on a couple of occasions. He'd got us into Colombia and back out. "I trust you."

"She'll go in under a fake name. I'm British, yeah, we've got our own problems with immigration, who hasn't? But I'm not going to be dobbing her in." I take it he means reporting her. "Carter's doing what he can. She needs surgery to get the artery patched or grafted, and a doctor needs to check how much damage the bullet might have done. Apart from giving her more transfusions."

"I'm staying with her."

"We all will," Drummer interrupts. "My brother's ol' lady's coming home with him, Devil. Not having any different outcome."

"I'll sort it." Devil's face is full of promise as he moves out of the way. "I told you. Trust me."

"Hold this, Mouse." Kleinman's now moved away, his face paler than before he started. Carter's passing me a bag. "It's saline," he explains. "Out of all other options now."

The plane flies on, the engine constantly droning. Carter uses his second, and last bag of the fluids I hope will keep her alive until we land.

By the time we touch down, the most I can say for Mariana is that she's still breathing. She hasn't come around. The ambulance is waiting, the medics come on board and have her hooked up to another drip before she's moved. Devil goes in the ambulance with her, I had to agree he was best to get her checked in.

The six of us get our bikes out of the hangar and are right behind it.

It's a small hospital, thank God; one I haven't been to before. They're expecting her and rush her straight in to surgery as Devil deals with the bureaucracy. Drummer gets me a coffee. For the first time in my life I wish I wasn't a teetotaller, longing for the oblivion to wipe this worry from my mind.

"I can't lose her," I suddenly announce to no one in particular.

"You won't," Drummer replies from beside me. "She's a fighter. She's strong."

"You saw the conditions she was kept in…"

"But not for too long, Mouse. Hold on to the positives."

Standing, I start to pace. "What's taking so fuckin' long?"

"It's only been half an hour, Mouse."

I glare at Viper, then cease walking, stopping and leaning my forehead against the wall. The smell of the disinfectant reminds me of the month we waited for Heart to come around, and the time we thought we were going to lose Slick and Beef. We're men, we're bikers. We signed up for this shit. An untimely end is likely for any one of us. Mariana's only twenty, she's got her whole life ahead of her.

"Should I tell Drew?"

Drummer closes his eyes and thinks about it. "Wait until we know more, Mouse. Don't want to worry the kid. He can do nothing to help. When we know what the prognosis is, you can prepare yourself to tell him."

"I haven't had a chance to get to know her," I complain out loud.

"You'll get your chance," Blade growls as he comes over. "Think positively."

Don't borrow trouble. Was it really only this morning I was saying that to Mariana? It seems so long ago. Why hadn't I said more to her? Why hadn't I told her how I felt? *Because my intensity would have scared her.*

Devil comes in and joins us. When I glance at him he raises his chin. I take it everything's sorted. My nightmare would be for her to come around only to be confronted with ICE.

Two hours pass, and a doctor comes in. "Family of Jane Smith?" he asks.

Devil gives that lopsided grin. "Tse Williamson's her fiancé." He points me out.

I walk toward him, my heart in my mouth. "The bullet wasn't easy to extract, and there is some nerve damage. She's lost a lot of blood, but the transfusions and fluids she was given gave her a chance."

I can barely make his words out. The one thing I want to know, he hasn't answered. "Is she going to make a full recovery?"

"She'll need to stay in for a few days. We're pumping her full of antibiotics, and giving her more blood. I think it's likely she'll need to go to a rehab centre for the physical therapy she's going to need."

My brain says no. As soon as she can, she's coming home. Not letting her out of my sight again, and anywhere she goes will run the risk of exposing her. Peg can help her with physical therapy, can't he? But I don't argue with him now. "Can I see her?"

"Give us a moment to move her to a room and then, yes." With that the doctor leaves.

Drummer puts his arm around me, and gives me a brief hug. "She's going to be fine." I notice him glaring at Devil.

"Jane Smith?" Blade bursts out laughing, and his mirth causes the tension to dissipate. "Couldn't you think of something more original, Devil?"

Devil shrugs as he stands. "Worked, didn't it?" He walks to the door, then turns. "I'll be in touch. Any problems? Drummer, Mouse, you know where to find me." Then he disappears into the night.

My brothers stay until I'm called in to sit with Mariana.

I enter the room, seeing her lying so still on the bed, and my anguish of the last few hours comes back to me. I take her hand, bend my head over it, and let tears flow. A fucking man and I'm crying; I must still be suffering from my own blood loss. Tears of relief, of recrimination, wondering why we relaxed our guard and weren't prepared for an ambush. *She should never have been shot.*

A nurse comes in to check her. She must notice my red-rimmed eyes. "She's going to be fine," she tells me comfortingly.

The monitor beeps reassuringly, telling me Mariana's still alive. With my hand grasping hers, my head lying on my other arm, I close my eyes.

"Tse?"

A tentative voice wakes me.

"Where am I? Oh, God. I'm in the hospital…"

"Don't worry, *Jane*," I tell her quickly. When her eyes widen in confusion, I quickly add, "Jane Smith. That's your name here. Devil worked everything out. You're back in the US, in Arizona."

"Did the drugs break?" she whispers.

I realise she doesn't remember what happened. "Nah, sweetheart. Someone shot you just before you got on the plane home. Reckon it was something to do with your father."

"Oh my God. Shot? Is anyone else hurt?" Trust her to think of other people when she's been flirting with death.

Stroking my hand over her forehead, "Just you seriously. You were shot in the upper thigh, nicked your femoral artery."

Her eyes open in confusion, but the next question she asks is again not about herself. "Are you alright?"

"Don't worry about me, darlin'. Just concentrate on you. Doctor wants to keep you in for a few days, and then you're coming home." I don't say we've got a battle on our hands to keep her out of rehab. It's too dangerous for her to go.

"Shot." The word seems to resonate with her. She takes away the hand I've been holding all night, and gingerly raises the sheet.

"In your upper thigh," I tell her again, in case it didn't register the first time. "You've got some nerve damage, but it will heal in time." She's got enough to deal with without talk of maybe being confined to a wheelchair. Guess we're going to have to get Sophie's out of storage again. "You'll be sore for a while and have a nice little scar, but it shouldn't cause long-term problems." *I hope.*

She yawns, her eyes are drooping. The anaesthetic is probably still in her system, and she'll take time to make up for the huge loss of blood. "Go back to sleep, darlin'. I'll be here."

"You don't have to stay," she mumbles. The expression on her face, and her tight grasp of my hand, tell me she's lying.

I stay. Where else would I be? She sleeps, I feast my eyes on the woman I had doubts I'd see back in the US again. I can't take my eyes off her as every emotion goes through me. The fear I'd felt when she was deported, that we wouldn't be able to find her. My elation when we did, and the anxiety I'd tried to hold from her that her body wouldn't rid itself of those fucking drugs without killing her. My joy when we saw the plane, knowing home was within reach. My terror when I saw her fall to the ground having been shot, my utter panic when I saw how much blood she'd lost.

"Mr Williamson?"

A voice speaks quietly. Looking up, I see the doctor who's been treating her. He's beckoning me, I stand, take a last glance at Mariana, then step to the door. *If he wants me to leave her he'll have a fight on his hands.*

"Mr Deville filled me in on some of what happened to Ms Smith. The first aid you gave her certainly saved her life."

It takes a second to realise Mr Deville is the man known to me as Devil. "It wasn't me, it was the medic who was with us."

He brushes my comment away. "I understand you gave blood to her. Just wanted to say, it wouldn't hurt for you to have a blood test, check your red cell count. In that situation, it's hard to tell how much you gave."

"I'm okay," I tell him with a slight shudder. Not going to have another needle poked in me again. "I'm fit and healthy, my body will heal itself."

His eyes must confirm what I'm saying, and after a swift perusal, he nods. "Take care of yourself. If you start feeling weak or dizzy…"

"I'll seek help."

Another rise and dip of his chin. "I'm not stupid, I just heal people. Don't get involved in politics or what's right or wrong. Don't want to know what happened, but that girl there, she didn't deserve to be shot. I'm not going to make things worse for her."

Reading between the lines, he knows something is wrong, but isn't going to report it.

"Thanks." It's a lame expression of my gratitude, but sometimes too many words are worse. I can't confirm he's right to be suspicious, and denying it could lead me to saying too much.

"Ms Smith's going to take a while to recover her strength and the use of her leg."

"Prepared for that."

Another glance at me, then at his charge lying sleeping in the bed, then he's gone.

Mariana sleeps the rest of the night. Eventually my tired body shuts down, and I doze myself.

Early the next morning, I have a visitor. Leaving Mariana's door ajar, I go out into the corridor.

"Blade." I raise my chin.

"Thought you'd be lost without this." He grins broadly as he hands my laptop over.

It's like getting back my lost child. I take it, thanking him profusely. "How's she doing?"

"Been sleeping a lot."

"Not unexpected. Not after what she's been through. Rest is what she needs. And plenty of pain meds. Don't let her try to be brave, Brother." His brows knit together. "Anything you need, Mouse. Anything, okay? I like her."

Today I don't feel like hitting him, but welcome his approval. She's going to be living with me on the compound and will need the support of my brothers. Which reminds me, I need to have a conversation with Peg.

"How's Drew doing?" I've been so tied up with worry about Mariana, I haven't given much thought to the boy, but then I knew he was safe and being well looked after.

"Upset Mariana's hurt. Wants to see her. But Drummer's persuaded him to be patient. Wouldn't do him any good to see her until she's awake."

CHAPTER 36

Mariana

A nurse fussing around wakes me up. I open my eyes to see I'm still attached to a monitor, but the drip has been removed. Tse is sitting by my side, studying something on his laptop.

The nurse finishes what she was doing, and quietly leaves.

"Tse?"

His face when he smiles is gorgeous. Putting aside his laptop, he pulls his chair closer, taking hold of my hand. "How are you feeling?"

"Like I've been hit by a train?"

"Doc says everything looks good. They were worried about infection, but your temperature's normal."

"When can I get out? I want to see Drew…"

"Drew's coming in later. Blade's bringing him along. You've been in and out of it for a couple of days." He studies me for a moment. "You look more with it now."

Two days? My mind is blurry, vague memories of Tse leaning over and pushing the pain med pump. I try a glare. "Think that might have been you pumping me full of morphine."

He grimaces. "Don't like to see you in pain. How is it now?"

I reach my hand down, but withdraw it when I touch the bandages. "Sore, but bearable."

"You hurt? You take something for it, okay?"

"I had some weird dreams." I had. I could swear there'd been a horse standing beside me. I remember reaching out to stroke its nose, but only hit air.

"That's the morphine, darlin'. It can do that."

I decide there and then I won't be using it, except as a last resort.

"Mariana, darlin', I know you're probably still a bit woozy, but I need to know some things. You know where your driver's licence and social security card are?"

Why does he want to know that? Why's it the first thing he's asking me? He's right, my head does still feel fuzzy. Rather than dwelling on the why, and probably receiving a convoluted response, it's easier just to answer his question. "My licence was in my purse, I suppose the cops took it. The social security card is in a box in the trailer."

"Hmm."

He seems disappointed with my answer. "Do you know your social security number?" He doesn't sound hopeful.

"I do." I was proud to get it, to be able to work, to pay my taxes.

His eyes light up. "Then it seems fairly simple to get a replacement licence. There's a form to fill in online." He starts tapping. "What's your date of birth?"

I tell him and give him the other information he needs. Including my address at the trailer park. I can't wait to be back there with Drew.

The pain in my leg is worsening. Tse's brow furrows as he shows me the pain pump but I've been sleeping so long I don't want to use it. For now, I'll try to put up with it. Gingerly I go to pull myself up, Tse's there immediately, raising the head of the bed.

I don't understand why he's completing online forms for me. "Tse, I don't even have a car. Why would I need a driver's licence? I can replace it eventually." *As long as I'm allowed to stay in the US.*

His face softens as he tells me, "So we can get married as soon as possible."

I hadn't thought he was serious. Or at least, I thought that he'd give us more time to get to know each other first. My jaw drops and my eyes open wide as I stare at him, pain fading as my brain struggles to work through the fog. "Tse, we can't get married."

He places his lips to my head, peering down through long dark eyelashes, a devilish twinkle in his eyes. "Why not?"

"We've never dated, never spoken about what we want out of life. We don't know each other."

"We might not have had a conventional relationship, but my soul calls to yours." As I'm stunned into silence by his poetic words, he continues. "I can't let you go, Mariana. I've claimed you in front of my club."

"I thought that was only to get them to help you."

"Definitely not," he protests. He takes in a breath audibly. "I can't explain it, but I feel a connection to you. I think we'd be good together."

I can't deny I'm attracted to him. But what would I know? He's the first man who's paid me any attention, or who I've allowed to get close. "I'm not saying I'd never marry you, but I can't say that now. I can't make a commitment when I don't know what's going to happen to me…"

"Mariana," he lifts my hand and places it over his heart. "I know what I want, I *want* you. As for the timing, well. As soon as we're married, I can sponsor you to get a green card."

His casual approach makes me angry. "That's stereotypical, isn't it? Marry to get citizenship. And even if that was what I wanted, I've been deported. And returned illegally. It won't work, Tse, whether we're married or not."

"I'm trying to find a way around that. You weren't deported legally, Mariana. You didn't have your day in front of the judge. He tried to get the plane back, but it had already landed." When I look at him in confusion, he shakes his head. "Forgot, babe. You couldn't have known what happened. Mix-up? Nah, you were on the wrong transport because someone was bribed to put you there. People paid to divert the plane. When it all went to shit, that's how we knew something was wrong."

I'd had my suspicions, but now he's confirmed it. "My father was behind it?"

"Had to have been," he admits, his lips thinning.

My leg is throbbing again, but I refuse to give in. This discussion is too important. "I can't marry you, Tse. We'd have to prove we were living together as husband and wife. I'm not sure…"

"Won't be any hardship on my part, Mariana." His eyes flare with desire.

He's so masculine he frightens me. He's talking about something he's probably done many times before. An act I hadn't allowed myself to think about, not when I couldn't let anyone in. The things I saw in that dungeon, men rutting with unwilling women, are my only experience of sex. Tse is overbearing. If we could date, take things slow… But jumping into marriage? Would he expect me to leap into his bed? My mouth twists. Not that I'm capable of leaping anywhere at the moment.

Not for the first time, he seems to read my mind. "Mariana, what we do, when we do it, is all up to you. I told you in Colombia, I'd never hurt you, or force you, or expect more than you want to give. If we have to pretend in other ways, we will. I want you with me, living beside me. I want to keep you safe." He indicates to where my bandaged thigh is under the sheet. "You need time to heal before we even think of doing anything physical. You need time to get your mobility back. Let me help you."

"I want to go back to the trailer…"

It's then he tells me it's trashed. He explains that while my father's on the loose, it would be dangerous for me to be on my own. That because they blew up the compound, my father is ruined, and it's likely he blames me. That shot didn't kill me. The next one might. He gives me a lot to think about, so much that at last I use the morphine pump, just to get the thoughts swirling around my brain to stop.

Next time I awake, Drew's come to visit. It's unfair, but my brother's relationship with Tse surprises me, and makes me a little jealous. When he comes through the door they exchange fist bumps and back slaps before Tse tactfully leaves us alone. It's easy to see Drew looks up to him, admires him, treats him as a cross between an older brother and a father, neither of which he's ever known. Tse seems to fill a gap in his life that I never even knew he had.

Drew's easy acceptance of him, and his eagerness for a legal union between Tse and myself, starts me thinking differently. When Drew's eyes fill with tears at the thought of me being deported again, I realise I need to do everything I can to prevent that. If that means tying myself to a man I don't really know, perhaps I should?

I spend eight days in that hospital. I'd expected to leave on my own two legs, instead the damage to my nerves means I'll need to use a combination of crutches and a wheelchair. I was only cleared for release when I demonstrated I could use crutches on stairs. *Bad leg down first, good leg up. Down to hell and up to heaven*, the nurse said to remind me.

The doctor wanted to send me to rehab. Being here was exposure enough. At times I feel so angry, I'd worked so hard to keep my DACA status, my father took away my chance to become a permanent resident by arranging for me to be deported before I had my day in court. Now I'm truly illegal, I can't take chances.

It took a meeting between the doctor and Peg, the burly sergeant-at-arms for the club, to persuade him that the compound was equipped and Peg experienced enough to provide the physical therapy I was going to need. I heard talk of flexion of foot, passive knee extensions and straight leg raises, which luckily seemed to mean something to Peg.

Peg's visit and intervention with the doctor resonated with me. When Tse said his brothers would be looking out for me, he meant it. Before leaving, Peg had come over to me, his tall frame seeming to tower over the bed. "You'll be safe with us," he promised.

Safe. I don't know, and if Tse does he isn't telling me, how much of a threat my father still is. He's alive, and on the loose. Would he really be able to send men after me again? Or has his empire been decimated? And if he comes for me, what about Drew? It's him he's really after.

The night before I leave the hospital, I speak once again to the man who's barely left my side.

"Tse. Marrying you doesn't guarantee anything," I start. "But if that's what you want, I will." I wave him down as he starts to speak. "On one condition. I don't think I, I…"

"You don't want to consummate our relationship? Just pretend that we have," he finishes for me. He gazes at me earnestly. "What I can promise is I'll never force you. Trust me on that?"

While I've been in the hospital, I've gradually got more details of just how much time and effort Tse put in to finding and rescuing me, and have come to understand how he and his brothers had put their lives on the line just to get me away from my father. How could I not trust the man who could have died saving me? Who's taken care of a boy who was nothing to him?

"I trust you."

The next morning I go with Tse, back to his compound. When I get out of the truck, or rather, when Tse lifts me out, I find a wheelchair ready and waiting for me. A grinning Blade standing behind it.

Wishing I could explore by myself on two legs, I let Tse push me around, introducing me to my new surroundings, and to the women and remainder of the brothers who I haven't yet met.

The compound is nothing like I expected. I thought bikers would live somewhere dull and dingy, not in an ex-vacation resort. There's even a swimming pool as well as a gym. As I spy the equipment, I realise why Peg was so adamant he could help me.

The living accommodation is spacious. Drew and Tse have suites side by side. I know I disappointed him when I adamantly stated I'd be sharing with my brother, and not sleeping in his. Although it means I'll be in close proximity with my brother, I'm not unhappy with the arrangement. Having half a king size bed is better than sleeping on the couch, which I did for years in that trailer. It's not as if Drew and I haven't shared before, when my mom was with us, she'd sleep on the couch, Drew and I taking the small and only bedroom.

I'm surprised to find the compound full of women and children, there's a five-year-old girl called Amy, Marcia's twins Jacob and Isabel, Darcy's boy Noah, Sophie's girl Olivia, Sam's handful of a toddler Eli, and Maya, who belongs to Joker and Lady. Sophie, Sam, and Slick's wife Ella are all pregnant. It's got a happy family vibe, and the women welcome me with open arms.

Drew seems particularly friendly with a girl here, Jayden, who's only a year older than him. He sighs when he tells me she and one of the members will be leaving the compound soon. He seems disappointed, and I guess he may have a crush on the girl.

Tse hovers around as I meet each new face, intuitively knowing I'll be feeling overwhelmed by all the attention. I try to learn everyone's name, and which woman is with which man. But everyone is so kind and friendly, it's not long before I start wondering why I was ever worried about coming here.

"Hey! It's Wheels all over again."

"Viper," Tse growls.

A heavily pregnant Sophie comes over and slaps Viper's arm. "Hey, that's my handle." Looking down at me, she explains, pointing at the wheelchair. "That was mine when I first came here. Peg got me back up on my feet, well, foot." She laughs. "You're in good hands with Peg." Then she glares at Viper, before stepping away.

"What?" Viper raises his hands.

Tse bends down, "You wouldn't know it, but Sophie's got a false leg."

Oh. He's right. Watching her managing even though her belly's so large she looks like she'll topple over, I start to feel optimistic. At least my injury should heal, maybe I'll be left with a slight limp, but if Sophie can manage, so can I.

I've only been here a few days when Sophie goes into labour. Her old man, Wraith, looks more worried than her when he takes her to the hospital. Included in their circle, I wait to hear the news, which seems to be a source of amusement to everyone when we hear she's given birth to another girl.

There's going to be quite an influx of babies on the compound. Sam's due to give birth in a few weeks, Ella a couple of months later, and Rock's woman, Becca, is pregnant too. It makes me wonder if there's something in the water.

Watching the bikers with their old ladies makes it easier to understand how they pulled together to rescue me from

Colombia. These men are fiercely protective. What I find so intense about Tse is mirrored in the rest of the guys. Slowly I begin to find him less domineering as I start to understand what drives him. It's about protecting their way of life as much as the people on the compound.

"Hey, Ma."

"Drew." He comes over to where I'm sitting on the couch. I wrinkle my nose. "You stink," I tell him.

"Yeah, just got back from Jacob's. I'll go shower in a moment."

"How did it go?" Tse, coming over, asks.

"Got a headcollar on Niyol and groomed him," my brother says proudly.

Tse slaps his back. "Good going, Buddy." His expression suggests he's impressed.

"You're going to have to come and see him, Ma."

I've heard so much about the stables Tse arranged for him to visit. First to give him something to think about while I was being rescued, and then simply because Drew enjoyed working with the horses so much. I'd love to meet Jacob as I've heard so much about him. Just got to get more mobile first.

"You ready, Mariana?"

As Peg's loud voice booms out, I pull the crutches toward me, shake my head when Tse goes to help, and gingerly get myself vertical, offering a smile of success as I achieve it. Peg's a hard taskmaster, but his help with the physical therapy is taking effect. I doubt if I'd have done any better in rehab.

As it turns out, when the trailer was trashed, Drew had looked for and found the box I'd kept hidden. It contained my precious social security card. A return visit to that trailer park by Tse had found my new driver's licence had arrived in the mail.

Just like that, I had everything I needed to apply for a marriage licence.

The two weeks I've spent in the clubhouse have helped me feel slightly easier about the man I've agreed to tie myself to, but I remain convinced I was getting the better half of the bargain. The more I learn about him, the more I admire him. When he appears, my heart misses a beat at his sheer beauty. When he's close, when he touches my hand, strokes my cheek, parts of me come alive. The way he treats Drew, the respect he has from his brothers, makes me appreciate him even more. That he's an honourable man is obvious.

Everything I've learned about him both excites me and worries me. Despite his protestations to the contrary, I remain convinced he's only marrying me as a step to try to make me a permanent resident. A way of fixing my problems, like he's always been doing since that first day when he mended my car's light. That somehow he's taken responsibility for me, and in doing so, has persuaded himself he can make this work. That makes more sense than anything. I can't deny there's sexual attraction between us, even though I'm too nervous to admit mine to him, but why else would he want me? I'm nothing exceptional, whereas he would take any woman's breath away. Ours has been as far from a conventional courtship as you could possibly imagine. Though my heart tells me I like him, more than that, already part of me loves him, but the future lies out long in front of us. How long would he be satisfied with a convenient wife he's only married as a final step toward saving her? By agreeing, am I backing him into a corner? Will he soon start having regrets?

"You ready?"

He's standing in the doorway to Drew's room. I shake my head.

"What's up, darlin'?" Coming over, he kneels in front of me.

Tears prick in the corners of my eyes. "Whenever I thought of getting married..." My voice falters. I hadn't really considered it at all. Knowing my future was so uncertain I couldn't plan anything.

He completes my sentence for me. "You thought you'd have a man in front of you on his knees." He grins, looks at the position he's in, and changes slightly so he's now on one knee. "Mariana, will you do me the honour of becoming my ol' lady, my wife?"

"You can't want me," I whisper, wishing this could be real.

"Oh, sweetheart. I want you enough to ask you to marry me. The question is, do you want me?"

Do I? I don't know tears are running down my face until he wipes them away. It's only then I look at him, see the question in his face. Read the expression in his eyes. *He's hurting*. I'm still uncertain, but the thought I'd be disappointing him if I said no, drives me to give him his answer.

"Yes."

Leaning forward, he plants a soft kiss to my forehead. Then his strong arms pull me up and hold me as he passes me my crutches. "Let's go do this, then."

It's simple enough. We drive into Tucson, show the necessary identification, obtain the marriage licence. The next day we go down to the city again and quietly get married in the registry office. No fanfare or celebration.

We're silent on the journey back to the clubhouse. Tse parks the truck, kills the engine, then turns to me.

"Mariana." He holds up my hand, admiring the simple band he put there, and kisses the back of my hand. "My wife." It may be his reverent tone, or the heated look in his eye, but his touch sends tingles through my body. "Will you move into my room, now?"

My eyes fly to his. *Move into his room?*

Seeing my consternation, he leans down and murmurs, "Keeping my promise, darlin'. Not going to move this on before you're ready. Appearance is important, remember? No one needs to know what we do or don't do behind closed doors."

He doesn't straighten, his lips are inches from mine. I hold my breath, wondering if he's going to kiss me, like he did that one time in Colombia. I've tried hard to put it to the back of my mind, but now I'm undecided. *If he tries to kiss me again, should I pull away? Respond?* A strange shiver runs down my spine, and there's a throbbing, like an itch I can't scratch. *I'll let him.*

He pulls back, stares at me for a moment, and then states as if it's a foregone conclusion, "We'll get your clothes moved later."

I'm in a state of shock, realising I hadn't thought through the implications of that hastily spoken 'yes' the day before or the vows I took today.

I follow his lead as he goes first into the clubhouse, he walks to the bar and holds up our joined hands. Light reflects off the new gold bands we're both wearing. Muted congratulations are given and received. A hug for us both from Drew. It's the least celebrated wedding in history. As Blade gets Tse's attention, I turn away, a feeling of shame coming over me. *Everyone knows this is a sham.*

What they don't know is what's slowly been creeping up on me. My soul-deep longing that this could be real. For Tse to feel as much for me as I do for him. *But surely I'm only feeling gratitude, how could it be anything else?* However much I tell myself that, as I sneak a look at the man conversing animatedly with Blade, I know I don't deserve him.

Tse could have anyone he wanted. In the long term, he's not going to settle for me. I don't feel ready to give up my virginity when I believe it would just be meaningless sex for him. It might not even be long before he gets fed up with me not putting out. I'm not blind, I've seen the sweet butts, seen the single men going off with them. He might have said his vows, but men have needs. Needs I can't meet.

"So you've made an honest man out of Mouse." Sam, Drummer's heavily pregnant wife has joined me. She nods at Allie, one of the sweet butts minding the bar tonight, and swiftly has a soda in her hand. "What do you want to drink?"

I'm not even twenty-one, I haven't tried alcohol before, and having noticed Tse doesn't drink, have already decided I'll probably follow his example. "A soda, please."

Allie smiles as she passes it over. "Congratulations, I didn't think anyone was going to be good enough for Mouse." She sounds sincere.

Sam smiles at both her and me. "Not wanting to gossip, but never seen Mouse with a woman before, have we, Allie?"

Allie frowns, "Well, he certainly didn't take any of us up."

Interesting. He didn't go with the women who were available here? I hadn't realised that.

When Sam indicates a free table, indicating Tse's conversation with Blade is getting intense as they argue about some bike component or other and its merits, I follow her over. The snippet she just dropped makes me wonder if she'll give me more information about the man I'm legally married to.

Tse turns, sees me sitting with Sam. Raising his eyebrow, he sends me a silent query. I wave my hand to show he should continue his discussion. *I'm fine.* He smiles that devastating smile, then his attention's on Blade once again.

"So, you and Mouse." Sam nudges me with her arm, her eyes sparkling. "You've got yourself a good one there."

Instead of responding in a like vein, my insecurities come to the fore. I shrug.

Sam's eyes stare into mine. "Okay, spill. What's eating you?"

I've kept to myself. Never opened up to anyone before. After giving me a shrewd look, she shouts out, "Allie? Bring a couple of shots, will you?"

What? Seeing the smirk on her face, I remind her. "I'm not old enough, and you're pregnant."

"No one's going to give a damn about your age here, Mariana. And I'm not drinking. They're both for you. Reckon you need to relax." When Allie puts the drinks on the table, she slides the first across to me. "Now drink. And tell Auntie Sam what the problem is."

I pick up my glass and take a sip. *God. It feels like my throat's on fire.* Under her encouraging eye, I take another. *That wasn't so bad.* It's probably psychological, but I immediately feel light headed.

Sam sits back, her hands resting on her swollen belly. She rubs it, and grins. "Think it's probably another boy. Wraith will lose his shit if Drum ends up with two boys when his are both girls."

I've noticed Wraith is a good father, loves both his babies. I narrow my eyes.

"Drummer will rib him mercilessly," she explains. "Bet he'll be boasting about his male sperm."

"You don't know the sex?"

"Nah. Prefer the surprise. Now if it's a girl, Drummer won't know what the fuck to do with it." She laughs. Personally, I don't think either of them care what they get. Their relationship is something I'd like for myself, but I can't expect that with the man who married me to keep me safe.

While she's been talking, the first shot has gone down. Sam pushes the other toward me. I've already got a pleasant buzz.

"Now I might be happily married, but that doesn't stop me wondering. What's Mouse like in the sack? He all dominant?"

My face glows. If it wasn't for the alcohol, I'd probably be more cautious, but I find myself saying, "I don't know."

Her eyebrows rise. "The way he looks at you, Mariana, I'm surprised."

"The way he looks at me?"

"Like a starving man, my dear."

I cast my eyes toward the man in question. "He does?"

"Yeah." She leans in conspiratorially, "If you can't see it, that leads me to suspect you haven't got much experience."

"None," the alcohol makes me admit.

"You could do a lot worse than him."

"He could do better," I retort.

After looking at me carefully, she starts to speak. "One night, before I got pregnant again, I was with Drummer and the guys. We all got a few drinks inside us. One of them, Beef I think it was, asked Mouse why he didn't go with the whores." When she pauses, I regard her eagerly, wanting to hear what his reply had been. "He might not have used the exact words, but he said, for him, sex had to mean something."

I gaze down at my shot, unable to understand what she's saying.

"If he wants you, and I put money on it that he does, it wouldn't just be because you're convenient. It would be because he really wants you."

I flick my eyes toward the bar again. Tse's still talking, but every so often he turns to check I'm okay. *Always looking out for me.* Like he's done from the first day we met. Taking care of me when I needed someone. *Is there more to it?* "He could break my heart," I admit.

"You could break his."

I shake my head. I doubt it.

Her hand covers mine. "Isn't it worth taking a chance? These men don't claim ol' ladies lightly. Oh, I know you got married. But to them, claiming you is a lot more than that."

My head tilts to the side. *Is it?* I didn't understand that. Tse told me he'd claimed me back in Colombia. Did he really mean something by it?

"I'm scared," I admit. "Those days when I was kept in the basement of my father's house. Men forced women right in front of me. I was so scared they'd hurt me next. They didn't, but those screams, the women…"

Sam pushes the remainder of my second shot in front of me. "If you are a virgin, no wonder you're traumatised by what you saw. Mouse isn't like that. He's not going to force you. He's never done anything to hurt you, has he?"

My head shakes side to side slowly. "He's not made a move on me."

Drummer comes in and beckons Sam to him. With an apologetic smile, awkwardly with one hand on her huge belly, she gets up and leaves. I pick up the almost empty glass and drain it. Her words echo through my brain; I sift through them selectively. *Tse wants sex to mean something.* Then my last response. *He's never made a move on me.*

That proves it, doesn't it? When he promised he wouldn't touch me, it wasn't hard for him at all. *He doesn't want me.*

He'd told me that consummating our marriage wouldn't be a problem for him.

But once he'd known I was a virgin, he'd backed right off.

I sit. Undecided. *Does he want me or not?*

CHAPTER 37

Mouse

Seeing Sam's left Mariana alone, I slap Blade on the back. "Gotta see to my ol' lady."

"Your wife." He grins. "Gotta keep her satisfied on your wedding night." He thrusts his hips leaving me in no doubt as to his meaning.

I turn, studying *my wife* for a moment. Our marriage had gone off without fanfare today, but only because that's the way I assumed she'd prefer it. She's got it in her head I'm doing this for all the wrong reasons, and I've no idea how to convince her otherwise. I love her, but I've never found the words to tell her in a way she'd accept. So we snuck off to the courthouse alone, running away as though we were doing something dirty.

Up to me, I'd have had all my brothers there, a party back at the clubhouse. The girls would have been all over that. Instead it's as though it's something that should be hidden, not celebrated. It feels a non-event to me, and probably means absolutely nothing to her. But she's mine now. Legally. That's a basis which I can work from.

Fuck, I care for her so much. My feelings have only amplified the more time I spend with her. I've become envious of the smiles she gives Drew, while always holding herself back with me. Yeah, I've tricked her. Got her to agree to move her shit into my room, when there was no need. Every man and woman here would give whatever testimony was needed if it came to it, our version of the truth. They'd never betray her or me.

Keep up appearances, I told her. When I'll be committing myself to taking numerous long cold showers from sleeping in the same bed, while not being allowed to touch her.

Now and then I get a glimpse of interest in her eyes. But since that day in Colombia I haven't even kissed her. The vibes coming from her indicating my advances are unwelcome.

It's our wedding night.

I've already claimed her. My brothers would die if they knew I hadn't even touched her. *She's mine.*

My Navajo blood tells me to break down her defences.

With a purposeful stride I walk toward her, eyeing the empty glasses on the table. "Are you sober?"

She looks up fast, puts her hand on the table and stands, pulling the crutches toward her. "I'm fine," she tells me.

"Your leg?"

"Barely hurting." She grins. "The shots helped."

My eyes sweep across her body, checking she's not swaying or any other sign to give inebriation away. My examination has another result. My cock lengthens and swells, blood rushing south making my voice husky. "Come, then."

I put my hand gently on her arm, above where she's holding the crutch. This touch she allows. Without saying more, I lead her up to *our* suite, and inside the door. Drew's staying with Sam and Drummer tonight, an offer to give us privacy.

"Drew's not here, I could sleep…"

"You're sleeping with me." My tone is wrong. I should be reassuring, not threatening, but it's hard when my pants feel too tight and everything in me just wants to hold her, to show her just how much I want her. But first, I want her to want me.

She's hesitating, as if on the verge of running. I turn to face her, and gently turn her head up to mine. Panic flares in her eyes, so I brush my lips over hers, barely touching her, then pull back.

"Not going to take anything you don't want to give," I murmur softly.

Her eyes flick wildly. "I can't," she replies.

"If you can't, you can't," I reassure her. Then my lips descend once more, hers feeling soft and yielding against mine. The Navajo plan of attack comes into my mind. *Advance and retreat, make them come after you.* I pull away.

She follows me, unwilling to break the contact. *She wants more.* I let her lips find mine, and this time, apply more pressure. She opens for me, my tongue slips inside, finding hers, toying with it. When my tongue withdraws, hers tracks it, I allow her to explore my mouth. This time when I back off, an involuntary moan comes from her mouth.

Feeling emboldened, I place my hand on the back of her head and pull her to me once more. *Attack when they're not expecting it.* Letting her believe this is all I want, lulling her into a false sense of security, I keep my hips away so she can't feel my hardness, and kiss her again, this time, more forcefully. Our mouths meet and mate, our tongues dance. She smells so good, her taste intoxicating. Her crutches fall to the ground, neither of us pay much attention. She's balancing on her good leg, but seems to be stable.

"You okay?"

"I, yes."

I can't fuck this up.

I force myself to pull back. My hands gently brush her hair back from her face. I place a quick kiss on the tip of her nose, curving my lips to smile at her. Her pupils have dilated, and I swear I glimpse disappointment there. *I've not given up. Just giving you time to process.*

Running my hands up and down her arms once, I move away. I go to the side of the bed, grab the back of my tee with my hand and pull it over my head. I hear an inhaled breath behind me as I expose my naked back.

"I, er, I haven't thought this through," she says in an undertone as though talking to herself. Then slightly louder, her voice dripping with concern, "Do you sleep naked?"

My lips curve again, my back still turned towards her, I reply, "If you want me to."

"No," she squeals.

I smile briefly, then turning, advance on her again. Her tongue flicks out to lick her lips, an unconscious move, and if I'm not mistaken, an admission that she's not unaffected by the sight of my naked chest. I work hard to keep myself in shape, not proud of my body as such, but know it wouldn't turn many women off.

"I, er." Again demonstrating being at a loss for the right words, I chuckle softly.

"My eyes are up here, sweetheart."

Her expression resembles a child caught with fingers in a cookie jar. Gently, I take hold of her hands, and place them on my pecs. Her warm touch causing the small nubs of my nipples to harden.

She glances at her hands, then up at me, her mouth opening. "Oh…" she breathes.

"All yours, darlin'," I say softly.

I step closer, she doesn't move back. There's only an inch between us. One hand on the small of her back, one around her head, I encourage her to me. She comes with no resistance, resting her face against my bare shoulder, enabling me to feel the warmth of her exhaled breath against my skin.

I hold her lightly, no pressure. Her hands start to explore. My cock swells even more, her innocent touches more exciting than any practised hands.

I lower the hand that's holding her head, still she doesn't move. *Fuck, I wish I knew what she was thinking.* It joins its partner on her back, and softly I start stroking. My hands sweep up, then back down, a barely there touch. Then stay on the hem of her tee.

"I want to see you." My voice is quiet, light, almost teasing. Issuing a challenge, I've no idea if she'll accept.

"Okay."

"Okay?" I want to make sure I've got permission.

"This doesn't mean…"

"Shush. Doesn't mean we'll do anything else." *Fuck, I hope that's where it's leading.*

She raises her arms and gives me the space to take off her tee, then her face is against my chest again as though she's feeling awkward. I close my eyes, relishing the sensation of her naked skin beneath my hands. For a moment, I just continue my previous movements, my hands moving slowly up and back down. A shiver runs through her, her skin rippling under my touch. My hands move around her sides, and then lower. When I reach her waist, she jumps.

"Ticklish?" I laugh softly. Then tickle her again. This time she almost leaps out of my arms, batting my hands away, losing her balance slightly.

"Okay, okay." After helping steady her, I hold out my palms. "Promise I won't do that again."

A stern assessing look, a moment of hesitation then, *thank fuck*, of her own volition she's approaching me again.

"Stop." My outstretched hands prevent her closing the distance.

"What?"

I nod down at her bra. "Fair's fair. You've been touching my breasts."

"Your breasts?" she sounds indignant. "You're a man."

I puff myself up. "What's the difference?"

One side of her mouth turns up as she struggles to find an answer. Having none close at hand, she freezes, then hesitantly reaches around, undoes the clasp and lets her bra slide off her shoulders.

For a moment, it's me who's speechless. "Fuckin' gorgeous," I at last say reverently. Understanding I'm the first man to see them, to appreciate them. She's not large, there's just enough to fit in my hands, tipped with brown areolae surrounding the tight buds of her nipples. Nipples which are already protruding. My first sign that she's aroused. I interpret the sight as permission to continue.

I trace the outline of her breasts, then lower my head and suck one of those perfect nipples into my mouth. She gasps loudly, her hands clutch at my arms.

"Tse…?"

When I go to her other nipple, her hand clasps my head, holding me to her. *She likes it.* I'm using my fingers on the tip I'm neglecting with my mouth, sucking and nibbling on one, while slightly pinching the other. If my cock wasn't throbbing so badly, I could play here all day. Her little appreciative sounds, the force with which she's holding me to her, making me groan.

"You're beautiful," I mouth against her, the vibration of my lips making her shiver again.

"Tse?"

"What, darlin'?"

"I want…"

"What do you want?"

I'm almost holding my breath for the answer. *To get dressed again? To stop? To go into Drew's room?*

"I don't know," she wails.

"Trust me?"

A delay, then a soft, "Yes."

While my impulse is to pick her up and throw her on the bed, mindful her recent and probably only experience of sex was watching it performed with violence, I still my baser instincts. Raising my head, I take her hand, and help her down onto the bed. Gently I push her, applying a little pressure until she's lying on her back.

"Now, where was I?" I murmur, before returning to worshipping her breasts once again.

When she's writhing beneath me, slowly, very carefully, I lower my body over hers, keeping my weight on one arm. I see the moment she feels my hardness, her eyes widening.

"That's what you do to me, darlin'. What you've done to me from the start. That first moment when you rode on my bike? I was rock hard."

I'm not expecting her to say anything at all, but she raises her hand to my cheek and cups her palm around it. "What you're doing to me now. It makes me feel like I did, when I rode behind you on your bike."

I can't help it. I grin, knowing it's probably too lecherous, but there's nothing I can do to gentle my expression. "Want me to make you feel even better?"

Her eyes flare, then look down to our joined hips. She bites her lip.

"He's going to stay zipped up. This is all for you, darlin'." I stay still, not making a move until she relaxes.

Eventually she does, giving a tentative nod.

"Going to take your pants off," I warn her, again giving her a chance to protest. She doesn't. Keeping my movements steady as though trying to coax a scared puppy, I inch my way down the bed. My eyes fixed on hers, my hands slowly pop the button and undo the zip of the loose slacks she's wearing. Then shuffling down again, I pull them right off, leaving her in her underwear. I risk a glance down; the material is soaked. I suppress my lascivious grin, not wanting my obvious hunger to scare her.

Desiring to take this slowly, I move up her body again, my lips falling on hers. She meets me, her mouth melding with mine. Her tongue coming out, not just receiving but giving. When her arms come around my neck, I move my hand down, softly smoothing across her belly. She tenses when I get to her panties, so I don't explore inside, just let my fingers trace the material down, feeling her already swollen clit through the cotton.

Going rigid, her eyes are wide, her mouth opens in an O as I gently rub it. She squirms against my touch, her features contorting as though she wants more, but doesn't know how to ask for it.

It's then I move the flimsy material aside, feeling the satin of her skin for the first time. Our foreplay has already excited her, my fingers doing their job ramps up her arousal. Soft moans are coming out of her mouth, but I doubt she knows she's making them. Reading the signs, feeling her skin rippling, her thigh muscles trying to strangle my hand, I know she's close.

Twisting my hand, I leave my thumb on her clit, and slip a finger inside her, when she pushes against me, I add another, then curl them around. When I reach the right spot an almost indescribable sound reaches my ears, a cross between a surprised squeak and a gasp. *Fuck, the power I feel. I'm the first man who's done this to her.*

It doesn't take long. Now her moans turn to keening, so I apply more pressure, her muscles tense more, she takes in a breath and holds it, then tries to curl her body up as she comes with a scream.

I keep rubbing that clit, trying to extend her first orgasm given by a man. Then when an evasive twitch tells me she's had enough and has become too sensitive, I remove my hand, bring it triumphantly to my mouth, and lick her sweet cream off my fingers.

Breathing heavily, she watches, her eyes once again showing her surprise as I lick each digit clean.

CHAPTER 38

Mariana

As I watch him licking his fingers, relishing the taste of me as though nothing could be sweeter, I feel my heart rate returning to normal, and a giggle escapes my mouth. Then, suddenly, I'm laughing. I throw my head back as my whole body shakes with mirth.

"Well, that's unusual," he grins down. "Not had that reaction before." My laughter must be infectious, as he's laughing too.

"It's just… it's…." I can barely speak. "When I came to your room, I didn't expect this. Didn't want it. Didn't think you'd…"

He rears back. "You didn't think I wanted you?"

Quickly I shake my head. "I thought you might want sex, but what you've done, given, not taken. It's more than that."

"I'm glad you know the difference. I'm in the middle of making love to my wife." He's gone serious, though his lips still curve slightly.

I shudder in nervous anticipation. "In the middle of…?"

He shrugs. "We can stop if you like."

I can still feel his hardness against my thigh. If we stop now… "But you?"

He places a kiss against my forehead. "I'll live. I'll take care of it in the shower. You come first, sweetheart."

He makes me feel confident enough to joke, "I think I just did."

"Minx."

While we've been talking, he's moved his hand down, circling his fingers over my clit once more. I'd been about to ask how he could expect to arouse me again, when I have my answer.

"I want to taste you," he whispers against my ear. What can I do but give my permission?

Intrigued to know what he's going to do, I watch as he slides down the bed and expertly removes my panties. He's brought me nothing but pleasure. While there's still a niggling doubt in my mind, I'd be crazy to stop him now. Although his dick must be straining against his zipper, he's still got his jeans on. He's showing no sign of just taking anything that I saw the women being forced to do. And, I remind myself, I could have sent him off for a cold lonely shower. *I'd have been crazy to.*

He's gazing at me, his broad shoulders stopping me from closing my thighs, even though I'm embarrassed when I see where he's so intently staring.

"Fuckin' gorgeous," he repeats.

I'm not expecting him to do what he does next. He puts his mouth on me. *There.* Sweeping his tongue inside. As I feel him lapping, the sensations make my toes curl and my hands fist. This is a different feeling to his fingers. The soft glide of his tongue from my slit to my clit, so arousing. I even feel a gush of excitement, which strikes me I'm making the bed wet, but that seems to be the last thing on his mind, and then on mine, when he makes a dual assault on my clit while his fingers reach inside.

Oh, Oh. I didn't think I could come again. But he's, he's… My stomach clenches, I clutch at the sheets with both hands. My thighs tighten, I try to relax them, afraid I'm hurting his head, but I'm beyond conscious control as my body, played so expertly by him, does as its master commands. I can't hold back my scream, my head comes off the bed as the strongest waves of pleasure wash over me.

This time, when I come down, he's already moved up the bed. A smirk on his face which glistens with my moisture. Then his lips crash down on mine, forcing me to taste myself on his mouth. *I didn't expect to like it.* The salty taste, though, seems to spark another chain reaction, and though I thought I was spent, my clit tingles again.

Wary of committing myself, when he pulls away I rasp, "I want to see you."

"Yeah?" Not waiting for another invitation, he stands, undoes his belt, sliding it through the loops with a hiss, then undoing his button. Putting a hand inside, he slowly and carefully lowers the zip, and I soon see why he's being careful. He's gone commando. As soon as it's freed, a long, thick cock bounces out.

My hand snakes out of its own accord. When my brain catches up, I know I want to touch him, to discover what it would feel like in my hand.

But he steps back and waggles his finger. "You said you wanted to see me, not touch."

The mock expression of shock on his face makes me giggle again.

"Laughing at my cock now, are you?"

The smirk that accompanies his words has me snorting with laughter. As I cover my mouth with my hand, I realise I didn't expect sex would be fun. *No, not sex. Making love.*

"It's funny, is it?" He stalks me, putting first one knee then the other on the bed. "I'll give you something to laugh about." His hands glide over me, my body so responsive he leaves goose bumps in their wake, until his fingers dig in to that place under my ribs.

I squeal, and try to push him off. My body arches up allowing me to see his cock in all its glory, with its... "What the...?" He kneels over me, his cock just above my groin. If I was weakening, thinking of letting him put that thing inside me, now I'm definitely having second thoughts.

He looks down as if he's only just noticed. "It's an Apadravya," he explains. "I swear it won't hurt you, just heighten your pleasure." As though to emphasise the point, he rubs it over my clit. I jump at the renewed assault on that bundle of nerves. Seeing my reaction, he continues to work his dick over the nub. My back arches, and my breathing speeds up, the piercing on the glans of his cock forgotten.

One hand still holding his cock, working it over my clit, he reaches over and snatches up a condom, using his teeth to tear open the packet, then he's covering himself in latex. I watch transfixed.

With his eyes firmly fixed on mine, he draws my uninjured leg up so it's bent at the knee, and falling open to the side. Then he very carefully tries to do the same to the other, watching my face for the moment it starts paining me. Then he stops. He's managed to create a lop-sided cradle for himself.

I don't move as he repositions himself, and I feel the head of his cock putting a gentle pressure against my slit.

"Tell me to stop. Tell me you don't want this."

"Don't hurt me," I say, at the same time squirming as though my body knows what it wants, my head's just not quite caught up.

"Look at me, Mariana. The last thing I want to do is to hurt you. Something you don't know about me—I don't fuck when it doesn't mean anything. And here, now, loving you means the world to me. I love you. Hear me? I love you. I'm serious about us. I want the whole thing. You're my wife." He pauses for a moment.

I don't know what to say, scared about the unknown, and that he could easily overpower me, do what he wants.

"Tell me to stop. Tell me what you want, Mariana." As he talks, I can feel his cock pressing against me, and my body automatically tries to bear down.

As though the floodgates have opened, emotions wash through my head, from my brain to my hands which reach out for him. Allowing, *permitting,* me to believe this future really could be mine if I'm brave enough to take it. To admit to loving this man as I know I have for so long. An unlikely relationship, two lost souls. Mine called to his as his to mine.

"I want you. I want this. I, I love you, Tse."

His eyes close and open, the creases disappear from his brow. His gaze now fixed on mine, he presses the head in and retreats, "You want this, eh? You want my cock?"

He's teasing me. I can feel my vagina muscles clenching, as if they're trying to guide him in. "I want you," I repeat breathlessly.

"You want my cock?"

"Yes," I gasp.

"You want this?" He teases again, the pressure that's there and then not.

"I want your cock!" I scream.

It's the incentive he wants. This time he doesn't torment, just proceeds to make ground. I'm being stretched in ways I never have before. It stings, burns, but when I look at the man above me with such an intense look on his face, his teeth gritted as though he's holding himself back, I try to relax and allow him in.

He advances, retreats, gradually conquering me, I swear I can feel that piercing over the spot he'd found with his fingers, the one that had sent me off like a rocket launched into space. One final push, then he stops moving.

"You've taken all of me." He looks pleased, proud, and tense all at the same time. "You okay?"

I'm full of my man. Shyly I nod.

He leans forward, giving me a gentle kiss. "Gonna make love to you now."

I know he's holding himself back, trying to make my first time good. As my discomfort fades, I find I want more. Automatically lifting my good leg and putting it around him, gasping as it allows him to go deeper. What experience have I of cocks? None at all. But I suspect that piercing, as he suggested, is adding to my pleasure. *Surely it can't always be this good?*

I thought he'd shown me what orgasms could be like. *I'd been wrong.* As I writhe with frustration, wanting a little more stimulation, he intuitively knows, reaching his hand down between us and pinching my clit.

I see stars, planets. The whole heavens in a burst of blinding light. Only just aware of his roar, his short pumps, as he empties himself into the condom.

I swear I lose consciousness for a moment. When I come back to myself, my body's throbbing in all sorts of delicious ways I've never experienced. I'm tingling, I feel weak, and my lungs are heaving as though I've just run a race. As his softening cock slips out of me, he holds the condom in place, then ties and discards it in a trash can by the side of the bed.

When he gets up and leaves me, I feel empty, wondering what I do now. But he's quickly back by my side carrying a damp cloth. I go to move, but he fixes me with his eyes, and gently wipes the evidence of our lovemaking away. Then he's back, lying next to me, and I'm in his arms, enclosed in a blanket of security and love. I've a feeling that I've come home, and that this is where I'm meant to be. There and then I decide I never want to be anywhere else.

"I'm married," I say, my voice full of wonder. After the courthouse, I'd felt trapped, now I feel content, at peace with myself.

"*We* are," he corrects. "We're in this together, partners now, Mariana. Okay, so we've got a lot to find out about each other, but we've got a lifetime to learn that shit. What I do know is we were meant to be together. Hey, in time, maybe we'll throw a kid or two into the mix." As I freeze, he looks puzzled. "What's the matter?"

"I don't want kids."

"Oh? Why not?" He doesn't sound angry or upset, just interested to hear my reasoning.

I take a second to pull my thoughts together. "Well, first there's the issue of me having returned to the country illegally. Even if there's a way around that, and my DACA status is given back to me, I'm still considered illegal. Getting a green card may not be easy. And even that's just a temporary fix, it doesn't give me long-term rights. If I get that, we need to be married a couple of years before I can apply for permanent residency. Nothing's guaranteed, Tse. We'll have to prove this marriage is genuine and even then they could change the rules."

"Wouldn't having a baby prove we're serious? Shows we've consummated the marriage at least."

I reach for his hand and hold it. "Tse, I can't even think of it. I've already gone through hell thinking I was separated from my brother. What would it be like with a baby? At least Drew was old enough to look after himself if he had to. A baby would be helpless. Then he or she would be looked on as an anchor baby, people would say I purposefully had a child to try to stay here. Just think. What if I was deported? I know I wouldn't want to be separated from my child. What if you didn't either? You could fight me for custody, and as the child would be a US citizen, have a good chance of winning. Perhaps that would be the best outcome, being deported is bad enough, but to be in a strange country with the responsibility of a child?" I shudder just thinking about it.

He sits up, propping himself on one elbow, turning my head to face him. "Mariana. Look at me, listen to me. I've married you, more than that, I've claimed you. You are mine. Should you fail to get residency, should you be deported, you will not be on your own. Do you understand me? I will come with you. Wherever you go."

My brow furrows, unable to understand what he's telling me. "You'd leave your brothers? The Satan's Devils? All that you love?"

"I love you, Mariana." He raises my hand wearing his ring and kisses it. "You and me against the world." He's so intense, it's not hard to believe him. His dark eyes shine down as he makes me one more promise. "You're not alone, Mariana. You'll never be alone again."

CHAPTER 39

Mouse

I'd made promises in the dead of the night and I meant every one of them. At first it had been a sexual attraction, then the more I learned about the life Mariana had to live, how she coped with it, how she looked after her brother, even though we were parted, my respect, my admiration for her had grown. Slowly turning into a deeper emotion, I'd spoken the truth, I'd spent far too much time unable to see her, I never want to be parted from her again.

She's still sleeping, I dredge through the facts in my head, joining dots, analysing data, thinking of all the things that can be done. She's lived with the fear of deportation all her life. Now there's a real threat to her person, her father is still on the loose, and he's intent on killing her and kidnapping Drew. Surely no judge would send her back to Colombia? But if they did, she wouldn't be going alone.

I knew she'd fit in my arms, and making love to her? That had exceeded my expectations. Maybe knowing I was the first man to touch her so intimately, but my possessive, protective instincts had been roused. *She's mine.* Forever.

She starts to stir, I watch her as she comes to, a yawn, her legs stretching out, her feet finding mine. A little startled expression as she remembers she's in my bed, waking up with a man for the first time.

"Good mornin'." I'm smiling, she's so adorable half asleep.

When I hold out my arms she comes into them, waking up fast when my morning wood meets the softness of her belly.

"Ignore it," I say softly. "After last night, you'll be too sore."

She grins cheekily, and her hand moves down, and touches my cock, her tiny hand trying to surround it. I groan, my head going back. As she squeezes gently, I can't resist, covering her fingers with my own, showing her the pressure and rhythm I like, my other hand reaching between us and rubbing her clit.

Now it's her turn to moan.

Fuck, it feels good, her jerking me off, her face starting to contort with her own pleasure. I'm close, so's she…

The door's flung open. "Mouse…" Drew's excited exclamation comes to an abrupt halt. Luckily the sheet's covering both of us, but our closeness, our expressions must give us away.

"Er, I'll come back later." He backs out of the door.

My now limp dick falls out of her hand, Mariana moves to the other side of the bed. I look at her, she at me, then suddenly we both laugh.

"I'm fuckin' lockin' the door next time," I growl.

"Do you think we've damaged him for life?" she asks, quite seriously.

Hell no. I don't tell her, but he's probably seen far worse in the clubhouse. I settle for, "Nah, he just didn't expect to walk in on us like that. Poor kid's probably embarrassed."

"He's embarrassed?" Her eyes open wide. "I'm mortified."

I kiss her, then slide my legs over the bed. "I'll have a quick shower, then get dressed, go see what he wants."

We end up showering together. Which means it's an hour or more before we're ready to go down to the clubhouse. Turns out Drew didn't want us for anything life or death. The room's abuzz with the news Horse is making his annual trip to the States and will be arriving next week, and Blade's suggested the talented airbrush artist would paint a design on the hood of

Drew's car. I raise my eyebrows and shake my head in Blade's direction when Drew tells me. Unapologetically he grins and shrugs. Drew's car's only one step away from the scrap heap as far as I'm concerned. But boys will be boys, and who am I to censure him for wanting to customise it? I ride a Harley with all manner of shit on it myself.

Sophie's in her element, another British person to speak to. Horse has been coming here for years, one time he turned up with her in tow as she needed protection. She stayed when she met Wraith, and married our VP. *Hmm.* They must have been through the green card shit. Maybe they'd know a thing or two and could give us some advice.

As brothers and old ladies mill around, and Mariana's sitting with Drew trying to tell him a skull on his car wouldn't be appropriate, I'm pleased to see how she seems to be settling in here. When I see Sophie join them, I smile. Mariana's probably never had friends before, she'd always been afraid to let anyone in.

Over the next couple of weeks, life's great. Mariana really starts coming out of her shell, proving to be more adventurous than I expected both in and out of bed. I fall a little bit more in love with her every day, and become even more committed to somehow giving her the peace of mind that she can relax and make her home here. One thing bothers me, she adores the babies in the clubhouse, always wanting a cuddle, and proving a help, even offering to change diapers. She'd make such a great mom. That conversation the first morning plays on my mind. She's sacrificing what she wants for all the right reasons, but it kills me she has to.

"Sam said you'd be here." Mariana walks across the rough ground. Her leg is now strong enough to move without crutches as long as she favours it and doesn't overdo it.

I pause, my hand in mid-air, then beckon her to me. Dutifully she raises her face, and I lean down to kiss her.

"Jeez, you two lovebirds." Blade's shielding his eyes.

I raise my mouth a fraction. "Shut it, Blade." Then in a stage whisper, "He's jealous, ignore him." Spurred by his reaction, I put down what I was holding, put both arms around her, and kiss the hell out of my old lady. When we finally come up for air, I give him a pointed look.

Her lips are swollen; she looks flustered and adorable. My assault seems to have made her forget why she wanted me. Instead, she looks around and asks, "What are you doing?"

"Target practice," Blade replies. As if to demonstrate, he picks up a knife and throws it at the target in front of us, frowning when he misses the cardboard man's heart.

I step forwards, taking a throwing knife, and aiming it. Grinning when I'm closer than he is.

"Can I have a go?" Mariana looks intrigued.

"You ever play darts?" Blade asks.

She shakes her head. No, she's probably never had much fun in her life.

I hand her a knife, and show her how to hold it, demonstrating the action she requires. Blade's eyes widen, then he pointedly comes to stand behind us. "You want to throw it that way." He points toward the target.

"She'll be fine," I respond, expecting I'll have to go retrieve the weapon from the undergrowth, but hey, I'm learning I'll do anything for my wife.

Biting her lip in concentration, Mariana steps up. She pulls back her arm just like I showed her, then lets that knife fly… It lands right in the middle of the heart.

"Beginner's luck," Blade growls, and hands her another.

Fuck me. She's done it again.

Blade and I exchange glances. "Here." I pass her a third. It knocks both her previous blades out.

"I'll be fucked," Blade exclaims.

It does rather put a damper on our practice time. She might be my wife, and I'm proud as fuck of her, but I'm a man after all. Blade and I make a few gestures, both agreeing we'll resume another day when it's just the two of us. Neither liking to be outdone by a woman.

That Blade was impressed is confirmed later that night, when there in the clubhouse he makes a show of presenting Mariana with one of his favourite knives. Her look of pleasure at the recognition of her abilities makes her glow. My chin raise sends him my thanks; he shrugs them off.

"What's the matter?" The day after she'd shown me and Blade up with her knife throwing skills, I walk into our suite, sliding out of my cut. Mariana's sitting on the bed with the new phone I'd bought for her in her hands.

"That was Carissa. I've got a hearing date."

She clearly needs me. I go to her, pulling her into my arms. I don't say platitudes or tell her everything will be fine. Nor do I tell her that I've been preparing for the worst, having already told Drummer, if she's deported, I'll be going with her. So I just hold her, letting her draw strength from me.

Over the next couple of weeks, I make sure she knows how much I love her, nights spent proving it to her in bed. Around us life goes on as usual, but I know she feels like the Sword of Damocles is hanging over her head.

"How's Mariana holdin' up?"

I pause a moment before answering the prez sitting at the head of the table. We've just gone through the normal church business. Lowering the lid of my laptop, I at last respond. "Much as you'd expect. We're both preparing for the worst, hoping for the best."

"No one in their right minds would send her back to Colombia," Beef protests. "We all know what's waiting for her there."

It's a who, not a what, but I don't correct him. "We expect ICE to come down pretty hard on her. She's back in the US, entered illegally again. That will count against her."

"Her skin's not the right colour for them," Marvel sneers.

I nod, it's strange, though her colouring is actually similar to mine.

"People are all riled up about illegal immigrants, expect them only to come here to commit crimes. From what I've seen of your ol' lady, most of them are like her. Afraid to put a foot out of line in case they're deported."

"Stats show unless they join a gang, and join's the wrong word, forced into them more like, they're more law abiding than folks who were born here." I nod at Rock as I answer him.

"Yeah, because citizens know the worst that can happen is jail time. Not being sent back to whatever shithole they came from," Shooter sneers.

Drummer lets Rock, Shooter and Marvel all have their say, eventually bringing it to a close. "Anything we can do, Mouse?"

"Nah. As much as possible, I've got it handled. We're taking some stuff for her in case the worst happens. I'll take some shit too; I'll be on the first plane I can and following her."

"You got a visa sorted?"

I have. I've kept it from Mariana as it would upset her to know how serious I think the threat of deportation is. "Yeah, Prez."

Drummer wipes his hand over his beard. "I don't know if everyone's realised, but if Mariana gets deported again, Mouse will be gone for years, if not forever. Unless you've changed your mind?"

I shake my head. "Sorry, Prez."

"No need for apologies, Brother. If it were Sam, I'd be doing the same thing."

"Losing too many good brothers lately. You'll be off yourself soon, won't you, Paladin?" Beef frowns, then turns to his neighbour. "I presume that's still happening?"

Slick shrugs. "Yeah. Drummer's setting it up." He doesn't seem happy.

"What about Drew?" Blade interjects, getting us back on topic.

I glance at Prez who replies, "Sam and I will take care of him. Least until we know the score. Mariana and Mouse will need to get shit organised for if, and when, he decides to join them. Seems like we're getting a reputation for picking up strays." There's a chuckle, though Heart looks uncomfortable. Drummer and Sam looked after his daughter when he couldn't after the death of his first ol' lady.

"Drew okay with that?"

I nod at Slick. "He knows he should finish his education. Once we get settled, he can come for visits. I'll need to check out the ground first, make sure it's safe."

"Don't like the idea of you being on your own down there, Brother."

Me neither, but I don't respond to Peg. What choice have I got? I'm not leaving Mariana to fend for herself.

"Her father's still out there," Wraith reminds me unnecessarily.

"There are MCs in Colombia. One in Bogotá. Might be safer if you joined up with them."

And start all over as a prospect. "I'll think about it, Prez."

"Leastways they might give you protection if you need it. Worst happens? I'll get in touch."

I raise my chin, showing my gratitude to Drummer. Fuck, this meeting is making me depressed. I've had these discussions with Mariana and Drew, but it's always been in a hypothetical sense, the worst-case scenario. Sitting around this table is bringing it home that I could very soon be leaving this brotherhood. Not for weeks or months, but as Drummer had said, years. It's possible I'll never be around this table again.

I glance at the faces around me, it looks like the seriousness of the situation is dawning on my brothers too. I try to imprint the features of the men I'll continue to call brothers wherever I end up, on my brain, committing them to memory. I might be thousands of miles away, but that won't change how I feel about them. I take in Wraith, Blade, Dollar, Viper, Beef, Slick, Road, Paladin and Shooter. Joker and Lady at the bottom of the table, then Marvel, Jekyll, Hyde, Bullet and Peg. A wave of emotion washes over me.

"Hey, I've got this picture in my mind. A ranch, horses and lots of them. Lush green scenery, mountains behind. Mouse and Mariana and a houseful of kids behind them." Beef grins at me. "Great place to come for a visit."

"Put like that," Road says. "May even come with you."

"You could grow your own marijuana," Hyde suggests, a quick glance shows he's serious.

As other comments come to me, some of course inane, I shake my head, my lips curving. I'll miss this.

"You'll get your dues paid, long as you're still our computer guy," Dollar reminds me.

Drummer bangs the gavel. "Let's hope it doesn't come to that."

The night before we set off for LA there's no party in the clubhouse. Just people telling us to get our asses back here fast, grumbling we're going to be away, all avoiding mentioning that we might not be coming home. We'll be leaving early the next morning. Drew wanted to come with us, Mariana persuaded him not to, thinking if the outcome wasn't what we were hoping, it would be too devastating for him. Both sister and brother are struggling to stay strong for each other.

We walk up to the suites together. Drew hugs Mariana, holding her tight, and I give them the space to say what they need to. At least I know he's got the horses and Jacob to keep him occupied. Old man and boy seem to have taken to each other.

When she comes into my room, she's crying. She grabs a tissue, blows her nose, and tries to wipe the tears away. "Make love to me, Tse?"

She doesn't need to ask me twice. Although I've vowed I won't be parted from her, I love her so gently, so reverently, scared something could happen that would upset our plans.

In the morning we leave.

CHAPTER 40

Mariana

Tse was so gentle and loving last night, giving me precisely what I needed. But even after our extended lovemaking, I couldn't sleep. I hate the tag that's hanging around my neck, *illegal*. It seems unfair, I'm as American as the next person, it wasn't my choice I was brought here as a child. My brief sojourn in Colombia left me with no desire to call that country home. *I want to stay here.* Chances are, that won't be allowed. I've avoided the subject with Tse, I'm certain he's banking on me being allowed to stay, I hadn't wanted to upset him by making him face up to the fact that I most likely won't.

We're separated when we arrive at the courthouse. I'm taken to a cell to wait for my time in front of the judge; Tse will be taking his place in the public gallery. I'm so glad he's here. He's reassured me, whatever happens, he'll be with me. Close behind if I'm deported. I believe he will, even though I worry about all he'll be leaving behind, and whether that would put too great a strain on our still embryonic relationship. But at least, to start with, I wouldn't be alone. That takes some of the fear away.

At last I'm called and go where indicated to the witness stand. There are two tables in front of me. From one, Carissa Beacham, my lawyer, gives me an encouraging smile. Sitting just behind her is a man I didn't expect to see here, Jason Deville, or Devil as he's better known. On the next table are stony faced men I don't recognise, but know who they are immediately. They're representatives from ICE. Their only desire is to see me, a statistic, not a person, sent back to the country where I was born.

We stand, then sit, as the judge takes his seat. The name card in front of him shows he's Judge Hawkins.

Having settled himself, he looks down at the information in front of him, and his eyes widen. His face is stony as he looks toward the men from ICE. "This is the case I was supposed to hear some weeks back. When a deportation was pre-empted without my determination."

One of the men from ICE gets to his feet. "Your Honour, I apologise for that. I must also add that Mariana De Souza has re-entered the country illegally…"

"Objection, Your Honour." Carissa's on her feet.

"That's fact," the ICE man snarls.

The judge raises an eyebrow and motions for Carissa to continue. "Mrs Williamson received a near fatal injury in Colombia. She was brought here for emergency treatment."

"She could have gone to a hospital in Colombia."

Carissa sends the government representative a scathing look. "Her life was in danger. Her safety couldn't be guaranteed in that country."

The judge bangs the gavel. "I believe we are getting ahead of ourselves. Please, Ms Beacham, let us start in a more orderly fashion. Your witness, I believe."

Carissa stands and approaches me. "Mrs Williamson. Can you explain to the court how you originally came to be in the US?"

"I was four years old," I begin, my voice shaky. "My mother had been brutally attacked by my father. He'd hit me too and broken my arm."

"You remember that?" the man from ICE questions. "Or is that what you were told?"

"I remember. You don't forget things like that." I rub my arm where it had been broken. "You're right, I don't remember much else. The panic of my mother though, that I do recall. The details of the journey, no."

"You arrived in Arizona?" Carissa takes over again, giving a look at the ICE man who I presume shouldn't have interrupted.

"I couldn't tell you exactly what happened, I was only four after all. But my mother managed to feed me, and we soon ended up with a one-bedroom trailer."

"The trailer you'd been living in with your brother, Drew?"

I nod, then confirm, "That's right."

The ICE men confer with each other. "We're not aware of a brother, Your Honour. May I ask, is he illegal too?"

"My brother," I answer, drawing my shoulders back, "is a US citizen. The night before we left, my father had raped my mother. She didn't know she was pregnant until some time after we arrived. That," I address myself to the judge, "I don't remember. But that's what I was told."

"Your mother told your father she was having another child?" Carissa prompts, already knowing the answer.

"No." I shudder. "We kept Drew's, that's my brother, existence quiet. My father is a dangerous man, and if he knew he had a son, he might have come after him."

"What's the current status of your mother?"

"My mother requested asylum, but it wasn't granted. She was deported six years ago when I was fourteen. One day she was there, one day she wasn't. Nobody came, so I looked after Drew. He was just nine at the time."

"Are you in contact with your mother? She's in Colombia?"

"She was killed almost immediately after she arrived. At the time, I believed it had been my father, but there was no evidence. However, when I met him, he admitted it himself."

"Objection, Your Honour. Hearsay at best."

Carissa smiles sweetly. "I have another witness to call in a minute, Your Honour. What he has to say will corroborate Mrs Williamson's assumption."

She continues to question me. My DACA status comes out, the fake accident and the proof of my innocence. She makes the point I'm only in front of the court because of the greed of the man who crashed into me. The judge refers to the evidence that's provided to support my case. She's done her homework, she's got reports from the community college about my diligence as a student, and how I'll make a good nurse.

The judge's face gives no indication he's been swayed by my testimony. The men from ICE look bored as if they've seen and heard it all before. One keeps looking at his watch as though he wants to wrap this up.

"Ms Beacham, I have a question, if I may?" The judge needn't ask for permission, and Carissa doesn't withhold it. "Mrs Williamson, your notes here refer to you in your maiden name. You married after you returned to the States?"

"I did." My eyes catch those of Tse, he's smiling at me.

I hear a murmur of derision from the ICE table. The judge ignores them. "This wedding was precipitous?"

"Tse proposed to me before I was deported. My near death scared us both, made us realise life was too short for delays."

"Did you marry so he could sponsor you for a green card?"

I shake my head, a smile for Tse on my face. "No, Your Honour. I married for love. I've already got a family member who could sponsor me, my brother Drew in another six years."

My smile disappears as the judge's face looks like I haven't convinced him. That's all before I'm dismissed, and I go and sit down. Carissa calls up Devil, and he takes my place in the witness box.

I watch with interest, not certain why he's here.

"Mr Deville, could you tell us a little about yourself?"

"I'll tell you what I can. Your Honour, I believe you have my credentials in front of you?" He waits for a signal from the judge, then continues. "I am a senior partner of an international security company with its headquarters in the UK. Most of my work is on a consultancy basis. I've worked in many countries, and for a number of years, have worked with the FBI and the CIA."

"Yes, I can see that. And at the highest levels. I understand some details are not appropriate for a public court?"

"Thank you, Your Honour, and yes, though I am a little freer than I used to be. I'm unable to go undercover nowadays." He doesn't need to draw attention to his scar, we can all see it.

"How did you get involved in this case, Mr Deville?"

"Mrs Williamson is married to a man I have dealt with in the past. A man who's provided some very useful information to the FBI on occasion. Mr Williamson enabled us to bring down a child smuggling ring."

"How did Mr Williamson obtain this information? Was he associated with the criminals?"

A glare from Devil would make most men crumble. Even the man from ICE looks contrite. "Mr Williamson is an expert with computers. He was able to go into the dark web to get what we needed. He was working with an ex-police officer at the time. Together they exposed several officers in the Tucson police force."

"There are notes of the case in the evidence pack," the judge points out. "Carry on, Ms Beacham. I think we've established how Mrs Williamson was able to enlist the help of Mr Deville."

Devil raises his hand. "It wasn't Mrs Williamson. By the time I got involved, she'd been deported. The plane she was on was diverted, and Mr Williamson had lost track of her." Devil's taken the floor, not waiting for questions. Nobody seems to object. "When I investigated I found two ICE agents at this end had been bribed to put her on the wrong transport from the

Service Processing Centre. The plane pilot had also been paid a rather large sum of money. The report of a problem with the traffic control system had been fake."

The judge's eyebrows rise, and he addresses the agents. "Are you aware of this?"

I'm interested in their answer. Studying their faces, to me it looks like they're sheepish. "We're conducting an internal investigation."

The judge just stares for a moment, then turns his attention back to Carissa. "Continue, Ms Beacham."

"Did you discover the reason for the change in destination?"

"I certainly did. The plane was diverted to a provincial airport. The rest of the deportees were bussed to the capital, but Ms De Souza, apologies, Mrs Williamson, was collected by her father's men and taken to his residence.

"Your Honour, you have to understand the man who's Mrs Williamson's father. She knew him as a violent man who broke her arm when she was young, and who raped her mother causing them to seek asylum in the United States. As we've heard, asylum wasn't granted for her mother, with dire consequences. Perhaps it would have been, were the facts of the matter known. Mrs Williamson's father is a man who falsely assumed the title of General De Souza. In fact, he had been dishonourably discharged from the army due to, let's say, his overzealous practices. He was responsible for the mass murders of civilians. A violent man with no regard for anyone's life, death or happiness other than his own. He later became known as the criminal *El Procurador*, supplying guns and drugs to the US, as well as slave trafficking. A man the CIA were extremely interested in.

"On learning he had a son in the US, he sent his men to collect the boy who he wanted to groom as his heir. The abduction was foiled by Mr Williamson and his friends. During questioning, we managed to discover the whereabouts of *El Procurador*, and where Mrs Williamson was being held."

Devil throws me a quick glance of sympathy. "I coordinated a dual-purpose strike. To rescue Mrs Williamson who was being held against her will, and to capture her father. We were successful on the former, destroyed a large portion of *El Procurador*'s organisation, and managed to free a number of women who were being prepared to be sold. Mrs Williamson, far from being in the loving hands of her father, was being kept in inhumane circumstances, and was about to be sold as a slave herself. Her only usefulness to her father, a means to get to his son."

The judge sends an unreadable look my way. I sigh with relief that Devil omitted to mention the drugs I'd been forced to swallow.

Without prompting from Carissa, Devil takes a sip of water, and resumes. "I made the decision it was too dangerous for Mrs Williamson to stay in Colombia. She was going to accompany me back to the US instead. I take full responsibility for that. Especially as she was shot, either by her father or one of his remaining men, when boarding the plane. An injury she would not have recovered from had I not had a medic on my team, and if two team members were not able to give blood to her during the flight. Mrs Williamson is extremely lucky to be alive today."

Carissa goes to speak; the judge raises his hand. "Mr Deville. Where is *El Procurador* now? Were you able to take him into custody?"

Devil's face grows dark. "We were not, Your Honour. The house and compound was equipped with a means of escape. In the confusion, he managed to get away. Where the man himself is now, we have no idea. We, as in the CIA and myself, believe he's trying to regroup in Colombia. But serious damage has been done to his organisation. There is a good chance he will place the blame for that at Mrs Williamson's door."

"You believe Mrs Williamson remains in danger?"

"If she returns to Colombia? Certainly, yes. And we can't rule out more of *El Procurador*'s remaining men crossing over into the US and trying to take the boy again. From what we discovered, we were able to close a number of his pipelines, but, well, where there's a will…"

The judge looks at the men from ICE. "Have you anything more you want to say or ask?"

"Your Honour. While we appreciate the circumstances, and that Mr Deville made the decision, the cold fact of the matter remains that having been deported, Mrs Williamson re-entered the States again as an illegal immigrant. The law says she should be deported immediately."

"You're trying to teach me the law?" the judge snaps. After his comment is left to echo for a moment, he turns to Carissa. "Ms Beacham. Do you have anything further to ask your witness?"

After she replies no, the judge turns to the other men. "Any questions from you?"

When the ICE representatives shake their heads, Devil returns to his seat.

The judge looks down at his notes, then back up. "In such a complicated case, I'd normally wait to deliver a written statement, and that will certainly follow. Normally Mrs Williamson would be detained in an immigration centre while I make my deliberations. Due to the number of errors in this case, I believe I can give the gist of my judgement now."

He takes off his glasses, swinging them in his hand. First, he glares at the men from ICE. "You contend Mrs Williamson re-entered the country illegally. I contend mistakes and collusion with a foreign party within ICE caused her to be deported prematurely. I, myself, issued instructions for her to be brought back immediately. The circumstances being as they are, I hereby waive her illegal re-entry." He breaks off, sips water, then continues. "Mrs Williamson has presented sufficient evidence that she has a clear case for asylum in the United States. To return her to Colombia would undoubtedly be signing her death sentence, or sending her to an unknown fate which could be worse.

"I do not support the recommendation for deportation, and I would request that ICE examine the mistakes made in this case, including why Mrs Williamson was able to be deported prior to the hearing to which she was entitled, and how government offi cials could be bribed to turn a blind eye to a plane being diverted from its course.

"Before my learned friend in ICE gets too agitated, I would like to remind him, this immigration court can hear cases of asylum. Mrs Williamson was presented to this court, or should have been, as an illegal immigrant a few weeks ago. That she was brought here was questionable due to her DACA status. Her innocence, once proven, should have been taken into account. I am well aware a claim for asylum should be made within one year of seeking such a status in the US. I am concluding that Mrs Williamson's asylum application should have been filed when she returned from Colombia, and that now, today, we are still well within that one year limitation.

"Mrs Williamson. You will receive my written judgement in due course, and may apply for a green card on your own merits after one year of residency.

"The application for deportation is hereby dismissed. Until such a time as she's able to start the process towards permanent residence, Mrs Williamson now has temporary residency in the United States."

While the judge has been delivering his judgement, I've been listening, but hardly able to take in what he's saying. The only part that I've hung onto is that I'm not going to be deported. I'm going home. With Tse. To be with him and my brother. I stand as instructed, but my legs are shaking so much they can't support me, and I put a hand on the bench in front of me. When it's indicated that I can step away as a free woman, my head goes completely dizzy.

Tse's there already, his arms supporting me.

Carissa's passing me a glass of water, Devil's smiling with half his face. Looking past him I see the ICE officials gathering up their paperwork. They catch my eye and both nod. They don't seem particularly upset. It's all in a day's work for them. Lose some, win some, I expect, though I also suspect they're more used to winning.

"Thank you," I offer lamely to Carissa and Devil. "Thank you so much."

They wave off my thanks, and then I'm walking out of the courtroom alongside my husband, my man. And stepping into my new life.

CHAPTER 41

Mouse

When Mariana started to stand, I saw her wobbling. I raced across that courtroom to catch her, ignoring my own shaking legs. It was hard to process what the judge had been saying. I'd been prepared to lose everything, now I had it all. I'm still a Satan's Devil, returning to my brothers tonight. Along with my old lady.

It's only when she's at last in my arms that I realised the enormity of what I'd been prepared to do. I thought I understood, but deep down I hadn't. I'm so fucking grateful she had a judge who had listened, the advantage being he'd entered the courtroom already annoyed she'd been deported before she'd had her day in court. In front of a different judge it could have been another story. *So fucking grateful.*

We walk out into the smoggy air of Los Angeles and I breathe it in as though it's the freshest I've ever taken into my lungs. Cars moving tortuously slow are lined up around us, a sight that I welcome rather than wanting to escape from.

My arm is around her as we walk down the block to where I left the truck. She's silent, taking her own time to let the news sink in.

Suddenly she stops. "I feel sick."

There's an alley up ahead, I take her down it, stepping back to give her privacy.

"I'm sorry. It's just…"

"Shush. No need to explain, darlin'. I feel like havin' a stiff drink myself."

"You don't drink."

"I know," I reply laughing. "It's a shock. Having built ourselves up to deal with the worst, well, I think we're both comin' down with a bang." She wipes her mouth with a tissue. "What?" she asks when she sees me examining her.

"You're not illegal any longer." When she tilts her head to one side, I add, "Judge said you could get a green card on your own merits."

Already pale from vomiting, her skin turns even sallower. "You saying you only married me so I could get a green card? That you want a divorce?"

Taking a deep breath, I correct her. "Fuck, Mariana. How the hell can you ask that? Not even thinkin' it. But," I pause, trying to find the right words. "But if it was a reason you married me…"

"Tse! How could *you* suggest that?"

I brush back her hair, and pull her closer. "Perhaps because I can't believe someone as perfect as you wants me?"

She bats at my arm. "You're joking, aren't you? Me? Perfect? I think you've got that the wrong way around."

Unable to help it, I smirk. "You think I'm perfect?"

"I love you, Tse." Then she gives me a cheeky smile. "I never know who I'm going to get. The white man, the computer nerd, the biker, or the wild untamed Indian."

I pull back. *She sees me. Sees all sides of me, and loves them all.*

Ignoring the fact that she's just been sick, I lower my head and kiss her, my cock having its predictable response, not caring she's just been ill either.

"Do you want to get a house in town, or live on the compound?" I ask her as we at last leave the traffic of LA behind. *Now* we can start talking about a future.

"I don't mind where we live. As long as I can complete my studies and then work as a nurse."

She's rung Drew and told him, he's over the moon excited. At the same time, I spoke to Drummer, told him he wasn't losing a man. The only thing to mar our journey is that I have to stop twice more when she feels ill again. *It must be all the tension of this morning.*

"You okay?" I ask her as I pull the truck around the back of the restored auto-shop at the entrance to our compound.

"Yeah, I don't know what's the matter with me, Tse. I feel fine again now."

"It's been a big day. Best get some food inside you. I'm sure there'll be leftovers from dinner."

"Food might help," she agrees. "I feel hungry again now."

As soon as I open the clubhouse door, and step back to allow her to go in first, I realise leftovers aren't going to be on the menu. There's a Welcome Home banner stretched over the bar, and food laid out along the top. Drew's standing in a prime position looking excited and happy.

Horse has obviously arrived during our absence today, and he raises his beer towards me as I give him a nod. Sophie's standing beside him, they'll be catching up in their own version of English, I expect. No one else will understand them.

Drummer steps forward, welcoming me back with a man hug, and then a shorter one for Mariana. Blade, Peg, Wraith, one by one all my brothers come over. No need for words, they're all telling me they're glad we've come home in their own ways.

"Mouse, got a minute?"

"Yeah, VP, what's up?"

"Everyone else knows now, so you should too. Didn't want to tell you this for obvious reasons, but a few days back, Sophie heard she's got permanent residency."

"That's great, Brother."

"Yeah. I was sort of knowing how you were feeling. Two years she's been temporary, but nothing's ever a shoo-in, is it? 'Specially not nowadays. So we're pretty excited she's permanent now. Still got a few years yet before she goes for citizenship."

"Brother, I never gave it a thought that you'd have any problems with Sophie being British. You were dealing with the same uncertainties as me?"

"Didn't want to share really. We've been going through the motions. But, yeah, I always had it in the back of my mind that something might go wrong. She is married to a criminal, after all."

I narrow my eyes. "Did Drummer know?"

Wraith nods. "He was the only one. Didn't seem worth talking about. Thought it would be easy. Been worried sick since we heard Mariana's story."

"I'm sorry."

"Not your fault, Brother. At least it's all worked out. For both of us."

"Let's do shots!" Sam shouts from beside me, her loud voice making me flinch.

"Mariana," I call out, and wave to the bar. "Better get some food in you first."

She nods, takes a step toward the buffet, puts her hand to her mouth and is suddenly pushing past to get to the bathroom.

"She okay?"

"I don't know. Think today's been too much," I reply thoughtfully. "She's been ill a few times now. If this keeps up, I'll call in Doc." Mariana's lived through hell these last few years, all her life really. Though her mother being deported must have made it worse. I put her illness down to a release of tension, but worry it could be too overwhelming, and she might need help. I start walking toward the bathroom.

Sam's hand stops me. "Mouse, I've got this. I'll go see what I can do."

Thinking Mariana might prefer a woman with her, I thank Sam then watch as she walks across the room. Sam stops and pulls Sophie away from Horse, and has a quick word with her. Sophie nods vigorously, then after excusing herself, hurriedly exits the clubhouse. *Women.* I don't bother worrying what's going on.

Now having lost his companion, Horse comes over to me. "Glad it all worked out for you."

"Mouse! Horse has agreed! A skull and go faster stripes."

I ruffle the hair of the boy who's appeared next to me. "Has he indeed?"

"Yeah, he told me it's going to look like the dog's bollocks."

I raise my eyes at the Englishman, who grins, then shrugs and explains, "Sophie's words, not mine. I just told him it would be an absolute doddle and look smashing when I'm done." He winks at Drew.

Drew looks at me seriously. "He means it will be easy and will look great."

"I'd assumed that," I say drily. "You here long, Horse?"

"Flying visit. Got loads of work booked in before Sturgis."

"That Dyna Glide yours?" I've seen a strange bike outside.

"Yeah, well, buying works out cheaper than renting in the long run, especially after I do it up and give it a good paint job. Probably sell it for a profit in the end."

I start to ask him a few questions. Growing bored, Drew wanders away while Horse and I go to the bar, I grab a soda and Horse a beer. I keep flicking my eyes toward the bathroom wondering why Mariana hasn't reappeared. *Hope she's okay.*

Ah. Here she comes. *Fuck. She looks whiter than ever.* I push my way over, take one look at her and pull out my phone. "I'm going to ring Doc."

"No, Mouse. I'm fine." Her eyes flick to Sam who shrugs. "The girls just gave me a scare, that's all. It's just stress." She goes to the bar and starts filling her plate. "What?" she asks me as I just stand watching her, my phone in my hand.

"What do you mean the girls scared you?" *What have they been saying?* She's mine, I'll protect her from anything, even the other old ladies if necessary.

Mariana tugs on my arm pulling me closer, when I lean down she whispers into my ear. "Sophie got me to do a pregnancy test."

My heart speeds up. Immediately imagining her belly rounded like Sam's with my baby in there. I don't see how it's possible, but, "You're pregnant?"

Her head shakes side to side rapidly. "No, thank God. But for a moment there…" She must see the way my face falls. "Tse. It's not the right time. I've got to get my head around everything that's happened. Still got a long way to go, things to prove, before I'm a permanent resident. Adding a baby to that right now is too much. But one day, I'd love to have your children."

She's right, I know it. Her upset stomach shows how much strain she's been under. "If you had been, I wouldn't have minded," I tell her, truthfully. "But all the stress wouldn't be good for a baby if you were. Let's just be us, for the moment." My attention is caught by laughter from the pool table. Drew is playing against Jayden and clearly the youngsters are having fun, Paladin is leaning against the wall, his arms folded, glaring at them. *Uh oh.* "I think," I tell her, "we're going to have enough trouble with one teenage boy."

She turns to see where I'm looking. "Hmm. Jayden's with Paladin, isn't she? I thought they were leaving, going to Colorado?"

I continue to watch Paladin. That's the plan. The young member won't want anything to happen to upset that. It's not hard to see what he's thinking. Drummer's given him instructions he's got to be hands off until she's eighteen. Drew's had no such warning, and may not, they're so much closer in age. Could be nothing, but from the look on Paladin's face, there could be trouble brewing. But I don't want to add to Mariana's stress tonight. I content myself with saying a simple, "Yeah."

The next night, as I'm walking into church, I find I was right to be concerned. Paladin puts himself in front of me.

"Tell your boy to keep away from Jayden," he snarls.

"Whoa." I hold my hands up in front of me. "They're around the same age. Kids are gonna get together if they've got things in common."

His hands make fists by his sides. "You know how long I've fuckin' waited for her," he hisses. "Might not be able to publicly claim her, but she's mine. Ain't havin' someone else fuck it up now. Not now we've got plans in place to leave for Colorado."

I top him by a couple of inches. Pulling myself up to my full height, I rasp out, "You can't claim someone who doesn't want to be claimed, *Brother*. I don't know what the fuck Drew thinks about Jayden, but it's up to her to tell him if she's not interested. Seems to me you might be taking things for granted. Need to work at it, if she's the one for you."

"You're not going to speak to him?"

"Nah. But if you lay one finger on him, Paladin, I'll break both your fuckin' legs. Man up, will you?" I place my palm on his chest, physically pushing him back. "Drew's not your problem, but maybe your assumptions about Jayden are. Seems it's her you should be focusing on, not my boy. You hearin' me?"

He spins on his heels and storms off.

"You're right, Brother." Slick steps out of the shadows behind me. "Jayden's growing up. Paladin never thought she might grow away from him."

"She's sixteen now, Brother. Maybe time to loosen the reins a little," I suggest.

Slick frowns. "Part of me agrees with you, part of me still remembers that broken little girl we rescued. And it's not me that needs to be convinced. Ella wants to keep her wrapped in cotton wool."

I gaze thoughtfully after Paladin. "Paladin's had his hands tied by both you and the prez. If Drew or anyone steps in when he's forbidden to make a move, there's going to be bloodshed." I just hope it's not Drew on the receiving end.

A loud sigh, then, "You're right," he repeats. "I'll have a word with Drummer. Won't be able to do much anyway when they go to Colorado."

"That still happening?"

Slick grimaces. "Much as I hate it, that's for the best. We live with the fear of Jayden being snatched off the street, hell, taken out of school under some pretence or another. The Herreras getting hold of her however careful we are. So, yeah. Hellfire has agreed. They'll be leaving in a few weeks. That will be your problem with Drew solved."

It will. But maybe it's opened Jayden's eyes as to there being other possibilities. I wonder how Paladin will cope if she sets her eyes on somebody else.

Conversation over, Slick slaps my back and we walk into church and take our seats just as Drummer bangs the gavel.

This time I can pay attention to what's going on. Blade's report is particularly interesting.

"Got the lease signed on the tattoo shop. Rock and I have been going through the applications for a couple of tattoo artists." Blade breaks off, spins his knife until it's pointing at me, his grin evil. "Brother there is a blank canvas. Thought we could use him to try them out."

"No fuckin' way," I snarl. "Not gonna have needles anywhere near me."

"Says the man who's got a fuckin' apadravya," Joker reminds them.

Once. It was one time I told them. Memories like fucking elephants around this table. "I was drunk," I explain through gritted teeth. I was. Woke up with a fucking hole and jewellery in my dick. Once it had healed though, I hadn't regretted it. I shift in my seat as I think of how much Mariana appreciates it, and my cock reacts.

"Come on, Mouse. Take one for the team. Have Mariana's name tatted over your heart." Now Lady's joining in.

"You fuckin' volunteer," I point my index finger at him. "You can have Joker's."

"Alright, alright." Drummer's loud voice brings our exchange to a halt. "No one's forcing anyone to get a tattoo." He jerks his chin toward Rock. "What about your back?"

"Be a few months yet, Prez. Doc reckoned to leave it a year so the skin's properly healed."

I send him a glance of sympathy. Poor fucker had his Satan's Devils tattoo flayed off his back. While Doc did what he could to minimise the scarring, he'll still need a good tattoo artist to replace that.

"I'll volunteer," Beef steps up. "Let me know when, Blade."

"Now that's sorted, I've got one thing I need to bring up." Prez tugs at his beard. When his eyes land on me, I brace myself for trouble. "Fuckin' glad the way things worked out with your ol' lady, Mouse."

"You givin' her a property patch now?"

Prez glares at Blade for interrupting him, but a grin comes to my face. Thought it would be tempting fate to give her one before. But now it's confirmed she's here to stay, yeah, that's next on my agenda. "Sure am."

"If I can finish?" It's that voice that makes you want to slide under the table. Even Blade shuts up. Instead he opens a pack of cigarettes, gets one out, and lights it.

"Devil's been in touch."

That name never carries anything good with it.

"They picked up the trail of *El Procurador*. Tracked him to Mexico. He went into a house in a town near the border. He never came out. Thought it was an ideal opportunity to take him, so they raided it." Drummer pauses. "Tore the place to shreds, found a tunnel starting under a bed. It led to a derelict building this side of the border."

My mind whirls with the information. The implications hitting me fast. "He's in the US?"

"Either that, or he's disappeared into thin air," Prez confirms.

"He's coming for Drew." *And for Mariana.*

"Mouse, he's not going to get him or your ol' lady," Peg peers around Heart and reassures me. His words are echoed and come at me from every chair.

"Drew goes nowhere alone. And Mariana's not going off the compound." *Fuck. Can I take him out of school?* Just when I thought everything was rosy, this shit happens.

"Feds are on the lookout for him. Hopefully it's only a matter of time until he's caught."

"He'll want to make a move quickly. He'll be feeling like a fish out of water here," I suggest. "I'll keep Drew and Mariana on lockdown." And make sure those security cameras are monitored day and night.

"Doubt he knows where they are," Blade puts in.

That's true. *El Procurador* knows nothing to link either of them to us.

"You need help, Mouse? We've got your back."

"I'm going to try to find him," I tell them. "Use my contacts. He must be hiding somewhere. I'd like to flush him out. He needs to pay for what he did to Mariana and her mother."

Again, Drummer's eyes watch the reactions of my brothers, then he sums up. "You do that, Mouse? Think you'll have a full house of volunteers to help you."

Blade's eyes light up. "Got plans to scalp him, Chief?"

I roll my eyes.

"Still think we ought to change your handle," Shooter suggests.

I push down my anger, knowing they don't understand. Perhaps it's time to put them right. "Using the title Chief is disrespectful. It's a name Anglos throw around and Natives hate it. Unless they are a chief, of course. I played a part to get a reaction, it was no more than that. As I've never been, or will be a chief, I'd be happy never to hear that handle again in my life."

Blade looks at me thoughtfully, his knife spinning in his hands. Suddenly he nods. "I didn't understand that."

"I know you didn't, Brother."

Drummer's glare lands on each man around the table. "That's the last time we're going to hear it, then. Mouse stays Mouse."

CHAPTER 42

Mariana

I thought once everything was over, I'd be able to go back to school and resume my training. But no such luck. At first the threat of *El Procurador* being in the country was enough to persuade me that both myself and Drew were safest not setting foot off the compound. But as the days pass and Tse can't pick up any chatter about where he might be, I begin to think even Devil's not infallible, and that he must have been mistaken. My father may not be in the country at all.

Drew's school's getting antsy that he's still recovering from the mythical illness I'd invented, and my college is making threats they can't hold my place open forever. We need to resume a normal life. Tonight, I'm going to plead my case. Get Tse to see reason. It's good timing, nature had seen to it that we had to take a natural break from our sexual activities. But tonight, I'm ready. I've showered, shaved, and groomed myself to perfection, still enjoying the luxury of hot water anytime I want it. Those days in the trailer seem so long ago now.

Drew's tucked up and asleep, Tse's working in his office, but he'll be back soon. In preparation, I'm daringly lying naked on the bed waiting.

Just in time. I hear the outside door open, then the one to the suite. In the light from the lamps on the bedside tables, I see Tse's eyes flare. He prowls toward me, his face dark with desire.

I prop myself up on my elbows. "Who am I going to get tonight?"

His lips curve. "Who do you want?"

"Hmm," I tap my finger to my lips. "Let's see. The white man who acts like a gentleman? The computer nerd who looks up instructions? The Indian who takes what he wants, or the rough biker who gives all he's got. What a decision." I giggle.

Already having discarded his cut and tee, his hands go to his belt. As he slides it out of the loops, he remarks, "How about just your husband who loves you?"

"That will work." Eyeing him taking down his jeans and boxers, my tongue licks my lips. I'm feeling greedy tonight. I peer up through my eyelashes. "Can I taste you?"

For an answer, his naked body approaches. Kneeling, I put my hands to his cock, and let my tongue flick over the end where pre-cum's already pooling. He places his hand gently on the back of my head. Opening my mouth, I take him inside, well, as much as I can, pausing to play a little with his piercing, an action which makes him hiss. I've no idea what I'm doing, but from the way his hand fists in my hair, and the guttural sounds he's making, it seems I'm on the right track.

With one hand on his cock, I slide my other down, cupping his ball sac. His body jerks, as my mouth moves up and down his shaft.

"Fuck, that feels good, darlin'. Too fuckin' good." His hands close in on the side of my head, and gently pull me away. He pushes me back on the bed.

"Was I doing it wrong?"

"Fuckin' perfect, babe. But I need to taste you, then I want to be inside you."

Two orgasms later and I'm sated. I've almost forgotten my name, let alone what I was going to ask. Almost.

"Tse?"

"Hmm?" he replies sleepily.

"Drew needs to go back to school, and I need to go to college."

"No."

His short response would annoy me, were it not that I know he's trying to keep us both safe. I keep my tone reasonable. "Tse, you've found no trace of my father being in this country. We could stay holed up for weeks, months. At some point we've got to start living again."

"You mean the world to me, Mariana. You know that. I couldn't cope if I lost you."

"You won't lose me. You're doing everything you can to prevent that. But please, let Drew go to school at least."

His arm slides under my head, and I snuggle into him. "Let me sleep on it."

Two days later, Drew goes back to school. Once again, either Matt or Truck goes with him. There's no sign of my father.

A week passes. The only excitement on the compound is a going away party for Paladin and Jayden. Drew misses her company, but returning to school has at least distracted him. He's taken up with all his activities again.

"What time does Drew need collecting?"

My eyes flit to my man as I answer. "In a couple of hours. He's got football practice today." My mouth curves as I remember how happy he'd been to get back into the swing of things. I now glance around, it's quiet here today. The clubhouse is quite empty. Half the men have gone on a run to Las Vegas, why I'm not sure, Matt's gone with them driving the crash truck, and Truck's on his firefighting shift. Mouse and I will be collecting Drew.

Mouse's phone rings. I can only hear his side of the conversation.

"Prez? Yeah. Hey, really? Yeah, I bet it is good fuckin' news. Hope everything goes well."

He listens for a moment, looking at me in consternation. "Prez, I was… Sure. I'll sort something out. Yeah. Course. And good luck."

Ending the call, he stares at me. "Sam's gone into labour. Prez is heading straight out to take her to the hospital."

I grin. "She'll be relieved." The baby is almost two weeks overdue, and she hadn't wanted to be induced.

"About fuckin' time." Blade comes over. First he grins, then he frowns. "Had that meet arranged with the Wretched Soulz."

"About that," Mouse tells him. "Prez asked if I would go with you."

Blade holds out his fist for Mouse to bump with his, "Appreciate that, Brother."

"Which leaves me a problem. Who's going to pick up Drew?"

"Me." It's the only option. One look at his face tells me he's not on board. "Look, Tse. I'll be picking up Drew along with all the other parents. Nothing's going to happen to me, right? There's been no sign of my father. I'll be quite safe."

He glances at Blade as if for reinforcement, but Blade shrugs. "Can't see what else you can do, Brother. Of course, I could go to the meet by myself." The look on his face suggests he'd rather have company.

Tse's hand snakes over my shoulder, he grabs hold of my hair, tugging it gently so I'm forced to look into his face. "Straight there and back, Mariana. No stopping."

When he releases me, I nod.

"Got an idea." Blade disappears out back, then returns a few minutes later.

I can't immediately see what he's holding, but Tse does. When Blade shows him the back, he bursts out laughing.

"What is it?" I screw up my eyes.

"A bullet-proof fuckin' vest," Tse grins. Then he shows me what Blade has chalked on the reverse.

Property of Mouse.

Blade sniggers. "Figured it's more protection than a property cut."

I huff, not certain whether they're serious or not. If they are, I don't like it. "You're being ridiculous. I'm not wearing that."

Tse and Blade look at each other, then in unison they tell me, "Yes, you are."

So an hour or so later, I'm driving into Tucson wearing a freaking armoured vest. When I make a promise, I keep it, even though I think it absurd. I've also got a gun in the glove box and the knife Blade had given to me in a sheath strapped to my ankle. Overkill. But there's no doubt Tse's concern gives me a warm feeling. He's doing his best to protect me, even when he can't be there to do it himself.

As I drive, I spare a thought for Sam, wondering how she's doing, and what gender she'll have. I've a sneaking suspicion she'd like a daughter, but will be a great mom again whatever she has. Eli is a little rascal, a handful, but then, with Drummer as his father that's not unexpected. Already he seems to assume people will jump to his demands. Could Sam handle two like that? Yes, she could.

My mind turns to thoughts of what it would be like to have a baby of my own. I've been a mom to Drew for six years. Once he's older and no longer such a responsibility, it would be nice to have a family with Tse.

I'm still full of happy thoughts as I turn into the parking lot for the school, parking close to the playing fields. I stay in the car as I'd promised Tse, listening to music on the radio and singing along.

The boys start coming up, one by one the cars leave the parking lot. I tap the steering wheel in time to the beat, appreciating the excellent sound system in my brother's car. I brought his, so he could drive it back and get in a bit more practice.

Come on, Drew. When half the cars have gone, I start to get impatient. When a few more leave, I begin to get worried.

Stay in the car. Tse's voice echoes in my head, reminding me. My hand goes to the door handle, then returns to my lap. Another car leaves. One more and I'll be the only one here. *He's probably stayed back to talk with Coach.*

My blood suddenly runs cold. I see Drew, but there's another man with him. A man Drew doesn't know, but who I recognise. *It's my father.*

I open the door, my heart beating frantically, and step out. The man's leading Drew toward the only other car in the lot. *Drew wouldn't go with him, would he?*

Drew's not looking at all comfortable, the man is too close. I can't immediately see what's happening, but need to get my brother to come toward me.

"Drew," I call out. "Over here. Now."

The urgency in my voice gets Drew's attention on me. His eyes widen, at the same time as my father turns the gun which had clearly been the persuasion he'd used on Drew, toward me. Our father chuckles, a sound which grates on my nerves. Then fires without any warning.

Christ! Drew screams as I feel like a horse has kicked me in the stomach. I go down hard on my knees, my hands immediately going to my belly to staunch the flow of blood, unable to comprehend my father's shot me again. *And this time there's no one to save me.*

It's only a split second later my fingers land on the vest I'm wearing beneath my jacket. *I'm not bleeding to death.* It might be hard to breathe, but I'm not fatally wounded.

Drew's trying to get to me. My father turns the gun back on him and is pushing him into the car.

I've got no time. I stretch out my hand, pull the knife from its ankle sheath, aim just how Tse had shown me and throw it. The blade catches my father in the back. The shock causes him to drop the gun. Thinking quickly, Drew grabs it, and now he's turned the tables on the man who was going to kidnap him.

Getting to my feet, ignoring the pain, I stumble over, taking the gun from Drew. My father's gasping, trying to turn around and pull out the knife that's protruding from under his left shoulder blade.

"This is him, isn't it?" Drew's caught on fast. "This is the sperm donor."

"I'm your father." *El Procurador*'s voice isn't as strong as I've heard it before.

"Shoot him, Ma."

My mind races through the facts. Sure, *El Procurador*'s a known and wanted criminal. But I'm on very dodgy ground here. What would the authorities say if I killed him? And if he was dead, my asylum case might be closed. Better keep him alive for now. "We'll take him back to the compound. You drive, Drew." To my father, I say, "Move."

"I shot you." He makes another effort, this time managing to pull the knife out, and tosses it.

"Pick it up, Drew," I don't want to leave any evidence. That bloody knife's got my fingerprints all over it.

He does, then backs away to the car.

I motion with the gun. "Move," I repeat.

"What does it take to fuckin' kill you, bitch?" My father's enraged.

The blood starts to flow faster now that he's pulled the blade out. He's going pale. Drew's gone to his car and has popped the trunk. It's a good idea, but I don't think my father would fit, even if we could manage to force him in there. I open my mouth to tell him, but my brother's got other ideas. My mouth drops open when I see what he's brought back.

"What?" he asks innocently, then grins. "Blade said I should be ready for all eventualities."

I'm really not at all sure why Blade had advised my brother to carry zip ties in his car, but I'm so pleased he did. If we survive this, a lot of thanks are due to the enforcer. My bullet-proof vest and the blade he gave me have come in handy today.

Drew's strong. He yanks our weakening father's arms behind him, and has his hands tied together in seconds. Then he pushes him, hard, towards the car.

"I won't hesitate to shoot you," I tell him, my tone leaving no doubt.

"Where are you taking me? What are you going to do with me? You'll kill me anyway, why not do it here?"

"I won't kill you." I might not know much about them, but I think the Satan's Devils will make him hurt more than a single bullet would. "So get in the car if you want to live."

"Patricide doesn't suit you." He gives me an assessing look. "You're not a killer."

"Proves I don't take after you. And neither does Drew. Now get in." I'm getting nervous someone might see me. The coach must be finishing up soon.

After a calculating look, which I interpret as he's weighing up his chances of somehow being able to take his son, at last he slides awkwardly into the back seat. Drew gets in the driver's side, I get in the passenger seat, turning so my gun is trained on my father.

"Drive carefully, Drew." I don't want to get pulled over on the way.

Holding the gun one handed, I reach into my purse for my phone. I place my call. "Tse, I've got *El Procurador*. We're bringing him back to the compound."

Tse's exclamation all but deafens me.

"We're both okay," I reassure him. "I'll see you soon. Love you, Tse. But I have to go. I need to keep this gun trained on him."

I end the call, not wanting to have any distraction.

I can feel how tense Drew is as he follows my instructions and makes sure he stops well in time at every red light, proceeding through junctions carefully. When we're out of town and on the 110, I breathe a sigh of relief. Then we're turning up the track which leads to the compound.

The gates are already open. Blade and Tse are standing waiting. I get out of the car, hand the gun to Blade and collapse into my man's arms. I don't know why, but tears are falling and I can't stop shaking. The pain in my stomach, ignored up to now, returns with a vengeance. I feel weak as a kitten.

Tse hugs me so tightly. When I wince, he sweeps me into his arms and carries me up to the clubroom. He sets me down carefully, then stands back, his dark eyes examining me. Worried Blade's been left with my father, I shoo him away. "*El Procurador*. You need to see to him."

"Yeah. You okay for a minute while I help Blade get him settled? Drew, can you watch her?"

"I'm fine," I reply fast, as Drew nods.

I expect Tse to be gone for ages, and lie back on the couch, my hands protectively over my stomach, as I try to calm my nerves. In fact, he's back surprisingly quickly.

"Where's my father?"

He grins. "Tied up."

"He shot Ma," Drew tells him.

Tse's face turns grim and he pales as he drops to his knees in front of me. "Why the fuck didn't you say? What happened?" His hands reach out, then hover. "Where? Where are you fuckin' hurt?"

I point to the vest I've just removed. "Blade's good idea saved me." Gingerly I pull up my tee shirt, and Tse's eyes widen, then he grimaces as he stares at the developing bruise.

"Fuck, woman. That must have hurt."

"Understatement," I tell him. Now the tension has gone, it's pain that's making me feel faint.

"She threw a knife. Got him in the back. He dropped the gun…"

Tse stands and ruffles Drew's hair. "Slow down. You can give me the details later. Run to my room, I've got some Tramadol in the drawer. Think your sister could do with a painkiller."

When Drew leaves, Tse again kneels in front of me and takes hold of my shaking hands. "It's over now, or will be. He's not leaving here alive."

"Make him disappear, Tse. If anyone knew he was dead, they might still deport me. If he drops out of sight, they'll still think he's out there."

"That's why you brought him back?" His eyes go wide, as if realising. "Fuck, Mariana, that was good thinking."

"I trust you and your brothers, Tse."

"You're one brave and clever fuckin' woman, Mariana. We know exactly what to do with scum like him."

"Make him hurt."

"What the fuck's going on, Mouse?" Wraith runs through the door of the clubroom. "You said it was an emergency? Thank fuck we were already well on our way back. Twisted throttles all the way from Casa Grande."

"Mouse?" Peg's appeared behind Wraith.

Tse stands. "We've got *El Procurador* hanging in the storage room. Blade's keeping him occupied. He tried to take Drew, Mariana here showed off her knife throwing skills and disarmed him. Oh, after she was shot."

"Shot?" Slick's now in the entrance too. "Doc on his way?"

Tse brushes his hands and grins at me, as if he's only now realising it's a long story. "Blade made her wear a bullet-proof vest."

Then the rest of them are there, and I tune out the remainder of his explanation. I don't need to hear it. *I lived it.*

CHAPTER 43

Mouse

"Comfy there, VP?" I joke, spying Wraith sitting in Drummer's space at the head of the table. I've left Drew with Mariana as Wraith decided to call everyone in here rather than continue the discussions in the clubroom.

Wraith grins, leans his chair back, and presses the sole of his shoe to the table. He tries to mimic Drummer's death stare, but fails. To give him his due, he doesn't fall that short.

Blade's the last to arrive, Matt having gone up to relieve him of his head-of-cartel-sitting duties. Taking his seat, he points his inevitable knife toward me. "If you hadn't married that girl, Mouse, I'd have taken her."

"She did fuckin' good," Peg observes.

"Thought fast, too. Only option she had was to bring him back here."

Brave, intelligent, quick thinking as well as sexy. My lips curve as I run through her qualities in my head.

"Any news, Wraith?"

"Spoke to Prez, updated him. Sam's got a ways to go yet. He said do what we have to do and bury the body."

Succinct and precise. That sounds like Prez.

"You want to scalp him?" Blade's looking hopeful. "Or want me to?"

"I just want him gone." That's the truth. Out of our lives for good. So I can get on with mine. Mine, Mariana's and Drew's.

"Peg him out and let the ants eat him?" Shooter enquires eagerly.

Wraith's watching me.

"Dead's dead, isn't it?" I jerk my chin toward the VP. "Don't think he deserves us wasting time on him. Got better things to do. Some of us should be at the hospital to support Prez, and I want to look after my ol' lady."

Beef's tilting his head. "It was a long ride today. Could do with a bit of torture myself." Rock reaches across the table and they bump their fists together.

"Ah, come on, Mouse. I haven't had a chance to play for ages," Blade whines like a two-year-old.

"Okay." Wraith bangs the gavel. "Mariana wants him to disappear. I've got a suggestion how we can do that. We won't even have to get our hands dirty."

Minutes later we're ready to put the VP's excellent idea into action. I wink at Mariana as we pile out of our meeting room, and head out the back of the clubhouse. She's resting on the couch, Drew's got his arm around her. She's in good hands.

In the storeroom Matt's looking bored, flicking through a bike magazine while the formerly fearsome Colombian cartel head is trying to bribe him to let him loose. When we walk in, Mariana's father turns his attention to us.

"Who's in charge?" he snaps. His face contorts with pain, but his voice has regained some strength.

"That would be me." Wraith steps up in front of him and folds his arms.

"I can make you a good deal." His eyes zoom in on our cuts. "You're a biker club. Probably in the same trade as me. I can send good drugs your way, make it worth your while. Good women too."

"In the same trade? We're not even in the same ballpark," Wraith sneers. "We earn our money legit. Don't need to get our kids hooked on heavy stuff, or trade in women. Nor guns before you offer them. You're not a man, you're a snake that needs to be put down."

El Procurador isn't used to being spoken to like that. His eyes flare. "Let me go. I'll pay you cash."

"Thing is," Wraith hooks his leg around a chair and pulls it to him. "We're rather fond of your daughter."

"That *puta*," he snarls.

"I object to her being called a whore," Blade tells Wraith casually.

The VP nods. "You can show him how much in a minute. Yeah, we like her. And her brother too. They're both under our protection. Way I see it, the best way of protecting them is to remove a vengeful bastard like you from their lives."

El Procurador tries to stare the VP down, it doesn't work. In the end, he sighs. "Alright. I'll leave her and the boy alone. I'll go back to Colombia."

"Yes," Wraith says, enigmatically. "You will leave her alone. She has no wish to see your fuckin' face again." He nods at Blade. "Get him down."

Blade does, and not too gently. *El Procurador* lands heavily on his knees, overbalancing as his hands are still tied together behind him. The man's slowly bleeding out, though he doesn't seem to know it. The back of his shirt is soaked, his pants too.

He pulls himself to his feet, grimacing as he straightens. "Glad you've seen sense."

While Blade removes the zip tie Drew had used, I think to myself, *Gonna have to have a word with him about why he thought a fifteen-year-old would need them.* I watch as he ties a blindfold around the man's head. Then, quick as a flash, has his hands held together again, this time to his front. He slips a rope between *El Procurador*'s wrists and knots it.

Experimentally, he tugs the rope. "Come."

"I can't see where I'm going," Mariana's father complains.

"Don't want you to see all our secrets now, do we?" the VP explains reasonably.

Blade tugs the rope again which gets him moving. He fails to warn him about the step out the door. "Oh, my bad," he says, as *El Procurador* goes down. He doesn't lend a hand, just waits for him to get back on his feet.

Yeah, the blood loss is getting to him as I thought, his movements are slowing. "Better hurry this up," I say quietly to Wraith.

"He's not going to last long, more's the pity," Slick agrees.

Hopefully long enough. Followed by all the club, with the exception of Drummer, and obviously, Paladin, Blade takes him up to the back of the compound, out through the gate, across the now well-maintained firebreak, and into the forest.

"Where are we going? Can you set me free now?" He trips over a log, stumbles, but doesn't go down.

"Not far now," Blade replies, reassuringly, sending an evil grin at us over his shoulder.

Not far. And not long. Then he'll be out of our lives forever.

In a few minutes, we come across Matt and Truck leaning on shovels looking pleased with themselves. It was perhaps a shit job to give Truck as soon as he came off shift, but the big man was up for it.

"Done?" Wraith asks.

"Done," the prospects confirm.

"Truck, better get yourself gone." The firefighter-come-prospect's neither blind nor stupid, he'll know what we're doing. But for some fucked up reason we keep him out of the worst of the shit that we do. *Plausible deniability.* What he can't see or hear, he can turn a blind eye to.

"Better not damage my track," Road grumbles.

"Look at it this way, whether there's a hump or a dip after, it will make it more fun."

The trail bike rider's eyes light up. "True, that."

Wraith nods at Blade who whips off the blindfold. *El Procurador* shows his intelligence. He puts two and two together fast and tries to back away, but Peg's right there behind him, giving him a hefty shove sending him into the deep grave that's been dug in the loose peaty earth.

Beef picks up the can and starts pouring gas over him. I'm content to stand and watch this bit, seeing the fear on his face as he realises what's going to happen. Relishing the begging that comes out of his mouth. *I bet Mariana's mother begged while he raped her. Mariana would have begged to prevent them from forcing drugs into her mouth.* He didn't listen to them. Same way we're not listening now.

He's fucking crying. Rock's got a flashlight on him, lighting Beef's task. I can see tears on his face, mingling with the gas that Beef's now pouring over his hair. Beef shakes the can when it's empty, cautious not to waste a drop.

"Mouse?" Wraith waves me forward, then his arm snakes out to halt me. "Sorry," he mouths, while taking out his phone and reading a text. He swears loudly. "Fuck me. Prez and Sam have got another son. Fuckin' asshole won't let me forget it either."

Hey, that's good news. We all start cheering, pumping fists in the air, slapping each other's backs.

"This calls for cigars," shouts Blade. "But I'll have to make do." He takes out his cigarettes.

"Be careful where you drop that match, Blade."

I happen to have a joint on me. "Spare a light?" I nod toward the enforcer. Blade grins as he passes the box over.

The man in the hole starts screaming. I put the flame to the end of my joint, light it, inhale deeply.

"So," I say conversationally to Wraith. "Another boy on the compound."

"You going to have another try, Wraith?" Shooter suggests.

"Well, I won't complain at getting more practice in," the VP replies. He's then supplied with some suggestions, including, apparently, doing it upside down. Blade helpfully suggesting he must have been doing it wrong all this time.

"Take some lessons from Drummer," Marvel supplies.

"I could give you some pointers," Peg's grinning widely. Yup, he's got a boy.

"What about you, Slick?" Dollar asks. "You know what you're havin'?"

"Not a fuckin' clue, Brother, and don't give a fuck."

"Let me out! You're a bunch of madmen." The screams I'd tuned out start up once again.

I raise my eyebrow at Blade. He glances at Wraith and gets a chin lift in return. When he nods at me, I take a match from the box I'm still holding, strike it, then let it drop, making sure to swiftly jump back.

Now the screams increase in volume. There's a thrashing sound as *El Procurador* tries to avoid his inevitable fate.

"Well," I say conversationally. "Mariana wanted him to disappear."

Shooter walks as close as he can to the flaming hole and looks over. "Won't be much of him left after that."

Jeez. I'm glad I'm smoking. It's helping to mellow me and covering up a little of the barbeque smell.

"Think he's gone," Shooter shouts back over his shoulder.

Wraith smiles. "Let it burn out. Then, Matt, cover him over."

"I'll help you, man," Hyde offers. As the last member to be patched in, he'll recall his prospecting duties.

The VP slaps me on the back. "It's over now, Mouse. He's finished."

"And no one will know whether he's dead or alive." Yeah, the CIA and the feds will continue chasing their tails trying to find him. Another thing, along with how to get rid of him, we'd agreed on in church. Without a body, no one would be sending my woman back to Colombia.

The flames have died down. Matt and Hyde are picking up shovels. I smoke the last of my joint and throw the stub on top of the burned, twisted body. Then I spit on it. Turning around, I see my brothers walking ahead in the distance.

I start to follow them. The light from the flashlights behind me fades, and those ahead are a long way in front. I start to lengthen my stride, knowing I'm lagging.

There's rustling in the trees around me. A Navajo wariness of being out in the dark creeps up on me. *Ch'įįdii.* The white in me disappears as I quicken my step, forcing myself not to look behind me, unable to empty my mind of the Navajo belief that all that's bad in a person leaves upon death, becoming a malevolent spirit, not lingering near the body, but searching out anyone who mentions the name of the dead to infect them with their evil. The dead man I'd left to my rear was likelier than most to have his *ch'įįdii* leave him.

I walk faster as the rustling grows louder.

"Boo!"

Fucking hell! My heart, I swear, has stopped as Blade's arm goes around my shoulder.

"Spooky out here, ain't it?" he laughs.

Knowing he doesn't know the fucking half of it, but not wanting to delay with a fist fight here, I just snarl, "Fuckin' not funny, Brother."

"Oooh. Made you startle, did I?"

Knowing he fucking knows he did, I just frown. He puts his flashlight under his chin and lights his face, looking like a Halloween figure. Fuck it. I can't help but laugh at his childishness.

"What's the hold up?" Wraith shouts back.

"Fuckin' Blade, being fuckin' Blade," I yell back.

Christ, but I'm glad to be back on the compound. One last look behind, then I'm going down the slope to see my woman.

"Alright, Grunt. Sit." Heart's being greeted as if he'd been away a month, I dodge around the man trying to get his dog to obey, and see Mariana where I'd left her on the couch.

Drew holds a finger to his lips, and I see she's sleeping.

"She alright?"

"Sore, but the painkillers helped."

Mariana begins to stir; our voices having disturbed her. She wakes slowly as normal, stretching, wincing as her bruised muscles pull, then her eyes widen when she sees she's in the clubhouse and not our room. I see the exact moment it all comes back to her.

"El…?" she begins to ask. But I've put my hand over her mouth, my eyes flaring in warning.

"Never, ever, speak his name again."

"Tse?"

"Never, understand? Wipe him from your mind."

Her eyes meet mine, seem to read it's important without understanding why. Another thing I love about my old lady.

"It's over. Finished," I reassure her.

Despite her pain, she smiles as she tells me, "I love you, Tse."

"Love you too." I'll tell her every day, fuck, a hundred times a day for the rest of our lives. Lives we can now get on with without fear.

Drew gives a teenage snort of disgust at our proclamations, and walks off grinning and shaking his head.

I take his place on the couch, and gently pull her into my side.

"I think I've got the Indian tonight," she tells me wryly. And perceptively.

I laugh. "You have. If you weren't sore, I'd be dragging you by the hair back to my hogan."

As my brothers start celebrating, I realise I haven't told her the news. "Sam's had her baby. Another boy."

"I thought Wraith was looking upset," she giggles.

We stay there, comfortable sitting in the middle of the club-house. My brothers come over, checking she's alright, giving her praise for what she did earlier. I stop any of them speaking the name before they can utter it.

When she's going over it yet again with an admiring Blade, I rest my head back, finally relaxing for the first time in weeks. *My woman's safe.* I'm still a Satan's Devil. All's good with the world.

I feel, strangely, that my white and Native American halves are finally melding together, finding harmony. That what I've always been searching for, I've found with her.

CHAPTER 44
Mariana

hat are you up to, Tse?" Narrowing my eyes, I watch as he *once again* quickly ends a phone call when I walk into the suite.

Standing, he comes over, leaning down to place a kiss on my forehead, before telling me, "Nothing to worry your pretty head about."

I glare. If something was wrong, he wouldn't be smirking. There are no lines of stress marring the beauty of his face. But something's going on. I don't like surprises, had enough of those over the past few months and none of them were good.

"Hey, Mouse. Have you..." Drew bursts in the door, his mouth snapping shut as soon as he sees I've returned from admiring the new babies in the clubhouse. It seems to me like the two men in my life had planned on me being away longer.

Pursing my lips, I shake my head, wondering if I should drop it, then I decide whatever's going on, I'd rather confront it.

"Just tell me, will you?" It's almost comical. Both look like they've been caught with their hands in the cookie jar, both guilty as sin. Drew's wide-open eyes find those of Tse, whose own appear shifty. I step over to the bed and sit down, crossing my arms over my chest. "Okay, who's going to start talking first? What are you up to? It's something."

"Mouse?" Drew sounds uncertain.

Tse sighs. "I was going to set it all up and surprise you," he sounds frustrated.

"Don't like things taking me unawares, Tse," I warn. "Had too much of that lately."

Chastised, he comes over, kneeling in front of me and taking hold of my hands. A chin jerk over his shoulder has Drew joining us and sitting beside me.

My brother's gone from appearing worried to buzzing with excitement. "You going to tell her now?"

Tse grins, and nods. "Yeah. Okay." He pauses. "Those phone calls you keep interrupting? I've been talkin' to my mother."

"*Hanálí* Lina," Drew puts in. I smile. The Navajo for grand-mother seems to take many forms, that's the one Drew's settled on for Tse's mom. My brother became close to her while he stayed on the Rez.

A quick smile for Drew, Tse seems to like that he's using a familial term for her, then he's back to his explanation. "She wants to meet you. Well, all my Navajo family do."

"I'd like that…" I start to tell him. To learn more about his heritage, and what makes my man tick. The white man is easy, the computer nerd as well. The biker, hmm, I'm starting to understand that, living here as I do. The Navajo part of him? That's still a mystery. Seeing where and how he lived as a teenager, meeting the woman who birthed him, that might give me more insight into the man I've married.

His hand's on my mouth, a sign I'm to let him finish. "Mom's upset I married you so quickly. Nah, sweetheart. Not that I took you as my wife, but that we, in her words, ran off and did it in secret. She wants us to get married again, this time do it properly. In front of our families."

The removal of his hand indicates I now have a chance to speak. "A second wedding?" I think back to the misgivings I'd had about the first, doubting at the time it was real. Then I snort a laugh. "In front of our families? Tse, I've only got Drew."

"No, you haven't!" Drew butts in impatiently.

"Drew," Mouse growls a warning, then laughs, saying to me, "I'm learning Drew can't keep secrets."

"Can I tell her now?" Drew's leg is bouncing, it's obviously hard for him to keep still. "Please, Mouse?"

Tse sends him an exasperated look, then with a shake of his head, says, "Go on."

"The Satan's Devils are coming with us. Well, not all of them, but some. They're our family now, Ma, aren't they?"

Glancing at Tse, I see him grinning. I still think they're more his than mine. But I'm not worried if a couple come along to a wedding I'm apparently not going to have much choice or hand in planning. "So, I just turn up?"

For the first time, Tse looks uncertain. "Sort of. I've just left everything to Mom and my grandmother. Since she got the idea in her head, she's been unstoppable." The tilt of his head shows he wants me to comment.

Biting my lip, I start to understand Drew's excitement. It sounds different, interesting. Intriguing. Something good after all the twisted shit we've been through. I place my hand against his cheek. "I really have married a Native, haven't I?"

He covers my fingers with his own. "Not yet," he smirks. "But you will." Then he grows serious, "Good surprise, or bad one?"

I'm cautious, having absolutely no idea what form this wedding will take. Tse and I have come such a long way from that first almost-nothing affair at City Hall. As I let the idea sink in, I realise we deserve to have people, *family*, around us when we fully commit to each other for life, a second time, with no doubts in our minds. Doing it for all the right reasons. I give him the answer he's waiting for. "Good." Then I come up with a problem. "What should I wear?"

"Mom's got that in hand." His reassurance comes quickly.

It's touching how much Drew's looking forward to returning to the Rez, his eagerness feeding my own curiosity to see where Tse had lived after his father had died.

A week later we set off, going a few days before whoever will be representing the Satan's Devils follows us up. I've no idea who will come along, but suspect from some of the words Blade's been having with Tse that the enforcer will be one of the party. I walked in on one conversation where Tse was rolling his eyes and telling Blade he wouldn't see any scalping at the reception. I had no idea what he was alluding too.

Drew wanted to drive his car. Luckily Tse dissuaded him, and borrowed one of the club's SUVs for the long journey. It's like travelling with two little boys, each excited in their own way and eager to show me the sights. Tse slows and it's Drew who points out we're entering the Navajo Nation. I look around at the bare scenery as if the sign would suddenly summon up tepees.

"Hogans, Ma," Drew corrects me, when laughing at myself I tell him what I'd been half expecting. "Navajo live in a hogan. Mouse, we going to see Billy and his horses?"

Tse grins over his shoulder at my brother in the back seat. "We might," he replies. "Just don't expect to ride."

As Drew pouts at Tse's response, I'm just pleased to see him enthusiastic and happy. These last few months have made him grow up fast. Sometimes it's nice to have the reminder he's still a kid.

I hadn't realised the reservation was so large. It takes quite a while before we're approaching signs to Window Rock, turning off the main road before we get to the town. After that it's not long before we're pulling up at his mother's house, *hogan*, I correct myself, needing to remember.

Tse stops the SUV, gets out unfolding his long limbs, and walks around to open my door. My eyes are focused on the woman who's coming out of the eight-sided building constructed of logs, suddenly nervous whether she will think I'm good enough for her son.

Drew doesn't hesitate at all. "*Hanáli* Lina," he cries. From the slight quirk of her lips I suspect he's butchering the pronunciation, but from the wide smile that quickly follows, see she appreciates the gesture, and holds her arms open for him.

Tse takes my hand and helps me step out. We've been driving for hours, a delicious cooking odour reaches my nostrils, making my mouth water and reminding me I'm hungry.

"Mom, meet Mariana," Tse introduces me. "Sweetheart, this is my mom."

"Mrs Williamson," I hold out my hand politely.

"Lina," she corrects, not standing on formalities and pulling me in for a hug. "You're beautiful. Just like I expected."

So's she. She has the same facial features as my man, and the same long hair frames her face.

Lina and her mother couldn't make me feel more welcome. Over the next few days I feel I've been allowed to open a window into their life. While Tse takes Drew off to visit Billy, with the strange promise to me he won't let him ride, I'm prodded and poked with pins while the finishing touches are put on my wedding clothes, and the ceremony is explained to me. I'm filled with excitement. *This* is what was missing before. We might already have the marriage certificate to prove it, but this sense of preparation, people witnessing our union, being happy for us will make me truly feel like Tse's wife.

If anything, Lina is even more excited than me. When I try to thank her for doing so much, while her mother looks on giving a snort of disgust, Lina explains she had a similar wedding to my first. City Hall in Tucson, no family around her. It's then I remember she'd run off with Tse's dad. Both women seem to be making up for her lack of a proper wedding now. Their excitement is infectious.

I spare a thought for my own mom, missing her dreadfully, wishing she was beside me, but feeling she's watching over me, and would be happy for me.

Tse's grandmother surprised me, reverently showing me a wedding vase made of clay with two spouts. In days past, she explained, a medicine man would prepare a love potion made of holy water and nectar, nowadays herbal tea or water is used instead. I admired it when she told me it was given to her on her marriage. I was taken aback when she said it was mine now. I could well understand how a vase such as this is treasured, and never sold, but passed down when, like in her case, a woman has lost her partner.

I held it so carefully, frightened I'd drop it, as she explained that the spouts are joined together by a looped handle representing the bridge that joins two lives. During the wedding Tse and I will drink from it, blessings will follow if we don't spill a drop.

Each stitch in my regalia increases the anticipation. By the time the day of our wedding arrives, I'm more than ready.

I wear a pleated cotton skirt with a Navajo pattern embroidered around the base, with a matching long-sleeve blouse topped by a shawl woven by Lina's mother. Knee-high moccasins made from soft buckskin which I personally love. I'm festooned with silver jewellery, made here on the reservation. My hair has been plaited in a loose braid which hangs to one side.

Once I'm dressed, Lina and her mother leave me, and Drew enters. Having no father, he'll walk beside me today.

"You know what to do?" Drew asks, a small frown on his face. He's taking this so seriously.

"I think so," I agree, hesitantly. Lina's been through it so many times, but I'm still worried about making a mistake. "Has anyone turned up from the Satan's Devils?"

"Yeah," he grins broadly. "Blade arrived while you were getting dressed. Mouse's uncle's been showing him how to shoot a bow and arrow. Think he likes learning new skills. Oh, and Mouse shut him down fast when he asked about scalping."

I shake my head, Blade's bloodthirsty, no doubting that.

"You look beautiful, Sis." He holds out his arm, and I link my free hand through it. Leaning over I pick up a special basket, one full of corn mush.

"Let's do this," I tell him. Worried I'm shaking so much I might drop my basket.

I know Tse and his family will already be inside the hogan that's used for ceremonies such as *'ahé'éské*, marriage. He and his mother will sit on the west side, his uncles and the rest of his family sitting to the north. All I have to do is enter and sit on his right side. Tse and I will both face east, toward the door. The basket I'm hanging onto so tightly will be placed in front of Tse. My relatives, or Drew and Blade in this case, will sit to the south.

I'm aware of voices behind me as I enter, but until I've placed that basket so carefully in front of Tse, I don't look up. It's only then I stare at my man who's smiling at me, love beaming out from his eyes. I can't fail to notice how handsome he looks in a velveteen shirt of a deep turquoise hue, his hair tied up in some sort of complicated bun, white wool keeping it in place.

I sit down, then hear voices. Looking up, I see numerous Devils and old ladies have followed me in. I see Sam and Sophie, both carrying their babies, Eli and Olivia toddling wide-eyed alongside. Then there's Drummer, Wraith, Blade, Peg, Darcy and Noah. Bullet's here with Carmen, Viper with Sandy.

Road, Jekyll and Hyde. The compound in Tucson must have been left nearly empty.

Blade sees my mouth dropping open and winks.

A cough brings me back to the ceremony which is about to begin. Tse nods at me in encouragement. Carefully picking up a jug in front of me, I pour water over Tse's outstretched hands, then he takes the jug and does the same to mine. That part of the ceremony completed, Tse's oldest uncle sprinkles corn pollen on the mush in the basket I'd brought in.

Remembering the order I have to eat it in, Tse and I take pinches of the corn mush, eating from the east, south, west and then north sides of the basket. Then the basket is passed to Tse's mom, his uncle instructs she's to always keep it safe.

One by one Tse's uncles stand and give us advice on our marriage ahead, the oldest and final speech talking about the fire we've lit between us that should never be allowed to go out. Reminding us that our marriage is a new beginning. A new life, a new family. Words said in Navajo then repeated in English.

Food is passed around, an Anglo style wedding cake appears from somewhere. People talk and laugh.

Tse leans over and whispers in my ear. "How do you feel, Mariana?"

I turn to face him, "Married." It's true. This time, I really do. Sitting forward, I address myself to the woman on his opposite side. "I don't know how I'll ever be able to thank you for this, Lina."

She smiles. Reaching around her son, she pats my hand. "I'm so pleased to welcome you to the family. Just be good to my son, that's all I can ask. Oh, and perhaps a grandchild or two?"

"In good time, Mother," Tse answers on my behalf, giving a squeeze to my fingers. "All in good time."

My brother clears his throat pointedly. Lina gives him a broad grin. "Oh, I've adopted you too, Drew. My first grandchild. Just a bit bigger than what I was expecting."

I giggle, Tse chuckles, and Drew gives a full-bellied laugh.

Mouse

se." Jacob walks over, grasps hold of both my hands in his and squeezes them hard. "It seems a long time."

"Too long, old man." I grin.

"Know the lad. You gonna introduce me to your woman?"

"Sure. Mariana, meet Jacob." She steps forward, her hand outstretched, a smile on her face.

"I remember you." He takes off his cap, looks at it, then puts it back on. "You're the desert sprite."

"I think you described me as looking like a sack of potatoes." Her mouth widens as her lips curve.

"That I did, didn't I?" He looks between Mariana and Drew.

"That's my sister," Drew informs him.

Jacob laughs. "Thought that as you look alike. But hey, tell you this, you got all the riding skills, boy."

"Oh, don't be mean, old man. She just needs some lessons." I stand up for my wife.

Drew's pulling at Mariana's arm, he wanted to show her the horses, especially Niyol who he's taken a fancy to. Lad's a bit like me when I was younger, and I reckon it's the challenge he likes.

As we watch them walk off, Jacob leans in close. "Boy reminds me of you. He's been a great help to me. Just like you used to be." He nods toward the office; I follow him over and take a seat I've sat in a million times before. Jacob leans back in the chair behind the desk that looks like it will fall apart at any moment. It's a contrast, the stables are modern, clean, everything well maintained. The horses looked after with love and attention. Jacob wastes no money on himself.

Jacob wants to tell me something. I just lean back, enjoying the smells and sounds of the yard, letting him get around to it in his own time.

Eventually he raises his eyes to me. "I won't be around forever," he begins. I open my mouth to contradict him with some platitude, when he resumes, "You've put so much money into this place over the years. All that new equipment? Down to you. The new fencing? The horse walker? Couldn't have done it without your help. I'm not saying tomorrow, but within the next few months, I'll be giving it up."

I frown. Not what I expected to hear, and not what I wanted.

"My age is catching up. Got to be honest here. I'll go on a bit longer, got to get my head around the idea myself."

"Where will you go?" I'll help, do what I can. Help rehome the horses? *Niyol.* Fuck, I'll miss him. *Can I keep a horse on the compound?*

"My daughter. She's bought a house with an annex down in Tucson. Makes sense."

I'm pleased to hear he'll be living with family. But it's going to take more than a minute to get my head around the fact my refuge will be gone.

"I'm signing the place over to you."

I'll really miss coming here, riding my horse. Shit, even the jobs like moving hay and mucking out. *Wait. What?*

"What did you say?" I growl.

"It's yours." He jerks his head in the direction of the window. "Kid's a natural around horses. Knock this building down, or just let it fall by itself," he grins, "build yourself a new house for you and your family."

"I don't, you can't…" I can't get the words out. Rapidly I'm thinking how I can manage the club and this place. Some brothers live off the compound, Viper and Bullet. They manage it easily. Yeah, get Viper's construction crew here, design something for ourselves, fix up a computer room… "You should sell. Keep the money."

He snorts. "You've bought this place twice over. Nah, it's yours. I'll stay on until you're ready to take it over."

"Not just my decision," I say fast. "Got a wife now, and…"

"Your kid will love it."

What a great place to bring up children.

"Think it over?"

Still stunned, I find myself shaking his hand and agreeing. Then going to find Mariana and Drew, and finding myself still incredulous as I enlighten them as to my discussion with Jacob.

As though in a dream, the three of us walk around, eyeing up what could become our new home.

Mariana puts her hand on my arm, I turn to look down at her. "It's so peaceful here, Tse. If Jacob means it…"

She's right. Before I lived on the Rez, and after it, to me this place always felt like home.

Data, information, puzzle pieces.

I breathe in deeply, watching Drew try to entice Niyol with a carrot, then looking down at my wife, realising this place is the last fragment I've been seeking. Here, I can make my home, a real home for Mariana, for her brother, and the children we'll have in the future.

I was nineteen when I became Jayden's knight in shining armour, her Paladin. At only fourteen, she developed a teenage crush on me, the man who rescued her.

I gave her time to grow, waiting for her feelings to mature. As years, when I was forbidden to touch her, passed, I never doubted she was mine. I just wasn't allowed to show it.

Circumstances send us to Colorado, away from the restrictions and over-protective brothers. At last we have a chance to be together.

What could be better?

What could be worse?

A new club. A new life. Out of my depth, I don't fit in.

A different president and his old lady with their own issues. For some reason, Hellfire and Moira want to force Jayden and I apart.

Jay and I are just beginning. Or is it the end?

After all this time, will we make it work? Or have the years I've spent waiting been wasted?

Satan's Devils: Colorado Chapter #1
PALADIN'S HELL

OTHER WORKS BY MANDA MELLETT

All books can be read as a standalone.

Blood Brothers

A series about sexy dominant sheikhs and their bodyguards

- *Stolen Lives* (#1 – Nijad & Cara)

- *Close Protection* (#2 – Jon & Mia)

- *Second Chances* (#3 – Kadar & Zoe)

- *Identity Crisis* (#4 – Sean & Vanessa)

- *Dark Horses* (#5 – Jasim & Janna)

- *Hard Choices* (#6 – Aiza)

SATAN'S DEVILS MC

- *Turning Wheels* (Blood Brothers #3.5, Satan's Devils #1 – Wraith & Sophie)

- *Drummer's Beat* (# 2 – Drummer & Sam)

- *Slick Running* (#3 – Slick & Ella)

- *Targeting Dart* (#4 – Dart & Alex)

- *Heart Broken* (#5 – Heart & Marc)

- *Peg's Stand* (#6 – Peg & Darcy)

- *Rock Bottom* (#7 – Rock & Becca)

- *Joker's Fool* (#8 – Joker & Lady)

- *Mouse Trapped* (#9 – Mouse & Mariana)

Coming soon:

SATAN'S DEVILS MC
Colorado Chapter

- *Paladin's Hell* (#1 – Paladin & Jayden)

Sign up for my newsletter to hear about new releases in the Blood Brothers and Satan's Devils series:
http://eepurl.com/b1PXO5

GLOSSARY

Motorcycle Club – An official motorcycle club in the U.S. is one which is sanctioned by the American Motorcyclist Association (AMA). The AMA has a set of rules its members must abide by. It is said that ninety-nine percent of motorcyclists in America belong to the AMA

Outlaw Motorcycle Club (MC) – The remaining one percent of motorcycling clubs are historically considered outlaws as they do not wish to be constrained by the rules of the AMA and have their own bylaws. There is no one formula followed by such clubs, but some not only reject the rulings of the AMA, but also that of society, forming tightly knit groups who fiercely protect their chosen ways of life. Outlaw MCs have a reputation for having a criminal element and supporting themselves by less than legal activities, dealing in drugs, gun running or prostitution. The one-percenter clubs are usually run under a strict hierarchy.

Brother – Typically members of the MC refer to themselves as brothers and regard the closely knit MC as their family.

Cage – The name bikers give to cars as they prefer riding their bikes.

Chapter – Some MCs have only one club based in one location. Other MCs have a number of clubs who follow the same bylaws and wear the same patch. Each club is known as a chapter and will normally carry the name of the area where they are based on their patch.

Church – Traditionally the name of the meeting where club business is discussed, either with all members present or with just those holding officer status.

Colours – When a member is wearing (or flying) his colours he will be wearing his cut proudly displaying his patch showing which club he is affiliated with.

Cut – The name given to the jacket or vest which has patches denoting the club that member belongs to.

Enforcer – The member who enforces the rules of the club.

Hang-around – This can apply to men wishing to join the club and who hang-around hoping to be become prospects. It is also used to women who are attracted by bikers and who are happy to make themselves available for sex at biker parties.

Mother Chapter – The founding chapter when a club has more than one chapter.

Patch – The patch or patches on a cut will show the club that member belongs to and other information such as the particular chapter and any role that may be held in the club. There can be a number of other patches with various meanings, including a one-percenter patch. Prospects will not be allowed to wear the club patch until they have been patched-in, instead they will have patches which denote their probationary status.

Patched-in/Patching-in – The term used when a prospect completes his probationary status and becomes a full club member.

President (Prez) – The officer in charge of that particular club or chapter.

Prospect – Anyone wishing to join a club must serve time as a probationer. During this period they have to prove their loyalty to the club. A probationary period can last a year or more. At the end of this period, if they've proved themselves a prospect will be patched-in.

Old Lady – The term given to a woman who enters into a permanent relationship with a biker.

RICO – The Racketeer Influenced and Corrupt Organisations Act primarily deals with organised crime. Under this Act the officers of a club could be held responsible for activities they order members to do and a conviction carries a potential jail service of twenty years as well as a large fine and the seizure of assets.

Road Captain – The road captain is responsible for the safety of the club on a run. He will organise routes and normally ride at the end of the column.

Ronin – A biker who travels alone, sometimes wearing a patch denoting he's Ronin. Not affiliated to any club, but often bearing a token which will help ensure safe passage through territories of different clubs.

Secretary – MCs are run like businesses and this officer will perform the secretarial duties such as recording decisions at meetings.

Sergeant-at-Arms – The sergeant-at-arms is responsible for the safety of the club as a whole and for keeping order.

Sweet Butt – A woman who makes her sexual services available to any member at any time. She may well live on the club premises and be fully supported by the club.

Treasurer – The officer responsible for keeping an eye on the club's money.

Vice President (VP) – The vice president will support the president, stepping into his role in his absence. He may be responsible for making sure the club runs smoothly, overseeing prospects etc.

Brothers protecting their own

ACKNOWLEDGEMENTS

Mouse has always intrigued me; his heritage, the way his mind works. I delayed writing his story (originally he was planned before Peg), but he wasn't talking to me. He remained a shadowy figure in the background.

While Mouse was lurking in the back of my brain, I continued to listen to the real world around me. Immigration was rearing its head over and over again – not just in the US, but in the UK and other countries. Two things struck me. Firstly, getting papers and becoming legal isn't easy at all, in some cases, it's downright impossible. I was reading lots of comments blaming illegal immigrants for being lazy and not getting citizenship as though it was as easy as registering for a college course. When I looked deeper, it takes absolute years, and, if you've entered a country illegally, probably unlikely will ever happen. The second thing that I began to think about was what if the country you were currently living in was all you'd ever known? What if your earliest memories were of the place you resided now, but the authorities turned around and said you had to return to a country you'd never known, and didn't even speak the language. Had no connection to. Does this happen in real life? All the time.

I knew there was a story lurking there in the background, and suddenly Mouse started to come to the fore. *I'm indigenous*, he was telling me. *I'm a Native.* That's when the idea of Mariana began to take shape. What would Mouse think of an illegal immigrant? Would he help her once he knew? Of course, he would.

I'm not saying I've got all the processes one hundred percent accurate. Immigration law is an absolute minefield, but I've done what research I can, and hopefully have it mostly correct. Please do not look on it as a step by step guide – it's not. As I said a couple of paragraphs above, it's not just the US that has a muddled-up system, where people fall through the cracks and sometimes the laws are applied a little too vigorously. But some of the more fanciful things you might think come from a writer's imagination are actually based on fact. Take Mariana being put on the wrong transport and being deported instead of having her day in court. Yes, that happened. The judge was furious, and as soon as the plane landed, in the real-life case, demanded the woman was immediately brought back so he could hear her case. I departed into fiction at that point and decided that Mariana wouldn't be so lucky.

Abuse is reported to be common in detention centres. Illegal immigrants are regarded as having few rights, even basic ones. Obviously there are many good people in the world, but in all walks of life, there are those who take advantage.

Above all, this book is a work of fiction that I hope you've enjoyed reading. If, as I found when researching the facts of immigration, it makes you think, well, I'm glad. We make the most of the life we're given through nothing more than accident of birth. There are many families like Mariana's, where one child has citizenship of one country, a sibling, another. Families are torn apart by paperwork.

I didn't produce this book on my own, so now I have to thank everyone who helped me. An author can't get anywhere without a good editor, and I'm lucky enough to have worked with Maggie Kern again. She's a good friend, we have a lot of laughs, and most importantly, her insight and suggestions are invaluable in knocking my first draft in to shape and helping me through the stages to produce a, hopefully, polished final result.

My amazing group of beta readers came through for me yet again. Particular mention must go to Danena who I shamelessly took advantage of. She reviewed the Native American bits carefully and kept me in line, as well as picking up lots of other stuff too. My very grateful thanks to her, and to Colleen, Sheri, Terra, Zoe, Nicole, Alex and my husband Steve. You all picked up something that helped me. Once again I have to say, couldn't do without you, beta team. Love you all to bits.

I hope everyone likes the amazing cover. This is the fifteenth cover Lia Rees has designed for me, and personally I think it's one of the best (though that may have something to do with the model). Lia's also been the proofreader for Mouse Trapped. I do love working with you, Lia. Thank you.

Next up will be the long-awaited story (or so readers tell me) of Paladin and Jayden – Paladin's Hell. In Mouse Trapped we learned they're heading off to Colorado. Will their dreams come true, or will they be forced apart? You'll have to read it to find out.

As Paladin's Hell mainly takes place in the compound in Pueblo and we meet a ton of new characters there, I'm kicking off the Satan's Devils MC Colorado Chapter series with this one. But don't worry, the bikers you've grown to love will have a big part to play too. I suspect you're going to find more you want to read about as well.

I'm rambled a bit here, I know, so please forgive me. As always, I've left the most important people to the end. So now please, every person who's taken a chance on this book, accept my heartfelt thanks. If you weren't buying my books, I wouldn't be able to write them.

You can help even more. If you liked this book, don't keep it to yourself. Tell a friend, hey, tell me. Every time a reader contacts me to express how much they enjoy any of my books, especially when they ask for more, it spurs me to continue writing. I appreciate every review, message or comment that you give me.

Know what's even better? Leave a review. On Amazon, Bookbub or Goodreads, or wherever you made your purchase. I don't care where. Just one or two words is helpful. Reviews help authors make sales, sales allow authors to pay editors, cover designers etc, and put food on the table.

To anyone asking the question, the Satan's Devils have a long way to go yet.

There'll be another Devil along very soon.

STAY IN TOUCH

Email: manda@mandamellett.com
Website: www.mandamellett.com

Connect with me on Facebook:
https://www.facebook.com/mandamellett

Sign up for my newsletter to hear about new releases in the
Blood Brothers and Satan's Devils series:

http://eepurl.com/b1PXO5

ABOUT THE AUTHOR

After commuting for too many years to London working in various senior management roles, Manda Mellett left the rat race and now fulfils her dream and writes full time. She draws on her background in psychology, the experience of working in different disciplines and personal life experiences in her books.

Manda lives in the beautiful countryside of North Essex with her husband and two slightly nutty Irish Setters. Walking her dogs gives her the thinking time to come up with plots for her novels, and she often dictates ideas onto her phone on the move, while looking over her shoulder hoping no one is around to listen to her. Manda's other main hobby is reading, and she devours as many books as she can.

Her biggest fan is her gay son (every mother should have one!). Her favourite pastime when he is home is the late night chatting sessions they enjoy, where no topic is taboo, and usually accompanied by a bottle of wine or two.

Photo by Carmel Jane Photography